SEEMINGLY PERFECT

A PENDULUM NOVEL

MARY STRAND

For Naomi —
Happy reading!
Mary Strand

tripleberry
press

This book is a work of fiction. Names, characters, places, and incidents are either the product of the author's imagination or are used fictitiously. Any resemblance to actual persons, living or dead, business establishments, events, or locales is entirely coincidental.

triple berry
press

Triple Berry Press P.O. Box 24733 Minneapolis,
Minnesota 55424

Cover Credits
Cover and Logo design: LB Hayden
Wooden table © kaisorn4/DepositPhotos
Red wine splash collection © stockfoto-graf/DepositPhotos
Lake of the Isles - © Bjoertvedt/Wikipedia

Electronic ISBN:978-1-944949-14-3
Paperback ISBN:978-1-944949-15-0

Printed in the United States of America

PRAISE FOR MARY STRAND

For *Seemingly Perfect*:

"With Mary Strand at the controls, readers are in for a flight of a lifetime, spiraling downward, seemingly out-of-control, pulling up at the last minute, and into a beautiful, perfect landing. Emotional. Heartwarming. Deliriously funny." —ROBYN CARR, #1 *New York Times* Bestselling Author

For *Driving with the Top Down*:

"*Driving with the Top Down* is like a margarita: tart, refreshing, and utterly intoxicating. At times funny, at times poignant, but always exhilarating, this is a novel you'll consume in lusty gulps. It's a journey full of twists and turns and surprising detours. The trip is a joy from beginning to end." —JUDITH ARNOLD, *USA Today* Bestselling Author

For *Sunsets on Catfish Bar*:

"Emotionally complex and deeply involving, this is the story of a woman dealing with impossible challenges—and finding grace and humanity in the journey." —SUSAN WIGGS, #1 *New York Times* Bestselling Author

For the other members of my own high school
"Fab Five"
(although we didn't call ourselves that):
Sue, Lisa, Lynn, and especially Nancee, who left us too soon.

With all my thanks to:

Lon Lutz, M.D., who helped me with the medical and drug issues in this novel, and who trusted me that the advice was for the book and not for me personally.

Frank Magill, Jr., who helped me with the issues involving money laundering and financial crimes in this novel, and who *also* trusted me that the advice was for the book and not for me personally.

Other friends who helped with various research questions for this novel, especially Carol Prescott (art galleries), Ann Barry Burns (trusts and trustees), and Debra Dixon (accounting software), all of whom blithely assumed without asking that the advice was for the book and not for me personally, which might of course mean that they're too trusting. (Kidding!)

Various bars and restaurants in downtown Minneapolis, which provided inspiration for the Pendulum restaurant in this book and the entire trilogy.

Mariam AlAdsani, my daughter Kate's friend at Boston University, who came up with the "Pendulum" name.

All of my friends who've provided critiques, edits, beta reads, blurb help, or brainstorming help on this book, including my Maui writers group, Just Cherry Writers, Romex, Ann Barry Burns, Jennifer Crusie, Tom Fraser, Barbara Keiler, Carol Prescott, and Laura Taylor.

Laura Hayden and Pam McCutcheon, my publishing team, collectively also known as Parker Hayden Media, LLC, who make my life much easier.

By the way, any mistakes I might've made in this novel – despite all the excellent research help I received from my friends noted above – are mine alone, and no crimes have been committed in the course of writing this. But I mean, you never know, right? (Ha ha!)

CHAPTER 1

As opening nights went, this one resembled the Titanic just as it clipped the iceberg.

Twisting the stem of a wineglass between her thumb and forefinger, Victoria Carlyle Bentley surveyed the chaos around her and felt herself sinking. Prickles of irritation teased her neck, and her constant smile edged toward brittle. From the Diet Coke an excited patron splashed on a canvas to the wastebasket her summer intern accidentally set on fire to a celebrity wannabe's Chihuahua that peed all over the floor, practically everything that could go wrong tonight already had.

She hoped.

Clients and strangers packed her Jasmine Gallery for the opening of Sean Roarke's collection of abstract and, okay, mildly bizarre paintings. Thank God for decent weather. Minneapolis didn't always offer balmy evenings on the twentieth of May, and foot traffic in the North Loop depended on them.

Pursing her lips, Vic watched her summer intern, Hope McCulloch, wobble a drink-filled tray. She took a step toward Hope, intent on shifting the tray to steadier hands, just as someone tapped her on the shoulder. She turned, and a sigh escaped her.

Mother. "Who's that girl, Victoria, and what has she done to her hair? Does she actually work for you? She looks so—" Her nose wrinkled. "Young, for one thing."

Vic closed her eyes, but she couldn't erase the vision of Hope's blue, purple, and blond spiked hair. She also couldn't turn down the volume on the formidable Patrice Carlyle. "She's my summer intern, Mother, and it's her first week. College students often like to be creative with their hair."

She wondered again what had happened to Hope's shoulder-length blond hair or to the competent young woman she'd interviewed on a Zoom call a few weeks ago. If Hope's work tonight was any indication, her first week at the gallery would be her last.

Mother made a tsking sound. "Can she handle that tray? I think you should let someone else take it. She looks clumsy." Before Vic could respond, Mother's gaze swept the room. "Sean painted all of this . . . what do you call it? Abstract art? I'm more accustomed to—"

"Now, now, Patrice." Vic's dad joined them, none too soon, murmuring just loud enough for Vic and her mother to hear. Quite unlike Mother, whose voice must've carried to St. Paul. "It's not every day that Vic hosts an opening for her assistant, and I suspect it's not quite as easy as you think."

"But Warren—"

"Let her do it. Vic can take care of herself."

She smiled her thanks as Dad led Mother away, shushing her protests. She glanced across the room, saw a couple of her favorite clients frown when Hope spoke to them, and headed in their direction to make sure the situation was under control.

"Vic! One sec?"

The voice, and the hand grasping her elbow, belonged to Sean, her highly capable assistant and tonight's artist of the moment. In retrospect, she almost wished Sean had held his opening at someone else's gallery, where someone else's assistant would be handling all the minor catastrophes that sometimes accompanied an art opening.

She turned to him, sizing up his anxiety level. Medium to spilling over. "You should be meeting and greeting, Sean, not handling crises. That's my job tonight."

He ran his fingers through his short brown hair. "Too much is going wrong, and I haven't seen any art critics."

She shrugged, acknowledging the unforeseen problems. "I must've given Hope more than she could handle, especially considering the large turnout. My mistake, and I'll deal with it."

He glanced around the room. "Is Ryder coming?"

"Sorry, I'm not expecting him." She frowned, thinking of the excuses her husband always gave for skipping her opening nights. It would be just like him to show up, finally, on the worst opening night she'd ever experienced.

Despite herself, she looked toward the front door, wondering if Ryder might appear. Her jaw dropped. "No. It can't be."

Sean's gaze followed hers. "What? You know the hot guy?"

Vic sneaked another glimpse of the man near the door. Tall, with longish brown hair, wearing jeans and a polo shirt in a room filled with dress shirts and jackets. As their gazes briefly locked, her hand flew to her throat. Jake? She hadn't seen him in twenty years.

She hadn't planned on ending that streak tonight.

She blinked, and he disappeared into the crowd. "If it's who I think it is, he's not your type." Even if she weren't married, Jake wasn't hers, either. "But let's talk about you, and then I need to deal with Hope. What's the matter?"

Sean grimaced. "Everything."

"That doesn't exactly narrow it." She headed again toward Hope, who looked exhausted and irritable, as Sean kept pace with her. "Anything that really needs fixing? Or are you just playing the temperamental artist?"

He caught her wry grin and snorted but didn't say anything. As he scanned the room, his head bobbed slightly in time to the strains of Puccini coming from the accordion player positioned next to a wall divider.

Another nightmare. She turned away from the musician, wishing he'd disappear. Right through the floor. "I told Hope to hire a flute and saxophone and even gave her the phone number. The accordion showed up." Puccini, Verdi, whatever. Tonight, everything sounded like a polka. "I'm so sorry. I can't imagine what happened."

Sean smirked. "I can. But picture the looks on the faces of the guys at the VFW. The sax and flute are probably being shoved down someone's throat as we speak."

Vic took her first sip of wine and nearly spit it out. A low-grade chardonnay, when she'd specifically ordered two cases of an expensive Sancerre. Jesus.

Sean pointed at Hope, who stumbled and almost dropped her tray. "Should she be serving wine? Isn't she nineteen or twenty?"

Vic groaned. "She grabbed the tray right after the waste-basket caught on fire. Whether she was trying to help or just distract me, I don't know." She handed her glass to Sean and hurried toward Hope.

In slow-motion horror, she saw the tray flip, then heard glasses shattering followed by a high-pitched screech. Heads whirled in the direction of Hope, who clutched the empty tray high above the broken, wine-splattered heap at her feet. Vic could see her intern's chin tremble as she inched away from the glittering mess.

Vic bit down on her lower lip, her normal urge to fix the problem warring with an unnerving desire to flee the scene. Hope stared at the floor in a daze while patrons moved away, some of them out the door. Grimacing, Vic glanced back at Sean. "I'll deal with it. Go. Talk to people." His feet didn't move. "That's an order."

She reached Hope, who squatted over the puddle, picking through shards of broken stemware. "Hope? You told me you had experience with parties."

Her intern stood up, but her head slumped forward. "I didn't know it'd be like this."

"Like what? Work?" Vic bit her tongue, wishing for more tact and fewer witnesses. She spoke quietly in Hope's ear. "This isn't the time or place, but we'll talk later." Like, say, about the credentials on Hope's résumé, the glowing references, and all the experience she'd claimed to have. And whether in reality she possessed any actual job skills.

Hope stared past Vic in the direction of the front door. Glancing over her shoulder, Vic thought she spied Jake again.

"Do you know who that is?"

She turned back to Hope, who was pointing at the man who looked like Jake. "It's a big crowd, and let's get our priorities straight. Right now, I need you to clean up this mess. Quickly."

As Hope nodded in mute terror, Vic felt a stab of sympathy for the girl. Maybe not enough to keep her from firing Hope, but her mind flickered back to her own first job and a few embarrassing mistakes she'd made.

"Getting tough on your slave labor, Vic?"

Startled, she whirled at the unexpected lilt of her husband's voice. "Ryder? What brings you here?"

He brushed his lips across her cheek. "I've heard so much about Sean's opening, I couldn't miss it."

"You've never listened before when I mentioned one." Of course, Sean was practically part of the family. *Family.* Vic frowned. "Where are the kids?"

Ryder chuckled. "They wanted to stay home alone."

Her eyebrows shot up. "They're ten and eight. They also want to drive my convertible, taste their first alcohol, and watch an R-rated movie. Yesterday."

He took her elbow, steering her across the room toward Sean. "Natalie stopped by and offered to stay."

Anxious about Hope's progress in cleaning up the mess, Vic glanced over her shoulder just as Ryder's words registered. She froze in alarm. "Nat? How long? Ten minutes?"

"Until one of us gets home."

Vic sighed. Should she call home and check on her sister and the kids? Despite her jangling nerves and annoyance and too many things that felt off, all three of them had to be in better shape than Hope, who was now swishing the catastrophe on the floor into a bigger one. With a broom.

Ryder stepped away to greet Sean, clapping him hard on the shoulder. Vic cringed, knowing exactly how little Sean enjoyed male-bonding rituals.

Sean grinned, surprising her, as Ryder's hand remained locked on his shoulder. Poor Sean. Clueless Ryder. She stepped deftly between the men, wrapping an arm around each of them. Ryder had fifteen years on Sean, tiny wire-rimmed glasses, and a touch of silver in his short black hair, but they were practically twins tonight in their black shirts and slacks.

"I'm glad you came, Ryder, but I'll be here late. After you take a look around, I hope you can relieve Natalie." She didn't wait for his acquiescence, knowing she had it. Her husband knew only too well about art openings, and they both knew Natalie's attention span. "Now, I have to check on Hope—" For Ryder's benefit, she nodded in the direction of her intern. She also tried not to look for Jake. "And Sean needs to make the rounds."

She glanced to her left, where a reviewer from the *Star Tribune* aimed a puzzled frown at one of Sean's paintings. She whispered in Sean's ear. "Recognize the jeans-and-sportcoat by the door?" He turned, stared a moment, and nodded. "Good. You know what to do. Knock 'im dead."

Leaving the two men, she headed back to Hope, smiling on all cylinders at friends and clients as she grabbed a dustpan for the shattered glass and a mop for the chardonnay. Despite the startlingly pink palazzo pants that Hope wore tonight—only after Vic told her that her usual jeans wouldn't suffice—the young intern was now kneeling in the mess.

Vic had never cleaned a floor in an Armani dress, but she'd also never hired someone like Hope.

Gazing at the ceiling, she almost prayed for salvation from Hope. No, God had enough problems. As Dad said, she could take care of herself.

Always.

———

SHE WAITED ten seconds after the last patrons left, three minutes shy of ten o'clock, and turned the deadbolt with a satisfying click. What a night. Nearly over, thank God.

After she cleared the worst of the debris and quickly checked the evening's receipts, she could head home. Relax.

Regroup. Rethink her employment of Hope—who was still here, wiped out and red-eyed, two hours after her tray fiasco and despite Vic repeatedly urging her to call it a night. For both their sakes.

Turning around, she jumped. Hope stood two inches behind her, silent. "Oh! I didn't see you."

"Is there anything else I can do?" The girl's chin drooped to her chest, and her legs looked close to buckling.

"You've done enough." Understatement of the evening. "I said you could go home an hour ago."

Hope looked almost queasy but stood her ground. Strange girl. Most other college kids would be more than ready to party at ten o'clock on a Thursday night.

She wished she'd hired one of them.

"Go home. Really." She jangled her keys in the air. "I can lock up."

Hope's feet remained in place but her body swayed. "Thanks for taking care of me—I mean, everything—tonight. The opening went well, right?"

Vic lifted one shoulder. "We survived." Barely.

"Sean cut out early."

"Yes." Only a little early, right after the last critic left, but a first for Sean—and at his own opening. Surprising, but it wasn't Hope's business. "It's his big night. I told him I could handle it." She nudged Hope closer to the door. "Do you need a ride home?"

No response.

"Sorry. I didn't ask whether you had a car."

"I don't—"

"Or, for that matter, whether you had anything to do with the horrible wine tonight." Vic clicked her teeth, remembering the putrid chardonnay. "I know what I ordered, but you signed for the delivery, right?"

Hope jerked her head in a nod. "I saw your notes of what you ordered and thought you were spending too much. I mean, wine is wine, right? So I called up yesterday and changed the order."

"Without asking me?" Frowning, Vic felt the beginnings of a migraine. "Not to mention that you're underage."

"I'm twenty." Hope stared at the floor, then back up at Vic, almost defiantly. "I'll be twenty-one on November twenty-four."

"That's six months from now." And not one of Vic's favorite anniversary dates, for that matter. She touched her throbbing temple. The pain was exquisite. "In any case, I can't believe you didn't ask. I would've said no."

She also would've had something worth drinking right now, unlike the crap she'd pour down the drain the moment Hope left. Sooner, if the girl didn't move her feet.

Another thought occurred to Vic. "And the accordion?"

Hope shrugged. "I called the musicians like you said, but they sounded expensive. I saw an ad for this guy . . ."

Vic's jaw dropped. "You're kidding."

"I'm just trying to be proactive."

"I didn't ask you to be proactive. I wanted you to do exactly what I said." She dragged a hand across her face, but when she opened her eyes again, Hope was still there.

Hope pointed at Vic's hair, oddly enough. "I guess we look a lot alike, huh? I mean, when my hair isn't dyed. Your mom mentioned it." She scuffed the toe of her cheap but sparkly flip-flop against the floor as Vic flinched, imagining Mother's conversation with Hope. "It must be nice to have such a supportive family."

Vic tapped Hope's shoulder to propel her toward the door. Even if she fired Hope, the odds of which kept climbing, she wasn't prepared to do it at ten o'clock on a Thursday night.

No movement. "You probably get together with your mom a lot. That'd be great."

Vic jangled her keys again. "Do you have a jacket?" She spied the ragged backpack that Hope carried instead of a purse, snatched it off a chair, and handed it to her.

One foot inched forward. "So I guess I'll be going."

"And you don't need a ride home?"

"Home?" Hope stared blankly at Vic. Disaster or not, the girl must be dead tired. "I guess not."

"If you're sure." She hurried to unlock the door before Hope changed her mind. "And you have tomorrow off." Perfect timing. It would give her a chance to candidly discuss the evening's wins and losses with Sean—and without Hope. "So I'll see you on Saturday?"

"Yeah. Eleven."

Hope paused in the doorway, almost as if expecting a response. Finally, she shuffled out.

Vic locked the door again, then leaned against it and sighed. At thirty-eight, maybe she no longer remembered what it was like to be twenty. Or Hope was simply inept or, despite her impressive résumé and references, unqualified. But Vic couldn't let the girl turn her gallery upside down.

She headed toward the small kitchen area next to her office, wrinkling her nose at several unopened bottles of Hope's wine. Tomorrow she'd talk to Sean about Hope. Between his insight into strange young people and her need for sanity, they'd soon be back to well-ordered perfection. Or else.

She picked up an open bottle and started to pour it into the sink. Stopping, she filled a plastic cup and swallowed it in one gulp. Vile. She sagged on the stool next to the sink and poured another. It followed the first down her throat.

She'd held it together tonight, a reasonable facsimile of serene competence. But not as easily as usual.

The thought frightened her more than a little.

———

VIC TURNED the key in the lock just as the door into the garage swung open.

"Finally! You're home."

"Nat?" Taking a step back, she eyed her sister, noting the pajamas she wore—Vic's—and the craziest hair she'd seen in ages. Even counting Hope's. "What are you doing here?"

Natalie rolled her eyes. "Taking care of your precious children. The ones who like to scalp unsuspecting babysitters."

"They didn't." Stepping into the kitchen and scanning a floor littered with books, paint, drawing pads, and food spills, Vic sucked in a breath and waited to hear the rest.

"They claimed they needed the scissors for a school project, but I wasn't born yesterday."

"Or the day before."

As Natalie ran a hand through her wild auburn hair, getting tangled in a snarl, Vic wondered whether two sisters could be more different. She didn't envy Nat's freckles, but she wouldn't mind the rosy cheeks or a sprinkling of her muscles. Being in the same room with Nat made her feel like a fragile twig.

"I saw your car on the street, but . . ." Vic peered back into the garage. "Since Ryder's BMW isn't here, I thought he must've let you borrow it for some reason. Where is he?"

Natalie shrugged. "No idea. I stopped by to drop off that skirt I borrowed last week—"

Vic grinned. "And pick up some new jammies?"

Her sister fingered the silk fabric of her latest in a long line of clothing thefts. "Megan spilled juice down the front of my shirt."

"Sure she did." Vic hung her keys on the hook next to the mini TV set in the kitchen, then pulled her cell phone from her purse and tried calling Ryder. No answer. She left a message before quickly texting him. "Are the kids in bed?"

Natalie nodded. "By ten." An hour past their bedtime, but not bad, all things considered. "When I stopped by, Ryder asked if I could stay for an hour, then took off before I could even say yes. He claimed he was going to Sean's opening."

"He did. And left over two hours ago." Vic glanced down at her silk dress, frowning at the splotches on it, and moved to the sink. Maybe if she put the kitchen in order, the jumpiness in her stomach would go away. "He should've been home by now."

Natalie didn't say anything, and Vic didn't look at her sister's face. Nat had never thought much of Ryder. But she'd also never gotten married, so she didn't understand how marriages worked. As she ran water in the sink, Vic wondered if anyone did.

Sighing, she pulled a large apron off a hook and draped herself. No point increasing the damage. "He obviously knew you were here with the kids, and I asked him to relieve you." She glanced at Natalie, who leaned against the wall, absent-mindedly peeling a gooey spaghetti noodle off of it. "Thanks, by the way."

Natalie flicked the noodle toward the sink, not blinking when it hit the floor. Vic stooped to pick it up, then moved to the rest of the debris. Déjà vu after tonight's tray incident with Hope, which kept replaying on hyperspeed in her mind.

Ten minutes later, the kitchen sparkled, Natalie maintained her position by the wall, and Ryder still hadn't called or texted her back, let alone returned.

"The, uh, play room might need work, too."

"It's called a living room." Vic poked her head around the corner and swallowed hard. Not pretty.

She bit her lip, wondering whether frustration—over Ryder, the house, and even Nat, for reasons that eluded her— would beat out exhaustion. But if she tidied things up now, she wouldn't have to do it tomorrow. She headed into the living room, straightening cushions and picking up a million books and toys while Natalie trailed behind. The cleaning service came tomorrow, and she couldn't shove a disastrous house in their faces.

As Mother would say, it simply wasn't done.

She added her mother to the list of things frustrating her.

"Where do you think Ryder is?" Natalie, ever helpful, asked the very question that was bugging the hell out of Vic just as she retrieved a porcelain vase from under a sofa cushion.

Time crawled in slow motion as the vase slipped from her grasp, bobbled once, twice, and shattered on the wooden floor.

"Damn it!" Shuddering, Vic closed her eyes and took a deep breath, then counted to ten as she slowly released it. "He obviously must've gone back to his office." Picking up a shard of porcelain with hands that refused to stop shaking, she examined the intricate pattern she'd loved until fifteen seconds ago. "For God's sake, Nat. He's in trial next week. He's always working."

"But he went to Sean's opening."

"To be supportive. He's paying attention to me. Finally." Vic bit her lip as the last word slipped out. "I mean, he finally had a free moment in his work schedule, and he came to see my gallery."

"No doubt."

Natalie dropped onto the now-clean sofa and propped her bare feet on the coffee table. Swatting them off, Vic stepped around the broken vase and moved to a painting that hung askew.

She felt Nat's gaze boring into her as she circled the room, straightening paintings. "I swear, Nat. We'll be married eleven years in June, and you've never given him a chance."

"Maybe you should ask Ryder why that is." Springing off the sofa, Nat forcibly removed Vic's hands from the fifth piece of artwork she hadn't needed to straighten, then dragged her over to the sofa. With a slight tap, she pushed her down onto it. "But I wish you'd stop cleaning around the elephant doing a tap dance in your living room. I'm getting tired just watching you."

Even as her whole body tensed, Vic raised one eyebrow.

Natalie headed back to the kitchen. "If this isn't the moment to discuss elephants or husbands, how about a glass of wine? You probably had a tough night."

Vic sank into the cushions and let herself do nothing. Just this once. Despite the shattered vase staring up at her from the floor. Despite the fact that Ryder was missing in action and Natalie wanted to discuss it and nothing made sense. "You don't know the half of it."

Nat's off-key whistling floated out from the kitchen as Vic heard the refrigerator door slam. Moments later, her sister sauntered back into the living room, a bottle in one hand and two crystal wineglasses in the other.

She plopped down next to Vic. "With you, I've never known the half of it. Even a quarter. But try me."

Vic's mouth opened and clamped shut again.

Nat shook her head. "One of these days, Vic, you need to break down and talk. To someone."

Vic leaned back on the plush sofa, a glass of wine in one hand, a sister she loved at her side. As a single tear slid down her cheek, she shook her head.

———

Hours later, Vic lay awake in bed, staring at a clock that stubbornly insisted it was two in the morning. Ryder still wasn't home, which was weird even for him. At what point was she supposed to call the police and report him missing?

She'd called him again and gotten voicemail, at his law firm and on his cell phone, which meant nothing. He tended to keep his office phone on call forward and his cell phone on silent, even at night or on weekends. He often worked until midnight when he prepared for trial, but not this late. Luckily, his cases didn't usually go all the way to trial. The kids missed him. She missed him.

Didn't she?

The beep-beep-beep of the house alarm sounded, and she heard the beeps as the code was punched in. Ryder. Home at last. Marriage to a litigator kept her awake too many nights.

Her eyes fluttered heavily, then closed.

———

"Good morning, sleepyhead."

As lips brushed across Vic's cheek, feeling like a pesky mosquito, her eyes flew open. "Ryder?"

He sat next to her on the bed, dressed for work, shoulders hunched, as he clutched one of her hands and played absently with her fingers. "I'm, ah, sorry about last night."

Her free hand waved in the air. "I know. Work, work, work." She'd always let him off the hook too easily, but it wasn't as if she didn't understand his deadlines. "It's just that you left Natalie—"

"—here with the kids. Yeah. I'm sorry."

"You just said 'sorry' twice in one minute." She smiled to

ease the sting of her words and reached up to touch the back of her hand to his forehead. "Are you sick or something?"

He grabbed that hand, holding both of hers now in his clammy ones. "Or something."

She ground her teeth. "It's okay."

It wasn't, not really, but she'd wait until after his trial to discuss schedules and kids and, oh, keeping promises. Like letting her know in advance when he was going to stay out half the night working. When she finished the basics, she might even move on to the big stuff. Them. No romance, passion, or sex in way too long. Did they need an adults-only vacation? Should they both cut back on work? Or was it deeper than that?

She shuddered, not relishing a conversation she'd avoided for too long. Maybe for eleven years.

His hands were gripping hers too tightly, but she hesitated to pull away. He hadn't held her hands this long since she'd been in labor with Connor. He'd missed Megan's birth altogether.

"Vic, I—"

"You have to get to work. I know." She glanced at the clock. Almost nine? "Ohmygod! The kids are late for school. Are they even up yet?" She rocketed to a sitting position, scrambling to untangle herself from the sheets as Ryder's legs blocked her.

He didn't move. "They're long gone. Dressed, ate breakfast, left for school an hour ago. I wanted to let you sleep."

She fell backward onto the pillow. Despite her pounding heart, she covered her eyes with one arm. "Who are you, and what have you done with my husband?"

Not even a chuckle. She peeked at him from beneath her arm. Checking his watch. Staring out the window.

No. Not an alien body snatcher. Same old Ryder.

"Vic, I—" Turning from the window, he blew out a shaky breath and reached again for her hand. "I can't keep doing this."

She frowned. "Staying late at work? Getting the kids to school for once in your life?"

He tried to hold her gaze but soon searched for some unknown something out the window. "Pretending to be married."

She lifted one eyebrow. "Last time I checked, you weren't pretending. You *are* married."

And then his words sank in. Oh, God. He'd found someone else. At work, undoubtedly. Some cute, adoring little fifteen-year-old associate or paralegal or secretary who giggled at his pathetic jokes and batted her eyelashes when he walked by.

Young women nowadays. Ryder. The sonofabitch.

She tugged out of his grasp and rolled over. When his hand went to her shoulder, she swatted it away. "Who is she, Ryder? Who the hell is she?"

He didn't answer. She pushed herself back up to sitting, crossing her arms as she waited to hear him name some woman she'd invited here to dinner, who'd probably rolled around in her own goddamned sheets.

"It's not a woman. It's Sean, Vic. Sean. I'm so sorry. I've struggled for so long, and I just can't anymore."

Words kept spilling out of his mouth, picking up speed as they blended and blurred and tripped over each other, while her jaw dropped and her mind went numb.

"It's not like you didn't know, Vic. I mean, we've been together so long and I always wanted something else, and you must've, too. Right? And I tried to talk about it, but you'd roll over or go wash your face or something. Hell. We don't even sleep in the same bed."

Her mind swam as she thought of his snoring, her allergies, the late nights and early mornings—all the reasons they'd both had for not sharing a bed. Normal reasons.

"And, uh, it's never been great in bed. I mean, you've got a great body, a great *woman's* body—"

Her stomach curdled.

"—but it's not what I want."

He stopped, blessedly, before she threw up. She sucked in a breath, tasted bile, and stared into hazel eyes that suddenly reminded her of birdshit.

"Are you through yet, Ryder? Or are you just warming up?"

He shook his head and swallowed hard, his Adam's apple throbbing on a scrawny throat she desperately wanted to strangle.

"Sean? Sean Roarke?" STDs and AIDS and utter disgust swirled through her mind, churning and spewing a volcano's worth of acid through every single inch of her.

The ramifications kept multiplying like some mutant, out-of-control gene in a horror flick. The kids. Dad, Mother, Natalie, her brother Drew, her friends. How would she tell them? The kids would lose their dad. She'd lose a husband *and* Sean—not only the world's greatest assistant but a close friend. Leaving her with Hope.

Double fuck.

"I won't ask how long." She shoved him away, off the bed, and he fell backward, landing on his pathetic butt. "I don't want to know. You make me sick."

"I—I thought you'd understand."

Nauseated, she clasped her stomach and pointed at the door. "Get out. Before I scream."

"Vic, I just had to—"

She screamed until the windows rattled, until her lungs

ached, until her fucking gay bastard of a cheating husband tore out of the room, thundered down the steps, and slammed the door.

When she heard the garage door open, she curled into a ball, rocked back and forth, and wept.

CHAPTER 2

A claw grabbed Vic, trying to pry her loose as she emerged from a pitch-black tunnel to dangle from a narrow ledge above a deep canyon. Sweat beaded her face, dripping off her chin, as she clung more tightly. She wouldn't fall. She couldn't.

The pressure on her shoulder intensified. Letting go of one hand, she tried to shake off her assailant. Her other hand slipped once, and again, before losing its grip. She screamed as she plummeted downward, a blur of motion, toward her final—

"Mom? Mo-o-om! Wake up!"

Huh?

A swarm of hands tugged at her shoulders, arms, knees. Vic froze, struggling to separate dream from reality. She wasn't falling. She wasn't about to die. No, her husband of eleven years was gay and sleeping with her assistant of seven years.

Scrunching her eyes shut, she tried to jump back into the dream.

"What'sa matter, Mom?" The roving hands wouldn't let her escape. Vic grabbed a pillow and stuffed it over her face. Suffocation might work. "Are you sick? Are you sleeping? Are you gonna make us dinner?"

Ahh. Cutting to the chase.

She lifted the pillow an inch or so. "Where's Larissa?"

"It's after six, Mom." Connor rolled his eyes, an omen of the teenage years to come. "She went home."

"After six?" She'd slept eight hours, after crying out every speck of water in her body and throwing a few things at the wall, a few more out the window.

All of them Ryder's, as luck would have it.

She'd also missed work, and Sean hadn't called to check on her. Figured. His gay lover—oh, yes, that would be Ryder—must've warned him, and Sean bolted. The gallery remained locked and shuttered for the first time in its existence.

A thousand nails pounded inside of Vic's head as Megan burrowed in next to her. "Where's Daddy? Is he gonna bring us dinner? We want pizza."

Connor shoved Megan, sending her off the bed. "He's still at work, stupid. He never comes home this early."

Sighing, Vic set aside the pillow. "Don't call her stupid, Connor." She heard a whispered "stupid" as her mind struggled to formulate an answer. "He's not coming home tonight."

"See? Told you so." Connor snickered at Megan, who head-butted him in the stomach. "Hey! Mom!"

Vic shook her head. "That's not what I meant, and quit bugging your sister." She flailed for words that wouldn't come. Finally, she pulled both kids into an awkward hug. "Your dad is, um, moving out. Staying somewhere else."

She closed her eyes, imagining the somewhere else, as Megan began to whimper.

"He's not gonna—"

She couldn't talk about it. Not yet. Not without screaming or smashing something. "Can you guys give me a minute?"

Neither one moved an inch.

"Please. I need a little time." She cringed at the flicker of hurt on her kids' faces as they scrambled off the bed and out the door. Megan, whose legs churned as she raced to catch up to Connor, slammed the door shut behind her.

Vic sank back on the pillow. Larissa, their nanny, was gone for the weekend. God knew when Ryder would dare set foot in the house. Sean had likely vanished. And no one else knew.

She had to take care of the kids, of course, but everything felt hollow inside. She wasn't eager to face a mirror, which would only reflect eyes that burned a glowing crimson, matted hair, and skin as white as death.

No wonder Ryder had turned to a man. No one wanted a dishrag. Not even Ryder, who'd been a limp dishrag himself more than once. She smiled grimly, trying to find the humor in having lived so long with a selfish, inaccessible . . . limp dishrag.

Throwing off the covers, she dragged both feet over the side of the bed and groaned to a standing position. Ten slow steps brought her to the bathroom. She gripped the sink, unable to see anything, the only light coming from the dull rays poking through the blinds of her bedroom windows.

She grabbed a toothbrush. Please, let it be hers, and not Ryder's, which had been in a mouth that had been in God knows whose mouth, which made her gag.

Numb, she ran cold water in the sink, one hand on her toothbrush, the other fumbling with the toothpaste. Her mouth tasted like last night's wine, only worse, and she couldn't bear it another second.

A minute later, she glanced down at her rumpled negligee and sniffed. Ew. She turned on the shower faucet, stripped off the offending garment, and pitched it in the hamper. Without giving the water a chance to warm up, she stepped inside the glassed-in shower and cringed against the blast of cold, crossing her arms over her chest and hopping on alternating feet. Torture.

Gradually, the water warmed. She shampooed, rinsed, added conditioner, rinsed, lathered the necessary body parts, rinsed again. And then curled up in a ball on the floor of the shower.

She wasn't quite cried out yet.

———

HER BODY in a fresh-smelling terrycloth bathrobe and a towel wrapped around her head in a turban, Vic headed downstairs just as the doorbell rang. Ryder or Sean or a solicitor or her mother. She froze, unable to face any of them.

Connor ran to the front door and flung it open before she could stop him.

"Connor! What have I told you about—"

"—letting in his aunt? Who comes bearing pizza?" Natalie stepped inside, loaded down with pizza boxes and ice cream. She deposited it all in Connor's skinny but eager arms, sent him tottering to the kitchen with a light slap on the butt, then skimmed her gaze the length of Vic. "Hmmm. Better than I expected."

"What brings you here?" Ryder wouldn't have told her. And Natalie hadn't called, as far as Vic knew, although she'd been out cold for hours.

"As it turns out, Connor knows how to dial a telephone, but he wasn't sure which pizza place to call. Or where to find money." Natalie shook her head. "The kid is ten, Vic. Time to teach him the facts of life."

"I think he already has them down cold. He knows his aunt has money to burn, is a sucker for pizza, and won't make him break into his allowance."

Her lips twitching, Natalie glanced toward the kitchen. "He's lucky he's my favorite nephew."

As Natalie laughed, Vic sank onto the bottom step and wrapped her arms around her knees. "He left me, Nat. For Sean, of all people."

Nat plopped down next to her, nudging Vic with her hip until she made room. "I figured. I was going to say something."

Vic's stomach clutched. "You knew?"

"Not definitely, but I saw them having lunch last week. Nothing funny, but I've wondered about Ryder for a long time."

"How long?"

Nat's arm came around her shoulders. "Probably since the beginning? He was so caught up with you, especially when you guys first dated, I figured my instincts must be off."

Vic brushed off Nat's arm and lurched to her feet, fighting the urge to smack something—like Nat, who acted so *casual* about it all. "Why didn't you tell me?"

Nat shrugged. "You never wanted to talk about Ryder."

"You never tried to talk to me about him. You never made me." Vic's fist balled, a red haze clouded her vision, and she punched the front door until the pain broke through. "Damn."

Nat scooted up a step on the staircase. "I did try, but this isn't about me. It's about Ryder, remember?"

Vic pressed her stinging knuckles against her mouth, then both of their heads swiveled at the sound of a crash in the kitchen.

Natalie turned back to Vic. "Maybe he loved you in his own way, and he wanted kids. Some gay men do that."

Vic crossed her arms. "So now you're a shrink. Isn't that Drew's job?"

When Nat flinched, Vic cursed herself. She kept treating

Natalie like a punching bag when she really just wanted to smack Ryder. "God, Nat. I'm sorry."

"I understand, really, but I think I'll skip the pizza." Nat creaked to her feet and moved to the door, calling out a goodbye to Connor and Megan. She turned back to Vic, not quite meeting her eyes. "And don't forget for a moment that Ryder is a lawyer, not to mention the kids' dad. Believe me, he knows his rights."

"Undoubtedly." Vic's nails dug into her palms as her mind added a nasty legal battle to everything else on her plate. "You and Dad are lawyers, too."

"You got that right." Natalie laid an awkward hand on her shoulder. "Right now, you're pissed. Fine. But don't do anything rash."

"Does 'rash' include throwing his crap out the window?"

Natalie snorted as she pulled open the front door and stepped outside. "And here I thought you were hosting the first-ever yard sale on Lake of the Isles."

———

"RISE AND SHINE, kid. It's already eight."

Vic held the phone to her ear as she rolled over in bed. "I'm sorry. You must have a wrong number."

Too late, she yanked the phone away as shrill laughter rang in her ears. Tess Adams, her best friend since eighth grade. Irritating twerp.

"Natalie warned me you'd be a bear."

She frowned. "Oh?"

"She knew you wouldn't call, even though you adore me almost as much as Chris Hemsworth." After she finally quit laughing at her own joke, as she tended to do, Tess cooed into the phone. "I'm here for you, Vic. Whatever you need."

"How are you with dead bodies?"

"Depends. Yours or his?"

"I'll let you know." Maybe after she woke up. Vic stretched her free hand over her head, hitting the lamp.

"In the meantime, we have things to do. Plans to make. A twentieth high-school reunion to organize."

"You're kidding, right?" Sucking in a deep breath, she held it for several seconds before releasing it. "Did I just get two whole minutes of sympathy from you? My husband left. With my assistant. Both of whom are gay, as it turns out."

"You already knew that about Sean."

"That's not the point." Twenty-four hours after Ryder's startling confession, she wondered if she had a point. "I can't pretend I'm okay, Tess. I'm . . . not."

"Thank God for that."

Stunned, Vic almost hung up. After several silent moments, she snapped. "What's that supposed to mean?"

"It means you're not perfect. I know, I know. The rest of the world may think so, but you're talking to me. Tess. The holder of your deepest, darkest secrets."

She froze. Aside from one whopper of a secret—unless having a gay husband sleeping with her gay assistant counted, which she supposed it might—she didn't have any secrets.

Tess cleared her throat. "You don't need to hold it all in, you know. Shit happens. Even to you."

Vic rolled her eyes. "Sorry, but I'm not up for a pop psychology lecture at eight in the morning. Wait until I've had a cup of coffee."

"You don't drink coffee."

"Exactly."

Tess hooted her approval. "Good. Your brain is still working." In Vic's silence, she quickly sobered. "But I suspect you need some company this weekend."

"I have two kids and a gallery that didn't open yesterday." She groaned. Hope would be back today, and Sean undoubtedly wouldn't. "Isn't that enough?"

"Not nearly. Natalie said she'd watch the kids."

"And take care of them three days in a row? No way."

"She talked your brother into helping. And before you object, stop. It's no hardship to Drew, and a few hours away from his brats has to be a blessing."

"Only to spend it with two more kids?"

"Cute kids. Whose mother isn't a twit."

Thinking of Babs and the twin terrors, Vic felt sorry for someone other than herself. Drew. "I can't believe he'll help, but I guess that's Natalie's problem." Yawning, she rolled over and glanced at the clock. "Mine is the gallery. Sean must be long gone, and I have the world's worst summer intern."

"I'll come in and help. Afterward, we'll grab a bottle or two of wine, round up Midge and Andrea, and have a party."

She must be insane. "Not today. Please."

"Too bad." Tess shushed Vic's protests. "Now get your butt out of bed, or I'll do it for you."

"No, Tess. I—" The phone clicked in her ear.

———

Patrice Carlyle tapped a freshly manicured nail on the writing desk in her bedroom as she stared at the message slip and counted the number of telephone rings. Four, five. She started to press the disconnect button just as someone picked up.

"I'm already moving! Now what do you want?"

"Victoria? Is that you?" Patrice frowned. It sounded like Natalie, in tone and words, but she wouldn't be up at this hour, let alone at Victoria's house. She glanced at her watch and wished she'd waited. Or perhaps not called at all.

"Mother?"

"Am I calling too early?" She held her breath as she picked up the slip of paper and looked again at the words Natalie had blurted out last night, when Warren had been tied up at work. *Have Dad call Vic ASAP.*

"Uh, no, but I need to get to work. I'm running late."

"Do you really need to? Can't you call in sick?"

"Mother, I own the gallery. Who would I call?"

Patrice's nerves jangled as she folded the message slip in half, fourths, eighths. Blinking, she unfolded it and smoothed out the creases. "It's just that, well, we never get to talk."

She thought she heard Victoria's teeth grind. "Was there anything you wanted?"

To be of use. To someone. "I just thought I should call."

"Because?"

"Natalie said that your father should call you. He's golfing this morning, and I thought I might be able to help."

She held her breath as the seconds ticked past.

"No, I can't think of anything I need."

Patrice sagged. "How are the children, dear? And Ryder?"

"The kids are fine." A pause, followed by the sound of swallowing. "Sorry, but I really do need to get to work."

She sighed.

"You know I own the gallery, Mother. It's what I do, and it takes time."

"Your children take time. And Ryder takes time." Or he would in the world Patrice inhabited. She cringed when she heard Victoria snort. "How is Ryder, dear?"

A slight pause. "I'm not quite sure. I mean, as well as can be expected, I guess, all things considered."

She nodded to herself. Marriage to a litigator could be difficult, but it gave her something in common with Victoria. A safe topic. "He has a trial soon?"

"So he says."

"I know how that is. Your father hates discussing his work, too." She leaned back in her chair and settled in for the unexpected delight of a real chat with Victoria.

"Like I said, Mother, I really need to go."

Patrice clutched the message slip in her hand. "Are you sure, dear? Not a single moment to spare?"

"Sorry. Not today."

Not ever, it seemed. She hung up, tore the message into a dozen pieces, and watched them flutter into the wastebasket.

———

Just past nine, the door to her gallery stood wide open, and Caribbean reggaeton music blared from the speaker in the corner. Vic covered her ears as Sean's hips swayed into view, bouncing to the beat as he swished a mop in wild patterns on the floor.

"Sean? What are you doing here?"

The hips stopped moving, and Sean turned in a slow circle. "Working? Just like yesterday, when no one else did?"

She blinked, startled that he'd shown up—and not exactly pleased about it. "That's all you have to say?"

He leaned on the mop as the thump-thump-thump of the reggaeton music continued, sending a fresh spurt of pain to her temples.

"What do you want me to say, Vic? That I'm sorry? Fine. That I wish it hadn't happened? Or happened this way?"

Agitated, she walked through the gallery, straightening

paintings, picking up a glass tucked behind a chair. "I thought you'd tell me you're leaving."

The mop handle clattered on the floor. "Thought or hoped?"

She bit her lip. "Both. Neither. I don't know."

Sean retrieved the mop and resumed the swirling motion, which didn't appear to be doing anything for the pristine floor. Arms crossed, Vic watched him, waiting for a response.

After several long moments, he gave a final swish and walked the mop back to the storage closet. When he finally turned to face her, Vic's hands were on her hips.

"I expected more from you. Loyalty." She glanced down at her Ferragamos, which were tapping a nervous beat. "Respect."

"You've always had my respect, boss." Sean approached her, palms out. "I love the gallery. I want to stay here, working for you. With you."

Vic's left eye twitched. "You're kidding."

He offered a shrewd grin. "Unless you want to promote Hope. With her business flair, she'll be ready in ten years, max."

The hollow pit in her stomach expanded and contracted in an undulating rhythm, and Vic clenched her fists. "That's not—"

"Yo!"

At the sound of a sharp rap on the door, they both turned. Tess strolled inside, purse swinging, heels clicking on the tile floor.

Stepping up to Vic, Tess gave her a quick squeeze, then looked from her to Sean. She ran a hand through golden hair, her latest color, newly shorn in a blunt cut, as she shimmied to the reggaeton beat. "Wrong music for a wake."

Sean strode to the office and shut the door.

"He's here?"

Vic nodded. "For the long haul, in his opinion."

Tess whistled. "He's got balls, I'll say that for him."

"If you don't mind, I'd rather not discuss his anatomy." She pursed her lips. "Perhaps you can take that up with Ryder."

"Ryder wouldn't dare come within fifty feet of me."

"He's a lawyer, Tess. Don't underestimate him."

"Good point." Tess tapped her chin. "One hundred feet."

The office door opened, and a sullen Sean stalked over to the stereo, shutting it off. A strained silence reigned, broken only by Tess's footsteps as she wandered the perimeter of the gallery, studying Sean's paintings. "You did these, right?"

He watched her, one eye half shut, probably waiting for the other Manolo Blahnik to drop. "Yeah."

"Not bad." Moving back a few feet from one, Tess tilted her head, a study in concentration. "Are you planning to keep painting?" She turned to Sean, smiling sweetly. "After all, if you hurt Vic, I'll stomp on you until you can't see straight, let alone paint. Seems like a pity."

He grinned, both surprising and irritating Vic. "Then I guess I'll have to avoid that."

"I guess you will." Tess walked over to Sean, looped an arm through his, and dragged him over to Vic. Grabbing their hands, she forced them into a limp, hostile handshake. "It's not much, but it's a start. Now get to work so I don't have to."

Vic choked. "Just like that? We're supposed to be pals? Despite everything?"

"Co-workers for now. Besides—" She looked pointedly at Sean. "I hear Ryder's not all that in bed. Before long, he'll be history and you two will still be together." She tipped Sean's jaw closed and ignored Vic's horrified glare. "He doesn't deserve either one of you, but you need each other."

When hell froze over. Vic clenched her fists to keep from slapping Tess. And Sean. And Tess again.

She stomped to her office and slammed the door. Even Tess couldn't write a happy ending to a tragedy.

———

A QUIET AFTERNOON. A few calls that Sean screened, a client with an appointment, several drop-in customers. One artist who stopped by, seeking representation.

The low hum of tension in the gallery increased when Hope spilled a pot of coffee and Tess took it as an omen that she needed a Starbucks run.

An hour later, Tess still hadn't returned.

Vic perched on the edge of her chair, skimming through financial ledgers and artists' catalogs while she half-listened to Sean and Hope bicker.

As she drummed her fingers on her desk, she pondered whether she could talk to Sean about her issues with Hope. She needed to take action, and it couldn't wait until she'd dealt with Ryder and Sean and her putrid life.

She jumped when the phone rang.

She wasn't ready to talk to anyone. The phone kept ringing, and she ignored it. Finally, blessedly, it stopped.

"Vic, call for you." Sean poked his head inside her office, pointing at the phone. "It's no one I recognized."

She picked up. "Victoria Bentley speaking."

"Victoria Carlyle Bentley?" The woman on the phone sounded shrill, bureaucratic, and oddly nervous.

Vic groaned. Tess must've begun planning their reunion. She'd lost track of most of her Vassar friends, and very few people except her Southwest High School classmates still used her maiden name. Her nose wrinkled. She hadn't yet focused on details. Like names.

"Is this Victoria Carlyle Bentley?" The nasal-voiced woman spoke again, startling Vic out of her momentary lapse.

"Yes. May I help you?"

"I hope so." Papers rustled on the other end of the line. "This is Marian Franklin. I'm a social worker with Oakview Hospital in Kalispell, Montana."

As Vic went numb, the phone clattered to the floor.

CHAPTER 3

Hours later, Vic leaned back on a white leather sofa at Tess's Sawmill Run townhouse and sipped an expensive glass of pinot noir that might as well be Boone's Farm. Her third glass? She wasn't sure, which wasn't like her. She'd stopped caring at whatever point she passed tipsy and started the long, helpless slide to blotto.

Sitting cross-legged on the Persian rug on the other side of the coffee table, Tess topped off her own glass and tilted the bottle toward Vic, who spread her fingers across the rim of her glass. "My eyes are already crossed. What more do you want?"

Tess poured between an opening in her fingers. "Some conversation. You haven't said anything since I came back with the popcorn fifteen minutes ago."

"I was too busy watching you eat it."

Tess pushed the bowl—empty now except for a few unpopped kernels—across the table. "Help yourself. I was starving."

"Apparently." Vic closed her eyes, then quickly reopened them when she realized that Tess would kill her if she sloshed red wine on the white sofa. She pushed herself up straighter. "That's okay. I'm not really hungry."

"You're already too damn skinny, and you can't afford to lose more weight just because some man turns out to be gay. Even if he *is* your husband. And just because—"

"—the hospital called. After all these years." Taking a sip, she almost choked. "Seems like a decent reason to me."

"But you said the woman didn't tell you anything. You hung up on her." Tess shook her head. "What could it be? The baby died. End of story."

Vic flinched. "It's never been the end of the story to me. Or to the hospital, apparently. Something must've happened. Something awful."

"You don't know that. And why don't you want to see Andrea and Midge?" Tess practically gulped down her glass of wine and poured another. She was certainly taking empathy to a new level. "They're your friends. Good friends. We all are."

"They wouldn't understand. They never knew—" Vic eyed Tess, wondering, but her friend made a vague criss-cross in the general direction of her chest. "And I can't tell them now."

"Why not?"

She shrugged. "Midge gets squeamish when she hears stuff like that."

Tess raised one eyebrow. "Even though she's a physician."

"And Andrea gets so smug. About everything. Her perfect husband, perfect kids, perfect life."

Tess retrieved another wine bottle from the sideboard. "Sounds like you, at least until yesterday."

"Except that I'm not smug."

Grinning, Tess zipped a leather coaster through the air at Vic, whapping her in the shoulder.

"I'm not!" Her cheeks flushed, and she felt chastened. "Okay, I've had a pretty good life until now, but I've never bragged about it. Besides, everything that happened yesterday and today more than made up for it."

"I'll drink to that." Leaning across the table, Tess clinked her glass against Vic's, then drained its contents.

As her stomach tightened, Vic set down her own glass and watched Tess in amazement. "How do you do that?"

"Drink? Quite easily, after years of reluctant practice."

"No. Handle everything so well. Two divorces—"

Tess waved a finger in the air. "You're forgetting the broken engagement. Far more traumatic, if you ask me." Her eyes twinkled, but Vic saw something else in them.

She studied her friend. Tall, athletic, gorgeous . . . and after two marriages to creeps with big money, more wealthy than God. "You always sail through all the horrible crap that life tosses out without blinking. Or crying." She swallowed hard. "Or running to me for comfort. Like I always do to you."

"Twice in twenty years isn't exactly a habit."

"But it's weak."

Tess rolled her eyes. "You're not weak, Vic, and if you'd run to me sooner about Ryder—like, before you got married— you wouldn't have Connor and Megan."

Missing the kids, she peered into the empty popcorn bowl. "When is the second course going to appear?"

"It would've appeared, frankly, with Midge. Or Andrea." Tess made a face. "I'd put my vote with Midge. Andrea is taking another cooking class."

They both wrinkled their noses.

"So you're stuck with me." Tess ran a finger around the rim of the bowl, then licked it. "But we should grab some dinner. Or if you're done wallowing, maybe a few reinforcements?"

Vic groaned. "Andrea and Midge? I'm not ready."

"When will you be?"

"Sooner than I can face my mother." She swirled her empty wineglass, staring into its bottom. "Drew must've told her by now. Babs probably announced it to the whole world on social media."

Tess frowned. "I thought you were done wallowing."

"I forgot about Babs. And Mother. And—"

"Ryder?"

She bit her lip. "For starters."

Laughing, Tess stood up again. "I've got an idea."

"If it involves Ryder or Sean, I don't want to hear it."

"It doesn't. But it needs to percolate a bit." She tapped the side of her head with a freshly manicured, hot-pink nail. "So have a glass of wine, my dear, and trust me."

Watching Tess's teeth gleam as she offered a sly grin, Vic lifted an eyebrow. "I'm not sure which would be worse."

———

"PENDULUM. YOU'RE KIDDING, RIGHT?"

As the Lyft eased to a stop, Vic crossed her arms and didn't budge. Next to her, Tess tapped her phone to finish paying the driver, then gave Vic a hard nudge with her elbow. Despite herself, she opened the door and stepped onto the curb. As couples and singles and utter dregs scurried past, Vic gazed up at the neon sign over the royal-blue awning. It flickered, summing up her opinion of the place.

Behind her, Tess mumbled something about tight-assed women who needed to get a life, but Vic's gaze fixated on an eighty-pound high schooler in red spandex and big boobs who tottered through the door on nosebleed heels, accompanied by a forty-something man in a pinstriped suit who looked too much like Ryder.

Of course, Ryder would be out with a man. Like Sean.

As the Lyft sedan squealed away from the curb, Tess

bumped her hip into Vic's, nudging her closer to Pendulum. Her definition of a Saturday night from hell.

It wasn't Pendulum itself, or not really. With a popular location in the heart of downtown Minneapolis—not too far, but far enough, from Target Center—it had a casually elegant décor and remarkably decent food for a place best known for its thick burgers and greasy fries.

But its popularity meant it was absolutely *packed* on weekend nights. Packed with people who wanted to get picked up.

Tess nodded at two men headed for the front door who tried to swagger like cowboys—despite their Sperry Topsiders —and came up a few rodeos short.

The men whistled as Tess tottered on stilettos that she could barely handle when she was sober. She'd changed into a tight black skirt and even tighter yellow stretchy top and, with a drunken hand, applied full battle paint. Vic didn't spare a glance down at her own outfit—jeans, an old pair of black Converse Chucks, and a T-shirt advertising her gallery. Without thinking, she touched her face. Mascara, but no lipstick.

One of the men held out his arm to Tess while the other rushed to open the door. Vic slipped through it first, nodding at the man, whose gaze was glued to Tess's chest. Two steps later, choking on pungent odors, Vic tried to walk back out the door, but the surging crowd pinned her in place.

Music blared through ceiling speakers the size of her convertible, the heavy bass beat of a Rolling Stones classic thumping through her body in time with her heart. A waitress threaded her way through the crowd, her tray perched high on one hand, the other hand dealing with men who got too close.

Someone splashed a drink on Vic just as a hand brushed her breast. With a quick flick of her wrist, a man yelped. Tess walked inside just then, sandwiched between the two idiots she'd found on the street. Vic frowned, wishing Tess had left them there. Preferably face down.

A voice screeched in her ear. "Vic!"

She turned to find Midge Covington next to her. "Midge?"

Her old friend from high school sipped a glass of lemonade through a straw. At barely over five feet tall, she probably couldn't convince a bartender to serve her anything stronger.

"Tess called." Midge's brown bangs hung over her glasses as she peered intently at her shoes. "She, uh, told me about Ryder."

Frowning, Vic looked past Midge, wondering who else Tess had called and whether she could murder Tess in front of such a large crowd. "Where's Andrea?"

"Andrea doesn't like Pendulum, and she was busy. So I came by myself." Midge fiddled with her large-framed glasses, grinding them into her nose.

It wasn't her fault, and she'd made the supreme effort. Driving downtown on a Saturday night and walking alone into the most crowded bar in Minneapolis must've given Midge hives.

Vic placed a hand on Midge's forearm. "Sorry we couldn't have met somewhere else. I didn't know Tess was bringing me here."

"I call it shock therapy." An arm draped itself over her shoulders, and Tess's heavy floral cologne wafted past her. "It'll be good for you."

Midge looked from one to the other. "Is there a problem? I mean, other than the Ryder thing?"

"The Ryder thing." Vic blinked. "Neutral, yet somehow makes him sound like a disease. Right up your alley."

Twin spots of pink dotted Midge's cheeks. "I'm sorry, Vic. I didn't mean it. I meant to say the—"

"The Ryder thing." Tess snickered. "Got it right in one."

Vic shrugged. "I'd rather laugh about it than cry. I've done enough of that already."

"No shit." Tess grabbed Midge and Vic by the arm and hurried them over to the only empty table in the bar. "It's time for Vic to start her therapy."

Midge glanced at Vic before picking up a menu lying on the table. "I'll stick with lemonade. And I can give you guys a ride home. Your designated driver."

She smiled quickly, brightly, before returning her gaze to the menu. Tess held up her hand to call a waitress.

Vic eyed Midge's glass. "Actually, that looks good." She placed her order while Tess ordered a scotch.

"So where's Andrea?" Vic looked pointedly at Tess. "Midge tells me that Andrea doesn't like Pendulum, but I didn't realize we had a choice."

"She couldn't make it." Tess tried to pick up her menu, but Vic flattened her palm on it. "Or, ah, Philip wouldn't let her."

Midge jumped in. "He's not so bad when you get to know him. He's just a little—"

"Stiff." Vic and Tess answered in unison.

Vic frowned. "They've been married sixteen years. I'm not sure when we're going to get to know him."

"No kidding." Tess stuck her hand into a basket of popcorn that had magically appeared on the table. *More* popcorn? "I mean, you and Ryder were married, what, eleven years? And how well did you—"

Too late, she clapped a buttery hand over her mouth.

Wide-eyed, Midge reached for the basket of popcorn.

Despite the knots twisting her stomach, Vic shrugged. "It's okay. Say whatever you want. I won't break."

Tess arched an eyebrow.

"Fine. I might need some pain medication for a while—"

She eyed the lemonade that their waitress had just delivered, wishing she'd ordered something stronger. Like morphine. "But I'll survive. Eventually."

"We'll help, won't we, Midge?"

Midge stared at Tess, a question in her eyes, before turning to Vic. "Whatever you want, Vic."

Vic drummed her fingers on the faux-marble-topped table, trying to imagine what could ease her bone-crushing depression. Peace. Quiet. A happy marriage to a man who wasn't gay and doing the wild thing with her assistant right this moment.

Midge nudged her arm. "Vic? Are you okay?"

She blinked, clearing the haze. "Sure. Of course."

"You looked angry." Midge's eyes widened. "I mean, not that you're not entitled to be. If I were married—"

Tess and Vic flicked a quick glance at each other.

"I'd just about die if I found out that he . . ."

"Preferred men in leather pants?" Tess snorted, coughing and choking on her drink.

Vic slapped her on the back a little harder than might be strictly necessary. "Just because Tess likes men in leather, she assumes other people do. Even someone who's—" She choked on "gay," and for once Tess didn't fill in the blank. "Like Ryder."

"Now, me, I hate leather pants." A man appeared at their table, set both of his hands on it, and looked around at the three women. "Too damned hard to get out of."

If that was an offer, she'd pass.

Then recognition hit. Vic wiped her hands on her jeans as her stomach did a horrified belly flop. On cue, Tess fluttered her eyelashes at the man, who smirked back at her and glanced at Vic and Midge, then again at Vic. His gaze tried to hold hers, but she blinked first and looked away.

Definitely him. And definitely someone she didn't want to

see again, tonight or ever. Still gorgeous, which was no huge surprise, and the golden streaks in his windblown hair came from the sun, not a bottle. Already tan before Memorial Day, so he must not spend much time working. She bit her lip, wondering why she was disappointed.

He talked in low tones to Tess but watched Vic out of the corner of his eye. She turned to Midge and sneaked peeks at him, too, feeling an unwanted buzz of familiarity.

A tap on her arm. "Aren't you going to say hi to Jake Trevor?" Tess laughed as Vic glared at her. "And here I thought I'd have to make introductions."

On the verge of losing what little she'd eaten today, Vic pushed away from the table and stumbled to the bathroom, only faintly hearing Tess and Midge calling after her.

Jake. Bad luck always came in threes.

———

"YOU'RE NOT READY YET? Still at the gallery?" Ryder sat on the edge of Sean's king-size bed, amid rumpled silk sheets and too many throw pillows, and clutched his cell phone to his ear. "It's Saturday night, Sean. Why are you at work this late?"

A low chuckle flowed into his ear. "Exactly how Vic always talked about you. All work, no play."

"I played."

Another rumble of laughter. "But not with her. We've been together only a few months, Ryder. Should I ask how long it's been since you've played with her?"

"Don't." He blew out a breath and wondered what he'd ever seen in Sean—besides the tight ass, the abs, the whole package. Trying to picture his lover, his wife's face kept appearing in his line of vision. Talk about guilt.

He couldn't think about mistakes, except maybe the

mistake of telling Vic. If he hadn't confessed, he wouldn't be sitting on the edge of someone else's less-than-clean bed on a Saturday night, wondering if he was going to get laid. If he hadn't confessed, he'd either be getting laid or putting his kids to bed.

Fuck. He'd be lucky to see Connor and Megan again. Ever. He knew his legal rights, but his law firm didn't know about his side interests. Vic had him by the balls.

Sean's voice interrupted his musings. "I said, what are you going to do about Vic?"

He gritted his teeth. "I told you. I finally told her about us. I said I wanted a divorce. I moved out."

"And in with me."

Sean's voice dropped lower, the way it usually did when sex was involved, but he was at goddamn work, not next to Ryder. Not here in his miniscule one-bedroom apartment in Uptown, where the kitchen was the size of Ryder's walk-in closet at home.

He ran a hand through his hair. "Sorry. I never asked. If you don't want me here—" Half of him wished Sean would kick him out, if only so he'd have to find a bigger place. "I'll grab my things. What's left of them."

Sean hooted. "I still can't believe she pitched it all out the window. It doesn't sound like the Vic we know and love."

Love. Yeah, he loved her, in his own screwed-up way. They'd been together so long. He hated spending his life in a farce, but Vic had always loved him, always been there. She didn't keep secrets. She also didn't work late on Saturday night.

"What are you doing at work, anyway? Is Vic there?"

"She left the minute we closed this afternoon. I think she was going out with girlfriends. Tess was in today."

Tess. After hearing what he'd done, she'd cut off his balls the first chance she got. He winced.

"So what are you doing down there?"

"I got behind lately, between my exhibit and supervising Vic's new intern, who's a nightmare. I'm catching up on paperwork and trying to fix the computer financials. Stuff like that."

"On a Saturday night?" It didn't make sense, and he damn sure wasn't getting laid. He stood up and pressed against the dull ache in his lower back.

"So we can hang out tomorrow. All day. Together."

"Maybe half the day." Max. And only if he made it into the office early. He had a brief due on Monday and a trial scheduled to begin Tuesday. Vic wouldn't have forgotten that or tried to schedule an entire Sunday with him. She knew better.

Sean laughed, dropped his voice again, and told Ryder exactly how he planned to spend the day with him. His breath caught as his body throbbed on a full hard-on. "Okay, maybe more than half the day. Come home soon, or I'll come to the gallery."

Sean breathed hard into the phone, promising heaven and reminding Ryder—vividly—exactly what he'd always seen in Sean. He stripped down to his shorts and collapsed on the bed, keyed up and buzzing for Sean's return.

Tomorrow's brief? Wasn't that what associates were for?

BENDING OVER THE CHROME SINK, Vic splashed water on her face, trying to avoid streaking mascara down her cheeks. Not that it mattered. She looked like death and, like a coward, had sprinted for safety at the sight of Jake.

He was back—or maybe he'd been here all along. He'd attended the opening. And Tess, damn her, didn't look surprised.

She tried to brush off the instant recognition that had

zoomed through her, the unwanted familiarity. Bottom line, she'd packed him away with her childhood things and mostly forgotten Jake. Her first love. Her worst nightmare.

He'd obviously forgotten her, which stung more than a little. She peered at her face in the dim light of the mirror. Puffy red eyes, pale cheeks. Wrinkles. A couple, at least.

The heavy door creaked open, the sound barely registering, followed by a faint "Vic?"

"Hey." Vic glanced again at the mirror, then mustered a smile for her old friend. Loyal, dependable Midge.

"Are you okay?"

"Sure." Not. "Just, uh, using the bathroom." She glanced around the room, barely large enough for two stalls and one measly sink, but she had to admit it was clean and even stylish in an unexpectedly funky way.

"I haven't seen Jake since—"

"High school." She nodded, wondering how often Tess saw him and when she'd planned to mention it to Vic. "I haven't either."

Midge scuffed the toe of her worn loafer against the yellow-and-black checkerboard tile. "I'm sorry about Ryder. You probably didn't need to see Jake right now, either."

"Nope. I could've waited on that." Like, say, until the end of time.

Midge didn't meet her gaze. Not unusual, but Vic wished it could be otherwise. She'd known Midge forever.

"I didn't know he'd be here."

She laughed, the sound gurgling in her throat. "Don't worry. We can both guess exactly who did. Tess. The troublemaker."

"She means well. It just doesn't—"

"—always work out?"

They shared a brief laugh, Midge's faint and Vic's rusty.

"I meant what I said." Midge glanced around the bathroom, then peered intently at her. "If I can help . . ."

Vic rinsed her hands again as wheels turned in her head, then she dried off with a designer paper towel. "I'm depressed. Upset." She tried to look more genuine than she felt. "You name it."

Midge fiddled with the bridge of her glasses. "Not unusual. But it's only been a day, you know. Take your time."

So much for offering to help.

Midge kept talking. Quietly. Earnestly. "A lot of people in your situation turn too quickly to alcohol, painkillers, and antidepressants. You're smart to drink lemonade. Exercise is good, too."

Vic touched a hand to her mouth, praying she didn't reek of wine. "I'm sure you're right. I just wish I could sleep." After sleeping all day Friday, she'd barely made it through last night, and only with a significant investment in alcohol.

She held her breath as Midge studied her with a clinical, detached gaze so different from her usual shy self. She could always cadge a few pills out of someone else, just to get through this. Drew? Her internist? Ob/gyn?

Finally, a slow nod. "I think I have a few samples of sleeping pills in my car. I could give you a week's worth, ten days tops. You shouldn't take them longer than that.

"I know. And I appreciate it." Vic tried to rein in her inexplicable elation before she started dancing right here in the bathroom at Pendulum.

"When you're taking sleeping pills, you shouldn't drink alcohol or take antidepressants or narcotics. They don't mix. Besides, you don't need them."

She crossed her fingers behind her back. "I can't imagine why I would."

Midge looked at her again, sizing her up. So professional,

even on a Saturday night. "You're going to be okay, Vic. You'll get through this."

"Thanks, Midge." Vic offered her one last smile before steeling herself to go back out into the bar. "I owe you."

———

SHE WAS THINNER than he remembered, even more waiflike than the skinny dancer she'd been in high school. Her long hair was now shoulder length and styled, less touchable. Hollow cheeks, pale eyes that looked through him when her gaze wasn't darting around the room, and hands that clenched and unclenched when she thought no one was looking. A smile that wasn't one.

Still beautiful, somehow, in a detached way that Jake hadn't appreciated in their teens or remembered in all the years since, when he'd reminisced about stupid young love and wondered what the hell had ever happened to her.

Even though he'd glimpsed her at the art gallery, he hadn't recognized Victoria at first tonight. After all the years he'd spent erasing her memory—or trying to, anyway—he might not have noticed her if she hadn't been with Tess. Tess stopped into Pendulum now and then, but never with Victoria. He chewed his lip, thinking back, thinking about what-ifs.

He wondered if she'd sent him the flyer for the art opening. And why he'd gone. Victoria had seemed like a mirage that night, and he'd left rather than face her. Tonight, she was flesh-and-blood reality. Or she had been for the five seconds before she bolted.

The minutes ticked by as Jake waited for Victoria to return from the safety of the bathroom.

After all these years, she still pulled disappearing acts.

Next to him, Tess patted his hand and told him to wait. His

gut told him not to, and—except when it came to Victoria—his gut had always served him pretty well. He waited anyway, drummed his fingers on his knee, and tried to think up an excuse to leave.

Giving Tess a sidelong glance, he wondered, not for the first time, why he'd wanted Victoria all those years ago and not Tess. Overpainted, yeah, but she'd aged well, and he enjoyed her easy chatter. As he rubbed at a knot in his neck, he reached the same conclusion he had back then. It was just something about Victoria.

Tess leaned back against her chair. "You've still got it bad." She shook her finger at him, trying and failing to look like their old algebra teacher. "Don't bother denying it."

"I'm not interested in Victoria. Ancient history." Despite himself, he glanced back toward the women's bathroom. "And a bad history. You never told me why—"

"It's her story to tell and none of my business."

"Since when?" Getting no reaction, he shifted gears and begged like a pathetic puppy. "C'mon. It's been twenty years."

Tess just laughed. "That reminds me. Since you've never come to any of our reunions, I put you on this year's committee."

He rolled his eyes. "What a thrill. Hard pass."

"Nice try." Her lips twitched as she glanced around at the nearby tables, then lowered her voice. "Tell you what—I'll talk Vic into it, too. It'll be a party."

"Speaking of parties, where's the rest of yours?"

She stared at him blankly and didn't answer.

"Andrea? Carrie? You guys were inseparable."

She gazed down at her lap for a moment before glancing back at him, dropping the flirtatious look she'd been born with. "Vic and I get together, sometimes with Andrea and Midge. No offense, but they just don't come in here." She gave him an arch look. "Andrea's never said so, but I suspect her *husband* wouldn't appreciate her coming to Pendulum."

He met her gaze without flinching. "Like I said. Ancient history." He tipped back the Coke he'd brought to the table and took a long gulp. "Does, uh, Victoria—"

She appeared out of nowhere, pausing a moment beside him before reclaiming her seat. After nearly spitting out his Coke, Jake started to get up just as Midge joined them.

Victoria looked at him oddly. "Don't leave on our account."

"Can't. I own the place." As he took another swallow and abruptly sat back down, he enjoyed the shock on Victoria's face, the hard glance she gave Tess. "Besides, I was just asking Tess about you guys. The Fab Five. Andrea and Carrie, too." Chuckling, he shook his head. "I can still hear Carrie screaming her head off at Coach Ryan every time he yanked me from a game. Man, what a pistol. I'll bet she hasn't changed."

Midge looked stricken, and Victoria and Tess exchanged a look he couldn't decipher. Finally, Tess tipped her glass toward her lips, swallowing the last of her drink before setting the glass carefully, almost methodically, on the table.

"Carrie died. In college. We don't talk about it much."

She reached for Victoria's and Midge's hands, forming a triangle of sorts. Feeling sick, he mumbled a quick "sorry" and pushed back from the table. No one spoke as he left.

They didn't have to. He'd always been the outsider in their crowd, and he always would be. Some things didn't change.

CHAPTER 4

Monday morning, Vic wandered through her gallery, clipboard in hand, pretending to catalog inventory but discovering after a half hour that she hadn't jotted down a single note.

Not much improvement over Sunday, when she hadn't made it farther than her kitchen, and then only to prevent Connor and Megan from starving to death.

Natalie and Drew stayed away on Sunday and hadn't called yet today. Vic tapped a pencil on her clipboard, wondering if she'd said anything unforgivable when she arrived home late Saturday night, mildly drunk and upset and trying very hard to forget that she'd run into Jake.

She vaguely remembered asking Drew about antidepressants, cringing when she recalled his pointed "no."

The phone rang a few times before the sound filtered into her brain. Dropping the clipboard, she ran to her office and caught it before the machine picked up.

Winded, she snapped into the phone. "Victoria Bentley."

"Ms. Bentley? Please don't hang up."

As greetings went, it was unusual. An anxious client? A

new artist? Vic slid the receiver into her left hand and reached for a pen. "Yes?"

"This is Marian Franklin." In her rush, the woman choked on the words, and Vic strained to hear her. "We spoke on Saturday and—" She coughed. "We got disconnected."

Vic reached out to press the "off" button on the phone.

"Don't! Don't hang up, please. We've worked so hard to find you." The woman actually screeched into the phone. "For months now!"

"I'm sorry. Where did you say you were calling from?"

"Kalispell. Montana. Oakview Hospital."

Vic closed her eyes as she gripped the receiver but kept her voice coolly professional. "And how can I help you?"

A pause. She'd surprised the woman. Vic heard a rustle of papers. "Er, didn't you deliver a baby here twenty-one years ago? November?"

November twenty-four. "Sorry, but you must be confusing me with someone else."

Someone she'd been a lifetime ago. Twenty-one years ago.

The rustle of papers grew more frantic. "Victoria Carlyle?"

"Victoria Bentley. Carlyle is my maiden name." And the name she might go back to sometime soon. But that dilemma paled in comparison to the one on the line. "I'm sure there are quite a few women with my name. Or at least one. The one you want."

"And your birthday is—?"

"Nothing I give out to strangers, which I'm sure you understand. Thank you for calling, Ms. —"

"Franklin." The woman wheezed into the phone before she spoke again, even faster. "Your daughter—I mean, the daughter of Victoria Carlyle—" She obviously hadn't believed Vic, which meant she wasn't stupid. "She wants to meet you. Or *her*. She's searched for her mother for quite a while."

A knife twisted inside of Vic. A daughter? She hadn't even known. Hours after her emergency C-section, she'd awakened in a stark room with no baby and no one willing to stand up to her mother and give her information. Anything.

Mother told her the baby had died.

She collapsed into a chair next to her desk. "I can only imagine, Ms. Franklin. Again, I wish you luck in finding your Victoria Carlyle. I'm sure she'd want to meet her daughter."

"But—"

"Thank you for calling, and goodbye."

With shaking hands, she let the phone fall gently into the cradle. She felt sick—for herself, and for the unknown girl who'd never meet her mom—but right now, with her life unraveling, she couldn't let this woman yank another thread. She had to take care of herself. She couldn't afford to let the girl within ten miles of her.

She wondered idly whether the girl had blue eyes and blond hair—an adult version of Megan and a youthful one of Vic—and then mentally slapped herself.

Crossing her arms on her desk, she laid down her head. An hour later, Sean found her that way when he arrived for work.

———

WEDNESDAY MORNING, Vic snatched the phone on the second ring and chirped "Victoria Bentley" into it—even though the odds grew worse every day that the caller would be a social worker, Ryder's divorce lawyer, or some other slimy cave dweller who wanted to ruin her life.

"Victoria?"

She slapped her forehead as the low voice washed over the phone line. Except for Mother, who insisted on formal names for her daughters, everyone she knew called her Vic. In other words, the man calling now was a stranger, which these days only meant trouble.

"It's Jake. Jake Trevor."

Not a stranger, but definitely trouble.

"May I help you?" She'd perfected the frosty voice so well, she was almost starting to enjoy it.

"From Saturday night. From, well, you know."

"From my past." Okay, a little melodramatic, especially at nine a.m. "Did Tess give you my number?"

He laughed, but it was shaky. "She refused. She also didn't tell me you had a new last name."

Maybe not for long. "And?"

"It was, uh, great. Seeing you. Saturday night. After so long. I mean—"

The cocky star quarterback of Southwest High School's football team hadn't stammered that badly since their first date.

"And Thursday night. At my art opening."

"That's how I got the number. A flyer for the gallery showed up in the mail, and I figured, you know, what the heck."

More likely, he'd done a quick Google search—unless, buried in his bar and memories of high school, Jake had never bothered to enter the computer age. Vic and the rest of the world had. She also knew for a fact that he wasn't on the gallery's mailing list.

"So you found me after all these years. Twenty?" As if she hadn't been aware, at some level, of every single year. She hadn't seen Jake since their graduation and hadn't *seen* him, in that way, since the day they finished junior year. The day before she left her whole life behind for Kalispell and six long months of hell.

"Yeah. Twenty. Twenty-one." So Jake could count, too. "I, uh, wondered if you wanted to go out." He cleared his throat into a silence filled only by her thumping heartbeat. "I mean, you're probably married or something, but we could get together as friends. I'm usually at Pendulum, if you wanted to stop in."

"At nine in the morning?"

He chuckled, sounding more like his old self now. Confident. Too confident? "I do happen to be here now. But whenever. Lunch or dinner or some evening. Bring your husband if you want. So you're married?"

His voice held both a question and hope—that she was married, or that she wasn't?

"At the moment." She blinked, surprised that she'd offered even that much. She popped the top on a bottle of Valium that her next-door neighbor had prescribed an hour after seeing a few dozen of Ryder's bowties hit the lawn. "I can't, Jake. I can't go back there."

"To Pendulum?"

She didn't relish that, either. The fries were greasy and the hamburgers probably contaminated, even if they *did* taste amazing. "Anywhere. You. Us. Whatever we had ended a long time ago."

"Did it? You're sure?" He asked, but Jake didn't beg. At least one person in her life hadn't changed.

"Positive." She rushed to get off the phone before she changed her mind. "I have to go. Thanks for calling."

She hung up, nerves taut, and jumped to find Hope standing in the doorway like a silent, creepy apparition.

Vic shook her head, clearing it of Jake, Ryder, long-ago babies, and strange interns. Even with Hope and her husband's gay lover as co-workers, work would save her.

She counted on it.

———

"You HAVE to let me see the kids, Vic. Be fair. I haven't even technically moved out."

At least Ryder had the decency to do this in person, in the gallery, when Sean and Hope were both conveniently absent, and not in front of the kids. Vic clutched the bottle of Valium, shook a couple of pills onto her desk, and surreptitiously counted the remaining ones. Seven. Her neighbor had prescribed two dozen, and she already had barely enough left to survive the day.

She popped two into her mouth and gulped them down with a swig of water. Ignoring Ryder, she pondered how to get more pills. Hmmm. She couldn't ask her neighbor again, she didn't want to offend Midge's medical ethics, and Drew had been a prick about it. Fine. She hadn't yet asked her internist or ob/gyn or even considered her other physician friends.

As soon as she got rid of Ryder, she'd make a few calls.

"I don't think you're in a position to talk about fair." She flipped through pages on her gallery calendar, which didn't even show most of her family events. "And don't get technical on me. You've moved out, believe me. Your things are gone."

She pursed her lips, waiting for a tirade about what she'd done to a pile of his clothes, not to mention his golf clubs, but it didn't come.

He raked a hand through his hair, then quickly smoothed it. "All I'm talking about is the kids. I want to see them."

"How does September sound? The third weekend?"

"September?" Ryder leaned over her desk, his cologne wafting past her in a way she couldn't describe as sexy. "It's May, Vic. Are you kidding?"

"The end of May. The kids are finishing school soon, and then they'll be at camp."

"For two weeks."

"Maybe longer." Unlikely, but she should keep her options

open. "There's an excellent Spanish camp in London this summer."

"London?" Ryder slammed a hand over her calendar as Vic tried to turn the page. It ripped. "Megan's eight, for God's sake, and Connor's only ten. Don't fuck with me."

"And don't use that language on me." She retrieved her calendar from under his hand, which shook despite his bravado. "I need to do what's best for the kids." She smiled sadly. "And what's best for me."

He dropped into the chair across from her. "So you're saying our eleven years of marriage don't mean anything."

"Excuse me?" She hadn't worn her contacts today and looked at him over the tops of her small blue wire-rims. "I wasn't, but now that you mention it, I spent eleven long years married to a gay man. That must be the definition of meaningless."

He flinched. "You don't mean that."

"And your lover of choice happens to be my assistant. What were you thinking? My heart wasn't enough? You decided to go for the jugular?"

"I didn't—"

Waving her hand in the air, she pushed away from the desk, stood, and paced back and forth in the small office. Sean would be back any moment from the artificial errand he'd suddenly had to run, and God only knew how long Hope had been on break.

"You'll see the kids when I'm ready. Before September? Fine. But not today. Not this week. Sometime soon. Make an appointment."

"To see my kids?" He looked upside-down at her calendar, and she slammed it shut on his nose.

"Get used to it." Her legs suddenly felt weak, and she dropped back down onto her chair. The hard-edged façade she kept pretending was growing increasingly difficult to maintain, and exhaustion overwhelmed her. "I'm sorry, Ryder. Try me sometime when I'm not busy hating you."

Eyes wide, he slunk out the door without another word. So unlike the high-priced litigator she'd married, who didn't lose many battles.

Without waiting for Sean and Hope to return, she locked up early and drove home. Connor and Megan needed her—or even if they didn't, she needed them. Almost desperately.

———

Larissa slipped out the door moments after being relieved early, and Vic went upstairs in search of the kids. She found them huddled on the couch in front of the TV, watching a violent but funny Bruce Willis movie. Vic shook her head. Connor was probably repaying Megan for insisting on an American Girls movie the last time it'd been her turn to pick.

She called out a hello, to which Connor grunted and Megan mumbled something that sounded like "Mom" through fingers spread wide over her eyes.

"Are you guys hungry? How about a pizza?"

Connor glanced at the clock over the TV, which read four p.m., and didn't respond. Megan held up the bag of chips she'd been munching.

"I guess it's early. Want to do something?"

"After the movie?"

She rolled her eyes. "How silly of me. Sure."

Connor spared her a glance. "Aren't'cha gonna be busy tonight? Or in bed or somethin'? We could call Dad."

Megan nodded. "Where's Daddy? Is he on a trip?"

"No, stupid." Connor elbowed her, and she shoved him

back. "You heard what Mom said. He's not gonna be here anymore. Like Joey's dad."

"And Emma's mom?" Megan's eyes went wide at the mention of two of their friends in the Kenwood neighborhood. There must be something in the water besides algae. "He's not gonna come home?"

"Never."

Connor returned to the show, ignoring his sister's wails. Remembering her own smug declaration today that Ryder might not see his kids before September, Vic felt a pang of guilt that even a gallon-size bottle of Valium wouldn't fix.

Maybe she'd call Ryder. Or she could ask Drew again for painkillers. Antidepressants. Anything to take this constant heartache away. She slid out of the room, heading for a phone, debating which number to call.

———

"Are you sure you're okay?" As Vic glanced at Hope, who'd just returned from her third bathroom break in the last hour, she caught Sean rolling his eyes and puffing out his cheeks in a barfing motion.

Hope looked a little green—but, then, she hadn't looked much different the last couple of weeks. Maybe the outfit she'd chosen today—nondescript, baggy, and somewhere on the puce side of lime green—created that effect.

"I'll be fine. I don't feel good, um, most mornings."

Out of the corner of her eye, Vic caught Sean patting his stomach. Maybe everyone was sick. She reached for the bottle of antidepressants that Drew had finally prescribed last night— and slapped her forehead. What an idiot. She'd noticed Hope's tired, clumsy demeanor, and now her sickness, but she'd been too caught up in her own issues. "Are you pregnant?"

Hope flicked a glance at Sean, then at the floor. "Yes."

"And the father—?"

Sean cleared his throat. "Isn't relevant to Hope's employment, sweetie."

Despite everything, he still called her "sweetie" in that way she'd once considered cute. Part of her hated it now, but it was familiar. Very little in her life was anymore.

Now Hope was pregnant. And, as far as Vic knew, without health insurance, since she hadn't offered it to a part-time intern she'd employ for only three months. If that.

She jotted a note to herself. *No more interns.*

As Hope took a tentative step closer, Vic slapped a hand over her notepad and scanned her desk for anything fragile. She moved her water glass back from the edge. Not that Hope, given the chance, wouldn't puke all over the whole damn desk.

"It's not like I'm a total moron or something."

Vic clasped her hands as Sean edged closer, not even pretending to ignore the situation unfolding before them. "I never said you were a moron, Hope."

Only because it didn't happen to be a word she typically used. Inept, incompetent, disaster—she glanced at the ceiling, trying to think of them all—but not moron.

It might be a good addition to the list.

"You know what it's like—"

Vic frowned and held up a hand. "Pregnancy isn't an excuse. It's a medical condition. Nothing more, nothing less." At least in a perfect world, something Vic no longer recognized or inhabited. "The fact that I have two kids doesn't make me any less your employer or the person ultimately responsible for everything that happens in this gallery."

Oh, dear. She hadn't intended to conduct a performance evaluation on Hope today. Although it *was* a Friday . . .

Sean gave his head a quick shake, reading and discouraging

her thoughts. Stupid employment laws. Annoyed, she shooed him away from the door, where he'd taken up residence.

"You're responsible for much more than this gallery." Hope sniffed, and Vic prayed she wouldn't cry.

"Don't worry." Eyeing Hope as she would a four-year-old on the verge of a tantrum, she softened her tone but refused to get sucked into a "we're all just moms" conversation. "As long as you get your job done with a minimum of disruption, everything will be fine."

Hope let loose with a big sniff just as Vic handed her a tissue. "Really? W-when?"

For Vic, when Hope finished her internship. "Eventually, things always work out as they should."

Nice platitude. She peered at the label on the bottle of antidepressants, barely able to read—let alone pronounce—the word "amitriptyline." Elavil. Appropriate only in low doses, according to Drew, not unlike most things in life. As she popped a couple of pills and assigned tasks to keep Sean and Hope out of her office, Vic wished things ever worked out for *her*.

———

LATER THAT AFTERNOON, after enduring hours of Hope's weepy bathroom breaks and Sean's snide remarks, Vic stashed the bottle in her top drawer a moment before Tess poked her head into Vic's office. Apparently, a moment too late.

One eyebrow went up, exposing an eyelid painted emerald to match the eye beneath it. "Midge is worried that you're popping a lot of pills."

"Define 'a lot.' And don't you work?"

"Not if I can help it." Tess propped a hip on Vic's desk, exposing several inches of thigh below her bright-yellow silk skirt, and heedless of the papers beneath her. "Now, let's see. A lot? How about more than I consumed in college?"

"Midge doesn't know what she's talking about."

Tess blinked. "There's a new one."

Prepared for a fight, Vic succumbed to a half-hearted grin. "Fine. Midge *does* know everything. Except about me."

Tess leaned over and pulled out the top drawer, withdrawing three bottles. "Maybe not on every topic, but the kid knows her drugs." She studied each of the labels with an intensity she wasn't known for. "Three doctors, three different prescriptions. A veritable pharmacy."

Vic shuffled through some papers on her desk. "Was there something you wanted?" She yanked a file from underneath Tess's butt. "In case you didn't notice, I'm a little busy."

"Let's see. You're too busy—" Tess leaned toward the door and shut it in Sean's startled face. Turning back, she counted off on her fingers. "To deal with Ryder, deal with the adoption woman, deal with Jake, deal—"

"How did you know that Jake called?"

"He asked for your number. Just because I didn't give it to him doesn't mean he wasn't going to call. Give the guy some credit."

"It took him twenty years to call."

"And you're avoiding the subject." Tess shook a finger at her. "You've spent the past week drunk or doped up, and you're not facing things. It's not even remotely like you."

"What am I not facing?" As if she didn't know.

"You name it. Ryder, Jake, the kid—"

"It's a girl." The words rushed out before she could stop them. A girl. She'd imagined so many things since the social worker called on Monday. What she looked like. Where she'd grown up. Her first step, first word, first date, first kiss. "The social worker called again. I-I had a girl."

"You had the baby a long time ago." Tess caught her gaze and held it. "And you thought it died. If it didn't die and you want to meet this girl, go for it. If you don't, don't. It's that simple."

Vic stopped her trembling fingers on the verge of reaching for a bottle. The delicious floaty feeling she'd held onto since lunch had dissipated in the span of this brief conversation. "Nothing in my life right now is simple."

Reaching for one of her hands, Tess caught it in her own. Vic couldn't stop the quavery movement.

"Then make it simple. It's called survival." Tess stared hard into her eyes. "I'm here for you, Andrea's here for you—" Right. Even though Vic hadn't heard from her in a week. "And Midge is here for you. But no more prescriptions."

Picking up the bottles, Tess dropped them in her purse, swung it over her shoulder, and hopped off the desk. After opening the door to Vic's office, Tess spun around to look back at her. "What are you doing tonight?"

Her mouth, frozen open, moved again. "Hanging out at home? With the kids?"

"Good. I'll call you tomorrow."

Vic watched her leave, then heard Sean's chattering goodbye and the click of the outer door. As she picked up the phone to dial another physician, she reached into her lower drawer—which Tess hadn't opened, thankfully—and pulled out the last bottle. She shook it, hearing only a few pills rattle inside.

Time to stock up. Another long night ahead.

———

HER HEAD SWAM, and she hadn't taken a pill in three hours. Two hours, at least. Vic bent over the gallery's financial ledger, her finger running down the columns and back up again. Nothing matched, nothing added up.

Noting the odd reference to a work—a sculpture?—in handwriting she didn't recognize and could barely read, she blinked a few times to try to clear her vision.

Leave it to Hope to find a way to mess with the books when she shouldn't even have access to them. After wrecking everything in the gallery that wasn't priceless, she must've moved on to bigger challenges. Or the girl was a thief or swindler or con artist—which was unthinkable. Hope didn't have the talent for high crime.

No, either Vic and Sean had crossed wires, or Vic had crossed her own wires. The drugs she was taking could account for it. Tapping her pencil on the ledger, she shook her head. Besides the fact that she found it increasingly difficult to drive, or walk, or even think, she could no longer handle the books.

She closed the ledger and tossed it in the file cabinet. No clients in sight, no appointments, and Sean and Hope weren't working, for reasons she could only vaguely recall. But the clear, sparkling Saturdays that usually accompanied Memorial Day weekend in Minnesota weren't meant to be spent indoors.

After stashing her remaining bottles of pills in her purse, she headed for the door, taking the steps instead of the creaky old elevator, and walked outdoors into bright sunshine.

A beautiful day. Maybe, just this once, it would stay that way. Crossing her fingers, she hopped into her convertible and headed home: her sanctuary from the hellhole that, in one long week, her life had become.

———

AFTER A WINDBLOWN RIDE home that felt so good she wanted to keep going, Vic opened the door from the garage into the house—and almost walked back out again.

"You're back. Thank God." Nat's hair stood on end, a glob of grape jelly smeared her cheek, and she looked like a pirate who'd be only too happy to walk the plank.

"Where are the kids?"

"Uh—"

"Upstairs? Watching TV?" Based on Nat's appearance, Vic would've expected to see them hovering nearby, looking guilty. She glanced toward the kitchen, shutting her eyes against the likely horror she'd find there. "Don't tell me. They're busy cleaning."

"None of the above." Nat glanced over her shoulder, then turned back to stare down at Vic's red espadrilles. "Nice shoes." She whistled, as if she cared about some forty-dollar specials that happened to be comfortable. "But now that you're home, I'd better be going. I have to, uh, head into work."

"Work?" Vic caught Nat's arm as she started, head down, toward the front door. "On a Saturday? Since when?"

"It's—"

"Memorial Day weekend." She tapped Nat under the chin, but her sister still didn't look up. "And you're going to Drew's barbecue. You already told me."

"Oh, right." Nat glanced up, grinning sheepishly, before resuming her perusal of the tile floor. "Don't want to be late. Catch you later."

She broke free of Vic's loose hold and grabbed the door-knob on the front door, turning it to no avail. Thank God for deadbolts.

"Nat, the kids? Where are they?"

"They're fine, Vic." She twisted the doorknob again, and Vic didn't hand her the key. "They're out . . . playing."

"Outside? Alone?" As Vic's heart skidded, she raced to the door, nudging Nat aside in her frantic effort to unlock it. Her keys clattered on the floor. "I can't believe you—"

Nat stood back, crossing her arms. "Let them play outside with their friends? Or let them go with Ryder?"

Vic slumped against the door, her butt sliding down to the floor to join the keys. She still hadn't called Ryder. He'd kidnapped Connor and Megan.

Nat held out her hand to Vic, who didn't take it. "Get off the floor. He's their dad, Vic, and—I've gotta say—a hell of a lot more sober than you've been lately."

"I haven't been drinking." Much.

Nat bent down to pick up the keys before scowling at her. "That would be a miracle. Or would alcohol interfere with all those nasty white pills you're taking?"

She frowned. They weren't all white. Yellow? "I don't know what you mean. I'm working. Taking care of the kids."

"Larissa's taking care of the kids. I'm taking care of the kids. Hell. The *kids* are taking care of the kids." Nat rolled her eyes. "And Sean's probably taking care of the gallery."

"Sean? Ryder's *boyfriend*?" She practically spit on the floor —but Vic didn't spit. Even drugged up, which she wasn't at the moment, thank you very much, she wasn't vulgar. "He's not taking care of a damn thing except himself. And Ryder. I—"

Can't stand it anymore.

She wrapped her arms around her knees, drew them up to her chin, and felt her whole body shake. She just wanted it over. Now. Everything. She felt Nat drop down onto the floor next to her, but she swatted her away. As Nat's arm snaked around her shoulders, Vic curled into a ball and shut out the world. She had to get rid of Nat and whatever else stood in the way of what she wanted.

Oblivion.

She wiped a snotty nose on the knee of her capris. "I'm going to take a nap."

A hand grabbed her elbow. "Like hell you are. You spent too much of last weekend in bed and probably half of this week."

"And your point is—?"

Nat tugged Vic to her feet and headed toward the garage, Vic in tow. "There are a lot of things worse than your life."

"Name one."

"Drew's life." Nat opened the door and, with a hard tap on her shoulder, sent Vic through it. "You might've married Ryder, but he married Babs."

She'd have to work on a response to that one.

CHAPTER 5

"D ad? Mother?" Vic's head swiveled, taking in the group
in Drew's backyard, a cozy little half acre of rolling
green lawn on the far edge of Edina. "Ryder?"

"Hey, Vic." Ryder waved hello, casually, from the brick
patio, as if he weren't sleeping God-knew-where and doing
God-didn't-want-to-know-what with Sean. As if he weren't the
most vile scum on the face of the earth. As if he hadn't stolen
their kids from right under Nat's untrustworthy nose this
afternoon.

Vic's dad, in plaid slacks and a bright-green polo shirt, held
up a hand in greeting. Mother—identical to Babs in skirt,
sweater set, and pearls—kept chatting with her daughter-in-
law, oblivious to the newcomers. Ryder fiddled with the bridge
of his glasses, the only sign he ever gave of nerves.

Drew's three-year-old twins, Scotty and Luke, streaked
across the patio, one wielding a hose and the other shouting
pint-sized obscenities, as the adults jumped back and tried to
stay dry.

"Mom!" "Mommy!" A moment after the twin terrors
vanished around the corner, Connor and Megan appeared
from behind a tree, charged up to Vic, and hurled their arms

around her waist before she could move closer to Ryder and possibly break his glasses.

The impact almost knocked her down. Bending, she scooped each of them into a big hug. After a mile-a-minute summary of their day, they ran off, headed for the tree house.

Eyeing Drew, who was walking through the sliding-glass door of his house bearing a platter of raw meat, Vic wondered how her brother tolerated his wife or kids—and how he did it without medication. She tapped her purse, comforted at the thought of the pills inside.

Nat slipped Vic's purse from her shoulder before she could protest, let alone grab it back. "Don't worry. I'll stash this somewhere."

"Oh, no need." Vic shot her a scathing look.

Nat batted her eyelashes. "Anything for you, sister dear."

Reaching Vic, Drew set down his tray and murmured in a low voice into her ear. "I haven't said anything. Even to Babs."

She opened her mouth.

Grinning, he tipped her jaw shut. "She can't keep a secret."

"No kidding." She laughed, feeling lighter somehow. "But why did you invite—"

"The asshole?"

"Drew!"

They both grinned at Mother's high-pitched voice. Drew held up his drink, saluting Patrice Carlyle. "Your hearing's as good as always, Mom."

Vic put her nose to his glass, sniffing. Scotch. "You got more where that came from?"

"Vic." Nat shook her head. "You shouldn't."

Drew studied Vic's eyes, clearly sizing her up. "Probably not. But just this once." With a few strides, he crossed the patio, poured a tumbler, and dropped a few ice cubes into it. "Want me to splash something over the top?"

"More scotch?"

He hesitated, then shrugged and added a splash. "It's a holiday, after all."

Natalie stormed inside the house with Vic's purse, which would be empty of a certain small bottle when Vic reclaimed it. Her heart fluttered, calming only when she reminded herself that she had more where those came from.

Her dad handed the tumbler to Vic. "How's my baby girl?"

"Nat's your baby. Not me."

"Can't I have two?"

"Warren, quit teasing Victoria. She hates it." Leaving Babs and Ryder, Vic's mother approached her husband and Vic just as a phone rang inside the house. Drew took a step toward it, halting when Nat shouted that she'd answer it. Conversation ceased while they waited for Nat to return outside.

A minute went by. Another. After a few more, Drew left them, sprinting for the house. When he reached the sliding-glass door, Nat appeared, shaken and staring at Vic.

"Nat?" Drew moved past her, headed inside. "Who called? Should I pick up?"

"No." Natalie blinked as if coming out of a trance when Drew grabbed her arm. "They—she—hung up."

"Who called, dear?" Their mother took a step toward Natalie, her nose wrinkled in consternation. "A wrong number?"

"A woman from Kalispell, Montana. Ms. Franklin." Nat spoke in a daze as Mother froze. "She's calling every Carlyle, looking for a Victoria Carlyle."

Vic's breath came out in a whoosh. "What did you say?"

Natalie kept her gaze on their mother's face, which had turned a greenish shade of gray. "I listened."

Vic's dad grabbed a chair and planted it beneath his wife, who fell backward into it, skirt and heels and all.

Nat gazed over Mother's head at Dad. "She told me that a young woman is searching for Vic. I mean, Victoria Carlyle."

His hands on the back of the chair, their dad leaned hard against it, looking confused. "But who is this young woman? Why would she want Vic?"

Mother closed her eyes and leaned back in the chair. Babs stepped closer, but Ryder hung back. Vic glanced at him, wondering whether she should've told him. Wondering if her secret had been bigger than his.

She gulped her drink and headed toward Natalie, intent on ending the conversation. Dad was obviously in the dark, which puzzled her, but Babs didn't need to hear this. At this point, Ryder didn't either.

Nat held up a hand, stopping her. "The young woman's name is—is Hope. Hope McCulloch." She peered intently at Vic. "Isn't that—?"

Her intern. Her pregnant, inept intern with freakish hair and a personality to match. Her daughter?

Vic's glass slipped from her hand, and her body followed it to the ground.

———

Tuesday morning, Hope didn't meet Vic's eyes when she walked in the door of the gallery, where Vic stood waiting, hands on her hips. Now, fifteen minutes later, slumped in a chair across from Vic in her office, Hope's downcast eyes held something that Vic couldn't quite put her finger on.

Another secret? Another problem to fling at a life already littered with them? Vic put a hand to her stomach, trying to tamp down the nausea she'd felt all weekend.

Hope gave the same response to all of Vic's questions, no

matter how she phrased them. "I just wanted to meet my mom."

"You have a mom. And dad. The McCullochs."

The couple from Bozeman, Montana, who'd adopted Hope right after birth, according to Ms. Franklin, who'd given Nat her phone number on Saturday. Vic had called first thing this morning—after swallowing a couple of pills—and Ms. Franklin had answered her questions with an unmistakable note of triumph.

No wonder her stomach ached. "Do they know you're here?"

Hope stared at her hands, folded over her slightly rounded stomach. "Uh, they don't mind."

Vic's gaze narrowed. "But do they know?"

"Not exactly?"

Sighing, she leaned back in her seat. "Tell me everything."

"Since birth?"

Vic laughed, a little shakily. She wasn't ready to go there. "Let's try more recent history. Like when you left Montana, or when you decided to find me."

"Ms. Franklin helped, and I'm pretty good on a computer."

An actual job skill? She tried to keep her face blank.

Hope's chin drooped. "You think I'm a loser." She jerked her head toward the gallery, even though the door to Vic's office was shut. "You and Sean make faces behind my back."

"We don't—"

"Yeah, you do." Hope ran a hand through her badly dyed hair, making it stand up higher. "It's tough being pregnant. I'm clumsy and tired and feel like a jerk. And I don't know much about art."

Indeed. "You might've mentioned that a little sooner."

"And lose the chance to work with you? No way."

"How did you find me? And the gallery?"

Even Ms. Franklin hadn't known. She'd coughed and sounded irritated when Vic admitted she already knew Hope and had hired her for the summer.

Hope rolled her eyes. "Like I said, I know computers. I could help with yours. I can—" Her face lit up as she jabbed her finger at the computer, then sagged backward when Vic shook her head. "Anyway, my boyfriend—" She frowned. "He has a buddy in Kalispell, where your cousin lives."

Her mother's cousin, Shelby Dawson, who'd been far more generous with Vic than Mother had been. "My cousin? How on earth did you track her down?"

Hope shrugged. "Kalispell is a small town. Everyone knows everyone else and everything that happens."

She nodded as understanding dawned. Even at a distance of a thousand miles and twenty-one years, her mother would be mortified. "Like a teenage pregnancy."

"Yeah."

"But that doesn't explain your parents. Or—" Vic paused, wondering how far she should probe. "Your boyfriend. Is he still in Bozeman?"

Hope sagged even lower in her chair. "Ex-boyfriend. He didn't wanna have a kid, and my parents—"

"—blew up?"

A small nod. "Something like that."

"So he dumped you?" Another nod. "And your parents?"

"They said I was just like my real mom." Hope drew in a breath and held it. Then the words rushed out. "Another sleazy tramp who slept around and deserved what she got."

Vic closed her eyes, briefly, and wished she hadn't asked.

She spoke softly, remembering. "But I didn't sleep around. Ja—" She caught herself on his name and mentally steered herself off the dreamy back road where her memories had detoured. "He was my first boyfriend. My first everything."

Including her first massive mistake. And, until ten days ago, her last one.

"That's what I said to my parents."

Vic flinched. "About me?"

"Naaa." Hope rolled her eyes. "About me. They said stupid young girls always say stuff like that." She hesitated. "Like you just did."

Someone knocked sharply on the door just as Vic started to object. She sat back, relieved by the distraction.

"Vic?" Sean opened the door a crack and poked his head in. "Sorry, but I need to interrupt."

As Hope stood up, he opened the door wider to let her leave. Two men in dark blue suits stood behind Sean, their arms crossed in unison.

Vic rose to greet them. "Can I help you, gentlemen?"

One stepped forward. "Victoria Carlyle Bentley?"

"Yes." Her left eye twitched. Something felt . . . wrong.

"FBI." The man flipped open a wallet to reveal a shiny badge that could as easily have been a Mickey Mouse decal, then flipped it closed before she could blink. "We need to ask you a few questions."

———

"Vic? What did they want?"

She swung her purse over her shoulder and brushed past Sean, her only thought to get some fresh air. Or a drink. More pills. An entire IV of morphine.

On autopilot, she left the building, retrieved her car, and drove home. Fast, but not so fast that she'd get pulled over. The pills she'd popped the moment the Feds left her gallery hadn't kicked in yet, but she couldn't take a chance. They might make an ordinary traffic stop look more like Russian roulette.

She blinked when she arrived—not at home, as intended, but at her dad's small law office on the edge of downtown Minneapolis. The receptionist waved her inside the marble-and-chrome lobby. People she'd never seen and didn't know called out greetings.

Dazed and confused didn't begin to describe it.

With her hands and arms tingling oddly, she stumbled into Dad's office. What little was left of her brain was floating in la-la land. Had she locked her car? For that matter, where had she parked it? *Had* she parked it?

Dad rose and walked around his desk to give her a hug. She pulled back and tapped the side of her head—once, twice, finally a good hard slap—to try to stop the buzzing.

"Are you okay, honey?" A frown creased his blurry face. "You look a little, well, I'm not sure what."

Turning away, she eyed a chair as if it were nirvana and wobbled over to it before her legs gave out. "Fine."

Dad grabbed another chair and drew it close. She sat on the far edge of her seat, knowing she didn't reek of whatever was running wild through her system, but not believing it.

"What brings you here at—" He checked his watch and smiled as if everything suddenly made sense. "Noon. Lunch?"

The thought made her want to vomit. She glanced at his desk, which was covered with files. "I obviously knew you kept an office here, but I thought you'd retired."

"I thought so, too." He ran a hand through the salt-and-pepper hair he'd had since forever. "But I didn't quite know what to do with myself."

"Or Mother with you?"

He didn't produce the answering chuckle she'd expected. "When I left my old firm—" The biggest in town, which also happened to employ Ryder, and which had demoted Dad into a smaller office when he turned sixty-five in March. "I realized

I wasn't really ready to quit. So I came here, but not just to read *The Wall Street Journal*. I joined a couple of fellows I've known longer than I care to think about, and some fresh young ones."

"All men?" Her nose wrinkled.

"No. Women tend to do better in law school, as Natalie always says." Finally, a genuine laugh. "Actually, as a big fan of nepotism—" He waggled his eyebrows. "I tried to snap up your sister, but she prefers the salt mines that don't pay."

"That's what you get for raising trust-fund babies."

"Not my doing." Her dad ran a hand over his face. "Your mother's family . . ." He shook his head.

"Had all the dough." It had paid for Vic's gallery and her initial purchases of artwork, but everything had a price. "Is that why you're still slaving away? Mother won't increase your allowance?" She grinned, taking peculiar pleasure in teasing a man who was feared by so many. A man who was just Dad.

Rising from the chair, he moved to the window, staring out at the downtown skyline. "That's not it. I told you I had the chance to work with old friends."

A little dizzy, she bit her lip, wondering where the conversation had veered in the wrong direction. Not that she'd been aiming. "I was teasing."

"I know." He clasped his hands behind his back, looking like the fearsome litigator he'd always been.

"But enough about you." With difficulty, she added a chirp to her voice. "Isn't this supposed to be about me?"

When he flinched, she rushed on before she lost her nerve. This was Dad. The man who'd fixed her scrapes and combed through her tangles when she'd been a little girl. Besides Drew, the only man she still trusted. "I need to talk about—"

"Your mother." He nodded soberly. "I guess I should've expected this, especially after Saturday."

"Saturday?" She felt a flush steal up her face at the memory of collapsing like an over-the-top actor on a soap opera. She'd picked herself up, but not quickly enough to avoid the prying questions from Babs, the cheerfully false explanations from her mother, or the confused looks from her dad and Ryder.

He nodded as if he could read the thoughts spinning through her drug-addled brain. "I'm sorry. I wasn't there when you needed me."

She frowned at him. "I was okay. A bit embarrassed, sure." She flushed again at her dramatic swoon.

"Nothing to be embarrassed about." He flexed the fingers of one hand. "I've seen worse things happen to my friends' kids." His lips twisted. "You were always a good kid, Vicki."

"You know I hate being called Vicki."

He chuckled. "Vic. I'll leave 'Victoria' to your mother."

"And to men who think it somehow sounds more exotic." Like Jake, who in high school wouldn't have known exotic if it bit him in the butt. She wondered why she thought of that.

"In any case, I'm sorry." Her dad stared down at his hands, held together as if by super glue. "I didn't know." He pursed his lips, measuring his words. "About the baby. That you had one."

Her jaw dropped.

"I mean, I knew you were pregnant. Of course. You told us." His shoulders slumped, and he stared at the floor. "But your mother told me the baby died."

Vic's breath caught, and she couldn't swallow. The vivid memory rushed back at her. Her mother's words. Her cold voice.

He shook his head. "At birth. The details were a little fuzzy, but once I heard, I just cared about my own little baby. You. I wanted to know you were okay."

"But why didn't you ever visit?"

He turned his back to her and again searched the skyline. "I knew you were embarrassed and didn't want to see me. I guess I understood."

"You're kidding, right?" He'd called a few times, always from work, but he'd never flown out to Montana. Not once in six long months. "I *wanted* to see you."

As the drugs and lack of food scrambled her brain, she struggled for air and wondered why everything anyone said came out sounding like gibberish.

"Vic?" She blinked, and Dad was next to her. "I'm here now, honey. Right where your dad should be."

"Dad, I—" She felt faint, or way beyond it, and she hadn't even told him what had brought her here. "I need to tell you about Ryder."

"Be honest with him, hon. Be honest with the kids." Her dad knelt by her chair, running a hand briskly over hers. "It's not too late. Your mother—"

"This isn't about Mother. Ryder is—"

"I heard enough on Saturday to guess he's moved out. I'm sorry, honey. And it's poor timing, because I'm—"

"—gay."

"—leaving, too. Your mother."

Speaking simultaneously, their words crossed in the air. A split second later, they heard each other.

Gasping, her dad pulled her into his arms. Her head spun as it pressed against his shoulder.

"But you—you love Mother." She'd always wondered how, but she figured love was like that. Inexplicable. She sniffed against his crisp cotton shirt. "Everything is crazy. I have a daughter, and she found me, she's working for me, she's awful, she's pregnant, Ryder's sleeping with Sean, and—"

Her dad held her close, stroking her hair. "Easy now."

"And the FBI thinks my gallery deals in stolen artwork. Or

fakes. Or something." And she was high as a kite, which didn't seem like a good thing to point out to Dad.

He straightened and pulled away, frowning, then spoke in slow, measured words. "You always had to top everyone for news." He tilted her chin up and looked her right in the eye, even though her own eyes were almost crossed. "But finally my baby gives me something I can fix."

————

"I THOUGHT HE FIXED THIS." Late Thursday afternoon, Vic mumbled to herself as she frowned at the computer screen, which held a swirl of numbers and symbols more closely resembling a Van Gogh than a balance sheet. And she hadn't even taken a single pill all day. She clicked on the "X" in the upper right-hand corner, trying to close the program. Nothing happened.

A quiet knock. "Need any help with that, Vic?"

Hope. The savior from the black lagoon.

Vic pursed her lips and tried pointing at a different box. She tapped on the mouse and random keys, clicking frantically. "Close, damn it!" Nothing. She glanced over her shoulder at Hope, who leaned against the doorjamb, a smug grin on her face.

"Hopeless."

Vic blinked.

"I mean, that program is hopeless." Hope pointed at the frozen screen. "Aren't those the gallery's financials? No wonder." Tsking loudly while Vic rolled her chair out of the way, Hope walked over to the keyboard, hit a couple of keys, and shut down the program. "You're not using true accounting software. You want a program that you can customize, so it can do more for you."

Vic's eyes glazed over, and Hope's advice drifted past her while she prayed frantically for Sean to appear. He'd promised to fix the financials yesterday. "I don't need more complexity, Hope. For starters, I just want a program that opens and closes."

"With better software, you can separate promotional costs by artist, by opening, and figure out how much money you're really making." Hope continued to hover near the computer, glancing at the financial printouts strewn across the desk. "You can book expenses and revenue separately, too. And inventory is a snap. I can show you."

Vic sighed. "Sean takes care of the financials."

"He can't do it as well as I can." Hope kept talking when Vic frowned, but she inched backward toward the door. "I mean, he's not even using the right software."

Vic held up a hand. "That's enough. I asked you to organize our catalogs and brochures, then compare the inventory list I gave you against the artwork on display and in the storage area. Have you finished that?"

Hope's mouth opened, then closed.

"I didn't think so. You need to do what I ask you to do, not what you'd rather be doing. If you wanted a computer job, you shouldn't have come to an art gallery." The phone rang. "Now, maybe you can get back to work?"

Head down, Hope shuffled out the door while Vic chirped her name into the phone.

"Vic? Got a minute?"

Ryder. She glanced at the clock. Just after five. "I'm a little busy. What do you want?"

"I, uh, had a great time with the kids on Saturday."

"I'm so happy for you." She stopped twirling the pencil in her fingers, nearly snapping it in half. "After stealing them from under Nat's nose? If I recall, you asked if you could see them, and I told you no."

"I didn't steal them. They're my kids, too."

Sean poked his head in the door of Vic's office, and she waved him away. Standing up, she walked over to the door and shut it. "Let's get real. You've never spent more than five minutes a day with the kids."

"That's not true."

"You're right. On vacation, it's more like ten minutes." He'd often disappeared during chunks of their vacations, and she'd assumed he'd been jogging. Vic grimaced, trying not to imagine where he'd actually been. "What is it you want? Fifteen minutes?"

"I want my fair share."

"Fair? You really want to talk about fair?" A knock on her door, followed by Sean poking his head inside again. Vic slammed it on Ryder's lover. "You didn't just wreck our marriage and our family, Ryder. You ruined my gallery. Everything."

She willed the tears not to fall. She was done with crying. Done with Ryder. Done, damn it.

"Let's be reasonable." Ryder's voice was calm and soothing, making her want to throw something. "The kids need both of us. If we can't reach a reasonable understanding, we'll have to get lawyers involved. Do you want that?"

Vic's hand went to her throat, but she kept her voice from trembling. "Spit it out, Ryder. What exactly do you want?"

"I just want to see the kids. Spend time with them. Share my life with them."

His life with Sean. No wonder Sean kept poking his head in the door. He was probably listening in on the extension.

She took a deep breath. "You spent all these years lying to

me and *not* spending time with the kids, and then you walked out on us. I asked *exactly* what you want. Try harder."

She slammed the receiver on her desk just as Sean opened the door again. "Vic? Sorry to keep bugging you, but Hope said you wanted to talk about the computer?" He frowned. "Her plans for new software?"

Screw the software. Screw Sean. Too late, she tried to erase that thought. Biting her lip, she shook her head and closed the door. Softly. She moved in a trance to her desk and slumped into her chair. One hand reached into the lower drawer for a bottle of pills. A minute later, her other hand shook as she punched in Tess's number.

———

"IF THE FEDS are after you, why would they admit it to you before showing up with a warrant for your arrest?"

Thursday evening, Tess sat on the floor in Vic's living room and blew a smoke ring in the air. Vic's gaze followed the trail of smoke to the ceiling, wondering what Ryder would say. Ryder, who'd always claimed that smoke triggered his asthma, even though he ran and biked and played basketball without wheezing.

Ryder, who'd also pretended to be straight.

Vic almost lit up a cigarette herself. It would be her first since she'd started dating Ryder. The thought made her smile.

"What's so funny about the Feds barking up your tree?"

The smile disappeared, quickly replaced by her almost-constant longing for pills. She turned to Tess. "I was thinking about smoking. And—" She waved her hands in circles, trying to capture the universe of her odd, disconnected musings.

Tess sucked on the cigarette, making the end of it glow

bright red. "Ahh. The random thoughts of a woman high as a kite."

"I'm not as high as a kite." Not since three this afternoon, when Sean had asked again about the FBI. "But I'm worried about the FBI."

Tess nodded. "What did they say? They're conducting an investigation? You're their suspect?"

She shrugged. "They asked about my family. And Sean. Even Hope. I don't exactly see her as a criminal mastermind." Or as a daughter. The concept was too disturbing. "They didn't ask about me, but maybe they're asking other people."

"No one called me."

"Do you think—"

"There's anything to it? No." Tess tapped the cigarette on the edge of a ceramic Tiffany box as Vic tried not to look. "But they must've heard something."

"From whom?"

"Got any enemies?" Tess tapped the fingers of one hand on the coffee table, as if counting all of Vic's enemies. "I can't imagine any unless we consider Babs, but Babs is as dumb as a tree stump."

"That's what I thought about Hope."

"And you've changed your mind? Now that she's supposedly your daughter?" Tess inhaled hard and started coughing. "Maybe she got Jake's gene pool."

"Jake's not dumb."

"Are you nuts? He let you go."

Vic sank into the sofa. "No, he didn't. I let him go."

"And he didn't chase after you." Tess shook her head. "I expected better of him. I sure never expected—"

She froze, then puffed hard on her cigarette and blew another smoke ring. The first that wasn't perfect.

"What didn't you expect? Tess? Tell me."

Thumbing through a large book of Impressionism, Tess touched the body of a fuzzy Degas dancer. One of Degas's later works, when the artist was blind and painting from memory. Just how Vic felt as she crawled through life right now.

Finally, Tess looked up. "Forget about Jake. He's not worth it. Probably married or something, anyway."

Married? "He asked me out."

"Ah-ha!" Nailed. Damn. "What did you say? 'Sorry, but I'm saving myself for my gay husband'?"

"Nothing. No excuses. Just no."

"Sweetie, when they said 'just say no,' they didn't mean Jake." Knees creaking, Tess got up from the floor. "Where are the kids? And a bottle of wine? And not in that order."

"The kids are upstairs in the TV room. Probably watching something rated R." Vic bounced off the sofa, stumbling forward a moment before catching her balance, and walked with Tess to the kitchen. "I might have a bottle of white in the fridge."

When they reached the kitchen, Tess headed straight to the refrigerator and started rummaging. "Half a bottle?" She held up the last bottle of pinot grigio and glanced over her shoulder at the empty wine rack. "And nothing to spare? Did Ryder take the rest as his divorce settlement?"

"No divorce settlement yet. Or papers, for that matter. I'm not sure if he's even officially moved out, although he's obviously not here."

Tess bumped the fridge shut with her hip and reached into the cupboard for a wineglass while Vic poured herself a glass of water.

"What about the kids? Are you doing joint custody?"

She frowned. "Joint? Why would I?"

"Because they're half Ryder's? Because you have a gallery

to run?" Tess's gaze went to Vic's purse on the counter, which held three small bottles of pills, not that Tess would know that. "Because you've got a little problem?"

"With the FBI?"

A brisk shake of the head. "With drugs. What are you trying to do? Kill yourself?"

The thought had crossed her mind. Daily. When she woke and when she closed her eyes at night and far too often in between.

"How could you even think that?"

"Just thought I'd ask." Tess took a sip, slid her arm around Vic, and led her back to the living room sofa. "That's what friends do."

"Friends don't suggest joint custody."

"Actually, they do. If your husband is a lawyer and has any inkling of the drugs I think you're taking, he might not stop at joint custody. He might go all the way."

"Even if he's hardly ever here? Even if he's never spent much time with them? Even if he's gay?" Vic's jaw clenched, even though she knew that being gay obviously had nothing to do with Ryder's ability to be a good dad. He'd be a lousy straight dad, too. "The courts might give him the kids?"

One perfectly sculpted eyebrow rose nearly to Tess's hairline. "There's nothing wrong with being gay, as you would've been the first to say until you found out that your husband is gay. He's not a bad person. He has a good job. Gay versus potential overdose? I wouldn't want to place bets."

She could lose Connor and Megan. Lose her home. Thanks to the FBI, maybe lose her gallery. The pills—in her purse, in her dresser, in a dozen other nooks and crannies— called to her, singing their siren song.

She bit her lip. Trembled. Tried to breathe deeply and tune out her fears.

An hour later, after pushing Tess out the door, Vic snuggled with Connor and Megan, who groaned over missing a movie they'd seen a hundred times. Tears filled her eyes as she brushed her cheek against her kids' hair, inhaling the semifresh sweetness, feeling the softness. Praying for an answer.

She kissed them goodnight and went to her bedroom, shut the door, and grabbed several bottles of pills from the back of the bottom drawer in her dresser.

As her heart pounded, she swallowed a handful of pills, took a swish of water, and waited. It didn't stop the pain, and she had to stop the pain. Another handful. More water when the pills lodged in her throat, choking her. Somehow, more pills anyway.

An empty bottle.

Her hand shook as she opened another bottle. Even more pills through blurry eyes that couldn't quite see them, hands that fumbled with the bottle and struggled to hang onto the glass of water. Water sloshed down her chin, soaking her shirt. Her mind stopped racing through all the horrid nightmares she'd lived with for a week. Two weeks? No idea.

She collapsed on the floor, her knees buckling awkwardly but painlessly beneath her. She felt so empty. Felt numb. Felt—

Oh, God. The kids. She'd never see them again. Her heart slammed in her chest, nearly exploding, and she jammed her fingers down her throat, trying to throw up the pills. Wanting her kids desperately. Loving them desperately. What the fuck had she done?

No pain. Oblivion.

CHAPTER 6

"What are you doing, Warren?" Thursday evening, Patrice Carlyle walked into her bedroom to find her husband packing a large suitcase. She wrinkled her nose. "You never mentioned a business trip. Remember, we're having dinner at the Kaplans' tomorrow night."

The slow, methodical movement of his hands from dresser to suitcase, closet to suitcase, unnerved her. After a dull evening of bridge, she'd come home early, hoping to catch Warren without a file or a book. Perhaps they could enjoy a late dinner at a restaurant, even though she'd nibbled at bridge. Food wasn't the point. She needed to talk.

They hadn't, not really, in too long.

Arms folded, she watched her silent husband. "Warren? Why are you packing? I thought you wouldn't be traveling so much anymore."

She'd looked forward to more time together when he left his large firm. After forty years of devoted service, they'd practically forced him out. Unimaginable. But at the moment, his utter refusal to speak to her was even more perplexing.

"Warren?" She moved closer, tapping him on the shoulder as she peeked past him into the mostly-full suitcase. Enough underwear for a month-long trip to Tahiti. Frowning, she saw now that another large suitcase stood next to the bed. She moved to the dresser and pulled out two drawers. Empty.

"Warren!" Her voice was shrill, even to her ears. "What are you doing?"

He finally turned, but his gaze didn't meet hers. "I'm leaving. I'm sorry, Patrice. Too many things have happened." He shook his head. "Too many lies."

"Lies? When did I ever lie?"

Clutching a pair of white boxers, he sat on the bed on top of a heap of socks. Patrice reached to pull them out from under him, snatching back her hand only when she realized she was helping her husband of forty years pack.

She sank onto the bed next to him, her hand reaching for his thigh, and winced when he removed her hand.

"Why didn't you tell me about Vic?"

"Victoria, dear. We didn't give her a boy's name." She smoothed the comforter with her trembling left hand, watching the large diamond he'd given her for their thirtieth anniversary glimmer. "What should I have told you?"

"You name it. The baby, Ryder—"

Her breath caught. "Ryder? What's wrong with Ryder?"

He stared at the boxers so intently that she snatched them away and tossed them in the suitcase. Better there than in his hands. There was something . . . vulgar about it.

He crossed his arms, drawing her gaze to a chest that had often held her so close. But not for ages. "You'd think I would've guessed. I worked with the guy. Late nights, weekends, trials, client trips. I got him his job there."

"I'm sure Victoria is grateful." With jerky movements, she reached for a pair of socks and refolded them.

"Not at the moment." He glanced sideways at her and shook his head. "Not that she'd hold it against me. Vic's a good kid. And Drew knew the guy at the University of Wisconsin. Hell. He introduced Ryder and Vic."

Patrice threw down the socks. "Why are we talking about Ryder and Victoria? You're leaving because of them?"

He shook his head. "Vic's having a tough go of it, poor kid. And Drew is stuck with that—" He curled his lip, as if he found something distasteful. "Babs."

"Barbara is quite pleasant in her own way."

"And Nat won't be caught dead with a guy. Hell. You don't think she's—what do you call women these days?—lesbian, do you?"

"Natalie? A—" She couldn't even say the word, even though their pastor was, and she liked their pastor. And her wife. A darling couple. "Don't be ridiculous, dear. Natalie just works too hard. I've tried to speak to her."

"No wonder." He slapped his thigh and stood up. "Both girls do the opposite of whatever you say. Hey, maybe you should tell Nat to work harder. She'd get married in short order."

Patrice felt her heart stop. Warren was obviously upset. About what, she had no idea. He wasn't a man who shared his feelings. She doubted any man truly did.

"Natalie loves her work, for reasons I don't always understand, and Victoria doesn't know her own mind." She clenched one fist, relaxing it when her nails dug into her palm. "But when were *you* ever here to give them advice?"

He bent his head. "I should've been. I wanted to give them everything, so I worked." He ran a hand through hair that needed trimming. "That's how it goes in most families."

"Not anymore." She lifted an eyebrow, imagining all the hours Victoria spent in her gallery. Yes, she had a fine collection, but she should've purchased it for her own home. Not for strangers. "Men and women both work. No one stays home to tend to the children."

Warren tossed a handful of socks at the suitcase, some of them not even matched or folded. "We had nannies taking care of the children. And the first time one of the kids did something wrong, you shipped her off to Siberia."

"My cousin lives in Kalispell. It was easier." She sniffed, wondering why everything was suddenly an issue. Just because that dreadful woman had called. "You're acting as though you approve of what she did."

"Have sex? Get pregnant?" He barked out a laugh. "Tell me again—how long after our wedding did Drew arrive?"

She bit her lip. "Five months. But we were engaged."

"We were talking about getting engaged. The way a lot of kids talk."

She waved a hand. "We'd been dating quite a while. We were serious. We weren't in high school."

"No, you were a sophomore in college. You never finished."

Her eyes went wide. "Is that what this is about? After all these years? I got pregnant with your child and never finished college?"

Pressing his lips together, he didn't say anything. Despite herself, Patrice folded socks and straightened his underwear in the suitcase. Warren would be lost without her, whether or not she had a college degree.

"It's not about you, Patrice. It's not always about you."

A hand went to her throat. "Have I been selfish? When? When have I been selfish?"

He just looked at her.

"I took care of the home and the children and, frankly, you. I packed for you. Did your laundry."

"The dry cleaners and the maid did it."

Utter nonsense. "I've been here for you for forty years. For you and the children."

"Were you there for Vic? Were you there when she had the baby, and you told her the baby died?" He slammed the suitcase shut. "For Christ's sake, how could you do that? How could you lie to all of us?"

"I didn't lie. The baby died in every sense of the word. I don't know what they're—" She stood, refusing to finish his packing. He could fend for himself. "I wanted to give Victoria a chance at a normal life. Go to college. Get married in the normal course. Have normal—"

"—children? Patrice, a kid's not normal just because his parents are married. That's no guaranty."

"No, but it's easier for everyone. For Victoria."

"Yeah, she's in great shape. A kid surprises her twenty years later, and her husband turns out to prefer men."

"He—" Her breath caught in her throat.

"Ryder is gay." Warren rolled both suitcases into the hall and started toward the bathroom. "He's moved out."

She followed him to the bathroom, where his shaving kit and sundries lay scattered around his sink.

"He's not—" She nearly choked on the word. "Gay. They have children. He was at Drew's on Saturday. Perhaps Victoria is involved with someone." She closed her eyes, sickened at the likely scandal.

"I don't know why he was there—knowing Ryder, probably just for show—but he's gone. He left her. He's gay."

"And . . . that's why you're leaving? Because Ryder is?"

"No." He paused in the middle of tucking a bottle of cologne in his shaving kit, making her nose twitch. Polo. Her favorite. A sudden, horrid thought occurred to her.

Dare she ask? "Then . . . why?"

"I'm sixty-five, Patrice, and I'm not sure I can spend the

rest of my life with you." He threw more things in his kit and wouldn't look at her. "And I'm not so sure you'd want to spend it with me, either, all things considered."

She stumbled backward before catching herself. Dignity. Always. "I can't imagine—"

The phone rang, jarring her. On wooden legs, Patrice walked to her bedside table to answer it. "Hello?"

"Mom? Thank God. It's Drew." Her son's words rushed out frantic, staccato, and garbled. "You and Dad need to get to the hospital. Kendall South. Right away. An ambulance is at Vic's house now and will be headed there as soon as they stabilize her. She OD'd on some pills and—"

Patrice shrieked as the phone clattered to the floor.

———

"She's not dead? She looks awful."

"Be quiet, Babs. She might be able to hear you."

"If she cared about hearing me, I don't think she'd have taken all those pills."

"No offense, but I doubt you were her first or last thought." Drew's brief chuckle sounded almost painful. "Or anywhere in between."

The words floated over Vic, spinning near her head, which ached terribly. Her arms and legs were numb, her eyelids glued shut. Babs had probably done that. Vic tried to laugh, but her stomach jolted. Ugh. It felt like some mad combination of being put through a meat grinder and having a couple of huge brutes tie a rope around her waist and pull hard from each end.

She'd died. A dazzling white light had glowed all around her and she'd flown like the wind through some bizarre tunnel. She could swear she'd actually seen Dad's parents and talked to Carrie, who looked almost exactly the same as she had the summer before college. Before Vic had left for Vassar. She'd never forget the October day when Carrie had gleefully called to tell her all about her brand-new truck. She'd been the first to buy her own wheels. She'd died that afternoon, four-wheeling over the top of a hill with nothing on the other side.

Great, wracking sobs rolled through Vic, exactly the same ones she'd offered up that day and for weeks, months, afterward—but this time the tears didn't even pool. No noise reached her ears or outward movement stirred her body. Except for the pain, she wasn't functioning.

If Babs was here, though, Vic hadn't reached heaven.

The annoying, whiny voice kept coming at her like a freight train at full speed. "I don't get it, Drew. What made her take all those pills? What could possibly be wrong with Little Miss Perfect that a trip to a spa wouldn't fix?"

One of Vic's fingers moved. A fraction of an inch, but it was a start. Four more fingers and she could strangle Babs.

"I told you to cut it out, Babs. Vic isn't any more perfect than you or—"

"Me? I'm not perfect?" Her voice went up an octave. "Where's that coming from? I told you I was going to lose the pregnancy weight, Drew, and I will. Now that the boys are three, I have more time."

Vic heard a small gurgling sound in her throat.

"Vic? Did you say something?" Someone bent over her, close, too close, as Vic felt a tickle of hair. "Did you hear that, Babs? That noise? I think it was Vic."

"Probably just one of the machines. There must be thirty of them in here." A tsking sound. "You'd think they would've given her a room with more than one chair. I don't know how they expect people to stay very long."

"They don't. It's intensive care. In fact, we should probably leave."

No. Don't. Please don't. Vic tried desperately to mouth the words, but she couldn't move, speak, even moan. She tried telepathy, mentally tuning into Drew and zapping thoughts in his direction. *Don't leave me alone here. Send Babs home.*

A door clicked open, and footsteps shuffled across the floor.

"Dr. Carlyle?" A woman's gentle voice. "I'm sorry, but I've already given you fifteen minutes."

"I understand."

Vic's thumb moved, and she tried to lift her hand to touch Drew. Nothing. Her hand might as well be a boulder.

The hair tickled her cheek again, and Drew spoke into her ear. "Hang in there, kid. We're here with you, right outside the door. Dad and Mom and Nat are on their way."

The kids? Where were her kids?

"K—" The effort exhausted her and yielded only that slight sound.

Apparently, no one heard it. As she struggled again to speak, to make Drew understand, Babs's shrill voice intruded. "We're staying? But the boys—"

"—are already in bed. And the babysitter is only too happy to rack up a few more bucks waiting for us to get home."

Silence. Then Vic heard a drawn-out sigh followed by a noise like keys jangling.

"Here. Take the car. I'll grab a Lyft or hitch a ride with someone. Later."

The keys clattered to the floor. "Are you sure?" A pause. "Well, uh, take care, Vic. That was a stupid thing you did, but I hope you get better. Not that you can hear me or anything. God, I can't believe I'm talking to a vegetable."

"She's not a vegetable!" Loud footsteps moved away from Vic, and she heard the sound of the door opening again. "Go home before you say something even more idiotic."

"I'm not—"

The door slammed. Just as Vic resigned herself to being desperately alone, more footsteps moved softly toward her, and someone's hand held hers. A man's hand.

"I'm so sorry, Vic." She heard the sound of sniffles that didn't come from her. Drew? "I even prescribed one of your antidepressants. Nat said something, and I should've listened. Paid more attention. Taken care of my sis."

She felt a single tear drizzle down from her eyes and, a moment later, a rough finger brush it away.

"Yeah, you're going to be okay. God, I'm sorry. This time I won't let you down."

She was the one who'd let everyone down. She'd failed everyone, but especially Connor and Megan. When more tears followed the first, Drew hugged her.

———

THE MUSICAL RINGING of a phone jarred Ryder out of a heavy, dreamless sleep. He reached out his hand, patting the nightstand next to his side of the bed for his glasses. Not there. His phone wasn't, either—where had he left it?—and the clock was too fuzzy to read. "Sean. I think it's your cell phone."

A grumble and snort and a few other unpleasant noises were the only response. Finally, Sean leaned over the bed and picked his cell phone up off the floor. "'lo?"

A moment later, he passed the phone to Ryder and went back to his face-down position on the pillow.

The people at work obviously didn't have Sean's number. No one did, or no one who'd call Sean, looking for him. Except Vic. Running a hand over his face, he put the phone to his ear and mumbled a greeting.

"Ryder? You'd better get your lame ass over to Kendall

South. Vic's in the intensive-care unit. She— Never mind. Just get there as soon as you can."

The woman's voice was fast and familiar. Natalie? "Kendall South? Vic? Who is this?"

"Tess, of course. The only person who'd bother calling you, and I don't know why I am. And of course you had your phone turned off. Worthless."

"But—"

"Just get there. Fast."

Frowning, he leaned across Sean to slip the phone back into its cradle. He landed on top of Sean's back, awkwardly, as Sean rolled over and pulled him into his arms. Squirming away, he folded himself into a sitting position. Vic?

Sean rolled over again, his words muffled by the pillow. "Wrong number? On my phone?"

He couldn't speak. His knees creaked as he rose, fumbled for his boxers, a pair of pants, a shirt. In the dark, he groped for his glasses with unsteady hands, finally knocking into them on the floor next to his nightstand.

"Ryder?"

"It wasn't a wrong number." His throat went dry, and he hacked up some phlegm. "Vic's in the hospital."

Sean sat up, rubbing his eyes. Ryder flipped on a lamp, and they both winced.

"What happened?" Sean sprang from the bed and grabbed some clothes. "Wait. I'll go with you to the hospital."

Already dressed, Ryder hopped on one foot as he tried to get his shoe on. "I don't think that's a good idea."

"Why? I work with Vic."

"And I'm her husband. At this point, anyway."

"YOU LOOK LIKE HELL, YOU KNOW."

Tess. Her hand gripped Vic's and held tight, nearly squeezing it to death. Vic still couldn't feel much below the hips, but her arms and hands tingled, almost a burning sensation, a small army marched through her stomach, and she could move her lips. She'd pay a small fortune for a glass of water.

Her eyelids peeked open, protesting the movement. Wearing the same clothes she'd had on earlier this evening— what time was it, anyway?—her friend stood grim and alert right next to her. Biting her lip and fighting back tears.

So many tears tonight, and from such unexpected quarters.

"You are such a stupid, selfish little shit." The effort to hold back her tears made Tess's words come out strangled. "But I won't tell you that now. I'm here to cheer you up. When you're feeling better, I'm gonna give you hell."

Vic started to smile, freezing when pain shot across her face. She vaguely wondered where she was, who'd found her, how she'd arrived here. She also wasn't convinced that being alive was such a good thing. She closed her eyes again.

"Hey." A finger poked her upper arm. "Don't even bother trying to avoid me. Open those baby blues, sweetie, or I'll pry them open."

This was why Midge had gone to med school and Tess had made a career out of marrying wealthy men. No bedside manner.

Vic's eyelids fluttered open. Without moving her head, she tried to peer around the room, taking in the machines and tubes connected to her or whirring softly in the background. A few beeped. The prongs of an oxygen tube were attached to her nose, irritating it.

She flicked a glance from Tess to the oxygen tube.

Tess crossed her arms. "Don't even think about it. After the trouble they went to just bringing you back from the edge—"

She shook a finger at Vic. "You're not going to touch a goddamn thing. And no one's going to help you."

Vic closed her eyes.

"And quit ignoring me." Another poke in the shoulder. "Not many people like to spend their valuable time hanging out with a rich and gorgeous blonde. It's thoroughly annoying, particularly when the blonde in question goes and fucks with everyone."

Her eyes flew open.

"I see your hearing is just fine. Good." Heedless of all the tubes that looked so intimidating, Tess propped on the edge of the bed. "You're lucky, you know."

Vic closed her eyes, unable to listen. Maybe when she felt a little less foggy. Maybe when her ears stopped ringing and her stomach stopped doing the jitterbug. Or maybe never.

Another damned poke.

"I'm going to keep talking no matter how rude you are." One eye opened. "Yes, you. You didn't want Ryder to have custody, so you tried killing yourself? No offense, babe, but you graduated summa cum laude. When did you lose your math skills?"

A tear trickled down Vic's cheek.

She'd been terrified of losing the kids, and now she'd almost certainly lost them. Despite Dad and the best legal team he could hire, she was dead. Or she might as well be. Ryder would have the kids. Ryder and Sean, together, going to PTA meetings.

Tess grabbed a tissue and dabbed it under her eyes. "Just so you know, your kids are damned smart. Connor heard a noise and went to check on you. He called 9-1-1, then Drew, and the brave little kid held your head in his lap until the ambulance arrived. Even then, Connor wouldn't let go of you. He told the paramedics he had to take care of you."

"Wh—" Vic's cheeks blew out, but nothing else happened.

Tess patted her. "Don't worry. You'll talk soon enough. The doctor thinks all the drugs put your body to sleep, and it'll wake up little by little."

As Tess spoke the words, Vic could feel her bladder spring to attention.

"The kids are fine. While the ambulance brought you here, Drew found Larissa's number and called her. She's staying at your house overnight."

Vic's mind swam with the information, and the dull ache in her head was accompanied by occasional sledgehammers.

Tess looked over her shoulder, then patted Vic's hand. "Now get better. Your parents just arrived, and I'll bet they want to see you before you toddle off to sleep."

She didn't want to sleep. The last time she had, she'd thought it was forever. Vic tried to shake her head, to stop Tess from leaving. She couldn't be left alone. Alone, for her, was way too terrifying.

Smiling, Tess got up and walked out the door.

———

"Vic? Okay if I come in?"

Her eyes, closed only for a moment after Tess's departure, flickered open. She tried nodding at her dad, but it made everything inside her head rattle.

He took a cautious step inside the room, then looked back out and motioned to someone before finally shutting the door behind him. He'd sprouted a few more gray hairs since she saw him a couple of days ago. Vic winced. She'd dumped all her problems on him, waltzed out of his office, and almost killed herself.

"Quite a week you've had." He walked to the side of her

bed, claiming Tess's place, never taking his gaze off of her. Her breath caught, and the oxygen tube dug into her nose. "You didn't believe me when I said I'd take care of your problems. Some high-priced lawyer I am. Some father."

Oh, Dad. Tears welled in her eyes, and her hand struggled to touch his arm. She felt . . . something. More tingling in her fingers, and she could almost swear they brushed against Dad. Startled, he looked down at her hand, confirming it.

"Not much of a husband, either. I packed my bags tonight, not knowing how rotten my timing was." He lightly clasped her hand, which strained against his. "Next time we'll have to coordinate our schedules."

She couldn't smile.

"Your, uh, mother is right outside." He glanced back through the glass in the wall, shaking his head, presumably at Mother. "She has trouble with hospitals."

And with children who turned out to be far from perfect.

"But she's here. She loves you very much, and she's worried about you." His gaze probed Vic's face, making her squirm. "What should I tell her?"

That I'm as close to the edge as I was a few hours ago? Closer, even? I know I can do it now.

She blinked.

"That good, huh?" He patted her hand and glanced at the monitors near her head, reading the numbers out loud. "But you're alive. We're going to keep you that way, sweetheart."

He stood up, giving her hand one last squeeze. "There's no problem that can't be fixed. If not by your dad, then by someone else. I promise."

She flashed back to the dad he'd been in her childhood. Big, strong, invincible. Utterly confident he could change the world for her happiness and convenience. Just how he looked right now. As if, for her, he could conjure a fairy tale and a happily-ever-after on demand.

She wished it worked that way in real life.

———

"Vic? Talk to me, Vic."

Five minutes or an hour or two—she had no idea—after her dad left, Vic found herself peering at a white-faced Ryder through eyelashes that stuck together. She groaned.

"Good, good." He paced back and forth at the end of her bed. "You're moving, making sounds. You'll be fine in no time."

When did he go to medical school?

He stopped suddenly, arms crossed on his chest. "But what happened?" He ran a hand through sleep-tousled hair that stuck out at odd angles. Not at all like Ryder. "Sorry. I forgot you can't talk yet." He snapped a finger. "But soon. We'll have you up and out of here before you can blink."

We? Had Ryder forgotten everything that had happened?

She tried feigning sleep.

"Yeah, you must be tired. Sleep. That's the ticket."

If he snapped his finger again, she'd break it off. If she could muster the energy.

"In the meantime, don't worry about the kids. Between Larissa and me, we'll handle them." Oh? "And Sean can cover for you at the gallery."

Her stomach lurched. She hadn't even thought about the gallery. She tried shaking her head, but a lightning bolt zapped her and she held still, praying for an end to the pain. Exactly what she'd prayed for a few hours ago, at home, but she hadn't imagined this kind of pain.

Her legs started to tingle. A moment later, it felt like they were on fire. Like bones regrowing themselves, shifting in place with the sole purpose of tormenting her. Maybe she'd died and gone to hell. Babs and Ryder had visited. It couldn't be a much farther drop from there.

"Oh, and Vic?" Ryder stepped closer, near her elbow, one foot nervously tapping the floor. "While you're laid up, I think I should move back home." Looking away, he didn't see her eyes grow wide with terror. "Maybe even on a permanent basis."

Skyrockets went off in her head. She should've swallowed more pills. Finding out about Ryder, and losing him, had been horrific. Getting him back would be even worse.

CHAPTER 7

"**K**nock, knock."
Friday morning, after somehow surviving the worst night of her life, Vic opened her eyes just as a tall, startling apparition stepped into her room. Jake.

She willed herself to keep her eyes open. Lord knew she couldn't run, or even hide, although her legs now wiggled and her hands were a marvel of independent movement.

"Hey." He leaned against the door frame, not looking even remotely awkward or uncomfortable. For some reason, it annoyed the hell out of her. "Sorry. About what happened."

"Good news travels fast." Her throat ached at her first words since last night's . . . event. She wasn't quite sure what to call it, but Mother would certainly find a euphemism before the day was out. "Tess?"

"Got it in one." When he grinned, dimples she didn't really remember dug a groove into the corners of his mouth. "She must've forgotten I run a bar. I think she called at seven a.m."

"Knowing Tess, she remembered."

"Yeah." Another flash of dimples, followed by a crease running down the middle of his forehead as he took a step closer. "You know, not wanting to see me again is okay. You didn't have to take it to such extreme lengths."

"Now you tell me."

"I'm good with advice. It comes with owning a bar." Clutching a baseball cap, he rounded the end of her bed and stopped near her knees, which quaked for reasons she couldn't begin to explain. Jake wasn't here to ask her out again. He was just visiting. As a friend.

An old friend.

But they hadn't been friends in too long to count. Maybe ever. Had they been friends before lovers? Somehow, she'd managed to block that out along with everything else from twenty-one years ago. Until Hope showed up on her doorstep.

She sighed.

"Pendulum isn't so bad." He moved closer to her hips, sending the tingling higher on her legs. "Actually, it's a great place, which I might say even if I didn't own it. I bought it with a friend ten years ago, but he bailed a few years back. Now it's just me and a couple dozen employees."

Vic thought of her own employees. Hope. Sean, Ryder's lover, who'd somehow need to keep the gallery open in her absence, preferably not while sleeping with Ryder in her house.

"Victoria?" Jake took another step closer.

She flushed at the scrutiny in his piercing blue eyes. Another step or two and he'd land in her face. She waved for him to sit. Turning, he grabbed the only chair in the room and dragged it next to the bed.

She wasn't up to this. Maybe not ever, but definitely not today. "I couldn't talk last night." Even now, the words croaked from a dry throat. "I guess I forgot how."

"Yeah. Pretty rough." He looked down at the hat he still gripped, and his hands—tanned, with long fingers and the slightest dusting of golden hair—arrested Vic's own gaze. "Tess didn't tell me much, but I filled in the blanks."

Nodding, she closed her eyes. He probably didn't *need* to imagine all the gruesome details. Tess wouldn't have spared many to Jake, a good-looking guy who owned a bar. The whole thing left a bitterly green taste in her mouth.

Not that she had any interest in Jake. Absolutely not.

"Hey. You're not falling asleep on me, are you? Just when I was going to ask you out again?"

Her eyes flew open.

"At least I know how to wake you up."

Meeting his steady gaze, she saw something in his eyes. Regret? Embarrassment? She had no idea.

All she knew was that acid or some animal was churning its way through her empty stomach, chewing it to ribbons and spitting them all back out, and trying to send something vile up her throat. Her hands still tingled, her body ached, and she kept having a steady stream of visitors, the latest one practically a stranger.

Hearing a tentative knock, Vic glanced past Jake to the door. Hope? And . . . Jake. Oh, God. Almighty. Hope and Jake. Daughter and father? If that social worker in Kalispell could be believed?

Hope stared at Jake as if she knew him. Probably just the imaginings of a psychotic mind, but knowing Hope, she'd found him. Somehow. Those damned computer skills the girl kept bragging about.

Jake jumped to his feet. "Another visitor, and they told me I couldn't stay more than a few minutes. You're pretty popular, Victoria." He kept his eyes on Vic, hardly noticing Hope as he shuffled out the door.

Hope held it open for him. Vic looked past her for a nurse, a doctor, anyone who would get people to leave her alone.

"Uh, Vic?" Thank God she didn't try calling her "Mom." "Sean called and asked if I could handle extra hours. I can, so don't worry about it."

"Thanks." She didn't even attempt to smile.

"Yeah." Hope stayed by the door, almost as if she sensed Vic's desire to have someone clear the room. "I'm sorry about what happened." She dropped her head, muffling her words. "I didn't mean to make you, uh, take all those pills."

"You didn't. At all." Or at a minimum, she'd already been on that road before Hope started traveling it.

"Who was that guy visiting you just now?"

Just as she'd feared. "A friend." Vic refused to utter his name in front of the self-proclaimed computer whiz.

"Oh." Hope kept looking out the door. Vic tilted her head to one side, trying to spot any other visitors, but the hallway appeared to be empty. "I was just wondering. He's—"

"—just a friend. Friend of a friend, actually." She didn't even have to cross her fingers. At this point, Tess seemed pretty cozy with Jake. Damn her.

Hope finally dragged her gaze away from the door.

As soon as a nurse appeared, Vic would give a list of acceptable visitors, and it'd be short. Mother wouldn't visit, undoubtedly, so that left Dad, Drew, Nat, and Tess. And the kids. She still hadn't seen them, and no one had mentioned them since Ryder's moving-home bombshell last night.

"So I guess I'd better go. The nurse said five minutes, tops, and only after I told her I was your daughter."

Only by birth. If that.

"I hope that's okay."

Vic struggled not to react, shutting down only with effort several body parts that had been dead last night. No nods, blinks, or other movements that could possibly indicate acquiescence.

Hope wasn't her daughter. She had two kids, Connor and Megan. Period. Two little kids who'd had to cope with major trauma last night, forcing them to grow up faster than she'd ever intended—and no one had thought to bring them here today. To their mom, who loved them desperately.

Despite all appearances to the contrary.

"Hope? When you leave, could you send in a nurse?"

Nodding, Hope shuffled out the door. Something about the movement resembled too much the man who'd done the same thing only a couple of minutes ago.

Jake.

———

"You'll be out soon. Promise." Drew bent over Vic, gingerly touching the skin around her eyes with a doctor's concern, even though the only doctoring he'd done since his internship year had been of people's minds. "Your stomach needs to recover from the assault of being suctioned." No kidding. "And the rest of you needs to recover from the assault of all those drugs."

"I'm tired of promises, Drew." She lay motionless, letting her brother pretend to be her physician. "I want to see my kids. I want to go home."

"The kids I can manage." He sounded less grim than last night. "In fact, they'll be here right after school." He glanced up at the clock, which ticked loudly, adding to the horrid pounding in Vic's head. "Just a couple more hours."

In other words, forever. She felt her limp body sag even further.

Drew jammed his hands in his pockets and started to pace. "But you need to get checked out by a psychiatrist before they can release you."

"You're kidding. Don't they know who my brother is?"

The pacing stopped. "Yeah. The schmo who prescribed some of the pills found next to your body last night. I don't think I'm in high esteem today."

"I got you in trouble." Vic closed her eyes, horrified that her failings extended much farther than the crimes for which she'd already pistol-whipped herself. She'd cadged prescriptions from Midge, Drew, and too many friends and acquaintances to count. The ambulance drivers had probably counted, though, and noted it in their report.

Midge would never speak to her again.

Drew had to, eventually. He was her brother.

"No permanent damage." He returned to her side and perched next to her on the edge of the bed. "I'm a big boy, Vic. I knew better—or at least I should've."

"But I—"

"—had me fooled." He whistled. "You must've had everyone fooled. How long, Vic?"

"How long what? That I took pills? Just a week or two." At his skeptical gaze, she flicked a crossing motion in the general vicinity of her heart. "Honest."

He shook his head. "That's not what I meant. How long have you—" He struggled for words, and she wasn't about to help him. Drew was the shrink. Let him figure it out. "Felt like this? Depressed, obviously. Suicidal tendencies that you acted on, unless you were just too doped up to know better."

How long? Since age seventeen? Maybe earlier?

She crossed her arms, or tried to. Too many tubes and wires. "I was exhausted and upset and took a few too many pills. It was an accident." Even more than she'd realized in her doped-up state. "But if you have this analyzed so well, I don't know why you bother asking."

"Sorry. Force of habit." He gave a sheepish grin but quickly sobered. "I do want to talk, Vic. And listen. I obviously don't know you as well as I thought, but better late than never."

She swallowed hard on the excess saliva creating a nasty puddle in her mouth. Never? She'd almost achieved that last night.

———

"Mom?" "Mommy!"

After a short nap, Vic's eyes fluttered open to the most wondrous sight imaginable. Megan rushed forward, collapsing in a hug that encompassed most of Vic's upper body. Connor, both older and more cautious since birth, hung back near the door, his eyes hidden behind bangs that had gotten too long.

She'd almost lost them.

She untangled one arm from Megan and held it out to Connor, who trudged to the opposite side of her bed. With a downward gaze, he quickly touched her hand and let go.

Megan, now rolling on top of Vic, was doing whatever damage to her stomach that last night's horror hadn't already done. Aside from a few pained blinks that escaped, she tried not to show it. She snuggled with Megan as she turned to Connor.

"I'm . . . so proud of you, honey. I heard you were brave and smart and did everything right."

Chin glued to his chest, Connor gave a quick nod and tried to pretend that a tear wasn't rolling down his cheek. "I was scared, Mom. I didn't know what to do."

"But you were perfect." She reached again for his hand, this time catching hold of it. "I'm sorry. About everything. That you had to be so grown up and take care of me."

"I'll always take care of you, Mom. I'm already grown up."

"I can see that."

Megan stilled her movement on top of Vic. Her high-pitched voice piped in. "I thought you were dead, Mommy. Were you dead?"

"No, stupid. Duh. We're talking to her, aren't we?"

"Connor, don't call your sister stupid." Vic ran a hand through Megan's hair. "I wasn't dead, sweetie." She thought again of Carrie, of the dazzling sights she'd experienced, but it wasn't the time to discuss it with an eight-year-old. And anyone older than eight probably wouldn't believe her. "I took too much medicine and got really sick, and Connor and you helped take care of me until the ambulance brought me to the hospital."

"I didn't help. I hid under your pillow."

Hearing the brutal honesty in the high-pitched little voice, Vic didn't know whether to laugh or cry. "That's okay, sweetie. You're eight, and Connor's ten. And if he hadn't been there, I bet you would've done a good job."

Connor rolled his eyes. "No, she woulda hid under the pillow anyway, and then Mom would be—"

He broke off suddenly, looking appalled, and Megan started to cry.

"I wouldn't be doing quite so well." Vic patted Connor's hand and rubbed small circles on Megan's back. "Don't be so hard on Megan. She's getting to be a big kid, too."

Connor snorted.

"Who's gonna stay with us?" He tugged his hand away from Vic and stuffed it in his pocket. "Larissa slept at our house last night, but I think she misses her boyfriend. An' stuff."

He flushed. Her son was more grown up than she'd realized.

"Don't worry. I'm feeling better already, so maybe the doctors will let me out soon. Your dad—"

Connor waved his hand. "Larissa said he's gonna stay at

our house again, but no way. He left us, an' you don't like him anymore. He makes you cry."

Vic bit her lip at the too-accurate assessment from such a small person. "I'm not quite sure what we're going to do." The thought of Ryder in the house, with or without Sean in the picture, almost sent up a round of dry heaves. "But your dad said he'll help. We both love you, and you're our top priority. Always. We'll work it out."

Shaking his head, Connor turned slightly to one side and brushed a hand across his cheek. "Promise, Mom? 'Cause I saw all those pills you took. You almost died."

"Oh, Connor." She reached for him, but he stood just beyond her grasp. She cuddled Megan instead, trying to comfort herself as much as the kids. "I love you to the moon and back. But sometimes I have problems. Everyone does."

"But you're gonna take care of us this time, aren't ya? Forever? An' not die?"

She crossed her fingers behind Megan's back, then uncrossed them. She had a fresh start. She couldn't fuck it up. "We'll all die sometime, but I'll do my very best."

She wondered if anyone in the room believed her.

———

"She's in intensive care. Patients aren't supposed to have many visitors, no one other than family, and she's probably had too many already." Midge took a deep breath, fidgeted with her glasses, and looked pointedly at the file she'd been studying when Tess burst into her France Avenue office late on Friday afternoon. "Her physicians won't want another."

Midge. Always following the rules. Particularly when they suited her.

Tess arched one eyebrow. "You have staff privileges there,

and we both know that isn't why you haven't gone to see Vic."

"I don't know what you're talking about."

Tess whistled. "Weren't you Phi Beta Kappa? Highest honors in med school? Your pick of any oncology residency in the country? And you don't understand English? Or am I speaking too far beneath you?"

"Cut it out." Midge pushed her glasses even higher on her nose. "You're just as smart. Maybe I studied more than most people."

"More than the rest of our class put together."

"What's your point?"

"That you did it as much as anything to hide, even from us. The same way you're hiding from Vic now." Tess twisted on the straight-backed chair in Midge's small office, its shelves lined with large books, and tried to get comfortable. Impossible. "She needs you, Midge. Who does she have? Ryder? Her mother?"

Midge answered in a small voice. "She has you. She always had you."

"You say that like it's a bad thing."

"It's not. I just—" Midge shook her head and looked again at the file before finally setting her elbows on it. "I could never compete with you guys. Or be anything like you."

"Bullshit." Tess waved a hand. "What is that, hindsight without glasses? Is that seriously why you're avoiding Vic?"

"I'm not avoiding her. She wasn't even admitted until late last night. I worked all day."

"So you have plans to see her? When?" Tess caught her gaze and held it until Midge flinched.

"I told you. She's in intensive care."

Tess slapped one leg. "Well, lucky you. She's already been moved to a regular floor."

"Oh?" The glasses ground into Midge's nose.

"So when are you off work?"

Midge glanced at her watch, then at the clock on her tidy desk. "I'm not sure. I still have more patients."

"Your receptionist didn't think so."

Midge almost squeaked. "Yes, well, I—" She shuffled papers on a desk that didn't have many and didn't need shuffling. "I'm not sure. Soon."

"By any chance does this have anything to do with you giving Vic some pills?" Tess waited for a reaction and was rewarded with a slight flinch. "So what? She practically had a pharmacy in her bedroom, and knowing you, you didn't give her much."

"H-how do you know?"

"One bottle? Something relatively mild? Maybe enough pills for a couple of days?"

Midge picked up the file and fanned herself with it.

"She probably hit you up first and used them long before last night. Drew prescribed some, too, and God knows how many other people." Tess stood up and headed for the door. Once there, she grabbed the knob but didn't turn it. She looked back at Midge. "You're cautious, Midge, and that's a good thing." Tess laughed. "Even in my opinion. But we need to take care of Vic right now. She's not taking care of herself."

She whipped open the door and sailed through, not waiting for Midge's response. Midge could protest all she wanted, but Tess knew she could rely on her. And so could Vic.

———

RYDER LET himself into the house, trying to shake the guilty feeling he'd had the moment he put the key in the lock, and let Larissa go at quarter to six. A full fifteen minutes early.

"Hey, guys." Connor and Megan stared blankly at him, even though he'd seen them last Saturday. He'd gone on business trips longer than that. "Don't I get a hug?"

Megan obliged with a full frontal assault at waist level. Connor hung back a moment, then ran into his arms.

He hadn't lost them yet.

"How was school?" He knew from Larissa that they'd seen Vic, but he'd work up to that. "Have a good day?"

"Fine." The voices chimed in unison.

"That's it? Fine? When's your last day of school?"

"Tuesday."

Connor headed back to the kitchen while Megan kept clinging to Ryder in a death grip.

"So what do you guys want to do tonight?"

Megan peered up at him. "Are you staying with us? Did Mommy say it was okay?"

"It's fine." He hadn't visited again today, and Vic probably didn't remember what he'd said last night. "I couldn't wait to see you guys. Want to go over to Kenwood Park? Bike around the lake?"

"I wanna watch a movie."

"A movie?" Probably some stupid cartoon they'd already seen a million times. "C'mon, let's go outside. It's a beautiful evening."

Connor reappeared, his mouth stuffed with a peanut-butter sandwich. "Are you gonna stay overnight? And tomorrow? Where do you stay the other nights? Why doesn't Larissa just stay with us?"

The questions flew at Ryder like bullets. He suspected Connor didn't care about the answers as much as Ryder's reaction. At ten, Connor liked getting reactions.

"I'm staying at least until your mom gets home from the hospital, maybe longer." He dropped to one knee and put his arm around Megan, looking from her to Connor. He drew in a breath, not even sure of his own answer to the next question. "How would you guys like it if I moved back in permanently?"

"Yeah. Sure." Taking another bite from his sandwich, Connor turned back toward the kitchen, which was soon filled with the sound of hard rock blaring on the radio.

Trying not to be disappointed, Ryder turned to Megan. "And you, missy? What do you think?"

Two skinny arms, so like her mother's, wrapped themselves around his neck. "Oh, Daddy. I miss you. I'd like it a lot."

That made three votes to one, assuming Vic hadn't forgiven him already, which was what Vic did. Forgive. Move on. Smooth over the little wrinkles in life.

Not that he was sure this wasn't a mistake, but he'd forgotten how demanding a lover could be. How exhausting. He had a tough job and too many deadlines lately that he'd missed or barely met.

He knew where he needed to be. Not with Sean, or at most in the odd hours when opportunity and need struck at the same time. Sean would relish getting his small apartment back to himself, and somehow he'd make this work. And he'd figure out what to do with Sean as he went along.

———

Monday morning, bright and early, Vic's savior appeared at the door to her hospital room.

"I don't know how you did it, but thanks." She perched on the edge of the bed, dressed in fresh clothes that Tess had brought her from home.

Standing next to the open door, Drew crossed his arms and tried to look stern. "I don't know what you're talking about." He shook his head at the flowers and other gifts that had flooded in over the weekend. Tess's phone skills in action. "And I hope you don't think I'm going to stuff all this crap in your car. It's not big enough, and I'm not into flowers."

"The flowers can stay." They only reminded her of how many people knew what she'd done. She waved her discharge papers. "But I meant springing me from jail. And taking time off from work to drive the getaway car."

She stuffed the papers in her purse, also courtesy of Tess, and thought about all the pills it had once held. Part of her still craved them. Another part was glad she had Tess in her life, even though Tess had undoubtedly scoured every possible inch of her gallery, house, and cars in search of contraband.

Drew took a step toward her, keys jangling in his hand. "I didn't do anything. The psychiatrist gave you a clean bill of health." He wagged a finger at her. "Which only means you flattered the guy until he couldn't see straight."

She bit her lip on a grin. Guilty as charged.

Bending down, he grabbed her overnight bag. "And I'm happy to cancel an appointment or two on a sunny summer day if it means I get to hijack your Porsche." He smacked his lips, even though the guy had more cars than his three-car garage could hold. "Besides, my patients are mostly paranoid-schizophrenics and other wackos. They'll figure they had it coming."

When Vic gasped, he quit laughing. "Sorry. I didn't mean you."

Everyone else would. She stood up, trying not to look as shaky as she felt. "Don't worry. If I get too upset, I can always take a pill."

The moment he started to object, she walked over and poked him in the ribs. "Just kidding, bro. Can't you take a joke? Tess cleaned me out, and you probably helped. Not that—" She mentally crossed her fingers. "I still want them."

He must have X-ray vision. "You probably *do* still want them. The craving doesn't go away instantaneously."

She gazed up at him, wishing he could end her craving as quickly as he'd gotten her released from the hospital. "But I want it to go away. I want to get back to normal."

Putting his arm around her, he stuck close to her side as they walked down the hall, past the nurses' station, and to the elevator. He waited until a couple of doctors passed. One nodded to him. "You've gone through something awful, Vic. Hell. We all went through it with you, and it didn't end when they pumped your guts out."

Not even close. Her stomach still felt like someone had taken a machete to it, although the headaches had subsided to an occasional ping.

The elevator arrived a moment after he pushed the button. "I'm going to make sure you get all the help you need."

Thoughts jumbled in her brain, quickly moving to Ryder. "Does that include getting rid of a man who thinks he had the right to move back into my house?"

"Ryder? Sure." The elevator reached the ground floor, and they headed out into the sunlight. Fresh air. "But you should think about it. I know you love Connor and Megan, but they need someone who's stable, and right now I'm not sure that's you."

The verbal shot hit her in the knees. "And Ryder is?"

Drew grinned. "Good point. I'm just saying that you should give it time. Don't make any rash decisions."

"Like selling the gallery, moving to California, and giving my kids up for adoption?"

She'd spent all weekend considering all her options—except for adoption—as the post-drug haze swirled through her, adding to the remorse and utter embarrassment. But her kids might like California.

"Exactly. And don't operate heavy machinery."

"Huh?"

"Sorry." They reached her Boxster, parked with the top down in a physician's space in the parking ramp, and Drew opened the door for her. "Standard medical advice."

As she climbed into the passenger seat and fastened her seatbelt, Drew popped the trunk and threw in her overnight bag. She heard something crunch and decided not to worry about it. A moment later, he folded himself behind the wheel, turned the key, and revved the engine.

He grinned sideways at her. "Gotta love this car."

She always had, but it felt foreign to her today. Maybe because she wasn't driving. Maybe because the sun dazzled, blinding her, while half of her still operated in a fog.

"Drew? Thanks."

"For what?"

"For being there for me." She stared out the window at all the nameless, faceless people scurrying by. "Not just Thursday night, and this weekend, and today, but—"

"Tomorrow? And next week?"

She swallowed hard, unable to say more. Scared to think more.

"I'm here for you for as long as it takes. Driving your Porsche." Turning, he wrapped an arm around her shoulders. "But you've got a fresh start and another chance to make things turn out whatever way you want. It's your life, Vic. Don't fuck it up."

She sucked in a breath as he spun the steering wheel and roared into traffic. Drew was right. She had a chance, but only if she made it home alive. With her brother behind the wheel, that wasn't necessarily a given.

She gripped the door handle and hung on tight.

CHAPTER 8

The doorbell rang, bringing another Bachman's delivery.
With a quick rip in the purple wrapping paper, Vic
peeked at yellow long-stemmed roses. Her favorite. She
pressed her nose against the paper, inhaled the sweet
fragrance, and wished she could buy stock in Bachman's. Or
that they'd send their flowers to the hospital, where she'd left
the other ones.

She also wished everyone would leave her alone. Not at
night, when darkness and a large, empty bed brought a deadly
disquiet. Right now. Before she received another goddamn
flower.

She trudged to the kitchen, set the vase on the counter
along with the unopened card, and glanced at the clock over
the sink. One-thirty. Drew had delivered her home by ten,
after a wild ride past the Sculpture Garden and along Mount
Curve. She still felt windblown and out of sorts, which was
just how Drew had looked when she'd finally sent him away
after a series of questions he'd hesitated to ask and she'd
avoided answering.

Poor, noble Drew had probably wanted to check her house
again for drugs. Part of her wanted to do the same thing, but

with different intentions. The rational part of her walked outside and onto the back deck, lighting a cigarette with trembling fingers every time she contemplated the alternative.

If Tess hadn't left a pack of cigarettes behind on Thursday night, she didn't know what she'd do. She hadn't smoked in a dozen years, and she craved an entire carton.

She paced the kitchen, flexing her agitated fingers. The kids would be home in a couple of hours, Larissa with them. That didn't give her much time to figure out how she'd survive the rest of her life. Despite the kids, she also wasn't yet entirely sure she wanted to.

The doorbell chimed again. Good grief. Couldn't Bachman's combine their deliveries? Couldn't her friends and family find a different charity?

Her shoes clattered an indignant beat as she stomped through the hallway. She flung open the front door, and the door's momentum made her stumble. Trying to catch her balance, she hopped on one foot.

Jake stood in front of her.

In jeans, Teva sandals, and a faded blue polo shirt he'd owned at least fifteen years. Possibly since high school. In fact, she thought she remembered that shirt.

"Nice moves." He glanced down at her feet and the traitorous flats she wore. "I'm not sure I can keep up."

She felt a dull red flush start at her neck and blossom upward—and crossed her arms to beat it back down. "I'm more of a solo act anyway."

At this point, maybe forever.

"Whew." He wiped the back of his hand across his forehead, as if the thought of dancing made him nervous. As if anything made him nervous. "I never was much of a dancer."

Biting her lip, she tried not to remember how he'd held her in his arms during slow dances in high school, and even a few fast dances when they'd found a rhythm unmatched by their classmates. He'd always claimed he couldn't dance. He'd always found excuses just to hold her.

She sighed. No one found excuses to hold her anymore.

She caught him angling his head to peer past her into the front hall. "Did you want something?" Too late, she tried to soften her snapping tone when she noticed the small box in his left hand, wrapped in what looked like an inside-out grocery bag. "Or—?"

He thrust the box toward her. "Here."

Her arms remained at her side as she stared at the box. She refused to look at his arm, at the flatness of his stomach beneath his polo shirt, at the way his jeans rode low on his hips. Tess would notice, and Vic in her youth would've noticed, which was why she'd gotten pregnant. Stupid wandering eyes.

Her gaze returned to his face, which frowned. He took a step closer, shoving the box into her hand as he looked past her and whistled. "After seeing your place, I realize there's probably not much you need, but I brought this. I didn't know what you wanted."

"Not a date." The words flew out of her mouth, sending her eyebrows up, too.

He took a step backward. "Sorry. I don't remember asking for one." He looked at her, then away, not holding her gaze. "I mean, I didn't ask for one today. That was last week." The grin he shot her was jauntier than she would've expected. "I figure it's your turn."

"Please. Don't." The box was burning a hole in her palm, even though she knew it had to be food or a silly trinket with some sort of Hallmark saying, like everyone else sent. "It's history, Jake. A bad one."

"I don't remember the bad part."

She waved a hand in the air. "Besides, I'm not dating. In fact, my husband is moving back in."

Flinching, he took another step backward, his heel tottering on the edge of the brick steps for a moment before he caught his balance. "But Tess—"

Blabbed a lot. Vic shook her head. "Trust me. I have it on the highest authority."

She thought back to the revolting sight that had awaited her this morning. Ryder's suitcase lay in the middle of her bed, half of its contents strewn on the bed and floor. It wasn't like Ryder at all. Very much like her new self, though, she'd dragged it all out of her room and dumped it in the guest bedroom.

Jake jammed his hands in his pockets, making tight quarters even tighter. She crossed and uncrossed her arms, trying not to fidget. Or stare. Or drool.

"I wasn't here to ask you out again." He glanced at her lips, catching her in the middle of licking them. Talk about embarrassing. It was also provocative in a way she hadn't even attempted since high school. Since Jake.

"You said that already."

"Yeah." He put one foot on a lower step, then the other on the sidewalk, and started backing toward the street. "Anyway. Hope you're doing okay. You're looking good." He ran a hand through his hair. "I mean, coming from the hospital. Not in a dating way at all."

"Right. Well, thanks again." She shook the box, which hardly weighed anything. "For this."

"Hope you like it. I thought it'd be useful."

He kept backing up, watching her as he did. Halfway down the front sidewalk, he turned and almost sprinted to the gleaming black pickup truck parked in front of her house. With a roar of the engine, he peeled out.

Dazed, she walked back into the house, tripping on the threshold. Sagging against the door, she tore off the makeshift paper wrapping and looked at the box inside. Her hand over her heart, she slid to the floor and shook with laughter.

The small box in her lap contained a Slinky.

———

SHE NEEDED TO CALL SEAN.

Half an hour after Jake's bizarre but cute delivery, Vic sat at the bottom of the steps to the second floor of her house, mumbling to herself, as she set her new Slinky in motion again. Down, curl over the top, down again. Mesmerizing.

It beat certain drugs she wasn't supposed to think about, and a victory was a victory. Especially today, the first day of the rest of her clichéd life, in which a Slinky constituted a major day-brightener.

The Slinky dropped off the bottom step and into her waiting hand, and she tipped it back and forth between her hands. Up, curl over, down. Repeat.

Sean had left a few messages on her cell phone, but the messages blurred after the first dozen. Eventually her phone must've run out of room, right in the middle of a halting speech by Mother, who probably hadn't appreciated being cut off. No messages from Dad. One message, loud and clear, from Ryder. He was back and intent on making a go of things, whatever that meant. With her, or Sean and her, or avoiding a sex life altogether.

Whatever.

She sent the Slinky on one last rhythmic tumble down the stairs and was in the kitchen before it hit bottom.

A single aborted attempt later, she dialed the gallery.

"Jasmine."

"Jasmine *Gallery*, Sean."

A low chuckle, which only made her teeth grate. "It's not a gun shop. I figured they'd know that."

"Not all of our customers." She thought of the walk-ins who wouldn't know a Cezanne from a Corona. "It's our image. Our brand."

Cringing, she pictured the nosedive her image would take after Thursday night. The clients she'd already lost. Worse, the ones who'd now visit the gallery only to see what a junkie or a suicidal wackjob looked like. She wasn't sure which role held more cachet, but both made her lip curl.

"Our image is just fine. No men in black suits or dark sunglasses today, either."

She'd forgotten about the FBI. Their investigation probably took time, though, and they wouldn't drop it just because she said she wasn't hiding anything.

"And—" She swallowed hard on a raw throat. "Hope?"

"Still here. Still working, in a manner of speaking." He dropped his voice. "She keeps trying to use the computer, which doesn't need her help, and she asks a lot of questions. Odd questions. Not that it's any of my business."

"Like what?"

She heard a door shut. A moment later, Sean's voice returned to its normal pitch.

"Like she's a plant for the FBI or CIA or whatever, except for the fact that they wouldn't hire her. Lots of questions. About Ryder." Sean was silent for a moment. "And your kids. Family. Friends from high school. Except for Tess, I don't even know who they are."

"You've met Midge."

"Right. The short, smart one." He cleared his throat. "Anyway, I haven't told Hope anything I wouldn't tell anyone else, but she's strange. Not that you didn't know that."

"For a while now." But she didn't have a clue what to do about Hope. "What else is happening?"

"Not too much. When are you coming back? Are you taking some time off?"

More time alone? She shuddered, knowing the mischief of which she was capable. "Just the rest of the day. I'll stop in tomorrow. If it feels good, I'll stay all day."

She glanced around the kitchen, taking in the tornado that had passed through in her short absence. She noticed a shirt, slung over the back of a chair, that looked like one of Sean's. She leaned hard against the counter and breathed deeply.

"Take it easy." Sean's voice came at her, reassuring and low, and Vic tried not to picture him in the shirt staring at her from ten feet away. "Take the week off. Give yourself time."

And a rope? "I had all weekend, and the gallery won't survive if I don't get back there. Clients must be—"

"Everything is fine. Perfect." He practically cooed at her, setting her teeth on edge. "Remember, your kids finish school tomorrow." Had she mentioned that to Sean? "You'll want to spend time with them before they head to camp."

Had she mentioned when camp began? A chill crept along the base of her spine, but she shook her head as worries nagged at her. This was Sean. Nosy, yes, but she'd always depended on his memory. Of course, she'd also depended on him in so many other ways she now couldn't imagine.

She told the shrill voices in her head to shut up. "The kids don't leave for camp until next week. Don't worry about me. I'll be in tomorrow."

"I don't think that's such a—"

"It's fine, Sean. I'm fine." Superficially, at least, which was all that mattered. At least to the rest of the world. "I'll see you tomorrow."

——————

By NINE-FIFTEEN TUESDAY MORNING, the sun hadn't yet zapped the sleep out of Jake's eyes, let alone his dumbass brain, when he climbed out of the cab of his Chevy and took a few steps closer to hell.

Blinking, he tried to rub the grit from his eyes. The same fucking mansion still rose up before him. He considered hopping back in his truck, gunning the engine, and getting the hell out of Dodge, but his shoes refused to go that direction.

Even though Victoria was married. According to Tess, the guy was a two-faced cheat who preferred men over women. He tried to get pissed about it, but he immediately sputtered out and kicked himself. Truth was, he had good friends who were gay. A couple of employees. A lot of customers.

Still, the guy must be wacked. Choosing men after he'd married Victoria and had kids with her. Watched her undress at night and dress in the morning, either of which would drive Jake wild. Slept with her—unless they didn't do anything that radical in a house this big. Maybe everyone had separate bedrooms in Kenwood. A neighborhood ordinance.

He gazed up at the house, taking the time to really study it. Yesterday he'd been too nervous. Today wasn't much different, and the sick feeling in the pit of his gut was growing.

He hoped Victoria was home and the husband wasn't. If he'd known yesterday that the guy was staying here, he never would've shown up. He knew it today, though, and it hadn't done more than stall him for five minutes.

It also made him question the stupid gifts he kept giving her. Not the gifts Tess had basically commanded. Just stuff. Stuff to make her smile again. He hadn't seen her smile, really smile, since high school.

He couldn't compete with this, though. Thousands of

perfect bricks, three stories' worth of gleaming windows, trees and shrubs and row after row of flowers, none of which would dare step a toe out of line. Every blade of grass exactly the same height. No dandelions, weeds, nothing. No bikes or skateboards or balls or toys scattered around.

Victoria's kids must be perfect, too. Nothing he'd pictured all those years ago—their sticky-faced little girl, who'd be an ace on a baseball diamond if Victoria didn't stick a damned tutu on the poor kid, and their little boy who'd be a holy terror.

But she'd married someone else.

He trudged up the sidewalk, head down, memorizing every inch. The front steps loomed, and he slowed his approach to a mind-numbing crawl, halting at the front door. A force outside of him reached out and rang the bell.

A married woman. A rich, gorgeous married woman with two-point-two kids, a ten-bedroom house, and everything she needed in life. He glanced down at the white bag in his hand and wished it held a diamond. Something he couldn't give her and wouldn't even if he could. She didn't want him.

Idiot. He turned to leave.

"Jake?"

The soft, hesitant voice stopped his escape, but for the life of him he couldn't think, couldn't even turn around again.

She repeated his name, then softly touched his shoulder. "What brings you here?"

She didn't mention the damned Slinky. Probably trying to ignore it, if she hadn't already forgotten it or thrown it away.

"Guess I'm your delivery boy this week."

"I think Bachman's has a lock on that."

He turned, slowly, trying not to stare up and down the length of her, but he caught a quick glimpse of bare toes, a hint of lace under a pink robe, and damp hair piled up under a towel. He glanced at her face, free of makeup, and grinned.

"Still the fresh-scrubbed kid, huh, Carlyle?"

She laughed, flushing slightly, and touched her cheek. "And you're still the charmer. I think that's the first thing you ever said to me."

Word for word, almost, the second day of junior year, and three days after he'd moved to south Minneapolis and a new high school. Victoria's school. She remembered.

"And I owe you a thanks. For the Slinky." She stepped to one side, pointing at the hallway behind her, where the object in question lay on the floor at the base of the stairs. "It's the most fun I've had in too long."

His eyebrows rose. "If that's true, you need to get out more."

"So I'm told." She pressed her pale lips together, and he stared at them, wondering how she'd taste, which showed how pathetic he got at nine in the morning.

He stared at his dirty running shoes. The right toe was beat up, and he scuffed it against the brick steps. "Sorry I keep stopping by." Feeling about twelve, he pressed a hand against the back of his neck. "It just seems like, uh, my life began again when you walked into Pendulum."

Idiot.

"Funny. Mine had just ended."

He couldn't look at her. Couldn't think of anything else to say. He thrust the small bag at her. "Anyway, here. Better open it soon. Gotta run."

He turned and trotted back down the sidewalk, trying to slow it down a notch from yesterday's world-record sprint. He told himself he wasn't a total chickenshit who had no business trying to play out of his league. Even with Victoria, a woman he'd held in his arms and loved. If he thought about it, he probably still loved her, which was why he tried *not* to think about it. A damn waste of time.

He really ought to quit lying to himself.

———

"A Slinky?"

Late afternoon on Wednesday, Vic's first full day at the gallery after barely surviving an hour and a half yesterday, she listened to Tess's incredulous laughter warble through the telephone.

She shifted her cell phone to her other hand. A Slinky. Tess wasn't the only one who found it funny. The kids had looked at her strangely, especially when she wouldn't let them use it, and she'd hidden it before Ryder got home after work. "Yesterday, he brought me a Dilly bar. Cherry. My favorite."

"But—"

"This morning he dropped a crossword puzzle book in my mail slot. No note. He didn't even ring the bell."

"How do you know he did it?"

She grinned at the yellowed book, propped on her desk at work. "The theme was teen heartthrobs from the early 2000s. Orlando Bloom on the cover. I have no idea where he could've found it."

Tess made a choking sound. "It can't be Jake."

"Why not?" She hadn't even considered the possibility of someone else. From someone else it'd be almost creepy.

Tess sputtered. "But I told him—"

"What?" Vic's stomach churned as she tried not to imagine what Tess had told him. Or where they'd talked. Or what Tess thought of Jake. She wasn't even sure what *she* thought of him, if anything, but she wanted it to be different from Tess. Completely different.

"To pamper you. Get just the perfect gift. You know, roses. Or something small and sparkly."

"Everyone did that." Vic ticked off on her fingers all the gifts she'd received. "Flowers galore. Three copies of *Chicken Soup for the Soul*. Ryder gave me a bracelet. My dad promised to take my kids and me on a trip to London. My girlfriends all bought lingerie, which probably says something about their own lives."

"Midge bought you lingerie?"

Vic laughed. "Okay. Flannel pajamas. But the thought was there."

"She came to see you?"

"She rang the doorbell, waited half a second, then made a mad dash for her car. I caught her a moment before she escaped down the street."

"That's our little professional." Tess hooted. "But what does Jake want?"

"You probably know better than I." Another thought she didn't want to ponder. "He keeps dropping off gifts and then ducking out. He hasn't asked me out again since that first time, and he knows Ryder moved back home."

"You told him? Chicken."

"It's the truth." She'd regretted spitting it out almost as soon as she had, but she didn't need entanglements right now, and the kids needed stability. "Ryder is there. Bags and baggage."

"And Sean?"

"Not living under my roof, thank you very much."

The mysterious shirt had disappeared Monday night shortly after Ryder got home, and she couldn't say for sure it wasn't his. Besides, if a man could change his sexual orientation, a change of clothing should be a piece of cake.

"How's the gallery?"

"Still humming along, amazingly enough. Hope keeps offering to set up a better website for the gallery—anything to avoid doing real work—but Sean has it under control. Whether or not I'm there."

"I'll bet he likes that."

The thought had already percolated in Vic's mind, and she didn't want it to start bubbling again. "He'll have to get over it. I'm back. Ready, willing, and able."

A slight pause. "Are you sure?"

"Why shouldn't I be?"

"No reason." Tess whistled off-key to show her deliberate change of subject. She didn't do subtle. "When are we going to get together? The first meeting of the reunion committee is this weekend. We're already late."

"Now, there's a shock."

"Saturday night. My place." Tess talked fast, her voice growing louder when Vic tried to give her excuses. "You don't have to bring anything. And you need to get out."

"I get out."

"To the gallery. The grocery store. And maybe walking around the lake."

Wasn't that enough? "Sometimes I rollerblade around the lake."

"Why? Are the demons that chase you getting faster?"

Tess knew her too well, a thought that had never troubled her before. "It's a change of pace. But you were talking about the reunion committee. Who's on it?"

"Oh, you know. The usual. Midge, Andrea. Liz Tanner and Piper Jamison. You remember them." She named a few other people, one or two Vic didn't remember. Had it been that long? "No one detestable. No one I can't bear to party with."

"That doesn't do much to shorten the list."

"Hmpf. You're lucky you're on it."

"I'm not sure I can get a babysitter." Or whether she should go. She wondered if everyone at the get-together would've heard about last weekend. Shaking her head, she flipped open her calendar. Saturday. June twelfth. Her eleventh wedding anniversary. Nothing she planned to celebrate.

"You've got four days and, last I heard, an on-again husband who can stay with the kids. And a son who's ten. Practically ready to babysit himself."

She pictured Connor pummeling Megan just as someone knocked on her door. "Gotta run. I still have customers."

"What about Saturday night?"

And face a roomful of almost-forgotten friends without the aid of drugs? She shuddered, then tried to imagine what Ryder had in mind for their anniversary. His plans probably didn't include her. "I'll let you know."

Tess snorted as the knock came again. "You do that, or I'll have someone drag you there."

From Tess, it wasn't an idle threat.

CHAPTER 9

Thursday flew past, and Friday somehow, letting Vic survive the week with only a few stumbles. No drugs, no alcohol. No joy, either, but she didn't expect it. Low expectations might see her through this thing.

Lying in bed Saturday morning, alone and not particularly caring whether Ryder had spent the whole night in the guest room or sneaked out of the house after she finally fell asleep, Vic felt the warmth of the sun streaming through the top half of the windows while she contemplated her world.

Sunshine aside, it mostly sucked.

She heard the patter of not-so-silent feet creeping into her room and tiptoeing to her side of the bed. She opened one eyelid a moment before two missiles launched themselves at her.

"Mom, we don't wanna go to camp."

"You're not going today, Connor. In a couple of days, you'll change your mind."

"I won't." Megan's little voice, muffled as she lay with her face planted on Vic's midsection, floated upward.

"You will if I torture you." Vic reached for both children, tickling until they dissolved in giggles. "Besides, you've been looking forward to it for months. You get to speak Spanish, have churros and hot chocolate for breakfast, and do all those crazy things you can't do when I'm watching you."

"For three whole weeks." Megan's lower lip quivered, and Vic questioned again the wisdom of sending both kids for a one-week session followed by a two-week session. Megan had barely lasted one short week last summer.

"You're eight now. Last year was your first time at camp."

"But we gotta take care of you." Connor, who hadn't wanted to leave at the end of his two-week session last year, was the bigger surprise. "Nobody's gonna be here."

"I'm a big girl." She smiled, trying to reassure herself as much as them. "Your dad's around when I'm not here." More or less, and less each day—and night—that went by. "And there's always Tess."

"You took all those pills after Tess left." Biting his lip, Connor looked away.

Vic blinked. "That's not Tess's fault, and you can't possibly think she needs to stay overnight with me to keep me safe."

Both kids nodded very seriously.

"I was kidding!" She tried tickling them again. Neither one giggled, but Megan's lips twitched. "Hey, if I miss you guys too much, I'll ask Tess to stay over. Maybe we'll have a slumber party and pretend we're at camp just like you."

"And speak Spanish?"

Only after massive quantities wine, which seemed unlikely at the moment. "Sí."

"And roast marshmallows?"

"Definitely. And slap them on top of graham crackers and Hershey bars. Mmm."

She rubbed her stomach, not even having to pretend. She'd love a s'more or two. Of course, after a week of Slinkys, Dilly bars, and Orlando Bloom, she was bound to revert to childhood.

Both kids squealed. "Can we stay home with you?"

"No way. I don't share s'mores." She tapped each of their noses. "Not even with my two favorite people in the whole world."

———

THE PHONE RANG as Vic dragged herself into the house in sweatsocks, her rollerblades tucked under one arm, two tired kids straggling behind her. The answering machine to their landline kicked on, and both rollerblades clunked to the floor as she picked up the phone in the kitchen. While her message played, she puffed out "I'm here—don't hang up."

Her dad responded with his unmistakable chuckle. "How's my baby doing?"

She ran the back of her hand over her dripping forehead. After a whirlwind shopping spree for camp, it might've been overly ambitious to also rollerblade around Lake of the Isles. She'd skipped a second time around, telling herself it was out of pity for Megan, who'd biked, but Vic still had trouble catching her breath.

As sweat trickled down her back and the kids tromped upstairs, she leaned against the kitchen counter. "I have a cell phone, Dad, and so do you. Why do you keep calling the landline?"

"I tried your cell first."

"Fair enough." She mostly kept it on silent these days. "But I'm not your baby. Do you mean Megan? Or Natalie, who's *your* baby, but not exactly handy?"

His chuckle sounded more strained now. "I guess you'll do."

"Your enthusiasm underwhelms me." But it didn't surprise her. She was really getting cranky, even with Dad now. As she pressed the phone to her ear, she reached for a handful of Hershey Nuggets in the bowl on the counter. "To what do I owe the honor of this call?"

"Is Ryder there?"

No sign of him all day. Maybe he *was* celebrating their anniversary in style. Irritation prickled at the base of her neck. "I just walked in, but I doubt it. Why? Did you want to talk to him?"

"Not in this lifetime."

"Oh?" Loyalty was nice, but Dad had practiced law with Ryder. He'd also been Ryder's father-in-law for eleven years and hadn't noticed in all those years that he was gay.

Not that she'd noticed, either, and she'd been the one sleeping with Ryder. At least for most of those years.

Dad cleared his throat. "I'm still a little peeved that I didn't realize things earlier. Drew said he's back there again. Living with you. In the house."

"True." The sweat started to congeal on her neck, and Vic desperately needed a shower, or at least a dry T-shirt. "He's back. He didn't ask, just announced he was moving in while I was in the hospital."

"When you couldn't do anything about it." Dad snorted.

"When I also couldn't do much about the kids. Someone needed to take care of them."

Out of the corner of her eye, she saw Connor and Megan standing in the front hall, just outside the kitchen, listening intently. She waved her hand to shoo them back upstairs.

"And I wasn't there for you. I didn't even offer."

She grimaced. "No offense, Dad, but you wouldn't know what to do with the kids after the first movie ended."

"I—" He paused a moment. "You're right. And you probably wouldn't want your mother watching them, either."

"I wouldn't know. She's never offered." Vic grabbed the somewhat-clean dishtowel hanging from the oven handle and wrapped it around her neck. "When I was pregnant with Connor, she said she'd already raised three kids and didn't plan to raise any more."

"Another reason I need to . . ." He trailed off, and Vic waited for him to continue, or maybe just explain where he'd been for the past week.

She'd never been patient. "Where are you, Dad? I haven't seen you since the hospital, and I wasn't exactly coherent."

His voice dropped. "I'm still at home. With your mother. She says she can't go on without me."

And he didn't want another hospital drama on his hands. "Oh, Dad."

"I know. After all these years you'd think I'd know what to do. I'm not sure I ever will."

"But you—" The wheels spun in her head. Like Ryder, he must've figured out the logistics before he announced his plan. "You must've rented a place. Found somewhere to stay."

"Just a friend's place. No lease." He chuckled, but Vic didn't hear any humor in it. "Your mother insists on marriage counseling. I told her to get some for herself. I don't think counseling can fix what's broken."

Vic shook her head. She had two stubborn parents. "What was her reaction?"

"She's busy cataloguing her grievances. Last I heard, I don't do enough laundry."

"So? She doesn't do much, either." Would Vic's divorce proceedings be equally petty? For that matter, did Ryder plan to file for divorce, or was that up to her? "Do you need a place to stay?"

"Er, no. I just wanted to check in. Oh, and I wondered what's happening at the gallery."

"Sean took care of things while I was out, but I came back on Tuesday." Bottom line, the gallery was in better shape than she was, and her spin around the lake had confirmed it. She pulled the dishtowel from around her neck, careful not to catch a whiff of whatever odors it held, and slid it down her arm.

"No more visits from the FBI?"

She flinched, wishing he hadn't brought up that topic on a day that had been hectic but actually nice. Time with the kids. Time away from the gallery. "No."

"Good." He cleared his throat, almost choking. "I've, er, been checking into things."

Her breath caught, but she pretended a carelessness she couldn't rationally feel. "And?"

"Someone is pretty intent on the investigation. Someone in the New York office. They think the gallery is involved in money laundering."

"The New York office? Don't they have a Minneapolis office?"

When her dad started to answer, at length, Vic burst out laughing. She even slapped the kitchen counter.

Connor called out from upstairs, asking if she was okay, and she called back that Papa had said something funny. The funniest thing she'd heard in two weeks.

"Come on, Dad. Get real." She finally stopped laughing as she wiped a tear from her eye. "I mean, fakes, sure. Every gallery has to deal with that. But money laundering? That's something they do in the Bahamas. Or Switzerland. See? I don't even know where you do it. What a joke."

"It's no joke. That's what they're investigating, and these guys don't kid around. Ever."

His voice shook on his last words, and dropped lower, as if

Mother were right around the corner and he didn't want to ruin her opinion of the daughter who'd always disappointed her anyway. As if he thought his daughter laundered money.

"Impossible. I don't do much more laundry than Mother. And except for a few occasional coins in Connor's pockets, no money."

"Money laundering." He kept repeating the damn term until it swirled in her suddenly throbbing head. "That's why I asked if Ryder was there. Because you said he's involved with your assistant. Sean."

"They *were* involved. I don't know if they still are." Or if they weren't, especially since she couldn't pinpoint Ryder's whereabouts after ten o'clock last night. "Are you saying that he or Sean is doing something illegal? I don't believe it."

"It may seem unlikely, I'll grant you. But we have to explore all avenues before the FBI digs any deeper."

She winced at the picture forming in her mind. "I'm sure it's not—"

"All I'm sure of is you." He paused, as if he *weren't* quite so sure, and Vic held her breath. "No one else. Ryder is acting a bit strangely." Any moment now, her overly protective dad might even try to claim that being gay signaled other issues, but she didn't need to move past the sexual ones. "He's had some issues at work. I've asked around. Discreetly, of course."

"As discreetly as a sledgehammer?"

He coughed. "Nothing to worry about if there's no real problem. I worked with George Osborn since around the time you were born. He's concerned about Ryder. He supervised him before Ryder made partner."

"That's a long time ago." Vic remembered George more as Dad's friend than Ryder's supervisor. Maybe Ryder saw him the same way and had been loosening the bond.

"Ryder usually consults with George, and he hasn't lately."

"Maybe he doesn't need to."

"You're never too smart or too experienced to consult with someone else. Everyone talks to George." He coughed again. "But that isn't the point. My point is that you need to consider everyone, including Sean and Ryder."

She rolled her eyes. "What about Hope?"

"I'd suspect that her problems at the gallery are more along the lines of making lousy coffee."

And spilling it. Dad had stopped into the gallery a week ago, maybe to check out his new granddaughter, Vic had guessed, but she hadn't officially introduced them. She still wondered whether she should have.

"Anyway. Keep an eye on Sean and Ryder. Let me know anything out of the ordinary." He lowered his voice again. "I'm here for you, Vic. But watch your back."

She hung up, shaken, and turned.

Ryder was standing right behind her.

———

Moving back home, if he could call it that, hadn't been the smartest thing he'd ever done. He should've planned better, considered all the variables, and formulated an exit strategy. From the wary look on Vic's glistening face, Ryder figured he might need one.

She hung up the landline after a mumbled goodbye, and he bent to kiss her on the cheek, pulling back when he tasted salt. She pushed off against the counter and strode across the room under the power of the long, lean legs he'd always admired.

She wiped one hand on the bottom of her T-shirt, and her left eye kept making that tiny tic she got when she was flustered or upset, which wasn't often. He also couldn't ignore her glare and crossed arms. "What's up? Who was that?"

She hesitated. "My dad."

"Yeah? What'd he want?"

"Just checking in." Head down, she fiddled with the piles of paper on the counter, moving them around. Nervously. "He wanted to talk about the gallery."

"Oh? It's doing okay, right?"

They'd never shared much about work, which suited him. He loosened the tie he'd found at Sean's place and worn for an impromptu meeting with clients this afternoon, then scanned the headlines of the business section of the *Star Tribune*.

He looked up when she didn't respond. Finally, she gave a tight nod. "Nothing I can't handle."

"That's my girl."

She looked oddly at him, probably because she didn't want to be called his girl anymore, even though at some level she'd always be, which was why he'd come home.

But they needed to talk. Maybe she could even help him figure out his life in that calm, cool way she had of analyzing everything. She would've made a great lawyer.

"So. Where have you been?" She dropped her head to study one of her random piles of paper. "I haven't seen you since last night. The kids were, uh, wondering."

He flinched, but her head was still down. Resolutely so. "I had a client meeting."

"How early?"

"I had to get to the office before the meeting. I hadn't prepared for it ahead of time." True enough. He'd gotten to the office by eleven for a one-o'clock appointment. It coincided nicely with Sean having to open the gallery by eleven. "The meeting just finished, and I'm home."

She stared through him, guilty conscience and all. But Vic was too classy to say anything. He loved that about her. He also sometimes hated it. Trying to compete with cool perfection could take a lot out of a guy.

"You never mentioned a client meeting."

He pulled off the tie before it strangled him. "They left a message on my voicemail, and I picked it up last night. After you went to bed."

She stood facing him, hands on her hips. "And?"

"And what?" He held up his hands in surrender. "I got up early this morning—everyone was still sleeping—and went to work out." In a manner of speaking. "Then I headed into the office. My Saturdays have been like this since you've known me."

She crossed her arms. "Did I ever know you?"

"Yeah. Maybe not everything—"

"You could say that again."

"—but yeah." And the fucking surprise of it was that she *did* know him. His likes and dislikes, even the petty ones, in a way that Sean didn't and never would. And she'd never complained or held him up to some standard he couldn't attain. "You knew me pretty well. Still do."

"Just like I'll bet you know it's our anniversary."

He sucked in a quick breath, recovering enough to nod a moment too late. June twelfth. He'd missed it last year, too. Another strike against him. Lucky thing he didn't play baseball.

Pursing her lips, Vic brushed past him into the hallway and ran up the stairs. When she reached the top, she stopped, panting from the slight exertion.

"Ryder?" She looked more tired than angry, and his shoulders relaxed as he moved to the foot of the stairs, where he almost tripped on a damn Slinky.

"Yeah?"

"You do remember I have a reunion meeting tonight at Tess's place, right? You said you'd watch the kids?"

He nodded, even though he'd forgotten and made plans with Sean. Kid duty was fine, come to think of it. Sean had gotten a little too clingy lately, and weirdly aloof at the same time, and it might be smart to put on the brakes.

For bonus points, it would also show Vic that he was responsible. That he cared.

He picked up the Slinky, opened the front hall closet, and tossed it in the junk box in the back. He'd start by cleaning up the house. And move on from there.

———

THAT DAMNED Tess could talk a guy into anything.

Jake glanced at her, sitting cross-legged on a monstrous rug in the middle of the biggest damned living room of the biggest condo he'd ever seen. The place even gave Victoria's mansion a run for its money. He'd found Tess's expensive Sawmill Run neighborhood only with help from his phone's GPS, and Tess must've sprung for two condos and combined them.

He closed his eyes, trying not to compare his dingy little house in south Minneapolis.

He opened them again, shaking his head, same as he had when he'd walked in the door tonight with a couple of takeout boxes of restaurant leftovers and realized he shouldn't have. His stomach had growled, though, when he spotted the ornate silver tray full of hors d'oeuvres that didn't look much bigger than bugs.

Every wall, every counter, every damned stick of furniture was white. Even Tess's outfit. Long, flowing, and white. The rest of the women weren't wearing white, but most of them pretty much dressed the same way. He glanced down at his jeans, grateful he'd bothered to shower and throw on a clean shirt.

He sat on the floor, trying not to touch anything, and glanced around at the other occupants of the living room. A dozen women. He'd kill Tess. Wrap his arms around her little white-scarved neck and strangle her.

After transferring to Southwest at the beginning of junior year, he'd mostly hung out with the other jocks and, miracle of miracles, Victoria's gang. And a few forgettable girls during senior year, while Vic had been gone and then after she returned second semester, too stuck up for words.

He didn't recognize any of those girls here, but he probably wouldn't anyway. When he'd walked in at seven to find only Tess, Midge, and Andrea, he'd almost walked right back out.

A few minutes later, Liz Tanner and Piper Jamison had shown up—wearing jeans, praise God—and for a few moments he'd hoped that Piper's husband, Brandon Carruthers, would be here. He'd played ball with Brandon at Southwest. But when he asked if Brandon was coming tonight, too, Piper rolled her eyes and reminded him that Brandon had been a year ahead of the rest of them at Southwest.

No excuse. And yep, he'd strangle Tess the first chance he got.

The doorbell chimed, and Jake took a swig of his Corona. Reinforcements had arrived. If he knew Tess, *some* guys would have to show up sooner or later. Until then, he'd keep drinking and ignore the chatter and cloying smell of perfume.

The doorbell chimed again, and Tess didn't answer it. Finally, Midge dug herself out from the pile of white pillows on the couch and went to the door. Good old Midge. He'd never known her well—hell, she'd never come close enough to give him a chance to talk to her—but she'd always been the one they all counted on to get stuff done.

The door opened. Jake froze, trying to hide his reaction. Perfect. Victoria had arrived.

Victoria, who wasn't supposed to be here tonight. Damn that Tess. Yeah, her eyes had twinkled when she said it, which should've been his first clue. And, yeah, he'd counted on it.

But faced with a crowd of women who'd probably all heard about the Slinky, the Dilly bar, and the other stupid stuff? He reached for the keys to his truck.

From out of nowhere, Tess grabbed them, then whispered in his ear. "She won't bite."

He yanked her elbow and dragged her out to a cavernous kitchen filled with gleaming appliances she'd probably never used. "You said she couldn't make it, and there are no other guys here." He hissed through his teeth. "You set me up."

"You're welcome." Winking at him, she drew her arm through his. "You want to go out with her. She turned you down once, but you haven't tried again."

"Her *husband* is still living with her."

She didn't blink. "Change of plans. He moved back in, but they're not sleeping together."

"Sorry, but my standards are a little higher than that."

"Good to know." She peeked around him at the crowd in the living room and dropped her voice to a conspiratorial whisper. "She's been through a lot, Jake. Stay with her, and don't let go."

He scrubbed a hand over his face, feeling stubble he hadn't had time to shave. "She doesn't want to see me."

"Maybe when she was seventeen." She angled her head to look at him, as if deciding for herself whether Vic should've dumped him all those years ago. "And maybe not. Vic went through some rough times in high school. She had reasons, which had to do with you. In some ways, though, they didn't."

"Thanks." He rolled his eyes, noting a cobweb in the

ceiling fixture and tempted to jump up and swipe at it. Just to annoy Tess. "That really clears things up."

"Anything for you, sweetie." She laughed in that throaty way of hers. "But, no, don't tell me you need to check on the bar. I already called the bartender on duty."

His jaw dropped. "Jed?"

"An old friend." She smiled sweetly. "Now, let's get back to the party."

"I thought it was a meeting to plan the reunion."

"Talk about dull." She shuddered. "Are you trying to ruin my reputation?"

He walked back to the living room with her, arm in arm, seeking security from the danger posed by a certain slim blonde who could blow his safe, structured world to smithereens.

Swallowing hard, he glanced sideways at Tess. "I wouldn't dream of it."

CHAPTER 10

V ic barely took two steps inside the door when Jake strolled off with Tess, arm in arm, cozy and bending heads together and probably discussing their plans to exchange bodily fluids later tonight.

Blinking, she finally noticed Midge. "Midge. Hi."

"You made it. I'm . . . glad." A practically effusive greeting, considering that Midge still avoided her like a case of Ebola, despite all of Vic's attempts to make up. Despite apologies that bordered on groveling.

She chided herself for expecting more. Midge had given her pills even though she wouldn't take a Tylenol for a triple bypass. She was loyal and sweet and kind. She also didn't steal former boyfriends or men who gave a woman a Slinky.

Vic couldn't find the Slinky anyway, despite a half hour of effort more intense than she'd ever admit.

"Am I late?" She kicked off her flats and dropped her purse next to a chair, then followed Midge into the living room. Tess and her new man were still missing in action, and she refused to even glance toward the kitchen.

"No, we're just getting started." Midge picked up a notepad from an end table, adjusted her glasses, and sat down.

With her pen poised over the pad, she looked around the living room. "What do people want to do for a reunion?"

"Let someone else plan it?"

"Postpone it until next year?"

"Have it tonight?"

"I'll drink to that!"

As the inane suggestions kept coming, Midge wrote something at the top of the page and underlined it. Twice.

After grabbing a Diet Coke from the bar, Vic found a spot on the rug next to Andrea, who gave her a quick hug. She glanced around at the group, actually glad she'd come. Despite herself. Despite the fact that Tess was probably making out with Jake twenty feet away.

The lovebirds returned, Tess calling out more useless ideas. Not saying anything, Jake gazed pointedly at Vic—whatever that meant—and then away. Probably regretting that he'd hit on two women in the same week and they'd both shown up in the same room.

Doubtful. He was a guy, after all.

He tipped his bottle in her direction. "Hey."

The chatter continued around them while Jake dropped onto the rug next to Vic, on the side opposite from Andrea. "I didn't know you were going to be here tonight. Really."

One eyebrow rose. "That's pretty obvious."

His brow furrowed. "What's wrong?"

"Nothing." Midge looked at her, and Vic asked her to repeat the question. She heard something about dates and places, but she shook her head. Someone else would have to figure it out. She turned back to Jake. "Thanks for, uh, everything. Especially Orlando."

"Orlando?"

"You didn't—?" She broke off, embarrassed. But he'd given her the Slinky and Dilly bar. She bit her lip, trying not to feel like an idiot. "Someone dropped a crossword puzzle book in my mail slot. I thought it was you."

He looked at her strangely for a moment—and then laughed. "I never knew what you saw in Orlando Bloom."

"You were just jealous." Head down, she picked at a thread on the rug and tried to sound blasé. Experienced. Basically, more like Tess than herself. "I mean, he was an elf *and* a pirate."

Jake whistled, causing more than one pair of eyelashes to flutter in his direction. He waited until the crowd looked back at Midge, their field general, before speaking again. "Aragorn was a better choice, but I never had a chance anyway."

He'd had a chance, and they'd both blown it.

"Vic?" Midge called to her again. Everyone turned to stare, and Vic's face lit up like a Christmas tree. "Tess asked about holding the reunion out at your parents' summer place. We should've planned this months ago—" She wrinkled her nose, clearly irritated. "And I'm worried that we won't be able to book anything else on short notice."

"Vic's place is also a lot cheaper." Tess laughed as she swirled the wine in her glass.

"Since when do you care about money?" Vic finally snapped, although she was more irritated about her friend's intentions toward Jake than anything else. Even though she didn't want Jake.

When Tess blanched, Vic bent her head to ignore her while she considered the idea. Dad wouldn't mind, and she wouldn't give Mother advance warning. Their place would be perfect for a party. Plenty of beach. Sailboats, a waterski boat, and miscellaneous water toys. Spare rooms if anyone needed to sleep something off.

She wasn't thinking at all about Jake.

Or imagining where he lived or what he did in his free time or what he'd be like. As a grown-up.

Midge's voice squeaked. "We don't have to hold it at your parents' place, Vic. It was just an idea." She glared at Tess. "Obviously not a good one."

Tess's eyes glimmered, and she looked away when Vic tried to catch her eye. Vic nodded at Midge. "It's a great idea if people don't mind the drive out to Lake Minnetonka."

"Which part are we supposed to mind?" The woman who spoke looked vaguely familiar, but Vic was sure she hadn't seen her since high school. "The beautiful drive out, the gorgeous house, or the shimmering lake?"

She rolled her eyes. "It's just a summer place. Nothing to write home about." A place she'd rarely visited since marrying Ryder. Eleven years ago today.

"You're sure, Vic?" Midge started scribbling again on her notepad. "I mean, Liz just said we could hold it at her summer house on the St. Croix River if you want us to find someplace else. We don't have to hold it at your parents' place."

Vic glanced around the room, finally spotting Liz Tanner, who hadn't changed much in twenty years. They hadn't seen each other since graduation, but Tess had mentioned running into her sometime last summer.

Liz waved at her. "Your place is totally fine by me, Vic. But if you don't want to do it, I'd be happy to have the reunion at our summer house." She glanced at Piper Jamison, who grinned back at her. "The only hassle is that everyone would have to catch a boat ride across the St. Croix to the Wisconsin side, and that's a lot of boat rides."

Piper laughed, but Midge's eyes got big. Midge was all about logistics.

Jake called out from beside Vic. "I vote for Victoria's place."

Especially if it means we don't need to have another reunion planning meeting."

The crowd tittered, probably because Jake was the only man and it was Saturday night and half the women were well on their way to tipsy and hadn't gotten laid in too long. Even the married ones. Especially the married ones.

Andrea, who'd been silent ever since Jake joined them, turned bright red. Maybe even a woman married to Mr. Perfect wasn't getting laid.

Vic knew how that went.

Midge stopped scribbling and frowned at Jake the way she might at a mosquito. "We'll need another meeting." She glanced around the room at the faces staring blankly back at her. "Maybe a smaller group, to work out the details."

Tess swirled her glass but wasn't as bubbly as she'd been a few minutes ago. "How about Vic and Midge and me?"

The perfect trio, and a foregone conclusion. Midge did all the work and Vic's parents owned the place. Brains and money, with Tess thrown in for comic relief. She wondered where Andrea fit into the scenario, but Tess hadn't mentioned her, and Andrea wasn't saying anything.

Awkward. Just like how it'd been when she first returned to Southwest for the second semester of senior year.

Jake raised his hand, acting like he was in a classroom again and Midge was the teacher. "Can I help?"

A dozen heads whipped in his direction. Andrea also held up her hand after Tess pointedly stared at her.

"Uh, sure." Midge looked down at her clipboard, oblivious to the electrical current that Vic felt zooming around the room. "Andrea, you can help with invitations." Which meant Midge would do them. "Jake, could you get the alcohol?"

"My domain? Am I being replaced?" Tess pretended to pout, but the gleam had returned to her eye.

Midge looked flustered. "It's just that Jake owns a bar. I figured he could get alcohol at cost or something."

Tess batted her eyelashes. "I have my sources, too."

"Fine." Midge blew out a breath as she scratched something out and scribbled something else. "You can work together."

Vic's upper teeth almost sliced through her tongue. When she glanced from Tess to Jake, Tess shot her an odd smirk and Jake stared at a vase of fresh-cut orchids on the grand piano. Andrea, on the other side of her, looked sick.

Perfect. It truly was just like high school. One way or other, she'd be getting screwed all over again.

———

"I don't wanna go to camp."

Vic glanced into the backseat of her SUV. "Connor, we're almost there." After four hours of driving, bathroom breaks, food fights, and bickering, Vic wanted nothing more than to pull into the nearest bar and order a martini or three.

But she wouldn't. It was already nearly two o'clock, thanks to last-minute crises and Ryder, who'd showered the kids with lavish, utterly impractical gifts for their three weeks at camp. She'd bought them underwear and swimsuits. He'd furnished cell phones and a ghastly amount of candy.

Rolling her eyes, she pictured Ryder as he ran out the door right after she mentioned the long drive to Bemidji and how much she'd appreciate a second driver, even if the second driver was Ryder. Same old Ryder. Trinkets but no staying power.

She sang along to the radio despite the kids' protests. After she dropped them off at camp, she'd tie herself to the steering wheel until the urge to drink subsided. She couldn't afford to take even one step along the garbage-strewn path to where she'd been a week ago.

She also had a long drive home and a full day of work tomorrow. Preferably a day that would begin early, long before Sean or Hope showed up. She needed to look through the books and talk to Dad. If someone was laundering money, she didn't have the faintest idea how she'd discover it.

"Are you gonna visit us at camp?" Megan's voice piped up from the backseat, mumbling the words past the Milk Duds gluing her teeth together.

"We'll see." It all depended on how well she made it through the coming days. She'd buried herself in work since leaving the hospital, but that wasn't a long-term strategy, and life without her miniature chaperones would be difficult. "I can ask, but I don't think parents are supposed to visit."

Except maybe on the weekend between the one-week camp and the two-week camp. As in, five days from now. Ugh.

"You don't wanna see us. You're gonna take more pills and lock yourself in your room and nobody's gonna find you." Connor sniffled through his bravely defiant words, and the knife went straight to Vic's heart.

Megan started wailing, and Connor punched her. Boxed in by too many cars headed in the same direction, Vic allowed herself another quick glance in the rearview mirror. "Connor, quit punching Megan, and quit upsetting her. You two are going to have a great time at camp. It'll fly by, and you'll be home before you know it."

"Yeah, but you won't be there. Or Dad either."

"We'll be there." She amended herself. "At least, I'll be there. Just like I promised."

A promise she hoped to keep. She crossed her fingers—for luck, or to prevent a lie, she wasn't sure which.

All she had to do was survive three weeks. And the FBI.

And a gay husband. And a daughter she hadn't known about until two weeks ago. By comparison, adding Jake to that list—if he was a problem, and not already Tess's latest victim—didn't seem like such a big deal.

"Mom?"

Snapped out of her daze, she caught Megan just as she stuck her tongue out at Connor.

"Yes, princess?"

Megan giggled at the title, which Vic hadn't used in a while. "Can I call you if I'm lonely? Or scared? Or if Connor hits me?"

Great. The new cell phones were already burning a hole in their backpacks. She'd throttle Ryder. "Sorry, but I don't think the camp allows cell phones." She'd been too annoyed at Ryder's "gifts" to remind him about the camp's rules against electronic devices. Would he even notice when he didn't get any calls from the kids? "Besides, you'll be having too much fun."

"But will you be home?"

"Or at work, I suppose." Or in Jake's bed? Blinking, she stopped just short of slapping herself.

"And you'll miss me?"

"Incredibly."

An hour later, she'd dropped off the kids and gotten them registered and settled in amid endless questions, kisses, hugs, and last-minute requests to visit the camp store and candy shop. Finally, Vic climbed into her SUV and headed home. She'd have three weeks without kids and most likely a husband, since Ryder wouldn't have an excuse to stay at the house.

She hoped she survived.

———

By four a.m. on Tuesday morning, after a sleepless night in a house devoid of children and wayward husbands, Vic admitted to herself that she wasn't going to get any sleep and Ryder wouldn't be coming home. She arrived at the gallery just before six-thirty.

She'd now killed an hour and a half poring over financials, drunk three cans of Diet Coke, and made a corresponding number of trips to the bathroom. Blurry-eyed, rubber-legged, and a little sick to her stomach, she raised her Diet Coke in a toast to her stupid, irritating, awful life.

Time to call Dad.

He picked up his own phone at work, a change from his old law firm. "Honey? What's the matter? Are you okay?"

"Nothing a good lawyer can't fix." She yawned into her Diet Coke, too tired to care about the FBI or anyone else.

Her dad chuckled. "Well, you've come to the right place. You're at work already?"

"I couldn't sleep." She winced as soon as she said it. Dad would probably camp out in her living room every night if it gave her a good night's sleep. "So I came in early, before everyone else, to look at the books."

"Good, good."

She could actually hear him rubbing his hands together. Sheesh. The things lawyers got excited about. "But I don't see anything that clearly looks wrong. Or, for that matter, anything that completely adds up."

"Have you looked at your bank statements?"

"Sure. Nothing out of the ordinary." She flipped through three months' worth of statements. They all looked alike.

"If they're investigating you for money laundering—"

At his words, she frowned. Weren't they?

He kept talking. "It means they're finding unexplained cash transactions. Banks have to report deposits of more than ten thousand dollars in one day or anything else that looks odd, like several separate deposits in the same day of nine thousand dollars."

"I have some large deposits." She rubbed her temples where they'd started to ache. "But no different from always. Big sales, especially after an art opening, mean big deposits."

"Do you take in all the cash, or just your commission?"

"It depends, but we do run a lot of cash through our accounts." She flipped through a list of sales since the first of the year. A list of artists she represented. A list of clients. Matching it all up was a pain in the butt. "Sometimes we act as broker. Sometimes we buy and sell. It depends on the artist and the client."

"And all the entries add up?"

She arched her neck, which practically groaned. "As far as I can tell. The financials are a mess, though, which means I should've been paying more attention. Sean is good with numbers, so he usually handles the books." She stared at her computer screen and almost slapped it. "He set up a program for the financials, but I almost crashed the computer when I pulled it up this morning. I can't figure it out."

Her dad snorted.

"He minored in accounting!"

"And he might be majoring in ripping off my little girl." The scorn in Dad's voice grew—and started to annoy Vic.

"I don't think so, Dad." She stared at the rows and columns of numbers, all of which started to blur. "But I wouldn't mind a second pair of eyes to look at this stuff."

"Is that a date?"

She laughed. "If your life is as dull as mine, consider it one. Some evening this week? Speaking of which—"

"I'm at the house. With your mother. She's driving me up a tree."

"And?" She tapped her pencil on the sheet in front of her. "What else is new?"

A heavy sigh, followed by a rustling of papers. "How does Thursday evening sound?"

"Empty." She didn't have to look at her own calendar. With very few exceptions, it was blank. "I mean, free."

"That's my girl. Think positive. We'll figure this out."

Figure what out? The FBI investigation, or all the other problems that had turned her pristine life upside down? The question made her head spin, and she reached for—

The bottle of Tylenol.

———

WEDNESDAY EVENING, a little after seven, Jake swabbed down the bar and wondered where his regulars were. Or, for that matter, a few of his employees, including the bartender whose shift he was covering on short notice. A Twins game? Saints game? Outside enjoying the warm summer evening?

Busy planning their summer reunions?

Doubtful. Midge had called him by noon on Sunday and, surprisingly, three times since. Tess had stopped into Pendulum twice, but her so-called help consisted of picking out the brands she wanted, which he'd done a time or two in his life.

Victoria hadn't called. He hadn't given her his cell phone number, but he wasn't exactly hard to find.

He frowned when a young woman appeared in front of him at the bar. Pretty young. Definitely young enough to need an ID.

He held out his hand, not even bothering to ask. She stared hard at him, her blue eyes crinkling a little like his own did, but the rest of her was a topsy-turvy mess of hair and clothes and pretty much everything. Something about her was familiar, like he'd seen her before, but he couldn't put his finger on it.

And she was pregnant, if he didn't miss his mark.

The girl didn't offer any identification, or even fumble in her backpack or pockets the way most kids did, as if they'd left it somewhere. He'd heard it all. And never fallen for it.

"Mr. Trevor? Jake Trevor?"

"Yeah, kid. Can I see an ID?"

"I'm, uh, not twenty-one."

That was a new one. Honesty. "Sorry, hon. Unless you want to eat, and not at the bar, you'll have to leave. You can't hang out up here at the bar."

She took a look around the mostly empty restaurant, down the length of the bar, and her feet didn't move an inch. "I'm not here for a drink."

He rested one elbow on the bar. "Yeah, well, that's not how the law works."

"I came to see you." Her chin jutted out, and something about her flickered through his brain. He *had* seen her. Somewhere. With—

Damn. For the life of him, he couldn't place her.

"Sorry." He shook his head, trying to look like he gave a rip. Minors were a curse, especially on a slow Wednesday night when they stuck out like a sore thumb in a thin crowd. He didn't need the hassle. "You can't work here, either, if you're a minor. And I don't need a new girlfriend." Especially jail bait. "Or anything else I can think of."

"You know Victoria Bentley, right? I saw you—"

At the hospital that morning when he'd visited her. Bells dinged in his head, but he wasn't sure he'd won a prize. "Yeah, I know her. Friend from high school. Why?"

"How, uh, good a friend?"

The kid oughta be a detective. "Old friend, but we lost

touch. I just saw her recently." The girl seemed intent on his every answer, and Jake swabbed down the bar again. "With a bunch of other friends from high school."

She gave him a shrewd look. "Interesting."

"Not very." Jed walked in, a few minutes late for his shift. Excusing himself, Jake brought the bartender up to speed, then turned back to the girl. "Like I said, kid. If you're not twenty-one, you can't hang out at the bar."

"I'll be twenty-one in November. November twenty-four."

He shrugged. "Good for you. But this is June sixteen, last time I checked, so you're coming up five months short."

Her face fell, and her lower lip edged into a pout. "Don't you realize what happened twenty-one years ago in November?"

He slapped the bar. "Don't tell me. You were born."

"In Montana. Kalispell, Montana. Oakview Hospital."

"Super." The kid hadn't even had a drink, and she talked like one of his drunken regulars. "I hear the skiing's good in Montana. Maybe a little cold."

She pressed against the bar. "None of this rings a bell?"

"Skiing?" He frowned, wondering if she *had* been drinking before she showed up. Great. All he needed was to get busted on a sale to an underage he hadn't sold a damned thing to. "I mean it, kid. You're not old enough to be here. This is a bar."

"It's a restaurant, too."

Smart kid. "I don't see you asking for a menu, and if you want one, you'll need to go sit at a table. Anything else you wanted?"

She leaned forward, not unlike too many women who pushed their chests halfway into his face and wanted something. And not necessarily a drink. Jake backed up a foot.

She gave an exasperated sigh. "If you don't want to answer my questions, maybe you won't mind taking a blood test."

Holy fuck. He'd never seen her before in his life—okay, at the hospital, but that didn't count—and he hadn't done anything with a twenty-year-old since he'd been twenty. Since before he'd been twenty, maybe. Hell. He hadn't done much of anything with *anyone*, let alone a dumb kid with punked-out hair, in too long to remember.

She looked up at him, smug and sure of herself. Yep. The more he thought about that swell in her stomach, definitely pregnant. And the baby wasn't his.

"Maybe if you've got a warrant, kid. I don't know you. Now get out of here."

CHAPTER 11

L ate in the afternoon on Thursday, Ryder stared at the latest draft of the Brief from Hell and groaned. It still looked as bad as it had at noon, and he'd spent the afternoon in meetings rather than fixing it. Four hours, minimum, before he could call it a night. And he'd promised Sean he'd go to a freaking party.

On a Thursday. Sure, it offered more room for excuses to Vic, but he'd forgotten all about this antitrust case when Sean batted his eyelashes and asked. He sighed. Sean had all the right working parts but was more trouble than a wife. More than Vic, at least, who'd never made him do a damn thing.

His intercom buzzed.

"Mr. Bentley? A visitor is in the lobby. Mr. Roarke."

Crap. Sean, two hours early and way too many hours before he could leave. The brief was due by five tomorrow, and his associate had called in sick today. In his younger days, he wouldn't have dared call in sick the day before a brief was due. Young lawyers today were different. And he hadn't been paying enough attention to fix the problem before it turned critical.

He buzzed back. "Thanks, Shirley. I'll be right out."

Buzz. "Should I bring him to your office?"

Where Sean would want to do something inventive on top of his desk? "No, thanks. Too much of a mess back here."

He ran his hands through his hair, then glanced at his reflection in the window behind him and straightened the mess he'd just made. Files and way too many papers were piled high in front of him. Trying to ignore them, he pushed back from his desk and walked past Shirley on his way to the lobby.

"Why haven't you left yet?" He glanced at his watch. "It's already five-thirty."

"I wanted to make sure you had secretarial coverage for tonight. Unless you're not working."

"I'm definitely working." He smiled at her, a loyal employee in a world not filled with them. "But you don't need to. I'll either ask a night secretary for help or make the changes myself. All good."

She pulled her purse from her bottom drawer, obviously relieved he wasn't asking her to stay late at the last minute, like he'd done too many times.

He headed to the lobby, where he found Sean chatting up the young male receptionist they'd recently hired. Ryder had wondered about the receptionist, but he obviously would never approach the guy. Mixing work with pleasure could get a man fired. Even a partner. Even the son-in-law of the former managing partner.

"Sean?"

Sean murmured something and got a flirtatious response. Ryder didn't have to wonder about the receptionist anymore. And now the guy wouldn't have to wonder about Ryder, either. Shit.

He tapped his foot against the marble floor and glanced at his watch. Less than twenty-four hours before a fifty-page brief was due at the federal courthouse. He walked up to Sean, stopped an inch short of grabbing him by the elbow, and nudged him out the glass doors that separated the lobby from the elevator banks. Sean called out a goodbye to the receptionist, receiving a pretty little wave in return.

Ryder shook his head. He'd probably gotten the guy's digits. Since Ryder couldn't spend more than one night a week at Sean's now, and even that was tough, Sean was likely trolling.

He ran a hand along his jaw and felt whiskers. Had he forgotten to shave this morning? He'd sprung out of bed, grabbed a gym bag, and headed over to Sean's before dawn. Despite his brief. Despite having a wife down the hall who prowled the house at night, obviously unable to sleep.

Sean grabbed his forearm. "I'm so ready for this party, but I'm not sure if I can go. I really ought to work."

Frowning, Ryder pulled his arm away and tried to talk softly without leaning close to Sean. "What do you mean?"

"Vic's still at work, and her dad arrived as I was leaving." Sean's voice warbled in a singsong way that usually enchanted Ryder but now made him grit his teeth. "Isn't that odd?"

He shrugged. "She's tight with her dad. Maybe they're going out to dinner."

"But she said she was working tonight."

Sean gripped his arm again until Ryder looked at it pointedly. "Don't. Please." At his words, Sean let go. "Maybe her dad is just stopping by. It's not a big deal."

"I don't know. I just feel uncomfortable." Sean paused when Ryder nodded at a lawyer who walked past, but he obviously didn't appreciate how dangerous this was for Ryder. "I shouldn't let her work so hard. I told her I'd take care of things."

"And you did." Sean had spent more hours at the gallery than usual in the past few weeks, leaving Ryder annoyed and unable to complain. "But she's back now and doing great. Maybe she wants to take a look at the books."

"But it's not month end, and I haven't had time to finish entering all the financial data into the computer."

"So? The kids are gone, and Vic's just trying to occupy herself." He kept mentioning her name as often as possible, trying not to hyperventilate when two partners joined them. One pushed the button for the elevator, and the other looked from Ryder to Sean and back again, a little too curious.

Starting to perspire, Ryder loosened his tie as the bell dinged twice for the elevator. Both men got on. Sean waved to them.

"Aren't you friendly." Ryder crossed his arms and thought about the brief. Maybe he'd cancel on Sean and go home to Vic at a decent hour. Like eleven. "Are you planning on getting to know everyone here?"

"Do you have a problem with that?"

"None at all." Except for the fact that one gay man could hide in a crowd, and two couldn't. "Anyway, quit worrying about the gallery. You practically live there."

"You ought to know. It's what you do here."

Sean's voice took on the snippy, whining quality that Ryder hadn't noticed before he'd left Vic and moved in with Sean.

He ran a finger around the inside of his collar, seeking and not finding relief. "Speaking of that, I have a deadline. Tomorrow. I really need to work."

Sean stared at him. "But you hate it when I work too much."

"Yeah, but that's—"

"—an art gallery?" Sean's hands went to his hips. So like Vic. "Are you saying my work isn't as important as yours?"

God. Exactly like Vic. He saw it in her face every time he claimed a deadline or a work emergency, especially when she had a conflict at the gallery. But she rarely said the words, let alone screeched them. The sound reverberated in the glassed-in elevator lobby, and the receptionist stared hard at them.

Ryder held up a hand and spoke softly. "Please. I wasn't saying that. We're both busy. We both have work obligations. I was just trying to say that I hadn't realized how bad mine were. Tonight. Just tonight."

"Fine." Sean crossed his arms, obviously still annoyed but a little less angry. "Should we meet at the party?"

Ryder glanced at his watch. Yikes. He needed to log several more hours, get a good night's sleep, and start all over again first thing tomorrow. "What time?"

"I'll be there by nine. Don't keep me waiting." With that, he swished to the elevator, his trim hips mesmerizing Ryder despite himself.

"Right. See you . . . soon."

Sooner or later. If later didn't happen until tomorrow, he'd just have to buy something expensive or mind-blowing to make Sean forgive him. If Sean was too angry, both.

He walked back to his office, not sparing a glance for the receptionist. He wanted Sean, but he had to handle him the way he'd always handled Vic. With bribes and surprises and, although he hated lies, an occasional snippet of misinformation.

He could still have it all.

———

"I'm not seeing anything, except maybe a mess. No smoking gun." Vic's dad peered at her over his reading glasses and scratched his head, right at the top in back where he had a slight bald spot.

"I told you."

"And you're a smart girl. Woman." He grinned. "A very capable woman with a great business."

"But I'm being investigated by the FBI." She tapped her finger on the tax returns they'd just reviewed, wondering whether the IRS was also involved. Guilty or not, she never won with those guys. "And God knows who else."

Her dad tipped back on the wobbly chair next to her crowded desk. At just under six feet tall and broadly built, he wasn't made for her narrow chairs or cramped office. She'd scrimped on it, leaving more room for the gallery and storage areas.

She wrinkled her nose. "What do you think they're after?"

"A crime of some sort, probably involving your bank accounts. You have just one?"

"Who needs more than that?" Vic frowned, not understanding the question. "I mean, one for home and one for the gallery. Actually, two for home. Ryder and I have separate accounts, but our names are on each other's accounts."

Her dad shook his head. "How often do you see his bank statements? Or his credit card statements?"

"He pays our credit card bills, which come to him at the office. It's more convenient." A headache threatened, and she squeezed the bridge of her nose.

"Very convenient. For Ryder."

"And for me." She didn't know why she was defending Ryder, but he wouldn't cheat her. Cheat *on* her, as it turned out, but that was just about sex. With a man. "I mean it, Dad. Ryder isn't doing anything illegal."

"Do you mind if I check with a few banks to make sure you don't have accounts you don't know about? As trustee of your old trust fund, I must still hold a power of attorney."

"That's right. The trust fund is in a separate account." It was nearly gone, and she hadn't touched the small remaining balance in a few years. "Maybe I should use what's left of it to start college accounts for the kids."

"Good idea." Dad nodded his agreement. "Yes, it's probably wise to check out your other accounts. But my little girl—" His eyes twinkled when she started to object to the term. "My *daughter* already has enough on her plate. Let me handle it."

She sighed, knowing it would be a waste of his time. "Can you do it discreetly?"

"Isn't that my middle name?"

"No. It's Francis."

"No wonder I keep trying to change it." He looked at his watch, causing Vic to check the clock on her desk. Almost seven-thirty. "Want to grab a bite to eat? Something quick?"

"Isn't Mother expecting you home?"

"Hardly." He took off his reading glasses and tucked them in the breast pocket of his suitcoat. "I'm sorry, honey. I think I waited too long to do something, and we might not stand a chance of fixing it anymore."

She shut off her computer and stowed the books in her file cabinet, locking it, even though she'd never locked it before. Her dad's dire warnings were getting to her. "Do what you have to do, Dad. But divorce isn't easy."

"Sometimes living together isn't so easy, either."

After turning off the lights and locking up, she followed him out to the street. She then climbed into the front seat of his Lexus as he held open the passenger door. "Lucky thing we have each other."

"Two perfect individuals." He slammed her door and moved around the front of the car to the driver's side.

She smiled at him as he opened his own door, slid into the driver's seat, and buckled up. Dad. The one guy who'd never let her down. Thank God for that.

———

"I CAN'T BELIEVE you dragged me in here again."

Vic had to shout over the noise of the crowd, even though Tess probably wasn't listening.

"Reunion planning meeting. A critical one." Tess turned to her and smiled. "We need all of our committee members."

They waded through the crowd filling Pendulum at eight o'clock on Saturday night. As someone grabbed her butt, Vic swatted blindly and drew a yelp from Tess.

Vic lifted one shoulder, not bothering to look apologetic. "I don't see Andrea, and you don't need me here, either. Do whatever you want to my parents' place. I don't care, and they won't know."

Tess shouted into her ear. "Just like high school? Are you sure they never found out about our parties?"

She shook her head. "The only neighbors anywhere nearby don't live out there in the winter. The last party we had was in March or April of junior year, and we cleaned up afterward."

She'd probably been pregnant by then, blissfully unaware of it, and drinking. She shuddered, thinking how cautious she'd been during her pregnancies with Connor and Megan. She also hadn't thrown another party after that during high school, or gone to any. Her mother watched her every move, but she wouldn't have tried.

She didn't need to learn her lesson twice.

"Hey." Tess grabbed her arm. "You're lost in that daze again. It's all you've done in the past few weeks."

Vic shrugged. "My life might suck, but at least I don't bitch about it." She amended herself. "Much."

"You should." Tess steered her toward a booth in the far corner, where Midge held down the fort. "Life must get lonely in that ivory tower. You should escape more often."

"I'm not trying to escape. You keep dragging me away."

She slid into the booth next to Midge, whose head was bent as she scribbled something on her long to-do list. Tess sat across from them and picked up a menu. Vic glanced around but couldn't see anyone in the crowd, especially when some huge guy stood right next to their booth.

"Nice place." She pursed her lips and thought of all the things she'd rather be doing tonight. Like scrubbing soap scum out of the shower. "Who else is joining us?"

"Me, for one." She jumped when Jake took the seat next to Tess, who grabbed his elbow. Cozy. "But only for stretches here and there. I have a big crowd tonight."

"I hadn't noticed." She picked up a menu and pretended to peruse it, even though she already knew she'd get a burger and fries.

Midge looked up from her notes. "Where's Andrea?"

Tess shook her head. "Couldn't make it."

As Vic frowned, Jake glanced over at the bar, ignoring them. Tess tugged on the short sleeve of his polo shirt, and Vic pretended not to watch.

"By the way, has Vic told you about her problem?"

"Tess!"

She patted Vic's clenched fist. "No, really. Jake has quite an inventory system for the bar, and it occurred to me this afternoon that he might be able to help."

Vic frowned, wondering how Tess had gotten such a close-up view of Jake's anything. "I don't need more alcohol."

A hooted response. "That's a fact. No, I meant that he has a lot of experience running a business, and he might be able to help with your little FBI issue."

"Tess!" Vic glared at her as Midge looked curiously at both women. "I have plenty of business experience, too. But I wasn't planning to share my, er, FBI issue with the whole world."

"Not even with friends? Friends who can help?"

"I doubt Jake can help." She cringed at her words when he started to get up, and Tess tugged him back down into his seat. "I mean, my dad is working on it." She glanced from Jake to Midge. "It's just a routine investigation."

He shook his head. "I don't think anything is routine with the Feds. What is it, Victoria? Maybe talking about it would help."

She'd talked about it with her dad until her head swam. And she couldn't imagine what Jake could add, except maybe a good, strong drink. "I don't think so. Thanks anyway."

"Whatever." He shrugged. "If you think about it, though, our businesses are pretty similar."

Her nose wrinkled.

"We both deal in commodities." He held up a hand before she could argue. "Mine is just a more *liquid* form of investment."

Expensive artwork and cheap liquor. Right. "Like I said, my dad is taking care of it."

"Suit yourself." He glanced again at the bar, signaling something to the bartender, but after a moment he looked back at Vic. "By the way, that kid who was visiting you in the hospital is pretty weird. How do you know her?"

She stared at him blankly. She'd had so many visitors, half of them when she was almost comatose. But the only two kids who'd visited, to her knowledge, were now at Spanish camp. "What do you mean? A kid?"

Jake blew out a breath. "You know. Twenty. Weird hair. Looks like she's pregnant, although I couldn't really tell with those grungy clothes she wore."

She caught Tess's eye. Midge, next to her, went back to scribbling. Finally, Vic spoke. Carefully. "She didn't say her name?"

"Nope. Too busy pumping me for information and telling me her damned birthday. Hell, if it's not at least twenty-one years ago, I'm not interested in knowing."

Tess moved away from Jake, a fraction of an inch. "What did she say?"

"That's about it. She came in here the other day, insisting she'd be twenty-one in November, like I cared, and asked me to take a blood test. Like I'd fool around with some kid." He leaned across the booth. "I'm not a total shit."

Midge had abandoned her notes by now and was pushing her glasses into her nose. Frozen, Vic had no idea what to say.

Jake stared at her. "I'm not."

"I know you're not."

"Thanks, but everyone seems to be acting like it. You won't go out with me." At this, Midge's gaze went back to her notes. "You won't even give me the time of day."

"That's not true."

"Yeah, it is." He slammed one palm on the table, and all three women jumped. Standing up, he jammed both hands in the front pockets of his jeans. "But it doesn't matter. I just thought you'd want to know what kind of nutjobs are hanging out with you. Who is she, anyway? Am I supposed to know the kid?"

"No." Vic squeaked the word and couldn't make herself meet his eyes. "I'm sorry. Not your fault."

"Damned right it's not." He whirled away from the group and returned to the bar. Despite herself, Vic watched his hips all the way there. She turned back to Tess, who was doing the same thing.

"Cut it out. He's not your type."

"Oh, ho!" Tess smirked as her head bobbed from side to side. "Staking a claim, are we?"

"A prehistoric claim. Nothing more." She rummaged in her

purse, searching for her keys. The evening couldn't end quickly enough for her taste.

Tess reached across the table and grabbed her hand. "You're not going anywhere. It's me. Tess. Teasing you. Unless I'm not allowed to do that anymore."

"It looks like the rules have changed all around." She stared pointedly at Tess. "Are you dating him?"

"Jake?" Tess glared right back at her.

"Were we talking about someone else?"

Midge set down her pen. Without breaking their locked gaze, both Vic and Tess laid a restraining hand on her.

"You're so full of it." Tess flicked a glance at Midge, seeking support, even though both Vic and Tess knew that Midge would rather be five tables away. "Geez, Vic. All these years. Even if Jake were my type, the guy has your name written all over him. I don't poach, and I don't take castoffs."

"Rules to live by, I'm sure." He suddenly reappeared but clearly wasn't about to sit down again in the middle of a hornet's nest. "But I'm no one's castoff."

Three mouths hung open before Tess recovered. "We weren't discussing you. Just analyzing Midge's love life." Gasping, Midge turned away from the entire group. Facing the wall. "See? I think she's too shy. That's why we dragged her down here tonight. To get out. Meet people."

Vic tried to hug Midge, the last person on earth who'd ever want to be the center of attention, and got elbowed for her trouble. She kicked Tess under the table.

Jake waved to someone, and a moment later a young woman with a shaved head came up to them, chomping gum and holding a tray in the air. Two minutes after that, they ordered. Jake left right behind the young woman.

Tess leaned forward. "And no, he's not after her, either." She turned to Midge and patted her hand, even though Midge was still facing the wall. "I'm sorry, sweetie. I was just teasing, but I do think you should get out more. Both of you." She nodded at Vic. "I guess you can call me your own personal social director. Lucky you."

Midge twisted in her seat and glanced at Vic, who raised her eyebrows. Both stuck their tongues out at Tess.

She laughed. "I'm glad we're in agreement."

Belatedly, Vic and Midge both joined in her laughter.

Midge shook her head. "Tess, when are you ever going to change?"

"The same day you guys do. And not a moment before."

With that, the tension broke. But Vic wondered which one would, indeed, be the first to change.

She had a feeling it wouldn't be her.

———

MONDAY MORNING, holed up in her office behind a closed door, Vic stared at numbers on the ledgers in front of her when she should've been finding new artists or artwork or selling something fabulous to someone with plenty of money.

And Dad was missing. She'd called him at home, and Mother had said in a frosty voice that he wasn't staying there. Thursday night, over dinner at J.D. Hoyt's, Dad had insisted he was still living at home with Mother—at least until something new happened.

She hadn't thought something new could happen so quickly.

She closed the ledger after deciding not to make her headache worse by poking around in the computer financial program. She'd leave that, at least, to Sean.

Almost eleven. Sean and Hope must be here by now, and

she needed to get out into the gallery. Last time she checked, she still had a business to run. It wouldn't run on fumes.

Someone knocked faintly on her door. "Come in."

Hope's head poked into her office. "Are you busy?"

"No more than usual." Getting up, Vic tried to look more friendly than under attack, which was how she actually felt. She tucked the ledger into the top drawer of her file cabinet and pushed the button to lock it, pocketing the key.

Hope stared at her pocket—or maybe it just felt that way to a woman overcome with paranoia—before pointing at the computer screen. "I can help you with your computer." She rushed on when Vic immediately started to say no. "I mean, not just a website, although you need a better one. Inventory, financial statements—"

Vic shook her head. "Not necessary." She glanced pointedly at the clock. A minute before eleven. "Time to open up. Is Sean taking care of that?"

"He's not here." Hope frowned. "And he hasn't called. I was wondering if we should check up on him."

"I'm sure he'll be here soon. It's summer, and Sean's been putting in extra hours lately."

"While you were in the hospital."

She brushed past Hope into the main room of the gallery. "And before and since. We've had several exhibits and new artists, and it all takes time. I don't mind if Sean's a little late. Neither should you."

Hope's shoulders sagged. Her stomach had grown, although it was still hardly noticeable except for the fact that she rubbed it whenever she mentioned something that irritated Vic. "I just thought you'd want to know about Sean."

"Thanks for the update." Vic moved to the door, turning the deadbolt to unlock it. Swarms of art lovers were not standing outside waiting to get in. "And we're open for business."

"I think Sean's been acting strange."

Spoken by the girl who wouldn't know what normal looked like if it walked up and smacked her in the face.

Vic moved along a wall of artwork, wondering whether she'd ever unload a couple of paintings that had been a rare impulse purchase. Hands on her hips, she stared at an oil painting by a hot young artist whose work reminded her of Dalí. Beautiful, in its strange, twisted way. Several customers had been on the verge of buying it but balked at the last minute.

"Um." At the sudden sound next to her, Vic jumped. Hope looked ready to follow her to the ends of the earth. "Sean seems to talk a lot to your husband. Ryder?"

"Ryder? Yes." The identity of her husband was hardly a secret, except perhaps to Ryder. But the tingling at the base of her neck made her want to run before Hope lobbed another hand grenade. "Sean has known Ryder and me since I've owned the gallery. He knows quite a few of my friends."

She moved on from the Dalí wannabe, mostly to see if she could shake her odd shadow.

Apparently not. "Does he know Jake?"

Vic arched one eyebrow. "Jake? Jake who?"

Hope swallowed hard, then stuck like glue to her as Vic moved down the row. She should've brought a clipboard to take notes. At the outset of this little impromptu inventory, she'd been trying only to get away from Hope.

She stopped in front of a sculpture on a high table. Tapping a finger on her chin, she tried and failed to remember the artist without looking at the information card. A first, and a sure sign that she was buckling under the pressure of the phantom intern/daughter who dogged her every step.

"Jake Trevor."

"Hmmm?" Her left eye twitched. Hope knew too much. Saw too much. And Vic didn't have a clue how she did it.

Good with computers, indeed.

"Jake Trevor." Hope squeezed between Vic and the sculpture, and Vic commanded her eye not to twitch. "An old friend, right?"

She brushed past Hope, moving on to a large tapestry that should've been paid for and picked up last week. The "sold" sign was gone. Hmmm.

"Vic? I'm asking about Jake Trevor."

Vic took a step backward and crossed her arms, aiming for the cold, haughty princess look she'd perfected in ninth grade and never fully abandoned. "Don't you have some work to do? Or are you here just to ask questions? Jake Trevor today, someone else tomorrow. It's becoming tiresome."

Hope looked at her slyly. "I visited him last week after seeing him at the hospital. I saw his name written down at the nurses' station, and everything fell into place."

"How nice for you." Hearing a click, Vic moved toward the door. The first customers of the day. No one she recognized, which typically meant browsers without wallets. She turned back to Hope, speaking in a low voice. "But I'm not sure he's in your league. Jake's good looking, I guess, but a little old for you. If that's what you want, Sean's a little closer to your age."

"And gay." Hope sidled closer as Vic called out a greeting to the customers. "But that's not what I mean, and you know it."

"I'm not sure I do know what you mean." The customers waved her off and wandered among the artwork, leaving Vic stuck with Hope. "But all that matters is that you do, I suppose."

"I thought Jake should know who I am. And maybe Ryder.

And your kids." She kept talking even when Vic frowned. "Connor and Megan, right? I could find them at camp."

A chill raced up her spine. "Why would you even say such a thing? To get a reaction out of me? What is it with you?"

"I'm your daughter, Vic. I want to be part of your life. All of your life. And my dad's life, too."

"And you think your dad is—?"

Hope rolled her eyes. "Jake Trevor. Duh."

Horrified, Vic stared at her blankly.

"Yeah." Hope nodded, looking somehow encouraged. "I found both of you with an Internet search, although Jake was tougher. I mean, he wasn't listed in the hospital's records. But I found him. That's why I invited him to Sean's art opening. I wanted to meet my dad and see both of you together."

As Vic's vision swam, she bit her lip to focus. Now or never, and Sean wasn't here to stop her. "You're out of line, Hope." She shook her head, remembering Jake's odd appearance at the opening. She had no idea how Hope could've found him, but she certainly wasn't going to thank the girl. "And I'm afraid you're also out of a job. Pack up your things. You're fired."

CHAPTER 12

"You can't fire me."

"Oh?" Vic straightened an already-neat pile of papers in the center of her desk. "Let's see. I own the gallery, I'm your employer, and you're a temporary, part-time summer intern who's not doing her job. What part of that do I have wrong?"

"I'm your daughter, Vic." Tears clustered in the corners of Hope's eyes, and her hand roved frantically over her stomach. "I just wanted to find you. And I need a job."

"There are other jobs. Perhaps one in the computer field?" She smiled helpfully, wishing someone had an opening that Hope could take immediately. She'd make a few calls, but she wouldn't sic Hope on anyone she actually liked. "You can't work here. It's been one problem after another since you arrived."

"You'd do that to your daughter?"

"I have no idea whether you're my daughter." She really needed to ask that woman in Kalispell for the paperwork, although the blue eyes and the patches of blond roots at the base of her horrid dye job were two points in Hope's favor.

"And even if you were, there's nothing wrong with a policy against nepotism."

Hope flinched. "You don't have a policy like that. And y-you only have two employees."

"One, at this point." Vic shook her head. "I'm sorry, Hope, but we've both seen this coming. Ever since Sean's opening, certainly. I've never had a worse one."

"B-but—"

"No. It's time for you to go." Relief surged through Vic, along with something she recognized as guilt. She brushed the latter away. "Now, if you'll give me a few minutes, I'll take care of your last paycheck."

"I don't have any money. Or—or a place to stay." Hope gripped the edge of the desk. "I need this job."

No. She wouldn't give in. Not when she'd finally summoned the nerve to make the right decision. "You had a place to stay before today. I suspect it's still there."

"Not without money."

"Ask your parents for money. The McCullochs." Vic's teeth ground together, but she was determined to stick this one out.

Head down, Hope trudged out of her office. The instant she left, Vic took a shallow breath. Somehow, the victory didn't taste as sweet as she'd expected.

———

TUESDAY MORNING, bright and early, Vic was back at her desk, behind a closed door, struggling to figure out what could possibly be wrong with financials and bank statements that didn't look any different from how they'd always looked.

Dad still hadn't called. The only other lawyer she could trust, Natalie, knew as much about financials as she did about art: enough to mention in passing at a cocktail party. At least Nat was a friendly voice. Vic picked up the phone and called Nat's St. Paul office. "Hey."

"Hey yourself." Already at work, and from the sound of it chewing her daily cinnamon-raisin bagel. No cream cheese. No worries about carbs, either, even just to be fashionable.

Vic cut to the chase. "Have you heard from Dad?"

"I've missed you, too. How are those kids of yours?"

"At camp. Four hours away in Bemidji." Thinking of Hope, she wished they were farther away than the Canadian border. "They can't call home, because the camp confiscated the cell phones Ryder gave them as a farewell gift."

Natalie laughed. "It serves him right. Nothing's too extravagant if it comes from his wife's trust fund."

Vic sucked in a breath. "Ryder makes good money."

"And you make even better money on your gallery and investments." Nat broke off a moment, and Vic heard the sound of a door closing. Nobody seemed to be able to have a conversation these days without someone closing a door. "Sorry. Face it, Vic, you and I both know those kids don't need cell phones. They need their mom and dad."

Her throat constricted. "Together?"

"Not unless you want that, and I don't see why you would."

"Speaking of which, what do you know about Mother and Dad?"

"Quite a bit, from Dad's perspective. He's staying in my spare room."

And no one had mentioned it to Vic. "He and I were working together on something. I haven't heard from him since last Thursday."

"He moved in Friday night, with about fifteen minutes' warning. I wondered why he's not staying with you."

"I asked a week or two ago if he needed a place to stay, and he said no."

He probably assumed she had enough pressure without a houseguest. Or he figured he'd get in Ryder's way, even though she hadn't seen much more of Ryder than she had of Dad. Bottom line, though, he could've asked her. Or at least called. Something.

"Well, it's ruining my love life." Nat jumped into the dead silence. "Not that I have one, mind you, but you never know. It's theoretically possible."

"So they say. Even about me." Well, Tess did.

"You? Are you dating again? Or is Ryder still back with you? I can't keep up."

Vic snorted. "I didn't know the two concepts were mutually exclusive. At least from Ryder's perspective."

"Ew. I didn't want to know that."

"Neither did I." She also hadn't meant to share it, even with Nat. Some things were better kept in the closet. "But at least now I know where Dad is."

"Feel free to claim him anytime. Surprise me."

"Has he told you what's going on with Mother?"

"Not really. You know—" Nat whispered into the phone, even though Vic could've sworn she'd already shut her door. "I'm not sure it's all about Mother."

Vic choked on a sip of coffee, almost spewing it over the papers on her desk. "Another woman?"

"That doesn't seem right, either. Not like Dad. But I think something's up." She paused, giving Vic's stomach time to churn. "I can't quite put my finger on it."

"This is what you get for reading all those Nancy Drews when we were kids." Vic shook her head, not wanting to think about it. "But I'm not sure it's such a mystery. Like I said, he's helping me figure something out."

"Which is—?"

"Not helping me get my beauty sleep." Her second line lit up. "I have to go. Ask Dad to call me, okay?"

"Anything for you, sis. I wouldn't even mind babysitting your kids this weekend."

She frowned. "They'll still be at camp."

"Like I said." Nat laughed before the phone clicked in Vic's ear.

———

TUESDAY EVENING, a little after six, Jake stepped out of the shower just in time to hear the doorbell. Late for work, dripping wet, buck naked. Perfect.

He ran a towel in a zigzag pattern down his body, hitting the highlights. He'd already thrown his filthy jeans in the hamper. Stumbling downstairs, he wrapped the towel around his waist as he went, hoping he didn't frighten some little old lady collecting for the charity of the week.

The doorbell rang again. "Coming!" He was panting by the time he made it to the front door, flipped the lock, and swung the door wide open.

Victoria stood outside.

She glanced at him, flushed, then swung her gaze to her shoes. Cute little pointy numbers that matched her red outfit, but he doubted that was what attracted her attention.

His hand gripped his towel a hell of a lot more tightly than when he'd tripped down the stairs. "C'mon in. Quickly. Before the woman across the street calls the cops."

She turned to look across the street at the white rambler with a manicured lawn and picket fence. And waved.

"Funny." He waited while she stepped inside, her head swiveling as she took in his shabby old furniture, mostly hand-me-downs from his parents. A few hand-me-ups from his kid sister, sadly enough. "But I don't need more trouble."

"Am I trouble?"

With those big baby blues, lips he still wanted to kiss, and a husband? Naaa. No trouble at all.

He watched as she finished her perusal of his furnishings, such as they were, and started to peruse him. Unless she wanted to get naked, though, he wasn't waiting. He headed back upstairs. She paused, then started to follow.

"Since when do you follow me into my bathroom? It's been a while, Victoria."

She stopped on the stairs. "Most people call me Vic."

"I always liked 'Victoria' better. Cool and classy."

Reaching the top, he stepped into the bathroom and shut the door. He listened for a telltale rattle, wondering whether she'd try the handle. Nothing. At seventeen she would've entered, turned bright red, and stared at the floor until he made a move. No, at seventeen his mom wouldn't have left him alone upstairs with Victoria. Smart mom.

He whipped off the towel, then glanced in the mirror and saw his tousled hair, his stubbly beard. Not the prettiest sight. No wonder she hadn't joined him.

He bent over the sink, shaving quickly. Ouch. Blood ran along the edge of his jaw on both sides, and it stung like a sono-fabitch. He splashed water over the cuts and rummaged in the drawer for a white stick to stop the bleeding. Finding a couple of condoms, he shoved them in the back of the drawer.

He also found his robe, right where it was supposed to be, on the back of the door. He knotted the belt around his waist and flung open the door, ready to trip over Victoria.

She wasn't there.

Talk about inflated expectations. He headed down the hall toward his bedroom, conjuring up a fantasy of her lying on his bed, her hair fanned across his pillow, wearing nothing but an impish grin. He stepped into the bedroom and—

She wasn't there, either.

"Victoria?"

No answer. He couldn't believe she'd left without saying goodbye. Not that it'd be such a surprise, come to think of it, since she'd done the same thing at seventeen. She had plenty of practice.

He slammed the bedroom door and grabbed a clean pair of jeans. Zipped them up, didn't bother with a shirt. It was his own damn house, no matter how pitiful, and he wasn't going to make an effort. Even for Victoria.

He whipped open the door and trotted down the steps, knowing she must be gone. Looked through the glass in the front door. Saw an eye-popping yellow Porsche Boxster parked in the driveway.

Passing through the living room, he noticed a couple of ratty pillows that were out of place, a few tarnished picture frames that she'd obviously picked up. The whole place must disgust her.

He finally found her at the kitchen table. Scratched and dented Formica with cubbyholes where he and his sister had stuffed food when Mom hadn't been looking. Squash, Spam, you name it. The crap might be in there still. No wonder Mom gave him the table.

Victoria ran her hands over the top of the table, an odd expression on her face.

"Victoria?" He took a step closer. "What are you doing?"

"Sorry. I, uh—" She broke off, and her hands abruptly stopped their circular movement. "I thought I'd just wait here until you got dressed."

He glanced down where his shirt should be. "I didn't know where you'd gone. If you'd left." He eyed the fridge, wondering if he should offer her some wine. But he didn't have any. "Or why you showed up in the first place."

She gazed at his chest, then quickly down at the table. Still seventeen, but in a thirty-eight-year-old's body. "I came over to . . . talk."

His gaze swept the kitchen, seeing the yellow linoleum floor, the avocado-green appliances, the faded wallpaper. He wished they'd talked somewhere else. Anywhere else.

"This is charming." She needed glasses. "I love these old places. Mine is about the same vintage."

"But different vintners." She hadn't seen the chipped dishes yet. For the first time, he couldn't bear to look at his own kitchen, which had always reminded him of hot cocoa and Victoria. "I've seen your house. Not the same league."

His shoulders felt heavy, and he swung a leg over the back of a kitchen chair. "But why are you here? Reunion stuff? It's not worth a trip to the slums."

She frowned. "South Minneapolis is hardly the slums. I live in south Minneapolis, too." She slid her hand along the top of the table. "We used to sit at this table, late at night after a date, talking to your parents."

"While I groped you under the table."

She smiled. "I didn't mind that part, either."

"My mom did. She's no fool. Never was."

Victoria leaned forward. "How is she? And your dad?"

He glanced at the window. The frame needed touching up, like everything else. "She's fine, mostly. Dad died last year."

Gasping, she started to offer condolences.

He brushed them off. "Liver cancer. He went pretty fast, a few months, really. He'd just retired, and he and Mom were planning a celebration trip."

"I'm sorry, Jake. I didn't know."

"Yeah. Whatever." He felt a little better, somehow, felt the easing of something he'd carried in his chest since the funeral, when Victoria hadn't shown up.

She traced figures on the table. He squinted, watching the movement of her delicate fingers. She finally spoke again. Quietly. "I thought I should stop by. I need to tell you about that girl who came into Pendulum last week. The one you mentioned."

"The loony tune?"

"I wouldn't call her that. But she's a problem I need to deal with, and I'm sorry she's trying to drag you in."

His head spun, trying to imagine what some kid could drag him into that involved Victoria. Until a few weeks ago, he hadn't even seen her since high school. Not much at all since junior year. Twenty-one years—

No. God, no.

His jaw dropped, and she reached out to touch him. He pulled away. "Don't tell me there's a connection between that kid and us. The only one I can think of—"

She waited.

"—would really piss me off. Big time."

She watched him, chewing on her lower lip before starting to speak. Haltingly. "We were just seventeen, Jake, and I wasn't ready for, well, for whatever that involved."

A sick feeling in the pit of his gut told him he wasn't going to like this. He kept his fists beneath the table, balled up, ready to slam into something.

"I also didn't realize I was pregnant until just before school let out. I told my mother, and the next thing I knew I was on a plane for Montana. Staying with relatives I'd never met. I-I had to go to the hospital a month early when I started bleeding heavily. Emergency C-section."

She rubbed her stomach as her eyes glazed over and she drifted back to a time, a world, he couldn't visit. Hell. She hadn't let him visit. Or told him she'd had a baby. His baby. His almost-twenty-one-year-old baby.

His teeth chewed a hole in the inside of his cheek, but he refused to make her confession any easier. Her whole damned life had been easy, and he wasn't going to be a co-conspirator.

"And . . . I don't know what happened after that."

"You had a baby. And you gave her up for adoption—also known as a dump and run. You should've told me about it and given me the chance to raise the kid."

Her face turned white. He slammed his fists on the kitchen table and shoved back from it, knocking over his chair. Stomped from the kitchen as fast as he could without calling it running. Barely.

"Jake!" Her voice called out, and he heard the scraping of chairs and her heels against the floor. Coming after him. Twenty-one years too late.

She caught him in the living room, where he'd stopped after realizing he didn't want this to end upstairs, anywhere near his bedroom, the scene of the crimes he'd hoped to commit with her in this house. Now, the thought of being in bed with her made him sick. The whole damned thing did.

"Jake, listen to me."

"I would've been happy to listen in high school. When you got pregnant and ran." He glanced at her, not caring that her face had frozen or that she'd fallen backward into a scuzzy chair with lousy springs. "You didn't leave town to go dance in some fancy show, like you told everyone. You had a fucking kid. My kid."

"I never meant to hurt you."

What an idiot. To think he'd given more than a passing thought to being her husband and having kids with her. Someday. When he grew up and figured out what he wanted to be. Something besides the kept husband of a rich girl.

He stood above her, arms crossed, as she lay half-sprawled in the chair his grandfather had made a zillion years ago. "You didn't mean to hurt me? Are you kidding?"

"I wrote you a letter the day I left for Montana. You never answered."

"I never—"

She waved her hand. "I know. My mother must've trashed it. She wouldn't let me call you, and I was stupid enough to give it to her when I left for the airport. I didn't know she never mailed it."

He squirmed. "Victoria, I—"

"I know. You don't ever want to see me again." Biting her lip, she ran her hand down the arm of the chair. "It was stupid to think anything could happen after twenty years."

"Twenty-one."

"But who's counting?" One of her eyebrows arched before she shook her head. "I'm sorry, Jake. I didn't know if I was going to keep the baby or give it up for adoption."

Frowning, he dropped onto the couch next to her chair. "What do you mean? You obviously gave her up for adoption."

"Hope." She laughed, the sound both hollow and brittle. "That's her name, you know. Hope. I just found out about her myself."

Right. Maybe she could hide the kid from *him* for twenty years, but a woman couldn't hide her own kids from herself. He'd taken tenth-grade biology.

Eyes closed, she spoke, so quietly that he had to lean sideways and strain to hear her. "They told me the baby died."

"Who did?"

"Everyone at the hospital, including my mother, who'd flown to Montana as soon as her cousin told her I was going to deliver early."

As she glanced out the window, her fingertips tapped a

rapid beat on the tabletop. He stared at her, the mother of his child, wondering which question to ask first.

"And you didn't ask to see it?" He would've. Just to see the fingers and toes and other tiny parts, even once, and hold the kid in his arms.

She shrugged, looking way more calm about it than he would've been. "I was out cold during the C-section and groggy afterward. And they told me no."

He shook his head, trying to remember what Hope looked like. Except for the wild hair and gut, he hadn't noticed much. Blue eyes like Victoria's. Like his. Like half the people he knew. Hell, this was Minnesota. Land of ten thousand lakes and blue-eyed Norwegians.

"What does she want? The kid. Hope."

Vic lifted her hands in the air. "I don't know. She's been so belligerent about the whole thing, I've mostly avoided her. Until yesterday, I ignored the issue."

"Ignored it all the way into the hospital?"

Her nose crinkled in confusion. "In Kalispell?"

He shook his head. "Right here in Minnesota. Three weeks ago. Is that when you found out?"

"Right around then, but I— I had a lot of things come up. Tough things." She pursed her lips, clearly not about to confess the real reason she'd done something so stupid.

"So what am I supposed to do? Meet her? What do you know about this . . . Hope?"

She gazed out the window, or maybe at the row of his mom's old coffee mugs on the windowsill. "She looked me up somehow and managed to snag an internship at my gallery for the summer." She shook her head, looking as if a million thoughts were going through it. "If she weren't my daughter, I would've fired her right after the art opening that you attended.

She invited you to the opening after she found you, too. She admitted it yesterday, about thirty seconds before I fired her."

His stomach lurched. "You fired our daughter?"

"I fired Hope." She held up a hand. "Now she's pregnant, out of work, and says she's out of money."

"A hat trick. Congrats." His mind reeled, grasping at straws, but Hope was too young to work in his bar. "What's she going to do?"

She bit the corner of her perfect lip. "I don't know, but right now I can't let it be my problem. Her adoptive parents bounced her out, and her boyfriend isn't treating her any better."

He dropped his head, examining his hands. "Like mother, like daughter. Both dated creeps at a young age."

Her voice dropped almost to a whisper. "I didn't date a creep. I dated a nice guy. I should've realized that you never got my letter. I should've known you were here, waiting."

Waiting. He drew in a breath. "I'm not some knight in shining armor."

She smiled, a little sadly. "You didn't need to be."

"Nobody's all good or bad. Like your mother."

One eyebrow rose. "She's a little more clear cut. She never sent my letter to you, she lied to me about the baby dying, and she gave our baby away without even telling me."

He clasped his hands between his knees. "Like I said. It's not all black and white. At least not about the letter you wrote."

"What do you mean?"

"I got it but never read it. I was so pissed that you hadn't called, I ripped it up and threw it away."

CHAPTER 13

Vic stomped around the first floor of her house on Wednesday morning, trying not to spew stomach acid all over the hardwood floor.

For twenty-one years, she'd lived a lie—of other people's making. She'd told herself that Jake didn't care. And, later, that he *had* cared, but her mother hadn't mailed the letter. It had certainly given her a handy target on which to focus all of her anger.

She'd told herself it didn't matter, because the baby died, so she hadn't had to choose between the harsh reality of young motherhood and the pain of giving up her own baby.

She'd been an idiot.

Her mother had mailed the letter, but she'd lied about the baby. And Jake received the letter, threw it away, and probably slept with a dozen girls while she'd been gone. He'd hardly even noticed her when she came back to school halfway through senior year.

And the baby lived. The baby she and Jake had produced was a living, breathing woman. Hope was breathing down their necks, sure, but Vic couldn't blame her. After all, Hope had a couple of complete fuck-ups as biological parents.

Everything was a lie and a disaster, and that was even before she considered the FBI and Ryder. She should've done a better job with the pills the first time. The kids were safe at camp, at least, and someone would help them work through her death. Someone they could count on, which limited the options.

Her cell phone had already rung a few times, but she'd ignored it. Now the landline rang just as she started upstairs. She let the answering machine take it.

She was out of breath by the time she reached the third floor, which held her home office, a bathroom, and the huge attic. She unlocked the door to the attic, fumbling in the darkness for the light switch. Flicked it on. Went to the box labeled "Christmas decorations," where she'd hidden an extra stash of pills. Opened the box, which held—

Christmas ornaments.

She sagged to the floor, then shook her head and tried to regroup. Obviously, she'd been in rough shape when she hid the pills, and there were a dozen boxes labeled "Christmas decorations." Her fingers flew as she threw off lids and dug through other boxes. Six, eight, ten. Nothing. Each box held a bunch of fucking Christmas decorations.

She could shoot herself.

Wait. No, she could. With the handgun she'd bought five years ago during that rash of neighborhood burglaries. Even though Dad had advised against it and Ryder had actually forbidden it.

If only she could remember where she'd hidden it.

She perched on a wooden floor beam in the attic, breathing in what smelled like—hmmm—asbestos, and quickly stood back up. If she had to die, she didn't want her last breath to be of asbestos. Her last breath—

The garage. The gun must be in the garage, the perfect

hiding place, because Ryder never ventured into it except to take out his BMW. If it wasn't there, or if her nasty little drug-busting squad had found the gun and gotten rid of it along with the drugs, she could start the engines on both of her cars and die there. It would stink like hell, but maybe she could pour herself a drink first. She always lost her sense of smell when she drank.

Her mind reeling with possibilities—and her heart not wanting to act on any of them—she stumbled down the stairs just as someone pounded on the front door. She stood on tiptoe to peek through the small window high on the door. Mistake. Natalie was staring right back at her. With Tess at her side.

"We know you're in there."

Rolling her eyes, she unlocked and opened the door. "Of course I am. I was just upstairs."

"Looking for your secret stashes of pills?"

The way Tess read minds was positively creepy.

Vic flipped a hand through her hair. "I was getting ready for work. Some people work, you know."

Natalie narrowed her gaze on Vic. "I do know, because I'm one of them. But when Tess tells me I'd better get my butt over here to help my sister, I leave work."

"And wasn't that silly? Here I am, right as rain."

"And talking like your mother." Tess looked genuinely worried, the way she'd looked so often since Vic had landed in the hospital. "That proves something is wrong. I could feel it."

"It's our fault, really." Nat drew alongside Tess, locking shoulders with her. "Your overdose was a cry for help, and we ignored it."

"We didn't ignore it, exactly." Tess didn't mind helping, but she never particularly relished taking the blame for anything.

Natalie nodded vigorously. "Yes, we did. We visited you in

the hospital and gave you gifts and flowers as if you were just there for a regular illness or something."

"And Slinkys. Don't forget Slinkys."

Nat shot a puzzled frown at Tess, who apparently hadn't told *everyone* about Jake's little gifts. Shocking. "But we never asked why you were so upset that you wanted to die. I know Drew talked to you a little bit." Perfect. The whole family was discussing her. "But nobody followed up. Nobody made sure you're okay."

"I'm fine." Vic held up her arms and twirled in place, letting them inspect her all they liked. "And I didn't really overdose. I just took too many pills."

Both Tess and Nat stared at her.

"Okay, technically that's an overdose. But an accidental one. I swear." She'd given up crossing her fingers behind her back, so she just smiled at them. Innocently.

Tess shook her head. "You're still in denial."

"I'm not in—"

"I agree." Natalie grabbed one of Vic's wrists, letting Tess take the other. "It's time we intervened in your life. The way we should've a couple weeks ago."

"Or much earlier. Much, much earlier."

Vic rolled her eyes. "Does this mean we have to hold hands and sing 'Kumbaya'?"

Tess tilted her head to one side. "We already nixed any Barry Manilow songs. It doesn't leave much."

This was really getting annoying. She yanked her arm out of Tess's grasp. "Why the sudden concern? I left the hospital over two weeks ago."

Nat shifted from one foot to another, looking uncomfortable, while Tess fluttered a hand in the air. They were playing God, damn them. Acting like they had all the solutions to a life that no longer mattered. Couldn't they see that?

In the awkward silence she spoke again, practically spitting out the words. "When do you think you should've intervened? Before I married Ryder? Or sooner than that?"

Tess shrugged. "You know better than we do, but we're here now. Are you going to let us help you through this, or do we have to get tough with you?"

Vic looked from one to the other. Sanctimonious, interfering twerps whose help she didn't need. "Do I have a choice?"

"Not particularly." "No."

"Then I guess it's settled." She twisted the wrist that Nat held, peering at her watch. "Just make sure we wrap this up in fifteen minutes. I have to get to work."

"Sean can cover for you." Natalie let go of Vic's wrist but stayed close to her. Too close. "Just like he did when you were in the hospital."

Just like he had, in Dad's opinion, far longer than she'd suspected. She shook her head. "It's my gallery, and I'm responsible for it."

"Who's responsible for you?" Tess reclaimed her grasp on Vic's other wrist, probably guessing too accurately that she planned to escape the first chance she got. Maybe not to the garage, as originally planned, but somewhere. Anywhere.

She feigned nonchalance. "I am. I'm an adult."

"That's right. Vic the adult." Nat shook her head. "You've been like this your whole life. Invincible. Not needing anyone's help. Not letting anyone take care of you."

Bullshit.

Just like that, she broke loose of Tess's grip and bolted for the stairs. Stunned, Nat and Tess remained rooted in place. She stumbled up the stairs, hearing them follow a beat later.

"Slow down, damn it!" Tess's wheezing breaths were

louder than her words, but Vic could hear Nat's feet sprinting to catch up. She kept going higher, aiming for the third floor.

Two steps from the top, her ankles were yanked out from under her, and she toppled, landing on the top step. Natalie landed face down on Vic's butt.

Nat laughed. "The things I do for my sister."

Vic rolled to one side, rubbing her knee where it had collided with the stair. "Can't you find someone else who needs your help? Maybe our brother?"

"Are you kidding? And leave you?" Nat puffed a little as Tess finally made it to the top of the stairs. "You're stuck with us, Vic. Yeah, we might be annoying, but so are you." Getting up, she tapped Vic's butt with the toe of her shoe. "And I, for one, couldn't have signed up for a better gig."

———

Thursday evening, Ryder stretched out on the leather couch at Sean's apartment, hands clasped behind his head, waiting for Sean to get out of the shower. A week or two ago, he would've been *with* Sean in the shower. Helping him lather up.

Now? He didn't feel quite right at Sean's, where he no longer lived, and felt worse in his own house, where even his clothes had been permanently relegated to the guest bedroom. Vic wouldn't even let him wash his hands in the master bathroom. No longer master of his domain.

What he was in Sean's domain, he had no clue.

The bathroom door opened, and Sean appeared, a towel slung low on his hips. Ryder grinned. Male or female, a twentysomething just looked better than someone hitting forty. Sean's bare chest glistened with drops of water, and the short hair on his head sprang out at odd angles, making him look charmingly boyish. And way too tempting.

"Why didn't you join me in the shower?" The pout was boyish, too, but a little less charming.

He pushed himself to a sitting position. "I need to get home. Vic's sister Natalie called me at work." Something she hadn't done since he'd moved out, and not often before that. "She said she can't stay at the house tonight. Tess can't, either. I'm the default choice."

Sean made a face. "She needs a babysitter? Why?"

He shrugged. Sean was his lover, but he was also Vic's employee. As a lawyer and Vic's husband, he had to respect the distinction. "She doesn't, really. But she misses the kids and feels out of sorts in the big house all by herself."

Sean rolled his eyes. "Maybe she should downsize—unless you're thinking about moving back there permanently." His voice took on a petulant tone, something Ryder had once found sexy. "You and I haven't ever talked about it, you know."

Except in bed, when rational thoughts always fled his brain, which was probably why Sean started most discussions there.

He got up and reached for his suitcoat. "I'm not sure what there is to talk about right now. Vic needs me, and I have to take care of her."

"Who'll take care of *me*?"

Anyone Sean wanted. He'd rather not think about it, knowing Sean would probably be in a bar, dancing in someone's arms, fifteen minutes after Ryder left.

He ran a hand over his face. "I don't think you need anyone taking care of you. Vic sings your praises at the gallery." Or she used to, before she found out about the two of them. "And we both know you look great."

His gaze roved over Sean. The towel dipped an inch or two, then dropped all the way to the floor.

Ryder sucked in a breath. Strength. He needed to pass up this temptation tonight. Maybe forever.

A moment later, Sean took him by the hand and led him to the bedroom. He supposed Vic would be fine on her own for a little while. Just this once.

———

THE DOORBELL RANG, surprising Vic in the middle of making dinner. Ryder should've been home a half hour ago, as promised, but he had a key. She walked into the front hall, wiping her damp hands on her shirt, and peeked out the window.

Jake. With Hope next to him.

Neither one looked particularly happy, which made three of them. The doorbell rang again. After considering and rejecting several escape options, she sighed, turned the dead-bolt, and opened the door.

Jake, his mouth a flat line and one hand jammed in a pocket of his jeans, shifted his gaze from left to right and up and down and everywhere but at Vic.

Hope looked smug and unsure and unhappy, all at the same time. Her wild hair was growing out, leaving blond roots and a frizzy mop that needed a gallon of conditioner. Her left hand held her protruding stomach, as if to protect it from the harm she seemed hell-bent on inflicting on all of them.

Jake's black truck stood at the curb, parked at a reckless angle, and he glanced at it as if ready to bolt. His keys bulged in his pocket, straining the fabric.

Vic wondered whether Hope, who must've forced Jake into

this, had a game plan. Did wreaking havoc with other people's lives constitute a game plan?

Hope finally opened her mouth, offering a grim smile as she nodded at Jake. "I know who he is."

Vic nodded back. "I do, too. That's Jake Trevor."

"He's my dad."

"He *might* be your biological father. But your real dad is somewhere in Montana now, probably missing you."

Hope scraped the front porch with the toe of her beat-up sneaker. "He doesn't miss me. He kicked me out."

"But he's your dad. He misses you, and he loves you, even when he's mad as hell at you. Believe me."

Hope's eyes flashed. "You don't know him. He and Mom never want to see me again. That's why I had to find you guys and get a job at your gallery. I want us to be a family."

"We're not a family." Vic rolled her eyes, then let the two of them inside and closed the door. Ryder would be here any minute now. Perfect. He could meet Vic's daughter and first lover in one fell swoop.

It was efficient, certainly.

She rubbed her stomach, feeling through her thin T-shirt the rough edges of the incision she'd always blamed on an appendectomy. Ryder had never questioned it, never even touched the scar except to brush past it in his cursory touching of her. Somehow, she should've figured him out a long time ago.

Hope looked all around, her head tilting to take in the kitchen, living room, and small study next to the bathroom. Jake stared at the sturdy leather shoes he probably wore in the bar to avoid cutting his feet on broken glass.

Vic walked back to the kitchen, crooking her finger when they didn't follow. She pointed at chairs and waited for them to sit. Hope did. Jake remained standing, arms crossed, defiant. Vic pulled a bottle of white wine out of the refrigerator.

She wasn't supposed to drink, but this seemed like an excellent moment to break that rule.

"Got a beer?"

She jumped at Jake's voice right behind her. "Geez! You didn't have to startle me."

"Seems like a good day for it." He squeezed in next to her, squatting to grab a bottle of Ryder's craft beer from the bottom shelf. Straightening, he twisted off the cap and chugged a third of the bottle in one swallow.

Vic looked over at Hope, who looked sullen, probably from feeling left out. "Do you want something? A lemonade?" She remembered the baby. "A glass of milk?"

"Diet Coke would be good if you have it."

Jake jumped in. "Is that good for the kid?"

Hope glared at him. "Why do you care? You act as if you're my—" She gulped. "Dad or something."

"So you say." Shrugging, he took another swig of beer.

"It's true."

Vic couldn't stand the tension. The daughter and short-lived employee. The ex-boyfriend she'd thought she would never see again. The bottle of wine she gripped in her hand and didn't know whether to open.

Jake grabbed the bottle from her and opened one cupboard door after another in pursuit of a wineglass. He poured, oblivious to the dark thoughts scrambling her brain. Shrugging, she popped the top on a can of Diet Coke for Hope, who refused a glass.

"What is it you want, exactly?" Vic tilted her head at the can of Diet Coke in Hope's hand. "Besides something to drink. And besides anything else I might scrounge up for you guys if you haven't had dinner." A baked ham sat in the oven, awaiting Ryder's arrival, and a pan of asparagus simmered on the stove.

Jake lifted the lid on the pan and scrunched his nose. "What are those? Green vegetables?"

Despite everything, he could still make her laugh. "Just like your mother made you eat."

"Yeah, but nobody's making *you*."

"My internal mother. It kicked in when I had—" She stopped abruptly, realizing where she was headed.

"Kids." Hope practically snarled the word as she slammed her soda can on the table. "When you had kids. Three of them, not two. You had three."

"I had three. And raised two." She touched a hand to her throat, where the sip of wine she'd swallowed was burning a liquid trail. "But please don't slam the can on the table. The wood will scratch."

Hope rubbed her hand in a circle on the smooth wood of the table, lost in thought.

"I asked what you wanted, Hope. I'm not a mind reader." Unlike Tess, who'd be invaluable at a time like this. "Jake and I produced you. Possibly."

He stuck his head in the refrigerator and rummaged for another bottle of beer. At this rate, she'd have to make a run to the liquor store just to finish the conversation.

She turned back to Hope. "But that's the end of the story. I was seventeen. We were both seventeen. And you were adopted. It doesn't matter why or how." Except that it did, of course, to Vic as much as to Hope. "You have a family."

Hope snorted.

"So your parents aren't being too understanding." She thought of her own mother. "A lot of parents aren't, quite frankly. I realize you might want to know about your medical or family history, but that's all Jake and I can do. You can't work at the gallery."

Hope stared into the hole in the top of her can, her eye two inches from it. "I need you. I need parents."

"I told you." Vic drew in a breath and let it out slowly. "You already have parents. The McCullochs."

"I need help with the baby."

Jake interrupted. "You could always—"

Vic silenced him with a look.

She didn't think he'd suggest an abortion, but she couldn't say for sure. She knew firsthand that adoption wasn't the easy solution that everyone claimed it was. It could also come back to bite a woman in the butt twenty years later.

Eying Hope warily, Vic spoke again. "What kind of help?"

She wasn't going to offer. She wasn't going to offer.

Hope met her gaze and raised her one. "Money. A place to stay. A flexible job."

"In other words, the world."

Jake shook his head. "Sounds like a problem, kid. What about the dad? He's responsible for the baby, and so are you. I don't see where we fit into this."

Hope smiled at him. "Let's just say that I could make your lives a little unpleasant."

"Hell. Mine already is." Tipping the bottle upward, Jake drew a long gulp, then wiped his mouth with the back of his hand. He smiled back at Hope, who looked startled at being called on her threat. "You can't make it worse, kid."

Hope looked at Vic, her eyes anxious, but Vic shook her head. "You can't stay here. Your internship is over, and I don't need more help." Not Hope's, anyway. "Other than a few baby gifts, I'm not sure what else I can do."

"I'll tell your kids. And your husband." Increasingly frantic, Hope was practically shouting now.

"That won't do you any good." She worried about Connor and Megan, but they were safe in Bemidji while she figured this out. And Ryder? She didn't particularly care. She turned off the oven, but by now the ham was probably crispy around the edges.

Hope lurched to her feet, her stomach bumping against the table's edge. "You never gave me up for adoption."

Vic blinked, thinking of the adoption papers. Someone must've forged her name and made up a signature and name for the father. Her mother, undoubtedly. Just another petty misdemeanor in a long crime spree.

She took a deep breath, pointedly keeping her voice calm even though Hope had just thrown quite a curveball at them. "Oh? Then how did you come to be adopted?"

Jake looked stunned. "Come to think of it, I didn't—"

"—object when the McCullochs adopted Hope. Isn't that right, Jake?" On the other side of the still-open refrigerator door, she kicked him in the shin.

Wincing, he nodded.

She turned back to Hope, trying to sound helpful despite Hope's obvious familiarity with the concept of extortion. "Besides, you're twenty, almost twenty-one, and responsible for yourself. You need to quit running. Go home to Montana, to your parents and boyfriend, and figure things out from there."

Hope's chin stuck out at a defiant angle.

"And if that doesn't work—" In the absence of anyone else saying a damn thing, Vic kept going. "Maybe you're not ready to raise a child by yourself. I can give you contacts with an adoption agency here in Minnesota."

"Just like you did." Jake and Hope spoke in unison, and Vic stared at them in turn. Like father, like daughter, in a creepy way she didn't want to contemplate.

"Not true. Everything was different." She glared at Jake,

wishing he understood. Wishing Hope weren't here, so they could talk about it. About everything. "And any further discussions of it, Jake, are between you and me."

"Agreed."

"I mean it. You can't just—"

He covered her mouth with his hand. "I said I agreed."

When she tried to bite his hand, he just grinned.

She jerked away, trying not to show either her embarrassment or her inexplicable elation at playing on the same team with Jake. As they shared a comfortable laugh, she heard a whimper coming from the direction of the kitchen table. Hope, looking like she wanted to be part of a trio, had been left outside the turnstiles without an admission ticket.

Yes, Vic felt sorry for her. Not much else, though, because this was Hope. But she'd been in Hope's shoes, and they weren't comfortable. She couldn't be Hope's mother, but maybe she could do something for her. She'd have to think about it.

She shook her head at the long list of things she needed to think about. The kids. Ryder. Hope. Jake. Sean and the FBI and the gallery. Herself.

Finally, at least, she'd made it onto the list.

"Anyone want some dinner?" At this point, she didn't care when or if Ryder showed up. As she pulled out an extra plate and silverware, setting it in front of Hope, she wondered what lay in store for the three of them.

For now, all she could handle was dinner.

CHAPTER 14

"Dad? What brings you here in the middle of the day?" Vic looked up from the stack of paintings she was trying to organize for an upcoming exhibit. Her dad, dressed in plaid slacks and a pink golf shirt, looked too casual even for a Friday.

His head swiveled from side to side. "Is anyone here?"

"Hope doesn't work here anymore." She held up a hand when her dad offered a puzzled frown. "Long story. And Sean is out running errands. I asked him to pick up some artwork from an eccentric artist who doesn't drive downtown."

"Can't blame him. Or her." Her dad looked around the gallery, almost furtively.

"Did Nat tell you I was looking for you?"

"No. Er, yes. I mean, I've been looking all over for you."

"Oh? I'm not hard to find." Unlike Ryder. She'd found him, finally, last night around eleven, sneaking in the door and probably hoping she was asleep.

Her dad fiddled with his watchband, twisting it around his wrist. He wasn't wearing his wedding ring.

"Have you found anything in the books?" He walked over to her office, poked his head inside, then turned back to her.

"Heard anything from the FBI? Given more thought to who might be responsible?"

"Responsible for what?" She and Dad had pored over the ledgers. They were a little sloppy, maybe, but nothing in them looked suspicious. "As far as I can tell, everything is fine. The FBI people haven't stopped by again. It must've been a mistake."

"A mistake." He nodded, considering. "Someone's mistake, certainly. But I don't believe the FBI has dropped the case. You should be more proactive."

She could feel the groove between her eyebrows deepen. "You already told me you were checking my bank accounts. I assume you didn't find anything?"

He moved around the room, his hands in constant motion at his sides. "I think you should keep an eye on Sean."

"I am." Against her better judgment, or mostly so, since Ryder's continued late nights irked her. Her logical mind knew it had nothing to do with Sean's performance at work, but part of her wanted to scratch out his eyes and boot his butt out the door. Leaving her alone.

Which was why she hadn't done anything. Yet.

"Why are you so sure about Sean?"

Her dad shrugged. "It's usually someone in a position of trust." He cleared his throat and glanced at the door. "Someone you wouldn't suspect."

Vic set the stack of paintings back in place against the wall. "I hate to say it, Dad, but I think you're wrong. We didn't find anything, and I'm sure we would've heard more by now if the FBI had."

"These things take time to develop."

"I can't fire someone just because there's a possibility that something's wrong. I don't even know what's wrong, let alone who might've done it." She'd had enough trouble firing Hope, despite an unending list of reasons for it.

"At least keep him away from your books and computer. You mentioned his accounting degree. That type of knowledge comes in handy in situations like this." He glanced again at his watch, and his face flushed. "Look, I have to go." Turning, he headed out the door without another word.

"Situations like what?"

Vic asked the question to an empty gallery.

———

BARELY FIVE MINUTES after her dad left, two men walked in. Vic thought she recognized one of them from the last FBI visit, but frankly, they all looked alike. Dark suits, white shirts, short dark hair, glasses. She wondered whether the glasses were prescription or just part of the uniform.

"Ms. Bentley?" One of them flipped open his wallet long enough to flash some gold at her, then flipped it closed. Just like in the movies, but without the popcorn or Milk Duds.

"Weren't you in here before? A few weeks ago?"

"I was. How're you doing, ma'am?" The other man stepped forward and touched a finger to his forehead, which must be some sort of strange greeting.

Vic crossed her arms. "If you're here on business, and not to tell me what a horrible mistake you've made, and how sorry you are for inconveniencing me—" She rattled through the list without stopping for breath. "Then I'm sorry, but you just missed my lawyer."

"Oh?" The man who'd been at the gallery earlier looked sideways at his partner. "And who might that be?"

"My father. Warren Carlyle."

The two men exchanged another glance.

Tired of it all, she glared at both of them. "I haven't done anything wrong. Nothing!" She stomped one foot, probably looking like a child. She didn't care. "But thanks to you people, I've wasted hours of valuable time staring at my books and records, trying to find any stupid mistakes I could've possibly made."

"And you didn't find any."

"No." She took a deep breath, not entirely relieved that the man had guessed her answer. "I don't steal money or art, I don't hide things, and I have only two employees. Actually, one." Hope wasn't this man's business. "My summer intern is no longer here, but believe me when I say that she couldn't possibly be responsible for anything you might be investigating. My other employee has worked here as long as I've owned the gallery."

Sean. A niggling seed of suspicion settled at the base of her neck, planted there by Dad and refusing to budge. She didn't have to say anything to these two goons, though, especially when she had no proof.

The man who'd visited earlier stepped forward. "No one is saying you've done anything wrong, ma'am."

Feeling her blood pressure skyrocket, she jammed her hands on her hips. "Then what the hell are you doing here?" She flung a hand through the air. "I realize you sometimes go after art galleries, thanks to the New York auction houses. But this is Minneapolis. We don't do business that way."

"I'm sure you don't."

"Then I repeat: what are you doing here?"

The man pulled out his wallet again, presumably to flip another gold badge at her. She brushed him off.

"I don't need to see your badges, not that you ever actually show them to me for more than two seconds. I can tell from your suits and silly matching shirts and ties who you are. FBI. Fine. I'm not even remotely impressed."

Startled, the men glanced the length of each other, laughed, then looked back at Vic. The one man smiled as he opened his wallet, pulled out a card, and offered it to her, but she didn't take it. "I haven't heard it put quite that way before, ma'am, but perhaps we do need to work on our ties."

She refused to be mollified, especially when she'd just made a complete ass out of herself.

The man pressed the card into her hand. "Here. I gave you one before, but we thought we should stop by. I'm not at liberty to share anything more about our investigation, but you're not the subject of it."

"It's ongoing? Even though I haven't done anything?"

"We don't believe you have." He glanced at the other man, then back at her. "I can't say anything else, but I advise you to report any suspicious activity."

The two men headed for the door, their footsteps in perfect unison.

She called to them. "The only suspicious activity I've seen is yours."

Their shoulders shook as they walked outside.

———

FRIDAY NIGHT AFTER WORK, Vic bent awkwardly over the drinking fountain by the Lake Harriet bandshell, wheezing as she tried to catch a mouthful of water before her rollerblades slipped out from under her. She glanced over her shoulder at Drew. "We've already gone halfway around three lakes, and we still need to skate back to my house." If she had her phone with her right now, she'd order a Lyft. "What are you trying to do—kill me?

A single bead of sweat dripped off her brother's forehead, the only evidence that he'd accompanied Vic on this idiotic adventure. Sweat soaked the front and back of her tank top and the back of her shorts, and her hair might as well be glued to her head.

"I'm trying to think of a response that doesn't sound like a shrink gave it."

"Or like my brother, who worries about me too much." She sidestepped to the nearest bench, collapsing onto it as one skate slid out in front of her. "Just like my Gestapo squad. Tess and Nat showed up without warning on Wednesday, determined to save me. From what, I don't know."

She studied him out of the corner of her eye, wondering if Tess and Nat had also prompted his invitation to go rollerblading on a Friday evening, when he'd usually have other plans. Drew skated backward, away from the drinking fountain, then lifted the bottom of his T-shirt and wiped his face on it.

He dropped onto the bench next to her. "No one can watch you 24/7. Your Gestapo squad means well—" He muttered something about Tess's "woo-woo" psychic abilities and rolled his eyes. "But it's up to you, Vic. Quit letting life slap you around. Make a decision."

Ouch. "I'm making decisions."

He ignored her. "Your kids need you. We all need you. But I can't stand watching you like this, like you're plotting your next death march every other day." When she didn't say anything—because what could she say?—he kept going. "I'll bet you can name half a dozen reasons to check out. I can name more reasons to stay in the game."

She knew the two most important ones. "I'm not much of a mom. Connor and Megan can do better."

"You're a great mom and have super kids. You also have

Nat and me, Dad and Mom." He wagged his finger when she scrunched her nose. "And your friends. You don't need Ryder. He's the kids' dad, but that's a different issue."

"A difficult issue." Custody, dividing everything, ending the life they'd shared for eleven years. Her mind reeled.

"Not really. He's gay, so obviously you're not going to stay together for the long haul. It wouldn't be fair to either of you."

She sniffed. No one understood what was happening to her. She didn't, either. "And Hope—"

"She's no longer your employee, and it's up to you to decide how much you want her in your life." He obviously hadn't seen the little Machiavelli in action. "Bottom line, you need to balance your short-term pain against the long-term benefits. It's an easy call for me."

"Spoken like a shrink." And like the brother who'd always glossed over Vic's problems, at least when he bothered to notice them.

Grinning, he nudged her arm. "I'm a damn good shrink, and I'm not even charging you for this. What a deal."

"But what do I do?"

"Let people in. Let Ryder out. One step after the other, but you need to take the first step." He turned sideways and looked at her so seriously, she shivered. "Make a move, Vic. Take a leap of faith in yourself."

"And when I fall?"

"I'll be holding the net."

With her luck, his so-called net would have holes in it.

———

BRIGHT AND TOO EARLY ON Saturday morning, exhausted after another night of tossing and turning, Vic sat on her front steps, listening to the sounds of a typical weekend morning in late June. Ear-splitting lawnmowers, chirping birds, the laughter and shrieks of children already hard at play.

Her life. A year ago, maybe.

She wrapped her arms around her upturned knees. She missed the kids. Two weeks of camp down, one week to go. She no longer worried—much—that she wouldn't see Connor and Megan again. She loved them. Realistically, she also had no interest in landing in the hospital again with a pumped-out stomach and a helluva hangover. It wasn't worth it.

Ryder wasn't worth it, either. After his late arrival home on Thursday night, he hadn't even bothered to show up last night.

Enough.

First thing Monday, she'd call a locksmith and change the deadbolts, then make an appointment with a divorce lawyer. Ryder might claim he didn't want a divorce, but she had to move on with her life. She also had to quit waiting for her fairy godmother to show up and fix everything.

She also had to deal with Sean. She hadn't been able to look at him when he returned from his errands yesterday, and she couldn't work like that. He obviously couldn't, either. He'd left early. Probably to go do some money laundering.

She laughed, the sound hollow in her throat.

"What's so funny?"

As Jake appeared before her without warning, she almost tipped over backward. She scooted forward, trying to recover her balance. "Just thinking about some problems at work."

"When I have problems at work, I usually can't laugh about them." He dropped down next to her, stretching out his long legs, and she admired them while trying not to notice them. For once, he wore shorts. Rugged hiking shorts with huge pockets.

She glanced at the street. No black truck or other car nearby. "How'd you get here?"

"I was out running." He laughed when she stared at him blankly. "Kidding. Tess said she had to borrow my truck." At eight in the morning? "So I picked her up, and she dropped me off at the end of the lake. I walked from there."

Vic gripped her knees even tighter. "You two sure are close." She stared straight ahead, her chin on her knees, her teeth grinding against each other.

"Until last summer, I hadn't seen her in all these years. Never made it to the reunions." He paused, probably wanting to know if she had. "Tess walked into Pendulum one evening, out with one of her men, and remembered me."

"How lucky for both of you."

"Yeah. I mean, sure." He looked sideways at her, but she didn't acknowledge it. "Is that a problem?"

"It's a free world."

"Not as far as I can tell." He leaned back on his elbows, his body almost forming a straight line. "A kid I never knew about shows up, demanding that I be her dad, probably so I'll fork over some money in exchange for the privilege."

She flinched. "I'm sorry."

"Forget it." His hand slashed through the air. "I'm glad I found out, even if it's too late to do much about it." He paused. "Or to do much about you."

"What do you—" She gulped. "Want to do about me?"

"I'm not sure. To be honest, I thought you were ancient history. And now you're back, or somewhat anyway, and you're available." He glanced behind them at the open door. "Or somewhat anyway. I never seem to catch your husband."

"Me either." She rolled her eyes.

"Are you? Still married?"

"Yes, but it's over." She hadn't told anyone yet, not even Ryder, and it felt odd to announce it to Jake of all people. "He claimed he wanted to make it work again." In his own way, which wasn't all that. "But since I lack a penis, reconciling seems a little problematic."

Jake made a face. "No comment."

"That's probably best." She shook her head. "In any case, my kids get home from camp in a week, and my problems at work won't go away anytime soon. It keeps me busy."

"And happy?"

"I'm not sure I signed up for happy. When I need a break, I rollerblade. Or walk. Or play tennis." Anything to keep busy. To calm her mind. "Or I eat chocolate."

He stared at her. "Not a lot of chocolate, from the looks of it. You're still as skinny as you were in high school."

Her hips weren't, but she wasn't in a position to turn down a compliment.

"And still as cute."

She let go of her knees and stretched out one leg. "And you've become a shameless flatterer. Quite a change, Trevor."

He grinned. "I was seventeen. I've been practicing."

"Well, stop. I liked you better before."

"But not enough. Not enough to stay."

A lawnmower started up, and they both flinched. "Stay here and have a baby? Drop out of school and become another teenage-pregnancy statistic?"

"Weren't you anyway?" He shrugged, oblivious to the sting he'd just delivered. "Even with Hope in the picture, I'm not sure what I would've wanted. I just wanted you to come back. Go out with me again."

"And get pregnant. Again."

"We were careful." They had been, which only proved that no precaution would've been enough. "I wanted you, Victoria." He looked away. "I think I still do."

She slapped her thighs and stood up. "When you decide

what you want, let me know. In the meantime, I have a life to fix."

He got up, too, grabbing her hand as she moved to the door. "It doesn't have to be this way, Victoria. We could try again. Hang out together. Date."

"Just like when we were seventeen."

His blue eyes stared into her own. "Pretty much."

She broke free of his grasp. "But I don't want to be seventeen again. It's been twenty years, Jake. In high school, you were a football star and a cute guy and someone I could talk to." Just not when it mattered, when everything went to hell. "I don't know you anymore."

He tugged on her hand, drawing her close to brush his lips across hers. Feeling like . . . Jake. An odd combination of the seventeen-year-old boy he'd been and the man who stood before her now. Her eyelids fluttered shut as if by magic.

Then he took a step backward. "Okay, so you've got kids and a husband and other problems. Even without kids—not to mention a husband—I guess I can relate. It's called being a grown-up. It doesn't mean your whole life has to end."

She rolled her eyes. "When you have a wife and kids and something other than a bar and restaurant to call trouble, we'll talk."

He looked over his shoulder at the empty street, probably wishing Tess would show up with his truck. "Maybe we could talk sooner than that. Up to you. As always."

He jumped down the steps in a single leap and swaggered out to the sidewalk, then toward the end of the lake.

Vic's shoulders sagged, and she wondered why she'd just pushed him away. Again.

———

JUST BEFORE ELEVEN on Saturday morning, Vic walked into her office at the gallery, still in a stupor over her unexpected conversation with Jake, and found Sean rifling through her desk.

"Sean? What are you doing?"

He looked up, distracted. "Oh, hi, Vic. Just looking for—" His hands kept moving through papers while his gaze locked on hers. He glanced back down at the desk and soon brandished a single sheet of paper. "Here it is. An invoice for that sale to the woman from Wisconsin. The sculpture."

He smiled at her, so like Sean. Honest and trustworthy. Her loyal employee since the day she'd opened the gallery. The man who'd slept with her husband.

"Let me see it." Her hand shaking despite herself, she pointed at the piece of paper.

He shoved the paper back in the drawer. "I was just making sure we had it. The woman called, asking if we got her payment. I thought so, but I had to check."

"Of course." She continued to hold out her hand. "And can I see it, please?"

He closed the drawer. "Vic, you don't need to. It's just a routine sale. Fifteen hundred dollars. Her check probably already cleared the bank by now, but I'll confirm. We haven't shipped the sculpture yet."

"Sean." Her voice cracked, embarrassing her, which angered her even more.

Moving to her side, he patted her arm. As if she were a child. As if he were *her* employer. "I know you've been a little stressed lately. I'm just trying to take some of the load off those skinny shoulders of yours."

"My shoulders are just fine, thank you." If they started discussing body parts, they'd end up sooner or later discussing Ryder, and that wouldn't go over well.

"I know." He stepped past her, almost as if he knew what she was thinking. "But you don't have to take on the whole world by yourself, Vic. Don't get so stressed out."

That was it. She boiled over.

"Well, if that isn't a load of crap coming from the man who stole my husband." She crossed her arms. "No, don't explain. Don't tell me that it was bound to happen, how these things happen. How shit happens."

"I wasn't going to."

"And don't pretend it hasn't been going on a long time. Much longer than I knew."

"It hasn't—" He cut himself off. "Okay, I won't."

"And don't try to tell me he wasn't at your apartment last night. All night. Why he didn't come home."

He finally held up a hand, cutting her off. "Is this about work, or is this about Ryder and me? Just so we're clear, boss."

Her breath caught. She had no idea what it was about—or whether Sean deserved to get served up a plate of her wrath. She just knew it was spilling over, and he was handy.

"It's supposed to be about work, but I guess I have a few things on my mind."

He put his hands on his hips. "If you can't handle it, Vic, just say so. Ryder and I— Well, it doesn't affect my performance at work. That's all I'll say."

She'd like to say more. Much more. "Actually, I'm a little concerned about your work."

"Oh? The part where I show up even when no one else does?" One of his eyebrows rose. "Or the part where I fix all the mistakes that keep getting made?"

By her? She'd already fired Hope, which certainly narrowed the possibilities. "I've taken a little time off lately, yes." Except for the hospital stay, though, she really hadn't spent much more time away from the gallery than usual in the summer. "But I don't know what mistakes you're referring to."

"You can't blame Hope, let alone me, for everything that's gone wrong this summer." His nose turned up. "Except for the coffee she made. And, of course, the things she dropped or broke or spilled something on. We can't forget that, I suppose."

"I suppose not." Vic turned her head to glance at the small gold clock on her desk. Her stomach rumbled, and she wouldn't mind grabbing an early lunch. If Sean kept haranguing her, she'd fire him, too. What the hell. She was on a roll.

He looked keenly at her. "Could you tell me again why it took you so long to fire her?"

Not easily. "I hired her for the summer, and summer interns make mistakes. That's why they're called internships."

"She seemed to make more mistakes than most. She's also—"

"Vic's daughter." Hope, always there when Vic didn't need her, popped her head into the office, chewing hard on a wad of gum. "Or didn't you know that?"

Sean's eyes widened. "It's true? This—" He gestured to Hope, apparently at a loss for words. "This kid is related to you?"

"I'm not a kid." Despite her declaration, Hope blew a bubble and popped it with her finger. "I'm almost twenty-one. Not much younger than you."

He rolled his eyes. "Don't try to compare us. Please."

Hope glanced from Vic to Sean. "I wouldn't. After all, I'm not sleeping with the boss's husband."

"Guys, please." Vic looked at each of them as they snarled at each other. "I don't know why you're here, Hope, but this is an art gallery, not a zoo." She turned to Sean. "I just found out who Hope is, or *might* be, a few weeks ago. It's a long story."

Hope piped up. "We'd both like to hear it."

Vic wanted to wipe the smirk off Hope's face. "It's not Sean's business, and Sean isn't your business. Neither is my husband or my kids or anything else of mine."

Her lower lip stuck out. "I'm your kid, too."

"We won't go into that again. Not here, not now." Waving her arms, she herded them out of her office. They all walked into the main room of the gallery just as the bell over the door chimed, heralding the first customers of the day. Hope hung around the perimeter of the room, sulking, but Sean's face lit up as if he were greeting the three wise men.

Vic glanced at Hope. She wasn't an employee anymore, and her presence wasn't likely to endear any customers. Whether or not Vic was Hope's biological mother, she had to deal with her.

A restraining order? She smiled grimly, shaking her head as she imagined the scandal. No, but she had to come up with something that kept Hope out of the gallery and out of her hair. Vic tapped her toe on the floor, considering.

Meanwhile, the chance to talk to Sean had passed. Something told her she had to deal with him even sooner.

———

"Tell me why we're at Pendulum again?" Vic sagged in the corner of the booth, wishing she were anywhere else.

"To plan the reunion?"

Midge looked hopefully at Tess, who hooted and slapped the table. "Not completely. It's Saturday night, and only a week until Vic has to retrieve her kids from camp, and both of you need to get out more. Take your pick."

Vic looked at Midge and then at her menu. Frowning, she set it down. "Let's go somewhere else. Please."

"Sorry." Tess called a waitress to their table and ordered a burger and fries, with a side order of tequila, while Midge and Vic each ordered a lemonade. "We need Jake for the planning, and he's working tonight."

Vic refused to ask how Tess knew Jake's work schedule.

Tess winked at her. "What's the matter? Don't you want us to see you playing kissy-face with your old boyfriend?" She nodded over at Jake, who was tending bar. "Too unseemly?"

"Too unrealistic." Vic refused to look at Jake. Or at least tried not to. "I'd consider it more likely that we'd see *you* kissing Jake."

"Tess is kissing Jake?"

"No." "Yes."

Grinning, Tess threw her hands in the air. "See? No one except you believes it."

"Midge doesn't count." Too late, Vic's hand flew to her mouth. She turned to Midge, shaking her head. "I'm sorry. That didn't come out right."

"It never does." Midge jotted a few more notes, then closed her ever-present notepad and edged sideways out of the booth. "I think we're set. The invitations are out, a few responses have already come in, and we've decided on food and drinks."

Vic reached out, touching her arm. Midge actually recoiled from her.

"Midge, please don't go. I didn't—"

Ignoring her, Midge looked at Tess. "Could you make sure that Jake is all set with the liquor and soft drinks? I haven't had a chance to ask him lately."

More likely, she hadn't tried to ask him. Midge undoubtedly still saw Jake as the star quarterback on the football team, even though she was now a renowned oncologist and he owned a place that served greasy french fries.

Tess nodded at her. "Don't worry about a thing, sweetie. But are you sure you want to leave?"

Midge adjusted the strap of her purse on her shoulder. "This way you guys can talk."

Vic felt like the sludge at the bottom of a coffee pot. "We can talk with you, too, Midge. Please stay." She ran a hand through her hair, wondering how to fix things. "I just get upset when Tess keeps teasing me about Jake, and—"

Midge backed away from the table. "I know. It's just like high school. Perfect timing for a reunion."

"Were we like that in high school?" Vic frowned, remembering only the Fab Five and how close they'd all been. Before she'd left for a semester. Before Carrie had died.

"Worse." Tess laughed as she stood up and pounced on Midge. "And we haven't improved over time. I'm sorry, Midge. When we're awful to you, feel free to slap Vic."

Startled, Midge laughed just as Jake came around the end of the bar and headed toward their table, relieved by the skinny, balding bartender that Vic now knew was Jed.

Jake slid behind Midge into the booth, claiming the seat next to Vic. He wanted her, or claimed he did—but the way she'd been at seventeen, not as she was now. His bar, despite the sleek refinishing, mostly played hits from their high school years. If he hadn't been taller and broader than she remembered, she would've even bet he still wore his old jeans and shirts.

Tess grabbed Midge and pulled her back into the booth, then turned to Jake, fluttering her eyelashes. "Midge thinks we were positively awful in high school."

"I didn't say that."

Tess bounced in her seat. "And we haven't changed a bit since. What do you think?"

Jake glanced around the table. "I think you all look the same." His eyebrows danced. "Only a lot older."

Tess slapped him, but even Midge laughed. Vic felt her shoulders relax. Midge, back to business now, pulled out her notepad. Vic eyed Tess, wondering which of them would be the one to take it away from Midge and burn it.

Leaning back in the booth, Jake glanced sideways at Vic. Easily. As if he hadn't asked her out this morning and she hadn't turned him down again. "So. Have you told Tess and Midge about Hope?"

Vic's heart stopped. "Jake, everyone doesn't know."

"Isn't it about time? Tess knows a hell of a lot more than I do, so that leaves Midge. Your good friend." He glanced at Midge, who smiled tremulously, as if she'd just seen her first action hero up close. He looked back at Vic. "You turn everything into a secret, and secrets always get found out."

"That's rich, coming from the man who helped create my worst secret."

"Having a baby isn't anyone's worst secret."

"Vic had a baby? Other than her two kids?" Midge's eyes were huge behind her glasses.

Tess nodded. "In high school."

"Tess!"

"Jake's right. Secrets should be shared with friends."

Vic eyed her best friend. "Does that mean we get to hear all of *your* secrets? Fair is fair."

"I have no secrets." She flinched under Vic's hard scrutiny. "Or almost none I'm able to keep."

Jake squeezed Vic's shoulders. "You and I produced a kid. A weird kid, sure, but not the worst thing in the world."

Vic edged closer to the far corner of the booth as Midge closed her notepad again.

"So that's why Jake went out with Andrea that summer. I always wondered."

As Vic felt the blood drain from her face, Jake jumped up, excusing himself to go help Jed. Tess started whistling.

"Which summer? After junior year?"

Midge nodded. "You didn't know? Tess didn't tell you?"

"No."

"So that was a secret, too." Midge shook her head. "I'm sorry. I don't know which secrets are good and which are bad."

"They're all bad." Tess bumped shoulders with Midge as Vic felt herself crumble. "Some are just worse."

"You never told me."

Tess looked Vic straight in the eye. "No, I didn't. I don't poach, but Andrea didn't hold herself to the same standards back then, if you'll recall. She made *me* look tame."

Midge piped up. "It's hard to figure, looking at her now."

"People change. Andrea more than most."

Vic pursed her lips, feeling stupid. Hurt. Mortified. "And some don't. Some are beneath contempt." She stood up, grabbed her purse, and started out the door.

Tess called after her. "I didn't want to upset you."

Upset? Tess didn't know the definition of the word.

CHAPTER 15

The grandfather clock chimed four times. Vic blinked as the first streaks of light filtered through the predawn darkness of Sunday morning and poked inside the living room.

Half-asleep on the sofa, with Megan's Care Bears blanket tucked around her legs, Vic heard the faint rumble of the garage door, followed by the soft thud of Ryder's car door and, a minute later, his key in the lock. He quickly shut off the beep-beep-beep of the house alarm and padded through the front hall toward the stairs, his shoes dangling from one hand.

"Welcome home." When his head jerked in her direction, she pushed herself upright and patted the space next to her on the sofa. "Hard at work this late?"

"I, uh, yeah, I—"

"Stop. Please." She smiled softly, patiently, realizing that in the still hours before dawn, her anger had faded. Something like acceptance—although maybe not quite that, not yet—was taking its place.

Not that she'd be competing with the Dalai Lama, or even Tess, for zen-like composure anytime soon.

Ryder glanced down at the tasseled loafers in his hand, then let them clunk onto the hallway floor. A moment later he joined her on the sofa. Not too close, but not the gap he'd consciously left between them in the past few weeks.

He reached for her hand, withdrawing his own when she hugged herself. "Vic, I—"

"No excuses, Ryder." She drew the blanket up to her chest. "It's not fair to either of us, and it's not fair to the kids."

When he opened his mouth to respond, she held up a hand. "Don't. Don't make more promises you can't keep. You can't turn this into something it's not."

"But I'm ready, Vic. Ready to change." His eyes widened, giving her that sincere look he'd tried once too often. "For them and for you. I'm home."

She looked pointedly at the grandfather clock and raised one eyebrow. "I'm not a naive sixteen-year-old girl, and you're not Prince Charming." At his flinch, she patted his cold hand. "At least, not mine."

"But the kids—"

"They'll be better off with two happy parents. Parents who would both be happier living separate lives."

"Wh-who is it, Vic?"

She thought about Jake. Thought about Ryder with Sean. Thought, for once, of herself. "I'm just talking about you and me. We'll both have time with the kids, but it'll be in separate houses, living separate lives. Let's take this week we have left while the kids are in camp, start the divorce proceedings, and figure out how to divide everything up. I assume we can work things out without a hassle."

She sent a silent prayer skyward. She hadn't done anything this summer without a battle.

"What if I don't want to?"

She sighed. "Then others will have to get involved."

His eyes clouded over. "Like . . . people at my law firm?"

She didn't plan to do that, but if he made her play hardball, possibly. "Like it or not, I'm hiring a lawyer tomorrow and filing for divorce. How you deal with it is up to you."

He squeezed her fingers so hard, she had to pry them away. "Wh-what do you mean?"

"You can make this easy or difficult. Think about it, Ryder. Even if you don't want a divorce for my sake or for yours, do it for Connor and Megan."

He pushed his glasses higher on his nose, and this time his wide eyes were real. "Do it for them? But they want us to be together. How can a divorce be best for them?"

"You keep coming and going, and it's confusing for everyone. Including you, I think." She shook her head. "You need to leave. Find your own home, and find real time for the kids."

When he started to object again, she cut him off with just a look. They both knew how little time he spent with the kids. She didn't need to spell it out. She also didn't need to argue over which one of them would be leaving this house.

She laughed softly. "Look at it this way. It's a much more practical gift to them than those silly cell phones."

————

"Sean knows about Hope? Then Ryder must know."

Sunday afternoon, as Vic sat with Tess at a sidewalk table in front of Sebastian Joe's, Tess stared openmouthed at her and swirled a finger around in her Irish Cream float. Vic took a delicate bite of her Pavarotti cone, savoring the caramel, banana, and chocolate chips while trying to pretend that Tess didn't have the loudest voice in south Minneapolis.

At least they were outside, enjoying the warm breeze and glorious sunshine—and, okay, the heady perfume of car exhaust along Franklin Avenue. She glanced around, wondering when Midge would appear. "Could you keep it down? I don't need everyone in town to know."

"They probably already do." Tess slapped the wrought-iron table, making it wobble. "Sorry. But you may as well face it. Sean must've told Ryder by now."

"It doesn't matter anymore. Weird, I know." Just like that, Vic realized that not caring was a new phenomenon for her. "After I guarded that secret so tightly all these years, first Hope blurted it out to Sean, and then Jake to Midge, and I just don't care."

"Good. That means you're moving on."

Vic licked around the sides of her cone, wishing she could inhale it. "That's what I told Ryder this morning."

She looked up, finally, when Tess didn't respond.

Tess blinked. "Ryder? This morning?"

"When he rolled home at four a.m., I told him it was over." Leaning forward, she tipped Tess's jaw shut. "I talked to Drew on Friday night, and thought about it some more yesterday, and it's over."

Tess sucked so hard on her straw, she almost snorted the float right out her nose. "And he agreed? He's moving out?"

"He didn't object."

Replaying her conversation with Ryder, she frowned. He hadn't said much of anything, actually, but it was the obvious solution. And they'd always agreed about the kids—or at least he'd never disagreed. Then she remembered the cell phones and candy he'd bought for them when they went to camp. But she hadn't told him *not* to.

Tess slowly nodded. "I'm surprised, I guess, but this is great. You're moving on." A red sports car drove by, honking, as Tess gave Vic a sly grin. "To anyone in particular?"

She shook her head. "I'm reclaiming my life. *My* life, and I don't need someone else to make it perfect again."

She decided not to mention that she'd kissed Jake yesterday. It was just a little kiss, and besides—

Whatever. Tess probably knew more about the kiss than Vic did. Just like she'd known all about Andrea.

She bit down hard on her cone.

Tess touched her forearm. "Are you sure 'perfect' is what you want? I mean, you've been down that road before."

"I'm sure." Vic eyed her half-eaten cone. This conversation was killing her appetite. "My life felt pretty perfect before I found out about Ryder." And Hope and the FBI and even Jake. "I can make it perfect again."

Tess took a subdued sip of her float without looking at Vic. "At least things are happening. Ryder's moving out, Hope's doing whatever she's doing, and you're not sitting up there in your ivory tower worrying about it."

She blinked. "Isn't that a little harsh?"

"Probably." Tess smiled, easing the sting of her words. Slightly. "It's just that you always think you're the only one with problems."

"Spoken by a woman who's never had a problem in her life."

"Like, say, an unplanned pregnancy." Tess practically dove into her float, tipping the glass upward and draining it.

Despite her jumpy stomach, Vic kept nibbling at her cone. "It's one thing to think about what you'd do if it happened. But it doesn't happen to most people. It happened to *me*."

"All I'm saying is that you're not the only one."

"Oh? Who else?" She leaned forward, ready for an argument she'd been itching to have—with someone—for over twenty years. "Who else had a baby long before any kind of suitable marriage partner came into view?"

Tess arched an eyebrow. "If that's your question, are you

still talking about yourself? Because I'm not sure Jake wasn't a suitable husband for you."

"He was seventeen. I was seventeen. End of story."

"And now he's thirty-eight. You're thirty-eight. Is the story really over?"

She frowned at her cone. "This isn't about Jake. We were talking about unplanned pregnancies. Before marriage, outside of marriage, whatever. People talk about it, but I don't actually know anyone else it's happened to. That's my point. I *do* have more problems than most people."

"If you're going to have an impromptu pity party, you forgot to mention that you also married a gay man."

"See what I mean? Something else that doesn't happen to anyone else I know."

"You've got me there."

"And on the first count."

Tess started licking the rim of her empty glass.

Vic tapped her nails on the table. "Aren't I right?"

"No." Just that. A quiet little "no" out of a woman whose voice usually registered on the Richter scale.

"Come on. Who?" Vic leaned closer. "Is it a secret? You can tell me. No one ever tells me secrets."

Tess opened her mouth. Closed it. Jiggled in her chair. And finally spoke. "Me. In college. I had an abortion. As you say, end of story."

A choked breath whooshed out of Vic's lungs just as Midge showed up at their table, buried under a pile of notepads and file folders.

"Hi, guys. Sorry I'm late. Did I miss anything?"

———

"I'm sorry, Ms. Bentley. As I already said—twice now—I can't represent you. I wish I could."

The dial tone buzzed in Vic's ear. Mesmerized by the sound, she stared at her list of names and phone numbers. With a slash of her pen, she crossed off the fifth consecutive one she'd tried so far. Only three left before she had to call Dad again, and she'd already called him twice this morning.

Thanks to Ryder, all of the top divorce lawyers in Minneapolis apparently had a conflict representing her. She tugged on a lock of hair, nearly yanking it out. How many firms could he have somehow come up with conflicts for? And so quickly? She'd mentioned the divorce to him yesterday morning, and it was now only nine a.m. on Monday. No, a little past nine-thirty. She'd already lost a half hour on this.

She ran her finger past two more names on the list and went straight to the last one. Eden St. John, also known—according to Dad—as a pit bull. At Vic's insistence, the first list of names hadn't included anyone much nastier than a springer spaniel. After all, she'd planned a friendly divorce as the prelude to her newly perfect life.

And she'd been a fool. Fine. If this lawyer didn't pan out, the next person she called would be Ryder.

"Eden St. John." The woman who'd founded her own boutique family-law firm five years ago and already grown it to fifteen lawyers, according to Dad, answered on the second ring.

After a short conversation, Vic scheduled an appointment with Ms. St. John for the next morning and hung up, satisfied and relieved. Ryder hadn't called the woman yet, and he'd live to regret it. She was eager to represent Vic.

A minute later, she placed calls to her banker and broker just to thwart any other preemptive strikes.

With those tasks off her list, she rubbed her hands, gearing up for the battle ahead, then glanced at the picture of Connor and Megan on her desk—the photo that had replaced the family photo she'd kept there until a month ago.

She thought of all the punches she'd rolled with, or been walloped by, this summer. No more. She was going to be happy again, damn it, and she wouldn't let Ryder stop her.

She picked up the phone one last time and called him, then proceeded to tell him, in painstaking detail over his sputtering denials, just what she planned to do if he didn't start cooperating. Immediately.

Message delivered. She slammed the phone in his ear and buzzed with an electrical current. Her life—complicated, painful, and impossible to sort out—had finally coughed up a scrap of hope. She sprang up from her chair and charged into the rest of her day.

———

JAKE SWABBED down the bar Tuesday evening as he waited for Jed to show up for his shift and for Victoria to show up for the rest of their life together.

Okay, so a little self-delusion never hurt a guy. Much.

The door to the restaurant opened, silhouetting a woman. He squinted against the sunlight streaming into the darkened dining area, unable to see more than that, but it wouldn't be Victoria. Or Vic. Or whatever the hell she wanted to be called.

A regular, slumped at the end of the bar and nursing a tonic water, waved his empty glass in the air. Jake poured a fresh glass, then turned back to the new arrival as she made her way through the light crowd to the bar.

Tess. Close, but no enchilada.

He tried not to look past her to the door, tried not to hope that Victoria was parking her car and running to meet her friend. "Another reunion planning meeting? When will that damn thing ever be done?"

Tess set her purse on the bar. "Not for another month and, no, she's not with me."

"Who?"

"Nice try, blue eyes. Vic. The object of your wildest dreams." While he tried to think of a response that wasn't a flat-out lie, her gaze darted around the bar. "I'm not meeting her here tonight."

"Like I care." Head down, he wiped the already shining bar. "Isn't she talking to you, either?"

Silence answered him, and he finally looked hard at Tess, who stared at the rows of liquor bottles behind him.

She gave a quick, almost imperceptible head shake. "It's more that life's a little difficult for her right now, so she's not as easy to talk to. And I—"

She broke off, her gaze caught by a movement behind Jake. His top bartender, Jed, eased behind the bar fifteen minutes late for his shift. It wasn't like Jed—or hadn't been until the last few weeks. He shrugged. Everyone around him was going to hell.

He watched curiously as Jed glanced at Tess with raised eyebrows, and she nodded. He poured a double Chivas on the rocks and slid it across the bar to her.

After clapping Jed on the back, Jake started toward the back room. He'd look at the books, then flip through the purchase orders that Jed had left for his approval. When he heard the front door open, though, he turned to check out the latest newcomer.

Two men. Shaking his head, he left the bar area for the sanctity of the back room before he wasted another hour watching the door. He'd watched the door all weekend and most of last night, and Victoria wasn't going to show up.

Half an hour later, he returned to the bar, claiming he needed to run through the purchase orders with Jed, who shrugged and mostly kept chatting up Tess, although he stopped every few minutes to answer a pointed question.

Tess leaned across the bar and whispered something to Jed, and they both laughed. Jake told himself their conversation didn't have anything to do with him, even if he *did* look like a pathetic jackass every time the door opened.

He moved closer to the two. "What's so funny?"

Tess tilted her head. "It's not about you, and—" She blushed slightly, unless the Chivas was lighting up her cheeks. "Well, it's not about you."

As Jed rubbed hard at a spill near the tap, Jake leaned over the bar toward Tess. "You said that already."

"Is this a private conversation?"

He froze. Leave it to Victoria to show up the one time he didn't watch the door.

Tess lifted a shoulder and glanced at Jed. "It was, but feel free to join us."

Victoria stood behind the stool next to Tess, not claiming it, then reached into her purse and dug out her keys. "Thanks, but I was just leaving."

Jake frowned. "Didn't you just get here?"

She turned and took a few halting steps, and Tess didn't try to stop her.

"Hey! Wait." Shoving the purchase orders into Jed's hands, Jake tore around the end of the bar and caught Victoria just as she reached the door. "I don't understand."

She pushed through the door, and he followed her outside, blinking hard against the late-day sun.

A small voice floated into his ears. It didn't sound like Victoria at all. "I don't understand, either." She shook her head. "No, I guess I do."

"That makes one of us." He started to clap her lightly, jokingly, on her shoulder—then pulled back his hand. He couldn't treat her like a guy, or even a female pal, which left him without a clue how to act around her. "What brought you in? Something tells me it's not the gourmet food."

"It doesn't matter. I wanted to—" She shook her head again and didn't meet his gaze. "It really doesn't matter."

"Of course it does." He stepped away from the middle of the sidewalk and tugged her along with him. "Tell me what's up, and we can discuss it."

"Like old times?"

"Sure."

"I was kidding." She stepped backward, shrinking into the entryway just as a knot of suits brushed past them into the restaurant. "We never talked then, either." She stared at her feet as the toe of her sandal made little circles on the pavement. "We, um, just made love."

"Not all the time." Unfortunately.

"Anyway." Her head lifted for a brief moment, long enough to catch his eye and look away again. "I didn't come here to talk about that."

"So come back inside, Victoria, and we'll talk about something else."

"I wish you'd call me Vic."

"Old habits die hard." He kicked his boot against the brick building, wondering what the hell they could talk about that wouldn't upset her. Like she already was.

"I should go. You're busy." Touching his sleeve, she looked up at him, the corner of her eye suspiciously wet.

He shook his head. "Jed's on duty, and I'm done with the books." For tonight, anyway, since he'd already wasted a half hour in the back room, mostly staring at the wall.

"And Tess—"

He held up a hand. "She's hanging out at the bar, talking to Jed, maybe waiting for a date. She's not with me."

She looked over her shoulder as if plotting her escape. Hell, no. Not again. Grabbing her hand, he tugged her back inside the door.

"If you think I'm fooling around with Tess—" He cut off her protests. "Then you sure as hell don't know either of us. If you're mad about something else, let's talk. All of us, if you want, or I'll leave you to Tess."

She pulled her hand free. "I don't want Tess."

They both turned toward Tess, who sat at the bar, holding hands with Jed as their heads huddled together.

He nudged her arm. "At least we know what Tess wants, and it's not me." He chuckled, shaking his head. "Tess and Jed. I guess that explains a couple of mysteries."

Victoria rolled her eyes before kicking him in the shin.

"Gee, thanks." Nothing like plain, direct communication. As he bent down to rub his leg, he grinned.

———

Late Wednesday afternoon, alone in the gallery, Vic glanced up from a stack of inventory sheets to see Hope hovering in the doorway. "Hope? What are you doing here?"

"I just thought I'd see if I could help. I heard about your problems with the FBI, and I—"

Vic held up a hand. "Stop right there. My problems with the FBI? Who have you been talking to?"

Hope's gaze darted around the office. "I, uh, just overheard. No one told me."

Vic tried to stifle a groan. Most of Minneapolis probably knew by now, along with a few western suburbs. "And no one asked for your help."

"I figure it's financial stuff, right? I could try to track it on your computer. Even using your outdated programs, I mean, and I could install new ones while I'm at it."

"You don't work here anymore, remember?" Sighing, Vic closed the open document on her computer. "Besides, I don't need help. I've handled the financials for seven years now, with help from Sean, and my dad is on top of any other issues."

Hope took a few more steps into the office, stopping to touch and stare at the framed photo of the kids on top of her desk. "But I could—"

Vic crossed her arms. "I thought you were looking for a job. Any luck?"

Doubtful. Even Vic had made a number of phone calls, almost groveling by the time she got to the last few, but she hadn't turned up more than a glimmer of a possibility.

Hope shook her head. "I feel like I should help you."

"You don't need to. Really, I've got it covered."

Hope continued to pace around the small room, touching this and that and generally unnerving Vic. When she moved behind Vic's chair, Vic waved her back to the door, where she could keep an eye on her without needing a rearview mirror.

"Where's Sean? He seems to be gone a lot lately."

Sighing, Vic rubbed her aching neck. Sean should be helping her slog through these inventory reports, but he'd been missing since taking a late lunch. He'd taken time off, unannounced, too often lately—just like Hope had shown up, unwanted, too often. She wished the two would reverse their roles.

"He's here when he needs to be." More or less. "I don't think Sean's whereabouts are any of your—"

"Come to think of it, he's been gone a lot ever since the FBI showed up here that one day. Remember?"

Vividly. But the FBI's first visit also coincided with everything else in Vic's life zooming straight to hell. "I don't see your point, Hope, and I need to get back to work."

Bending her head, she buried her nose in the damned inventory sheets.

"Are you picking your kids up at camp this Saturday?"

She frowned. Hope's ability to discover all the things she did bothered her more than a little. "Again, if you'll excuse me, I really need to finish going over this."

Finally, Hope trudged out of her office. "I'll let myself out."

Don't let the door hit you in the butt as you leave. Biting back the retort, she concentrated again on inventory. It beat worrying about Hope or Sean or the FBI or anything else in her crazy, confusing life. But not by much.

———

"Need anything else before I go?" Sean leaned against the doorjamb, eyebrows raised, as Vic glanced up at him and shook her head. "I'll lock up on the way out."

"Thanks." Hearing the click of the deadbolt, she leaned back in her chair and stretched her arms over her head. It'd been a long day, but finally a fairly normal one. Sean had arrived on time, worked hard, chatted pleasantly, and stayed for the duration. Customers visited—and spent money—in a steady rhythm. Neither Hope nor the FBI showed their faces.

What more could a girl ask for?

The doorbell buzzed, and she glanced at the clock. Five after six, and she'd promised herself a rollerblade around Lake of the Isles followed by a joyride to Cold Stone Creamery for some cake-batter ice cream. Closing her eyes, she could almost taste it.

Another buzz. Ugh. Force of habit sent her scurrying to the front door. Her heels skidded on the tile floor at the sight of

Jake—who was wearing shorts, a shirt, and hiking boots and carrying an armful of outdoorsy equipment.

She opened the door anyway.

"Sorry, but this is an art gallery. The REI store is on 494 in Bloomington, but Midwest Mountaineering is much closer. You know how to find Seven Corners?"

"Funny." He shook his head at her silent invitation to step inside, juggling a couple of water bottles while he shifted his backpack from one shoulder to the other. "I already have plenty of equipment, thanks."

Remembering his equipment only too well, she blushed and glanced down at her feet. Scuff marks on her favorite sandals stared back at her, sending her gaze back up to Jake's face.

He, too, was staring at her sandals.

"Anyway." He scraped the heel of his hiking boots against the floor. "It's a beautiful evening, and we didn't talk much the other night." When they discovered Tess with her latest love interest, all further conversation had screeched to a halt. "I thought you might want to go hiking."

Stunned, Vic gazed down at her white silk blouse and yellow linen skirt, past them to her yellow sandals, and then back to Jake.

"I mean, you might want to change first."

"No kidding." Confused, she shook her head. "But hiking? Did we make plans I didn't know about?"

"Not exactly." He slid the backpack off his shoulder and dropped it onto the floor. The water bottles joined it. "I already asked you on a date, and that didn't work, and you're not the biggest fan of Pendulum. And if a guy's trying to impress a woman, it's hard to top a Slinky."

He was trying to impress her? In hiking boots? "And?"

"I figured you'd say no if I asked in advance. Or you'd say

yes, then think about it, and end up calling to say you had to wash your hair or something."

Looking as if he still expected her to say no, he jammed his hands in the huge pockets of his shorts, sending Vic's thoughts in the wrong direction.

She touched the blunt ends of her hair, which could probably use a trim. "My hair is clean, sorry to say, but why aren't you at Pendulum? I thought Thursday nights were pretty busy in the summer."

"And fall, winter, and spring. Jed's on duty, probably with Tess's supervision." He rolled his eyes. "And I needed a night off. And exercise. I hoped you might want to join me." Picking up his backpack, he slung it back over his shoulder. "C'mon. It'll be fun."

She eyed his accessories skeptically. "I don't remember the last time I went hiking. I'd planned to go rollerblading and treat myself to some ice cream."

"Borrrring."

"Speak for yourself. My kids come home from camp on Saturday, and I won't have many more nights to myself. Besides, it beats getting eaten alive by mosquitoes, ticks, and tree bark."

His eyebrows rose. "Tree bark?"

"Long story, and it involves poison ivy." She screwed up her face, remembering her one and only hiking expedition with Ryder. "Rollerblading is more my style."

"I don't mind rollerblading, but I wanted to do something different. I thought about fishing." He grinned when a loud groan escaped her. "But then we'd have to get up early in the morning, and I'd rather spend my mornings in bed with you."

Her eyes went wide.

"But I might be getting ahead of myself."

She held up a hand. "Way, way ahead."

"Yeah." His eyes twinkled. "So maybe a hike for starters. We can go fishing another time."

An hour later, she swatted at a mosquito as she followed Jake's annoyingly trim butt along a narrow, winding trail on the banks of the Mississippi. The setting sun danced on the river, a soft breeze tickled the back of her neck, and Jake's butt wasn't so bad, either. But the guy walked way too fast.

"Could we stop for a minute? Please?" Not caring whether he did, she bent over and propped her hands on her thighs, sucking in air and a few gnats.

"That's not how you do it." His arm came around her waist, and he pressed on her spine, forcing her to stand up straight. "Your lungs get more air if you're upright. And keep moving, even if it's small steps, so your legs don't get stiff."

"Too late." She put a hand on his forearm to steady herself while she slipped off one running shoe to get rid of what felt like a rock in it. A small mound of pebbles and sand cascaded out. "My legs started out stiff, and chasing after you doesn't help."

He grinned. "At least you're finally chasing me."

"Cute." He was, but she'd still rather rollerblade. "If you hadn't asked me to go hiking, I'd be zipping out to Cold Stone right now in my convertible, driving too fast for the mosquitoes to get me."

"Fine." He watched her shake out her second shoe, then grabbed her hand, spun her around, and led her back the way they'd come. "You've sold me. Time for ice cream."

She sputtered as he practically trotted along the trail. "Just like that? We're done hiking?" Letting go of his hand, she grabbed at the huge backpack he toted, trying without success to slow him down. The thing felt like it held bricks. "After you packed enough provisions for two months?"

"Give or take a couple weeks, yeah."

He kept walking in silence with her tripping behind him. Fifteen minutes later, they reached his truck. He threw his backpack in the back and helped her into the cab.

She waited while he walked around the front of the truck and climbed into the driver's side. "You didn't like the hike?"

Steep climbs and bloodthirsty bugs weren't high on her list, but all in all it hadn't been so bad. The hiking relaxed her, she'd felt surprisingly comfortable with him, and they'd talked a bit when she hadn't been gasping for air.

The engine rumbled to life. He put the truck in gear and swung a U-turn on the empty road while Vic waited for him to answer her question. Her simple question, damn it.

"Yeah."

Swallowing hard, she looked out the passenger window as gravel spun under their wheels and trees flew past. "Even though you suddenly couldn't bear to hike another minute and set a new land speed record racing up that trail."

He winked at her. "At least we missed the tree bark. And poison ivy."

"Hmpf." She leaned back against the headrest.

The truck rolled to a stop in the middle of a street lined with houses, none of which she recognized. Jake turned sideways and grabbed her hand. "I'm sorry."

She yanked her hand away.

"I didn't like the hike as much as I thought I would."

"Oh." She stared at her hands in her lap.

"Because I realized about halfway up the hill that I wanted to be doing something else."

"Rollerblading? Treating me to Cold Stone?"

"Or something. Like kissing you. Holding you." He lifted one shoulder as a shiver raced up her spine. "I figured if I started kissing you on the trail, we might wind up naked on the banks of the Mississippi."

She felt her cheeks flush as she tried not to imagine it. At the same time, she wondered when they might go hiking again.

Grinning, he reached for her hand. This time, she let him keep it. "Would you mind skipping Cold Stone and heading over to my house?"

She bit her lip as a seventeen-year-old's memories warred with a thirty-eight-year-old's desires. No clear winner emerged. "Let's go to mine. I have Ben & Jerry's in the freezer."

CHAPTER 16

"Half Baked or Americone Dream?"

Jake stared at the pints of Ben & Jerry's in Victoria's hands and wondered when the romantic evening he'd envisioned had turned into an ice-cream fest.

She'd changed into microscopic pink shorts and a wisp of a black top as soon as they got to her place, while he'd pulled a clean, rumpled T-shirt out of his backpack and tossed it on. Standing close together in front of the open freezer, he saw the hairs on her arms standing straight up. She'd skipped a bra, praise God, and her nipples were also standing at attention, not to mention doing weird things to his heart rate.

He tapped her shoulder and pointed into the freezer at a pint of Karamel Sutra. "Saving that for yourself?"

A faint blush stole up her cheeks, and he realized with a chuckle that she *was* saving it. Either that, or she thought the name was too erotic to say out loud.

Grinning, he reached past her for the Karamel Sutra and pried off the lid. "Next best thing to Vanilla Caramel Fudge, but I could probably think of something that tastes even better."

Her jaw dropped. "You like that, too? Why did they ever

stop selling Vanilla Caramel Fudge, at least around here? It drives me crazy."

He peeled off the plastic film on top, grabbed a spoon, and dug into the pint—even as he gave up on getting Victoria excited about anything besides ice cream.

With a sheepish smile, she stole the pint from his hand and set it in the microwave. "It's better when it's a little soft."

He pressed his lips together. No comment.

The microwave dinged, and he watched in disbelief as she scooped a few puny little bits of Karamel Sutra into cartoon-character bowls, Scooby-Doo and some princess, then handed him Scooby-Doo. Shaking his head, he grabbed the open pint off the counter and filled his bowl.

Her eyebrows rose.

"Hey, I'm a growing boy."

She glanced the length of him, a quick up and down, then dipped the tip of her spoon into her bowl and touched the spoon to her lips. At this rate, they'd be standing in her kitchen for hours. Not kissing. Not doing a damn thing except waiting for her to finish her ice cream.

Shaking his head, he slammed both their bowls on the table and grabbed her hand. "You like soft ice cream? Good. It's about to get really soft."

He half-dragged her into the living room and pulled her down next to him onto a cream-colored couch, one of her legs splayed over his, all while ignoring her sputtered protests. Realizing what he'd just done, he scrubbed a hand over his face and groaned. "The caveman style doesn't really work, does it?"

"Maybe in high school." She pulled his hand away from his face and ruffled his hair. The way she'd always done in high school. "What should I say? On you, caveman looks good?"

As they shared a laugh, he glanced around the room, taking in the oriental rug, the designer furniture, the expensive art and knickknacks. The bay windows. As dusk started to fall, the complete lack of curtains. Beyond them, a steady rumble of cars, trucks, and motorcycles cruised along the parkway.

"Should I turn on a lamp?" Victoria must've noticed the darkness, too, but maybe she'd never noticed that she needed curtains.

"What? And let a million strangers see me?"

She shook her head. "Just a few hundred. I had to get used to that when we moved in. Most of the houses on the lakes don't have drapes or blinds on the first floor."

"Sorry I dragged you in here like that." Taking her hand, he played with her fingers. "I just wanted to kiss you."

She lifted one shoulder in an elegant shrug. "Maybe you could try that."

"And your husband won't show up? Or come after me with a shotgun?"

Laughing, she inched closer. "He's not exactly the gun type and, no, he won't show up. I filed the divorce papers this week. He's not living here."

He swallowed hard. Ask about the divorce? Don't ask?

Or take her advice and kiss her?

His arm snaked around her shoulders, and his cheek touched the top of her head. Soft, clean-smelling hair with a hint of oranges. Turning sideways, his other hand touched her waist, and his lips moved closer.

But he stopped halfway there.

"Are you sure this is okay? You really want this?"

She locked her arms around him, hauled him in tight, and planted one on him—then pushed him away and leaned back against the couch.

Grinning, he tapped her nose. "I'll take that as a yes."

"Smart man." She reached out a tentative hand, touching his chest, but didn't meet his gaze. "Your turn now. But you might want to be more imaginative than I just was. I was a little nervous."

"Aye aye, captain. Imaginative."

"Within reason."

"Hate to say it, but my definition of 'reason' is pretty broad." He pulled her closer, getting used to the feel of her again. A brush of skin against skin tantalized him, and his hands ran the length of her bare arms, fiddling with the skinny straps of her top, moving to her neck. She shivered.

"Cold?"

Shaking her head, her tongue circled her lips. He moved closer, nuzzling her neck, and she wriggled under his touch. One hand strayed to her breast. She caught his hand and held it.

He went still, his mind spinning at the mixed messages. "Are you sure you want this?"

Biting her lip, she relaxed against his side and tilted her head to look at him. "I guess it depends on what 'this' is. I do want to kiss you. Very much." She glanced away, turning a faint shade of pink. "Beyond that, I'm not sure. It's been a long time, Jake. And it didn't end well."

"It didn't end at all. You just vanished."

She tucked her feet under her on the couch and finger-combed her hair. "We've already talked about that. It doesn't matter anymore." Yeah, it did, but he could wait on that conversation. Maybe until breakfast. "In any case, we need to get to know each other again."

"But you want me to kiss you? Like this?" He cupped her face as their lips softly brushed together. "Or like this?" He went deeper, letting their tongues dance. He forgot the way she used to taste, discovering instead the way she tasted now.

Pretty much like Karamel Sutra.

She closed her eyes, and a soft sigh floated out of her. "I do want that, but I also want—"

"—to get closer? Like this?" He shifted her legs until she straddled him on the couch. Her arms went around his shoulders, holding on tight. His own hands stayed at her waist for about two seconds, then stole under her flimsy black top and sneaked up the front of her until they held her breasts. Soft and still perfect and a little heavier than he remembered. "Maybe we should explore our, um, feelings?"

Her breath caught as she arched her back, then pressed the weight of her breasts against his hands. "I—oh—guess we could explore those, too."

His hands kept wandering while she wriggled on his lap, moving against him in an unconscious rhythm. She leaned forward and nibbled at his ear, his neck, making tiny little moans when he lifted the hem of her top and his mouth moved to her breast. As she swayed faster against him, he felt himself go hard. He gave silent thanks for baggy hiking shorts.

The honk of a horn jolted him, and he twisted to glance past her out the window. A thousand cars drove by while he made out in the semi-dark with Victoria on her couch. The thought would've excited him in high school. Now, it nearly gave him a heart attack.

His lips moved back to her mouth, pressing kisses there, before he whispered against her lips.

"I want—" "I want—" Their voices merged.

"—to take this to a bedroom."

"—to slow this down."

Breathing hard, she pulled a few inches away from him just as her cell phone rang. Yanking her shirt back into place, she leaped off his lap.

"You don't have to answer it."

She scurried around the corner and into the kitchen. "It might be the kids."

Right. The kids way up in Bemidji. The kids she'd be picking up on Saturday morning. The kids she'd forgotten until he'd gone too far too fast. He slapped his forehead. They spent all those months together junior year, in bed and in cars and damn near everywhere else they could think of, making love so urgently that they couldn't see straight. Twenty years later, she fumbled and blushed and offered him a tray of mixed signals.

Tight-lipped, she returned, carrying the two bowls of ice cream. She'd had a quick conversation, obviously, and they were back to square one. "You're right. It got soft."

It wasn't the only thing that had. Shaking his head, he reached for Scooby-Doo. "Who called?"

She tilted her head to one side. "As a matter of fact, it was a mutual friend with excellent timing. Andrea."

In the blink of an eye, his chances of making it anywhere near Victoria's bedroom tonight plummeted to zero.

Groaning to his feet, he set the untouched ice cream on the coffee table, then shifted the bowl onto a coaster after a moment's thought. "I guess I should go."

Her hands went to her hips. "Because Andrea called?"

"No. Because you have to make it all so damned difficult. High school wasn't this hard."

She stared at her bare feet. He'd noticed the blue toenail polish earlier, and it still startled him that the grown-up Victoria would do anything even remotely wild.

She spoke so softly, he barely caught the words. "High school was harder for me than it was for you."

He blinked, remembering his parents' financial struggles, his own struggles to fit in at a school where a lot of the kids he'd hung out with came from wealth and didn't seem to realize that any other life existed. Yeah. The gorgeous, rich, homecoming queen had it real tough.

In her own mind.

"Because you got pregnant." At her nod, he jammed his hands in his pockets and padded past her to the front door, where he pulled on his hiking boots and picked up his backpack. "Well, you've got me there. And you always will."

Leaving her to wallow in her self-pity, he let himself out and pulled the door closed behind him. He walked to his truck, tossed his stuff in the back, and peeled out from the curb as fast as he could.

———

By midafternoon on Friday, Vic nearly unplugged the phone in her office. Calls all day, and none from Jake.

She kept asking herself if she preferred it that way. He'd bolted almost as soon as she first hinted at "no," and she couldn't stand men like that. She needed someone who respected boundaries. Who talked as well as he kissed. Who didn't vanish the minute his ex-fling's name was mentioned.

Shaking her head, she realized the truth. Last night, at least, she'd wanted him. Warts and muddy hiking boots and all.

The phone rang again, and she glared at it. As the ringing persisted, she called out into the gallery for Sean. No answer. Another long afternoon break. His third this week.

"Victoria Carlyle Bentley." A mouthful, but between reunion planning and sorting through her divorce, it was the best solution she'd come up with so far.

"Victoria? You're still at work? Don't you have to pick up the children early tomorrow morning?"

Mother. Sounding tired and stressed and something else that Vic couldn't quite put her finger on.

"I'm here all afternoon." Alone, as it turned out. Damn that Sean. "I decided to get up early rather than make the drive to Bemidji tonight."

The sleepless nights weren't getting any shorter, and she was just being practical. She hadn't factored a possible make-out *or* make-up session with Jake into the equation at all.

Liar.

"Would you like company on the long drive?"

Vic frowned. Mother liked car trips even less than Ryder did. Even less than she liked fast food or dirt or snakes or cheap wine or designer knockoffs.

"I'm leaving at five a.m. Thanks, but I can manage."

"Oh. Well."

The silence on the line grew until Vic couldn't stand it.

"Mother, it's at least four hours each way. And Connor and Megan will probably be a little rambunctious on the way home." Another thing that wouldn't thrill her mother.

"I understand, dear. It's just that—" A long pause, during which Vic started gnawing on her knuckles. "Never mind."

Despite herself, she pushed a pile of papers to one side. "Is Dad still staying at Nat's?

"I'm . . . not quite sure." Mother hesitated over each word, as if pondering what she could reveal. "Natalie's apartment is so small. I thought he might be staying with you."

"He hasn't asked." Something—irritation? jealousy?—bit at Vic, just as it had when Nat had first mentioned Dad's current sleeping arrangements.

"Well, he doesn't return my calls. Even though I've offered to help."

"Help?" Dad helped Mother, not the other way around. Vic shook her head, irritated at herself for letting the conversation go even this far. "You're each going your own way right now, and maybe he doesn't want your advice."

"My advice?" Mother laughed, the sound brittle in Vic's ear. "No, I suspect money would be an easier solution." At Mother's deep sigh, Vic rolled her eyes. "But he's never wanted my money. Even now, when he needs it."

"Look, I really should get back to work."

"Please don't go, Victoria. I need your advice."

If she had to pick sides, and she didn't, the wrong person had called. "I can't get in the middle of this." As she thought about Mother and Dad, and those thoughts strayed to other unpleasant topics, her stomach churned. "And if you wanted my input, you'd have asked me what to do about Hope. Twenty-one years ago."

Another pause. "Hope?"

"My daughter? You know—the one you hid from me?" A niggle of regret pinched her. With Mother already in obvious distress, her timing was awful. But she'd never reclaim her life if she balked now. In theory, she knew she was right. In practice, she heard a sniffle on the other end of the line.

"I told you, Victoria. Your baby died."

"All evidence to the contrary. I may have been seventeen, but it was my decision to make. My baby."

"You don't believe me? Your mother? I can't believe you'd take the word of—"

Vic's second line blinked, and the unknown caller had to be preferable to Mother. "I'm sorry, really, but I need to take a call. Talk to you later."

"Victoria—"

She hit the button for the second line, disconnecting her mother. Something that didn't feel at all like relief slammed into her stomach as she chirped her name into the phone.

"Vic? It's Andrea again."

"Oh, hi. Sorry I forgot to call back."

She winced, realizing she should've just unplugged the damn phone. Her finger inched toward the disconnect button.

"You must really hate me."

Yes, now that she mentioned it. "Why would I?" Besides the fact that Andrea had been a snake all these years. "But I'm really buried in work. I need to drive to Bemidji early tomorrow to pick up the kids at camp, and you know how that goes."

Except that Andrea didn't work and usually didn't understand other people's hassles. Tess didn't work, either, except for the fundraising she did for a slew of charitable organizations, but Tess was Tess.

Andrea was the one who'd slept with Jake.

"Vic, we really need to talk. Jake called me today."

She clutched a hand to her throat and stopped breathing. No wonder Jake hadn't called or stopped by or even sent flowers, like any self-respecting louse would. He'd been too busy burning up the phone lines with Andrea. Sonofabitch.

"Vic? Are you still there?"

She coughed, sending the air whooshing out of her lungs. "Sure. Just busy. What were you saying?"

"I didn't know you guys were together again. I mean, I wondered . . ."

As Andrea paused, Vic imagined the side of Andrea's face and simulated a slapping motion.

"We're not." Last night had just been a hike "with benefits" —and, actually, not that many benefits.

"Really? Jake acted like you were, and anyway, I'm sorry. I should've told you. Someone should've. I was just so embarrassed about the whole thing."

Vic wanted to clap her hands over her ears and hum something loud, a favorite technique from childhood. "Whatever."

"I'm sorry, Vic."

"You already said that. It's fine, Andrea. Ancient history." She thought about holding her breath until she passed out. Maybe she could just slam down the receiver.

"He still likes you. It was always you." Andrea sniffed, sounding too much like Vic's mother and too little like the villain in this scenario. "That's why he wanted to go out with me that summer. All he did was talk about you."

As Vic's eyebrows rose, the slightest flutter of relief teased her. "That's all he did?"

"I mean, you know. Pretty much."

Biting her lip, she wondered why she hadn't already left for Bemidji. Without a phone. "Did you sleep with him?"

The long pause spoke volumes. "Like I said. I'm sorry."

"Tell me again why you called? To rub it in?"

Andrea sighed. "Because Jake asked. And because I've known you since grade school. I want us to be friends again."

The reasonable part of Vic that had always liked Andrea—despite a few of her mildly ugly traits—wanted it, too. But not today. "Anyway, thanks for calling. Right now, someone's on my other line."

"Vic, I—"

"Gotta run. Bye."

She hit the disconnect button. Enough. Grabbing her purse, she swung around her desk and headed out into the gallery—and bumped into Tess, who was hovering near her office.

"Geez, Tess! You scared me."

"Serves you right. With phone etiquette like that, you must've vanquished at least half a dozen helpless souls today." Shaking her head, Tess grabbed Vic's arm and started to drag her back into the office. "Let's talk about it, shall we?"

"Not in here." She shook her arm loose and headed back to the main door of the gallery. "And if this is going to be another one of your interventions, I already gave at the office."

Tess waited while she locked up and flipped the sign on the door to "closed." They walked in tandem down the stairs to street level, where Tess's new blue Mercedes gleamed at the curb. "Where to?"

Vic shrugged. "Home."

Keys jangled in Tess's hand as she walked around to the driver's side. "Meet you there?"

"Only if this is your lucky day."

"I'm counting on it." With a quick wave, Tess slipped into the car and took off at turbo speed. Much more slowly, Vic trudged to her parking ramp, eased out of her stall, and drove a meandering route home—where, leaning against the hood of the Mercedes, Tess waited for her.

Vic cruised past her and into the garage, idling a moment as she pondered shutting the garage door and hiding inside her house. But Tess probably knew how to pick locks.

Leaving the car and garage, she walked around the front of the house to the front steps, where Tess gave her a quick up-and-down glance. "You're sober, which is good, but you seem to have acquired a nasty habit of ripping people's heads off. Starting with Ryder's head, I hear."

Vic frowned. How did she—?

Tess waved a hand in the air. "You hired Eden St. John."

"Only after Ryder took a running start at every other divorce lawyer in town."

"And she served papers on Ryder at his office, and quite flamboyantly, I gather."

Vic sat on the steps, stretching her legs out in front of her as Tess did the same. "I don't tell her how to do her job. Divorces aren't pretty."

"But you want the rest of your life to be perfect again."

Pursing her lips, she nodded.

"Even though it never was."

Twisting sideways, she glared at Tess.

"It wasn't, and you know it. Ryder was always gay, even

though the subject never came up. So to speak." She patted Vic's leg. "Not that my life is perfect, either."

"Tell me about it. A fabulous condo, all the money in the world, and no gay husband."

Tess snorted. "I'm dating a balding guy you wouldn't look twice at, who tends bar for a living, and he's lived in the same one-bedroom apartment in Uptown since he graduated from college." Despite her unvarnished description of Jed, Tess's eyes had a dreamy, faraway look that Vic had rarely seen on her best friend with any of her wealthy ex-husbands. Even during the honeymoon stage.

She frowned, for once in her life realizing she didn't understand Tess's choices and wasn't quite sure what to ask. At least Jake *owned* the restaurant. "You forgot to mention that bomb you dropped about the abortion, which we still haven't discussed."

"Nothing to discuss. Jonathan and I didn't—" She waved her hand, and the dreamy look vanished. "But enough about me. Everyone in your life has messes that you can't fix. Your brother and Babs. Your parents. Nat tells me that your mother is clinging to one of the rungs of hell, but you can't be bothered. By the way, it took guts for Andrea to call, and you stomped all over her." She shook her head. "The path to perfection doesn't look like that."

"How long were you eavesdropping?"

"All summer, babe." Tess draped an arm casually over her shoulders. "You've gotten rid of the booze and drugs, not to mention Ryder, but you're so busy striving for perfection that you're losing the best parts of you, too."

"Such as?"

"The imperfect, utterly cool Vic. A woman whose Porsche once held kids' car seats. A woman who's bitched all her life about her mom but once spent hours at Tiffany's picking out

the perfect birthday gift for her. A woman who dropped every-thing to bring me chicken noodle soup that time I got so sick."
She winked. "Next time, I'd prefer wonton soup."

Vic rolled her eyes. "There won't be a next time."

"If you insist on tossing away or avoiding all the pieces of your life that aren't perfect, like your mother or Andrea or Jake —" She looked meaningfully at Vic, who looked away. "You won't have much left."

"I'll have my kids. And you." She hoped so, at least, despite Tess's unfortunate tendency to poke sticks in her eye. "And Dad and Nat and Drew."

"Not even Midge?"

Vic shrugged. "I don't think she's speaking to me."

Tess rested her elbows on her knees and propped her chin on her hands just as a loud motorcycle rumbled by and the man driving it honked at them. Tess waved at him before turning back to Vic. "No one's life is perfect, Vic. It's not supposed to be. But what you seek is inside of you, and you need to find it before your world gets even smaller and it's too late."

"Too late for what?"

"Patience, Grasshopper. You'll figure it out."

Vic groaned. Just once, she wished Tess would save the Buddha crap for a willing victim.

———

"Are you sure this is okay with Victoria?"

Jake rubbed his rough jaw as Hope turned the key in the lock of Jasmine Gallery just after seven on Saturday morning, way too early for his taste. He wondered how he kept getting into messes with Victoria. And now Hope. Their daughter. At least Hope had a key to the place. That must count for something.

"I'm positive." A click. Hope turned the handle, pushed open the glass door, and flipped on the overhead switch. "Sean's having trouble with the computer, and Vic won't be back from Bemidji until this evening." She glanced sideways at him, as if she suspected he'd be seeing Victoria, but he just yawned. Hell hadn't frozen over. "She said she'd appreciate any help we could give, but she didn't want us to bother Sean or be here when the gallery is open."

"That's not exactly how she put it to me." The only time they'd discussed it, she'd turned him down flat. Now Victoria probably wasn't even speaking to him.

"She changed her mind."

About a lot of things, apparently. Last thing he'd heard, Victoria had fired Hope and was trying to keep her out of her life. The FBI investigation must really be heating up. Victoria was obviously getting desperate.

Desperate enough to ask him for help. Except she hadn't asked him. She'd asked Hope.

He sighed. "What do you know about her books?"

"I know where they are." She led him to a small office, then jiggled the key ring, peering at a few keys before deciding on one and unlocking a file cabinet. She pulled open a drawer, then moved to the desk and turned on the computer. "I figured you could go through the books and bank statements while I poke around in the computer files."

"And you're sure that's okay?"

"Like I said. Vic is going to be more than grateful."

An hour later, a stack of inventory sheets and ledgers with incomprehensible scribbling grew high next to Jake on the floor, threatening to topple over, and he whistled as he flipped through a wad of bank statements. Victoria needed an accountant to audit the mess, but he wouldn't be the fool who suggested it.

Skimming down a column of numbers on another statement, he shut his eyes, overwhelmed by the amount of money in the gallery's accounts. If he'd thought Victoria was out of his league before, he now knew it for a fact.

He tossed the statements on a new stack. Even if he found something in all these piles, he couldn't admit to Victoria that he'd gone through her financial information. No matter what Hope claimed, Victoria would blow sky high.

His knees creaked to a standing position, then he pulled open the top drawer of the file cabinet and reached inside. Only a couple unopened bank statements left. Curious, he slit open the envelopes and read the account names. Personal trust accounts for her and her kids. He stuffed the statements back in the envelopes and returned them to the top drawer.

"What's that?" Hope spun in her chair and pointed at the top drawer just as Jake slid it closed.

"Personal stuff of Victoria's." He pressed his hand against the drawer as Hope reached for it. "It's not our business, Hope. We're just helping Victoria with whatever the FBI is doing, not going on a fishing expedition."

Hope kept trying to grasp the handle. "Vic doesn't know what the FBI is looking for. She told me we should look at everything in her office."

Something didn't feel right, but he shook his head and moved away from the file cabinet. Victoria had apparently asked Hope to check out her financials and even gave her the damn key to the place. Who was he to say no? The man Victoria wasn't even speaking to?

"Fine. Take a look, but I don't want to hear about it. It looks like trust statements for Victoria and her kids." Too late, he cringed as his words registered. "She hadn't even opened them."

Hope's eyes flashed. "I'm her kid, too."

"So you keep saying." He moved to the desk and sank into the plush chair. Swiveling, he faced the computer screen. "While you're checking those statements, I'll take a look here. You didn't find anything on the computer?"

Distracted, Hope shook her head as she peered at the bank statements, then glanced at a photo of what he assumed were Victoria's kids on top of the file cabinet.

He picked up another photo, propped on Victoria's desk next to the phone. Cute kids. Just like their mom.

Turning again to the computer screen, he groaned as he scanned a bunch of entries. Another mess. He spun in the chair and faced Hope, who sat cross-legged on the floor. "This is how she keeps her financials? Why the hell doesn't she get a decent computer program?"

Hope frowned up at him. "I know. I mean, I talk to her about computer stuff all the time. I suggested a couple of programs, but she never takes my advice. She just listens to Sean."

"He's worked here a while." And Victoria had fired Hope, which made him wonder exactly how long ago Hope had talked about computers with Victoria. He shook his head as he turned back to the computer, not understanding a damn thing. "But I agree she needs a better program. Like the one I use at Pendulum."

"Really?"

The note of surprise in her voice pissed him off. Just a little. "I'm not a dinosaur."

"Maybe we could both talk to Vic about her computer."

Yeah. The same day he'd tell Victoria he'd gone through her bank statements. The day after never.

He played around with the computer without changing or deleting anything. He couldn't actually see anything wrong, but maybe Hope had fixed it while Jake pored through everything else. He glanced up at the clock. Almost nine.

"Jake! I think I found it." Clutching the bank statements, Hope leaped to her feet, tripping and slamming backward into the file cabinet. Moaning, she rubbed her large stomach while she took a few deep breaths.

"Found what?" Money that Hope thought she deserved along with Victoria's other kids?

"What the FBI is looking for. Maybe they already found it." She waved a crumpled bank statement in his face, then peered at it again, grimacing. "I'm just surprised. I really thought it would be Sean. He's such a jerk."

"It's not?"

She shook her head. "Take a look. Money moving into the accounts, day after day for a few weeks in late March, from different accounts in the same bank. Each time, just under ten thousand dollars. And then, starting in April, it moves right back out, into a single account. Or most of it, anyway."

"So? What does that mean?"

"I don't think trust accounts work like that. The money mostly sits there, except for occasional payouts for tuition or a house or car or whatever. Or living expenses."

Jake felt a headache coming on. "How do you know? You've got a trust account?"

She snorted. "Funny. They talked about trust accounts in freshman accounting. And it just makes sense."

Probably true. "But why would Vic do that?"

"She didn't. She's not the trustee, so she can't move the money without the trustee's permission. The trustee is the only one who can do it. At least, I think so."

"So? Who's the trustee?"

Hope pointed at the top of the statement. "Vic's dad."

CHAPTER 17

"*Maravilloso.*" Vic clapped as Connor and Megan took a bow along with dozens of their new friends at Spanish camp, then set down their mementos from the end-of-camp program and bounced around slapping high-fives at each other.

Tan and giddy and babbling in high-pitched Spanish that Vic could barely understand, Megan raced over to Vic and gave her a breath-choking hug.

Connor ambled toward them, hands stuffed in his pockets. "Yo, Mom. What's up?" He swung his head from side to side as Vic blinked at the change in him. He seemed closer to fifteen than ten. "Where's Dad? He said he'd be here. He promised."

Megan looked expectant, Connor ready to be disappointed. Watching their two young faces, Vic had a glimmer of how a prisoner might feel when facing a firing squad. She wished she had a blindfold.

"He wanted to come." She pursed her lips at the small lie. Ryder hadn't wanted to endure the long drive, especially at Vic's side, but he'd offered. A small victory in a battle from which she'd withdrawn.

"Yeah, right." Connor's hair, bleached white from three

weeks of sunshine, hung in his eyes. "Dad didn't show again. Like, no surprise there."

Vic bit her lip. "That's not true." She glanced at Megan, who chattered in makeshift Spanish with the dark, pigtailed girl next to her. The girl's parents tapped their feet and looked at their watches.

Connor stared straight at Vic. "Yeah? Since when?"

She thought of all the excuses she'd made for Ryder over the years. Why he couldn't attend school functions, sporting events, family get-togethers. Because of work. Or had there been a Sean in his life all along? "I asked him not to come."

Connor's eyes widened a moment before he whipped his head to one side, letting his bangs fly. "No way, Mom. That blows."

"Connor Bentley."

He shrank a moment, then looked at her with a new defiance. "It sucks."

"Try again." She shook her head. "No, don't." She drew a shaky breath, coughing when she tried to hold it. "I'm sorry your dad isn't here. He did offer to come." Barely.

"So why didn't you let him?"

"Because I needed to talk to you." She waited while Megan gave her friend a goodbye hug and the girl's parents dragged her away. "Both of you."

His face turned wary. Age ten going on twenty. Vic worried that it'd be thirty after the conversation they needed to have. She wondered again whether she should speak separately to Connor and Megan, but she kept reaching the same conclusion. She'd only make it through this conversation once.

But not in front of the crowd of campers, parents, and counselors still milling around. After retrieving the kids' duffle bags and bedding and taking photos of them with their favorite counselors, she steered them to her SUV and steered her SUV to the nearest Dairy Queen. Connor ordered a Blizzard and Megan a cherry Dilly bar. Vic got a Diet Coke for her jumpy stomach.

It didn't really help, but after a moment she dove in anyway.

"Your dad and I—"

"Is Daddy waiting for us at home, Mommy? I missed you both!" Squealing, Megan waved her Dilly in the air.

When Connor slouched in his seat and just stared at his untouched Blizzard, Vic reached for both kids' hands. "Your dad and I can't live together anymore."

Connor rolled his eyes. "Does he really like guys? I mean, that blows, Mom."

"Connor!"

He hung his head, scuffing the toe of his sneaker on the floor. Megan frowned, then drew close to Vic, whispering in her ear. "Does Daddy like boys, Mommy? Like Connor, and Uncle Drew, and Papa? Me too."

The kids' two-year age gap had never felt wider. She stroked Megan's hair as her mind whirled. "Connor didn't mean *those* boys, Megan, but I'll talk to him later." If she could manage it. Connor looked ready to bolt—or to tell the world about Ryder's sexuality. "Your dad and I both love you. We just can't stay together."

"Do we hafta go live in a dumpy little house? Will we ever see Dad again? Are we gonna be poor?" Questions streamed out of Connor's mouth as Vic listened, debating her answer on some, nodding or shaking her head on others.

"The three of us will stay in our house, but you can still see your dad. He can visit us, or you can visit him. How does that sound?"

Having to spend much time around Ryder after the crap he'd pulled so far in their divorce proceedings didn't sound particularly good to *her*, but she'd decided to be civil about this. No matter what he did.

Megan nodded eagerly. Connor just looked at Vic, arms crossed over his narrow chest.

Drawing a breath, she prayed for strength to broach the second part of her talk. A subject she'd rather not discuss in front of Ryder, even though he undoubtedly knew by now. After swallowing hard on a dry throat, she took a few sips of her Diet Coke. "There's something else I need to talk to you about."

"You like girls?" Connor screwed up his face. "Yuck!"

She laughed. "I have plenty of girlfriends." Or at least one who still spoke to her, if she didn't count Natalie. "But I don't like them that way."

"I do, Mommy." Megan nodded vehemently. "I like lots of girls."

Vic wondered whether they should start the drive home. No, she had to finish this—if she could get a word in edgewise over Connor's defiance and Megan's eager lack of understanding.

She plunged in. "When we get home, there's someone I'd like you to meet."

"Oh, man. You've got a boyfriend, Mom? Is that why you didn't visit us? That—"

She stared at Connor, silently, daring him to utter the word. She also tried not to think about Jake. She'd spent time with him, taken a few steps forward—along with a dozen painful steps back. "No, I'm talking about someone I never mentioned to you, because I didn't know about her until this summer."

Frowns crossed both kids' faces. "Who?"

"Her name is Hope. She worked at my art gallery this summer. She's in college."

Connor shrugged, then stuck his spoon in his Blizzard. "Whatever."

"And—" She couldn't do this. No, she had to. Before Hope did it for her. "And it's possible that she's your sister."

"No way, Mom."

"A sister!" Megan squealed. "You had a baby?"

Connor rolled his eyes. "You are, like, so stupid."

"Don't call your sister stupid."

Megan tucked a thumb in her mouth, withdrawing it only when she noticed Vic watching her.

"She's all grown up, sweetie." Vic frowned a warning at Connor. "I had a baby a long time ago, but I didn't know she was alive, and I guess she might be your sister." Half-sister, but this little talk was already sailing high over Megan's head.

"When?" Connor frowned, and Vic could practically see the wheels turning in his head.

"When did I have her?" A tight nod. She lifted one shoulder. "When I was seventeen."

"In high school?"

She nodded. "I really liked a boy, and—"

"You had sex in high school." He glared at her. "And Dad has it with guys. Man, this blows."

"This does not blow, Connor!"

She flushed as half a dozen heads turned in their direction. Reaching across the table, she grasped one hand of each child. She had to make them understand. In basic terms, at least. "It's not what you think."

"You said we shouldn't even think about sex."

"You're ten, Connor. Of course not."

"For a long time. Like college or marriage or when we're old, like thirty."

They hadn't had much of a sex talk yet, frankly, since she'd hoped to throw that particular chore on Ryder. Yet another thing he probably wouldn't do. "You're definitely too young now." As Megan's eyes widened, she tapped her on the nose. "But some day. It's something we need to talk about." Like, say, before Connor turned eleven.

"Were you too young?" His gaze pinned her.

"Yes. No." She bit her lip, thinking back. "Yes. High school was definitely too young. I hope you'll do better."

"But you had a baby."

She nodded.

"And that baby is our sister now? How old is she? Is she gonna live with us?"

Vic shook her head as her stomach lurched at the thought of Hope living in her house. Occupying the same work space this summer had been bad enough. "She's almost twenty-one. She has her own place."

"Will she give me birthday presents?" Megan clapped her hands and squealed.

"No, stupid."

"Connor . . ."

He shrugged. "I don't need another sister. I already have a sister, and a mom, and that's enough."

"Don't forget your dad, too."

He crossed his skinny arms, his lower lip defiant. "Do we hafta meet her, Mom? I don't wanna, and I don't wanna meet any of your boyfriends, either."

She gritted her teeth, realizing that Connor already knew Ryder's boyfriend. *Ew*, as Connor would say.

"I don't have a boyfriend." She thought of Jake, relieved that she hadn't said yes to him. Or not enough of a yes to count. "You can meet Hope when you want. When you're ready."

"I'll never be ready."

She prayed that Hope didn't have other ideas.

———

VIC CHECKED HER WATCH AGAIN, then shook it hard and held it against her ear, catching the faintest sound of ticking. Yes, eight forty-five. Her watch was working.

Larissa, however, didn't appear to be.

She paced in the front hall as she called Larissa's cell phone, getting voicemail twice. She left a message. Twice. She wondered again why she'd scheduled back-to-back meetings on the fifth of July, when most people gave themselves a three-day weekend. Including Larissa, apparently.

Larissa's weekend had now extended to three weeks and three days, she amended herself. With the kids at camp, Vic hadn't needed a nanny.

Megan scurried up to her, one hand clinging to her pants leg, while Connor looked out the front window.

Larissa couldn't be sick. Not today. Vic could reschedule a couple of meetings, but one was with her biggest client, who might take his business elsewhere.

"Someone's parking in front of the house, Mom!" Connor stumbled and fell backward off the sofa.

Someone? Not Larissa, then. Vic tried her again. As the phone rang, she made a half-hearted attempt to stop Connor from answering the door, but to no avail.

No answer. She hung up, hoping that Larissa was on her way, maybe almost here, and just wasn't picking up her cell phone. Right. The young woman whose phone, most days, might as well be surgically attached to her ear.

The doorbell rang just as Connor whipped open the door to admit Hope.

"Hey." In a pair of stretched-out athletic shorts and a tent for a top, Hope bent down to eye level with Connor. It always irritated him when an adult did it, and he took a step backward, unwittingly inviting her inside. "You must be Connor. Ten, huh?"

Megan peeked at Hope from her safety zone behind Vic. "I'm Megan. I'm eight."

Hope waved at her. "Hi, Megan. I'm Hope."

As Connor frowned and Megan clutched Vic's pants, the air caught in her throat. She coughed hard into her hand. "Megan and Connor, please go into the kitchen. Now."

Hope's face fell as Megan scampered into the kitchen and a sullen Connor followed a few slow steps behind.

"What are you doing here, Hope? You know I'm usually at work by now. If you need something—" Vic fervently hoped she didn't, because she wouldn't be providing it. "You should call me at work. This is my home."

Hope's gaze swung around the first floor, much as it had the time she'd practically forced Jake here at gunpoint.

"Nice place."

"Thanks, but I really don't have time right now."

Her cell phone rang, the display showing Larissa's name. Thank God. "Hello? Larissa? Where are you?"

"Uh, San Francisco?"

"What?" Biting her lip, Vic smacked the phone against her palm. Just in case she hadn't heard right. She turned her back on Hope and tried again. "You're where? Did you say—"

"San Francisco." Vic could hear noises in the background. "That's why I didn't call until now. I'm a couple hours behind you, and I tried setting my alarm and . . ."

"How long have you been there?"

"How long have I been here, Tony?" Laughter and mumbled words floated into Vic's ear, annoying her in the midst of her confusion. "Eight or nine days, I guess. I met this guy, Tony, and he has a bike."

"And you pedaled all the way to San Francisco?"

Another spurt of laughter. "Too funny, Vic. He has a motorcycle. A Harley. We rode it here, and then we—"

Her formerly responsible nanny of two years wasn't coming back. Not today, certainly, and after pulling this stunt, when hell froze over.

"Thanks for calling, Larissa. The kids will miss you." She hung up, sagged against the wall, and closed her eyes.

What had she done to deserve this summer?

"Anything I can help with? Was that your nanny?"

Hope. Right behind Vic. She sagged even harder against the wall and wrapped her arms around herself. Her first meeting started at nine-thirty. No nanny. No husband. Only Hope.

Come to think of it, how did Hope know who'd been calling? How did she happen to show up at the moment Vic lost her nanny? A shiver ran down her spine. She already had a psychic friend in Tess. She didn't need a psychic pseudo-daughter. Or any pseudo-daughter at all.

She turned slowly, pushing off against the wall. "What are you doing here? And before nine in the morning?"

Hope shrugged and dropped her beach bag of a purse in the front hall. "I knew the kids would be home from camp, and I figured you might be taking the day off."

"No."

"And I wanted to meet them."

Good Lord, the girl was intrepid. In a terrifying way. "That's all?"

Hope didn't meet her gaze. "Pretty much."

Vic raised an eyebrow. She took in Hope's outfit—maternity grunge—and sighed. No. She couldn't do this to herself.

She glanced at her watch and shook her head. Nearly nine. No, no, no. She *really* couldn't do this to herself. "I hate to ask —" A thousand times more than Hope could possibly imagine.

"But I'm in a bit of a pinch. By any chance could you spend the morning with the kids? My nanny can't make it here this morning."

Or this afternoon, or tomorrow or the next day, but Hope didn't have to know that. Vic could rearrange meetings, get the bare minimum done at the gallery this morning, and regroup this afternoon—starting with a call to her nanny agency, which she hoped could find a temp for her by tomorrow.

"Really? You'd let me stay with them?"

She hadn't even wanted Hope to meet them. Now she'd be handing Hope a key to her house *and* kids. Apparently, hell really *had* frozen over.

"You won't regret this, Vic."

She already did.

———

At quarter to eleven, Vic got up from her chair, shook David Andretti's hand, and showed him to the door of the gallery. A client satisfied, another bullet dodged. Smiling and chatty, David paused by one of Sean's paintings and nodded when Vic quoted the price. Sold.

Except for Larissa's unexpected departure, Hope's unexpected appearance, and the fact that Sean was two hours late for work, she could almost call the morning successful.

The phone rang, and she ran back to her office after letting David out the door. Greeting the caller, the owner of her nanny agency, she sighed in relief.

"Sorry, Vic. No one is immediately available, but we have a few good prospects who can start by August first."

"August first? That's it?" She skimmed her finger down her calendar, counting four long weeks. "What about a temp?"

"I don't have anyone. Wait." Vic heard the rustle of papers. "Maybe the last week in July."

It would still mean three weeks without a nanny. She groaned.

"It's a tough month. Should I send you the résumés of the candidates who can start in August or possibly late July?"

She sighed. "I suppose. To my office email."

Hanging up, she scoured the internet for other nanny agencies. She already worked with the best in town, so anything else would be a few notches down. But, then, so was Hope.

Ten minutes later, she reached for her bottle of Tylenol. One agency had no one available, the receptionist at another sounded drunk or stoned, and the third didn't answer. Time to call Ryder? She closed her eyes. He worked all day, too, and she didn't know where he was staying. Or with whom.

The phone rang at eleven-thirty. Still no Sean. Shaking her head, she picked up the phone.

"Vic? This is Eve at the Prescott Gallery. How are you?"

"Fine." She hadn't talked to Eve in months, and the last time hadn't been pleasant.

"Good, good. Well, I was calling about Sean."

"Sorry. He's not here right now." The hairs on the back of her neck stood on end. "Can he call you back?"

A trill of laughter. "Oh, no need. I was just calling to check references." As Eve waxed enthusiastic, Vic slumped against the edge of her desk. "We've known him for ages, of course, and think he'd be perfect for the job."

A loud buzzing roared through her head. She held the phone away from her ear, but the buzzing didn't stop.

"Vic? Still there? So why is Sean leaving your gallery? And will you still be representing his artwork?"

She closed her eyes, and a collage of images flashed past. Sean, practically a boy when she'd hired him part-time during his freshman year at St. Thomas. Sean the growing artist. Sean celebrating with Ryder at his side at his art opening. Sean bickering with Hope. Vic bickering with Sean. The FBI agents. Vic's dad, advising her to fire Sean.

Despite Dad, she hadn't fired him, but the Prescott Gallery was offering to take his head away on a silver platter. She ought to leap at the opportunity. A problem solved.

Eve's voice continued to prattle in her ear, asking questions to which she had no answers. Was he a good employee? The best—before his relationship with Ryder, before the FBI started calling, before he stopped showing up.

Remembering Tess's advice, Vic sighed. Sean was one of the many things in her life that weren't perfect. Far from it, when she thought of Ryder. But the gallery wouldn't be the same without him. Somehow, she had to convince him of that.

After drawing a deep breath and releasing it, she made up her mind. "Eve? I'm sorry. I really can't give you a reference on Sean. I'd like him to stay right here."

She nodded to herself. A good decision.

"Sorry, Vic. He's already accepted our offer."

———

VIC PACED the perimeter of the gallery, her hands clasped behind her back, as she considered and rejected a dozen possible solutions to her nightmares. Say good riddance to Sean. Bribe and beg Sean to reconsider. Rehire Hope and somehow find a different nanny. Hire the children in the gallery and forget a nanny altogether. Ask Mother to help.

Each possibility was more terrifying and/or ridiculous than the one before it.

In the meantime, she'd left Hope with the children only for the morning, and the clock on the wall inched toward noon.

Sean wasn't coming back today, Larissa wasn't coming back ever, and her kids needed her more than the gallery did.

Squaring her shoulders, she headed to her office for her purse just as the door to the gallery opened.

Sean. Three hours late, wearing shorts and beach sandals, and not likely to apologize for anything. "Hey, Vic."

Eyebrows raised, she waited. He sauntered toward her, his only sign of nervousness the bottle of fruit juice he guzzled every ten seconds while he caught and held her gaze.

She blinked first. "I got a call this morning. From Eve at the Prescott Gallery."

"Yeah?"

"Yes. She tells me you're working there now."

Rocking back and forth on the heels of his sandals, he nodded.

Her arms hung ramrod straight at her sides as she fought the urge to cross them. "You couldn't tell me yourself? After all these years? I thought we—" As Sean's jaw jutted out, she shook her head. "I thought we were friends."

"We were. Before this summer."

"Before Ryder."

He shrugged. "Before a lot of things."

One hand clenched as she remembered all the things that had gone wrong this summer—starting with Ryder leaving her for Sean. "You haven't even given two weeks' notice."

"I thought of that, but then I remembered that I have some vacation time saved up." He took a final swig from his bottle, then crossed the room to the recycling bin and tossed it in. "I guess I'm on vacation. Starting today."

"But that's—"

He held up a hand, stopping her. "You're right, I know, but it's been one thing after another. You can't deal with Ryder and me, and it has nothing to do with work. And you finally got rid of Hope, but the Vic I used to know is gone, too."

She paused, trying to formulate a nonviolent response, when all she really wanted was to smack her husband's lover upside the head.

"Please don't do this, Sean. My nanny left, and I had to leave Hope with my kids this morning."

He smirked. "You're bringing your personal problems to the gallery, Vic, just like you told Hope not to do. Tsk, tsk."

If he took a step closer, she'd choke him. "Please. Stay for the afternoon?" She bit her lip, wondering whether he had a change of clothes in his car, but beggars couldn't always insist on proper attire. "If not for me, do it for my kids. You always liked Connor and Megan."

"Dirty pool, Vic." He grinned, finally looking like the Sean she used to know. "Okay, just for the afternoon. If I were you, I'd spend it finding a new nanny."

"I'm trying, believe me." Her face felt flushed from the strain of the conversation, but she kept going. "But I'd really like you to think about staying. Permanently."

"Vic—"

"No, wait. You're right. It's been a hard summer. For all of us." But Sean and Ryder had started the whole thing, damn it, and she refused to apologize to him. "We haven't talked the way we used to. We haven't—" Gotten together for dinner or drinks. The Ryder issue again. "We haven't made this work. You've been a wonderful employee and friend. If you give this another chance, we can put it all back together."

There. She'd made her not-quite-an-apology without throwing up.

He rubbed a hand on the back of his neck. "I really appreciate that, Vic. More than you know. We've had some good times here, and I've missed that. I've missed it a lot."

"Then you'll stay?"

"Nope. Still leaving after today. It's time."

———

VIC RACED inside the open door of her house a few minutes after twelve-thirty, windblown and out of breath and wondering what on earth had happened to her front yard. Bikes and scooters and skateboards and balls and bats were strewn everywhere. Despite the lack of silk boxers, it looked as if she were hosting another yard sale.

The view from the front hall wasn't much better.

"Hello? Anyone here?"

Shaking her head when no one answered, she shut and locked the door. Passing through the kitchen, she noticed the smudges of chocolate on the counter, the flour dotting the cupboards, the—ew—oil spreading across the tile floor, and the patter of no-longer-so-small feet scurrying around the corner.

She tiptoed through the mess, careful to sidestep the worst of it and save her Ferragamos, and caught the tail end of Connor's baseball jersey as he started toward the dining room.

"Busted, mister."

"Aw, Mom." Connor's high-pitched protest floated up at her, and she squelched it as she drew him into a sticky hug. "We were just cleaning up."

Her eyebrows rose. "Where are Megan and Hope?"

"Uh, trying to hide?"

She rolled her eyes. She'd left three children to watch each other for the morning. And she now needed one of those children to act as a nanny for an entire month.

After a few moments, Hope appeared from wherever she'd been hiding, followed by Megan, both looking like Connor. A mess.

Vic called the three of them back to the scene of their crime, where she pointed at the floor. "What's going on? And someone left the front door wide open."

Hope frowned. "It's such a nice day, I thought we'd let some air in. We burned the first batch of brownies."

That explained the acrid stench and Vic's twitching nose. "We open windows for air and keep the doors shut and locked. This isn't Montana, Hope. Robberies happen. Even in this neighborhood."

Megan's eyes grew wide. "Bad guys?"

Vic held out her hand to Megan, who grasped it with sticky fingers. "We can keep them away if we lock the doors." She glanced at Hope. "All the time."

"Weird."

She bit her lip on a retort. She probably wouldn't have a nanny until August. She had a feeling she'd be reminding herself of that constantly in the coming weeks.

"Speaking of weird, I spoke to my nanny agency today. They don't have any nannies available until the end of July."

Hope stared blankly at her. "But you said your nanny was just gone this morning."

Unfortunately, no. "As it turns out, she'll be gone much longer than that."

Megan grabbed Vic's leg, leaving a large patch of brown goop on her pants. "When is Larissa coming back, Mommy? I miss her."

Vic ran a hand through Megan's hair. "I'm not sure, honey. I don't think she'll be coming back at all."

Megan wailed, Connor stomped out of the kitchen, and Hope continued to stare blankly.

Despite her huge misgivings, Vic turned to Hope. "If you're still looking for work, I was wondering if you'd mind filling in for her. As my nanny. Just until the end of the month."

"No way!" As Hope started to nod, Vic's head whirled in the direction of the angry shout. Connor charged back into the kitchen. "She's not a nanny, Mom." He glared at Hope, who took a step backward. "She's just some dumb *girl* you had when you were a teenager. You said I didn't have to meet her, or see her, or anything."

"Connor—"

He ran from the room, his footsteps soon thumping up the stairs. Megan sat cross-legged in the middle of the sticky mess on the floor, whimpering. Vic turned toward Hope, whose face had gone white.

"I'm sorry. I told the kids about you on Saturday, and this is still a bit of a shock for them."

"So they didn't want to meet me. Gee, thanks."

Vic pursed her lips. She needed to extract Megan from the mess and find a way to calm Connor. And she needed a nanny.

She started with Megan. "Sweetie, would you show Hope your bathroom? I need you to take a shower and get cleaned up."

Megan's lower lip curled. "Is she gonna be our nanny?"

"Just for a while." If she said yes.

Hope held out a hand to Megan, who didn't take it.

"Do we get to go to the pool and the park and stuff?"

Vic nodded. Remembering the junker parked at the curb, she turned to Hope. "Is that your car out front?"

She shook her head. "My roommate's. She let me borrow it this morning."

"Doesn't she need it?"

"Uh, yeah. By two."

Vic glanced at the clock, which now read twelve forty-five. "We'll take it back to her. Can you drive an SUV? It's an automatic." Her nanny agency would've checked Hope's driving record, a luxury Vic couldn't afford right now.

Hope's eyes grew wide, but she nodded. "I think so."

"Let's try it this afternoon." She turned again to Megan. "Would you let Hope supervise your shower? Please?"

The lip uncurled, and Megan shot to her feet, pranced from the room, and soon slammed a door. Unless that was Connor. Vic turned to Hope. "If you'll deal with her, I'll manage Connor."

A quick nod. As Vic's world spun on a shaky axis, she headed upstairs with Hope following. "We'll drop off your roommate's car, then get the kids' hair cut. They both look a little shaggy." Hope looked even more shaggy. "I'll call my hairdresser on the way to your place." She'd schedule an appointment for Hope along with ones for the kids.

Maybe she could do something for Hope after all.

CHAPTER 18

"Forget it. It's not going to work."

"It won't if you don't try."

Jake glared across the bar at Tess, who responded with an annoying twinkle in her eye. Next to her, Victoria's little sis, Natalie, sipped at a draft beer and watched him, pretty much the same way she'd watched him when she'd been in eighth grade and they'd been in eleventh. Like she knew something he didn't.

It wouldn't take much.

He slashed a hand through the air. "Like I told you. I took Victoria hiking, and now she's not talking to me."

Tess choked on her bottle of designer water, then turned to Natalie. "Wanna bet he's leaving out a few details?"

He refused to meet Natalie's curious gaze. Bottom line, Victoria's life didn't include him. Never really had, never would.

"Have you tried calling her Vic?" When Natalie finally spoke, he flinched. "Actually getting to know her and letting her down from that pedestal? She isn't the pedestal type."

Turning his back on the women, he made a martini for another customer at the bar and smiled as he pictured Victoria on a tall pedestal, wearing a slinky see-through nothing. He groaned softly to himself. "I've always called her Victoria."

Natalie kept watching him over the rim of her glass. "The only other person who calls her Victoria is our mother. Believe me, it hasn't helped her, either."

"That's different."

"Not from where I'm sitting. How long is it since you talked to Vic? A week?"

He nodded. "Last Thursday. But then she went to pick up her kids at camp."

"On Saturday."

"Yeah, and she's probably been busy with them ever since."

Tess shook her head. "With Hope as her new nanny, I would guess she's busier than she wants to think about."

Both women laughed, but Jake choked on his can of Coke. Hope was Victoria's—Vic's—nanny? Had the whole world gone crazy?

"If you want my advice, Jake—" He didn't, but Natalie spouted it anyway. "Take her hiking or bowling or whatever. Meet her kids, and give Vic some relief from Hope."

"Why don't you guys do that?"

Natalie looked sideways at Tess, while Tess did the same to Natalie. Laughing, Tess slapped the bar. "Because we don't look like you. And Vic knows the difference."

They didn't know a damn thing. "She doesn't want me."

"Get over it." Finishing her beer, Natalie touched a napkin to her lips. "And for God's sake, start calling her Vic."

———

"THIS IS STUPID."

Friday evening, when she'd rather be lounging in the back-yard with a margarita or even a glass of lemonade, Vic tried to keep Connor and Megan in sight and her temper in check. Hope stood in front of the three-paneled mirror in the maternity boutique, twisting in every direction while making faces and muttering under her breath. Or pretty loudly, actually.

"Pregnancy is no excuse to give up on how you look. You just have to work a little harder at it. Everyone does."

Hope tugged on the hem of the flowered top she'd grabbed after rejecting all of Vic's suggestions. "This does look pretty gross."

Vic held up a short-sleeved, stylish black top that would hide a multitude of sins. "Did you see this one?"

Hope's nose wrinkled. "In July? And isn't it too old?"

"There's nothing young or old about dressing well." God, she was starting to sound like her mother. "And it's lightweight. But they have yellow and blue ones, too."

She pointed at a rack of expensive clothing, relieved when Hope's face finally lit up. If Hope got excited enough, maybe she'd even let Vic burn her ragged T-shirts. They could roast marshmallows over the bonfire.

Hope glanced again at the butt-ugly flowered tent she was wearing. "This is more in line with my budget."

"Consider it an early baby gift."

Hope ran a hand through her hair, newly blond again and cut in a semi-sleek bob. So much like Vic's, it was startling. "But you already paid for my hair. And you're paying me to watch your kids, even though it seems like you watch them as much as I do."

More. But they'd have to work on that.

"Don't worry about the cost. If you have some nice things to wear, you'll feel better." So would Vic, which made it a win-win situation. "I guarantee it."

Taking a last glance in the mirror at the flowered fashion

crime, Hope chewed on her lip. "The clothes you picked out look more like you than me."

Okay, she couldn't exactly disagree with that.

"But they look good on you, right?" Unwilling to wait any longer for Hope to realize her good luck, let alone thank her for it, Vic handed her credit card to the hovering salesclerk and pointed to several outfits, a few pairs of shorts with coordinating summer tops, and even a swimsuit. "We'll take all of those."

After sending Hope to search for Connor and Megan, who hadn't responded to her last few shouts, Vic watched the salesclerk ring up her purchases and tried not to think about how much it was costing her to have a semi-presentable nanny.

Her cell phone rang, and she dug through a tangle of charge slips in her purse to find it. "Hello?"

"Vic?" She frowned as Ryder shouted over the blare of traffic. "I know I was supposed to take the kids this weekend, but I'm jammed up on a case and can't make it."

No. Not again. Seriously? "But you promised—"

"Explain to the kids, will you?"

She flinched as Ryder's cell phone went silent.

"Bastard." He'd moved on from generally ruining her life to specifically ruining her weekends. Including this one, when Sean wouldn't be covering the gallery, and she'd promised to go with Drew and Nat to Mother's house on Sunday. Without kids. Well, at least now she didn't have to visit Mother.

"Excuse me?" A line creased the center of the salesclerk's forehead, as if she'd never heard an off-color word before.

Tired of explaining her unkempt life to curious strangers, Vic dropped her phone back into her purse. She finished the purchase, picked up two stuffed bags, and headed into the mall to find her kids.

No, her kids and Hope. Her kids and their nanny, the frightful young woman Vic needed in her life right now.

She spied the trio coming out of a gardening store, of all places. Catching up to them, she sent Connor and Megan to look at the latest cool toys in the window of the gadget store.

Alone with Hope, she bit her lip and made herself speak the words before good sense intruded. "Ryder called, and there's a small favor I need to ask."

———

"You what?"

Vic ground her teeth, reminding herself that at least she'd escaped a face-to-face visit, despite her siblings' heated protests. Leaning back in her Adirondack chair in the backyard on Sunday afternoon, her feet propped on the wooden ottoman, she took another long drink of her fruit water before answering.

"You heard me, Mother. I needed Hope's help this weekend when Ryder cancelled at the last minute, and it's just easier this way."

For everyone. Hope didn't have a car, the bus routes between Vic's house and Hope's apartment were problematic, and Vic's ability to trust Hope with her SUV didn't extend to overnights or weekends.

Nodding to convince herself, she realized that her mother hadn't responded. "Mother?"

"I think you're being foolish. Letting a stranger take care of your children, and now letting a stranger move into your house. Have you asked for her references?"

She blew out a frustrated breath. "I checked them before I hired her as an intern." Much good that had done. "And she's hardly a stranger. The hospital in Kalispell said that Hope is my daughter, remember?"

"And I've told you repeatedly that she's not, but you won't believe me. Now she's found her way into your house."

"That's not how I phrased it." Vic glanced at the backyard playground, where Hope aimed a hose at a shrieking Connor as he slid down the slide and Megan squealed in delight. Happy and safe. "Hope is helping me out, and I'm letting her stay here. Just until the end of July."

"So she says."

"You've been reading too many mysteries again."

"I only wish I had more time to read." Her mother sighed, loudly, and Vic realized with a start that she probably had far too much time to read now, ever since Dad left. "Speaking of which, has your father talked to you?"

Vic frowned. He hadn't. "Why? Is he there?"

"No, dear. I was, er, hoping he'd talk to you. He promised he would." As Mother coughed, Vic's head spun. Dad must be talking to Mother. To everyone in the world but Vic. "Drew and Natalie tell me that you're seeing your young man again. Your friend from high school."

Traitors. "His name is Jake, but I'm not seeing him."

A pause. "I know his name, Victoria, but I just like to know what's happening in your life."

Fat chance.

"I worry about you, dear." As a slight sniffle reached Vic's ears, she frowned and held the phone closer. "I only want what's best for you. I want you to make good choices."

A stream of water from the hose landed perilously near Vic's bare feet. Smiling, she shook a fist at Megan. "I'm sure you do. It's just that we often disagree on the details."

"Not as much as you think."

The water splashed Vic's shorts, and she leaped to her feet. "I really need to go. The kids are trying to drench me."

"Tell them to be careful."

Rolling her eyes, Vic disconnected the call, then ran to the hose, snatching it out of Connor's hands and dousing both of them in the process. She grinned. Beside a dose of reality, maybe all Mother needed was a good blast with the hose.

IN THE MIDDLE OF JULY, with temperatures and the humidity index in the upper nineties, even Vic's usual customers stayed home. Just where Vic would rather be—except that she wasn't. She sat behind her desk on a sweltering Monday afternoon, wearing as little as she could without being arrested or turning away the few customers who wandered in, and fanned herself. Despite the air conditioning.

She was paying Hope good money to tote Connor and Megan to a pool every day while she bided her time here, alone in the gallery, where nothing seemed quite right without Sean. Ryder's lover. She repeated the phrase, trying to get angry so she wouldn't miss Sean. But she missed him.

She didn't miss Ryder, but the kids did. They'd been home from camp over a week now, while he stayed away, sending snotty demands through his divorce lawyer. Vic wondered why she'd bothered changing the locks.

And Jake? Missing in action. She told herself she liked it that way. The old boyfriend who crawls back under the rock. Knowing him, though, he hadn't actually crawled under a rock. He was probably busy playing kissy-face at someone else's rock.

So be it.

Besides, she needed to focus on finding a replacement for

Sean, interview nanny candidates later this week, then fix the rest of her imperfect life. One item at a time.

The phone rang, interrupting her musing. "Jasmine Gallery."

"How's my little girl?"

"Dad? Where are you?" He was no longer staying with Natalie, luckily for Nat, but she didn't think he'd moved back in with Mother. Vic had no idea where he might be.

"At work. Boy, it's hot today."

"In your office? Don't you have air conditioning?" His building was relatively new, unlike the old pile of bricks she rented space in, so he shouldn't have any complaints. At least, none she couldn't top.

"Sure. It just seems hot, though." No kidding. It was ninety-five degrees outside. He cleared his throat. "Have you heard anything more from the FBI?"

"Nothing." Over two weeks since their last slimy visit. "Maybe they dropped their case."

"We hoped that before, and they didn't, did they? Is Sean still there? Still working for you?"

"He quit." Because she'd been suspicious and hadn't appreciated him enough. Because she hadn't been able to handle the fact that he slept with her husband—which, really, was fairly understandable. "He's working at another gallery now, and no, I still don't think he had anything to do with the FBI investigation. If that's what it is."

She glanced out her half-open door, wishing Sean would magically appear.

"It's probably good that you didn't fire him, what with Ryder and all."

"No doubt." Even without a lawyer's input, she'd known the employment laws at stake. On top of everything else in her life, she didn't need a lawsuit.

"Anyway, I wanted to let you know where I was. I'm staying at our Minnetonka place. No one else is using it."

Oh, no. So much for sneaking a couple hundred people in for the reunion. "That's great." It wasn't, but it wasn't his fault. He and Mother owned the place, after all. "I'll bring the kids out sometime soon. If you don't mind driving the boat, it's been ages since I've waterskied."

"Sure. Sounds . . . wonderful."

He didn't sound thrilled. Without Mother there to put things in shape, or hire it done, the place must be a complete mess. "How are things with you and Mother? Are you talking?"

"Not much."

"May I ask why?"

"It's complicated." He sighed heavily. "It's been a long time coming. What she did in that, er, business with you in Montana was the last straw. Certainly not the first."

Vic thought of Hope and all the entanglements she'd caused this summer. But causing the breakup of her parents' marriage? It didn't make sense. "Hope is grown up now, Dad, and Mother did what she thought best."

He snorted. "Best for her."

"I have no idea about that, but it's ancient history." She resented Mother's interference, and quite a few other things, but wasn't that what analysts were for? "I can't help thinking there must be something else going on."

"Like . . . what?"

"I don't know." Maybe he'd had an affair. She cringed, unable to imagine it of Dad. "You tell me."

"I'm sorry I've said as much as I have." Which was nothing, basically. "The issues are between your mother and me. I really am sorry, Vic. I didn't mean to involve you."

"I'm not a child. And no offense, but I think you involved Nat when you took possession of her spare bedroom."

"Lumpy damn bed. You'd think she could afford a better one with all that money in her trust fund, like you—" He broke off suddenly, startling her. "Anyway, I just wanted to check in on my baby girl. Make sure you're okay."

"I'm fine. And I'm not your baby girl."

"Take care of yourself."

"Like always."

"That's what I'm worried about."

She laughed as she hung up. Same old Dad. New place of residence but otherwise unchanged. Just the way everything else in her life should be. And wasn't.

———

"BAD NEWS. We have to find a different place for the class reunion. Or else we'll have an unexpected guest." Wednesday evening after work, Vic sat in a booth in Pendulum and tried to pretend Jake didn't exist, let alone own the place. She still wondered why Nat had been so eager to babysit. In fact, she should've sent Nat here in her place.

Midge's pen clattered onto the table, and her eyes bulged behind her glasses. "The invitations are already out, and we have a lot of people coming. The reunion is two weeks from Saturday, Vic. It's too late to change."

Tess stuck her finger in her drink and swirled an ice cube in it. "Don't tell me. Ryder. And he's bringing Sean."

"Worse. My dad."

Midge sank down in the booth. "Is that a problem?"

Tess kept swirling the ice cube. "Not at all."

Vic frowned at her. "Yes, it is."

"Why?" Tess dipped her hand into her second basket of

popcorn, and they'd been here only ten minutes. "You're close to your dad. Ask him, and let him join the party."

"I can't do that. He's— He and my mother are separated. It's not a good time."

Midge was hyperventilating, and Tess patted her shoulder before turning back to Vic. "It's never a good time to spring a huge party on your parents, no matter how old you are."

"And you're pretty old." Jake slid into the booth next to Vic, as if everything was cozy between them. As if they were even speaking. "But in a good way."

Tess pointed a long, bright-red fingernail at Jake. "And you need to be nice. You might consider shameless flattery."

He shook his head. "I thought you had the lock on that."

"Only with the men in my life." She blew a kiss at Jed, who stood behind the bar waving back at her. "I meant that you should try it on Vic."

Vic shrank into her corner of the booth, wishing her first conversation with Jake in two weeks could occur without an audience. She also wished she could ignore the way Tess flirted so easily with him. She reminded herself that Tess was dating Jed.

"I don't think Vic is the shameless-flattery type." Jake twisted sideways, sizing her up. "Nope. She's not."

Her eyebrows rose. "You called me Vic."

He sipped his ever-present can of Coke and slid his arm over the back of their booth, just brushing her shoulders. "A guy can change, Victoria—I mean, Vic." He slammed a fist on the table. "Damn. I've been practicing 'Vic' for a week."

She laughed, feeling the knot of tension at the base of her neck start to dissolve. "Keep practicing."

"Yeah."

The weight of his arm rested more heavily on her now, and she resisted the sudden urge to snuggle against him. Barely.

Midge cleared her throat. "Jake, are you all set with the liquor? For the reunion?"

He nodded. "Despite Tess's help."

Tess flicked him with her fingernails.

Midge jotted something on her infernal notepad, then looked at Jake, her nose crinkling. "Vic doesn't think we can use her parents' place because her dad is staying there now." Hearing the words, Vic sucked in a breath, not happy to hang her family's dirty laundry in front of Jake's nose. "But Tess thinks she's just kidding. I mean, she has to be kidding, right?"

He nodded at her again. "She's kidding. Don't worry about it."

Bristling, Vic edged away from him. "Don't worry about it? Is there anything you *do* worry about?"

"Not much. If I can fix things, I do. When I can't, I don't lose sleep over them."

"Nice philosophy. It must save you a lot of trouble."

He frowned at her. "What do you mean? I don't see all your worrying about Hope doing you a damn bit of good. You fired her from your gallery, but now she's your nanny, isn't she? Staying with your kids in your house? While you go to work every day with your husband's boyfriend?"

As her mouth hung open, Vic saw a mental picture of all the gross underwear imaginable flapping in the breeze. She glanced at Midge, who looked at Tess, who looked amused.

"Sean isn't working for me anymore, and I needed a nanny on a temporary, emergency basis."

"And you're not speaking to Andrea."

Turning, she shoved Jake's arm off her shoulders. He yelped when his hand smacked against the edge of the table. Rubbing it, he stood up.

She offered him a tight smile. "If you want to avoid other sore subjects, you might not want to mention Andrea again."

"Oh, get over it, Vic."

Three heads whirled in Midge's direction.

She fiddled nervously with her glasses. "Well, it's true. Whatever Andrea did with Jake happened twenty years ago— while you were off having a baby." She nodded at Vic, whose jaw dropped. "All these secrets, and your troubles this summer, and I'm tired of hearing about it. You need to forgive Andrea." She bent her head. "Like I forgave you."

Vic felt a tear at the corner of her eye. "You did?"

A quick nod, followed by a soft whisper that forced Vic to lean forward in her seat to catch the words. "For the pills. For everything you did. That's what friends do."

For once in her life, Tess was speechless.

Jake eased back down into the booth, perching on the far edge of it and keeping his pseudo-injured hand away from Vic. "Listen to her, Vic. After all, Midge is the smartest person we know."

"Hey!"

He reached across the table to pat Tess's hand. "Don't worry. You're not even in second place, but Jed loves you."

This time, Midge slapped him, but then she grinned. "I've always wanted to do that."

He shook his head at her. "You have to quit hanging out with these two. You're starting to go downhill." He turned back to Vic, who eyed him warily. "So. Midge is fixing all your personal problems." He gave Midge a thumbs up. "And Hope solved your financial mess. Life is good, right?"

"What financial mess?"

He waved a hand. "You know. The FBI." He leaned close and whispered in her ear. "Your dad."

She froze. "What about my dad?"

"Uh, the trust account? The money he moved around?" He grimaced. "I thought she would've told you by now."

Her mind started churning along with her stomach. She shot a quick glance at Midge and Tess, who both looked equally puzzled. In an embarrassed daze, she replayed her recent conversations with Mother and Dad. Mother, who'd said that Dad had promised to talk to her. Dad, who'd chatted with her the same as always, or at least mostly. Hadn't he?

Grabbing her purse, she prodded Jake to let her out of the booth. "I have no idea what you're talking about, or how you and Hope are mixed up in this when I never asked for your help, but I'm going to find out."

"Wait, Vic. I can explain."

She turned back to him on her way out the door. "And you've known whatever this is for how long? Don't bother. It's too late now."

———

"You're home early." Natalie looked up from the book she was reading on the bottom of the stairs. Her hair was in tangles, and something that looked like blood or ketchup smeared the front of her T-shirt. "Did you have fun?"

"Not much." Vic dropped her purse in the middle of the front hall, cringing when she heard something break. "You look like someone scalped you. We should've traded."

Nat touched her hair and winced. "They're under house arrest at the moment." She jabbed her thumb toward upstairs. "Watching a movie."

"Tough cop."

"It's a gift." Pushing herself to a standing position, Nat stretched her arms over her head and yawned. "What brings you home early?"

Vic looked around the messy first floor. "Where's Hope?"

"Out. A girl picked her up. I think it might've been her

roommate." Nat wandered beside Vic into the kitchen, where an open bottle of ketchup lay in the middle of the floor. "What's the matter, Vic? Is something wrong?"

Other than the house? She rolled her eyes, trying to summon her normal urge to clean up the mess. "Jake and I—"

Nat grabbed her arm. "Yes?"

She jerked her arm away. "We got into a fight. About a lot of things. And I had to talk to you right away."

"Me? Why?"

Vic shook her head. "I was so surprised, not to mention pissed, I didn't stay long enough to find out what he was talking about. But Jake said that Hope found out something about Dad. And our trust accounts. He thinks it's the answer to the question the FBI is asking."

"The FBI?"

"Sorry." She stared at the ketchup bottle, surrounded by red ooze, before gingerly picking it up and setting it in the sink. She grabbed a wad of paper towels and took a swipe at the glob on the floor. "The FBI has visited the gallery a couple of times, and Dad was checking into it for me. Or so he said." Couldn't she believe anyone anymore? Not even her dad? "Jake seems to think that they're actually after Dad."

Nat went to the refrigerator, relieving it of an old, half-empty bottle of white wine. "That doesn't make sense. How would Jake know, anyway? Or Hope?"

"I don't know. I don't understand it at all. Is anything funny going on with your trust? Dad started to mention it the other day, in passing, but he cut himself off." After a final swipe, Vic straightened, then tossed the paper towel at the wastebasket, missing it by a foot. So much for cleaning up. "I don't get it."

"As beneficiaries, we don't usually see the trust statements. The bank sends them to Dad as trustee."

"Then I really can't imagine how Jake and Hope think they know something."

Nat frowned. "I did get one or two trust statements earlier this summer, after a different banker got assigned to the trusts. I think he goofed up." She poured a glass of wine, not bothering to offer Vic any. "Anyway, I read them. No activity in the account except for some interest."

"I haven't used my trust account in ages, either."

"Then there's no problem." Nat swirled the wine in her glass, then peered closely at it and extracted a sliver of cork. "Talk to Dad."

Vic eyed her sister's glass, wondering how long she had to avoid alcohol. The issues with Jake and Hope and Dad, whatever they were, would usually call for a soothing glass of wine. But . . . no. "I will. First thing tomorrow, after I figure out what I should ask."

CHAPTER 19

The early-morning smell of the lake, fifty yards behind him, wafted into Jake's nostrils as he stood on Victoria's front step and waited for someone to open the damn door.

He rang the bell again and started to feel stupid. Maybe they heard the doorbell, peeked through a window, and opted not to open the door to the crazy guy in the musty fishing vest. Except they couldn't smell him from behind closed windows.

Hearing the click of the lock, he took a step backward. And another one when Hope answered the door, wearing a pup tent masquerading as a Disney T-shirt.

"Jake?" Yawning, she looked past him to his truck, then up and down the parkway. "Is Vic expecting you?"

"Is she here? I mean, is she up?" When Hope frowned and didn't invite him inside, it finally occurred to him that showing up at Victoria's house at seven a.m. wasn't one of his smartest ideas. Or one of Tess's, damn her anyway. "Can I come in?"

"Uh—" As the sound of movement filtered outside, Hope looked over her shoulder and stepped to one side.

"Jake? Why are you here?" Victoria gripped the lapel of her thin robe with one hand as her other hand tried to squelch an unruly tangle in her hair. On her, tangled looked good.

He mustered a feeble grin. "I'm here to pick you up. We're already a couple hours late." When she squinted at him, he talked faster, tripping over his words. "It's better if you go early, before the fish know what hit 'em."

"Are you nuts? It's seven in the morning. On a Thursday." One of Victoria's hands waved wildly in the air, punctuating her sentences with exclamation marks, until she glanced down and saw her robe gapping. She yanked it back together and held on tight. "We were all in bed, Jake. Sleeping. And I have to be at work in two hours."

Two sleep-tousled blond heads appeared behind Vic. The older one, the boy, spoke. "Mom? Who's this guy?"

"An old friend. It's okay." Victoria tried to shoo them away. No one budged.

Despite the audience and his own instincts for self-preservation, Jake kept talking. "You don't have to work this morning. Besides, the smart fishermen go out midweek, when the amateurs aren't hogging the good fishing spots."

"The amateurs must be the ones who actually hold jobs."

At Victoria's less-than-enchanted look, all the lines Tess had suggested flew right out of his brain and into the pit of his stomach. He wished he hadn't left his cell phone in the truck. He'd dial Tess right now and hand the damn phone to Victoria.

"I have a gallery, Jake. And no employees." She glanced sideways at Hope and bit her lip. "I can't help it if your working hours are much later than mine."

"That's not what I meant. I found you an employee." At the stunned look on Victoria's face, he considered dropping to his knees and begging. "Tess offered to handle your gallery for the day. She said she owes you."

"That's what I get for leaving the bar early? Moronic little schemes cooked up by you and Tess?"

He shrugged. "Midge helped."

She glanced down again at the front of her robe, then stepped outside and shut the door behind her. Hope and the two kids pressed against the windows on either side of the door, and she waved them away. When she turned back to Jake, the three faces returned to the glass.

Victoria clutched her robe even more tightly before plunking down on the top step. When he dropped down next to her, she sighed. "What are you doing here, Jake?"

"I'm not really sure." He stared at his hands and wondered whether he should just leave. "Trying to get you to like me?"

"By asking me to go fishing?" She rolled her eyes. "I'm not quite sure which is lower on my hit parade at the moment—you or the concept of fishing."

"Have you ever gone fishing?"

She stared out at the lake. "It's not one of my life goals, sorry. I *did* try hiking with you."

"And refused to speak to me afterward."

"But not because of the hiking." After a moment's thought, she shook her head. "If you hope to get back together by showing me your world and not spending time in mine, this isn't going to work. Tess keeps dragging me to Pendulum, and you want me to go fishing."

He watched the slow procession of cars driving past, even at this hour, probably on their way to work. "You're right. We're in two different worlds. But the more I see of yours, the more I appreciate mine."

Her cute little nose scrunched up. "Oh?"

"I fish or hike to relax. You don't relax, period." He leaned back, bracing his weight on his arms. "My point is, you need to stop and breathe, chill out once in a while. Your current life landed you in the hospital."

"And yours landed you in a bar." She drew in a sharp breath as her jab hit his gut. "I'm sorry. Honestly. But I keep getting advice on how to fix my life from you, from Tess—even from Midge last night—and I'm tired of it."

Remembering, he absently rubbed his gut. "Next thing you know, you'll be getting it from Hope."

She frowned. "She wants to fix my problems by pointing a finger at my dad. As if."

He paused, not wanting to go there but knowing he had to. "I think she's right. She said you asked her to look through her files and computer."

"*What?*"

"I know. At least, I'm starting to." Closing his eyes, he heard her teeth grinding. "The day you went to pick up your kids at camp. She had the keys to the gallery, and she seemed to know what she was doing, so I went along with it." He looked sideways at her, feeling way beyond stupid. "Bad move, huh?"

"Not your wisest."

"We went through everything, and it all seemed fine."

"I know. I'd already looked at it. Several times."

"But then I found a couple of bank statements that weren't for your gallery. They were for your trust account."

Her back stiffened, and she started to get up. With a hand on her thigh, he pressed her back down again.

"As soon as I saw what they were, I put them back in the drawer and told Hope they were personal."

Her eyebrows rose, but she stayed where she was. "Kind of like setting candy in front of my kids and telling them not to eat it."

"Or waving a bottle of my best scotch in front of Tess." He grinned. "At least until she met Jed. Her bar tab isn't quite so heavy these days."

She lifted one eyebrow.

"Anyway, Hope looked at the statements. Someone made a

lot of deposits into the account a few months ago, then with-drew the money. The statements say your dad is the trustee."

Victoria frowned. "It sounds like another mistake by the bank. Nat told me that a new banker was handling our trust accounts, and he shouldn't have even sent us the bank state-ments. Maybe he goofed this up, too, and then fixed it."

"Or maybe your dad did something wrong."

She wrapped her arms around her legs and rocked back and forth on the steps. "I can't believe it." She suddenly stopped rocking. "Why is Hope doing this? Hasn't she done enough?"

"Vic—" He reached for her.

She pushed his hand away. "I mean, I don't even know her. She somehow got her hands on the keys to my gallery and talked you into sneaking in there with her."

"Does she also hate your dad?"

She shook her head. "I haven't figured that part out. The one thing I know is that my dad couldn't possibly have done anything wrong."

"Just like that?"

"He loves me." She gazed at the lake, caught in a dream world he didn't dare enter, and trembled slightly. "I mean, he'd do anything for me."

"Even take you fishing?"

Getting up, she waved at him to follow her into the house. "Come on in. You might as well meet Connor and Megan. Maybe you can talk *them* into going fishing."

"With their mom?"

"Not in a million years."

SHE'D SURVIVED the introduction of her kids to her high-school boyfriend, in the presence of the young woman supposedly conceived with her high-school boyfriend, so the day had to be looking up.

Vic only wished it felt that way.

Connor and Megan stared at Jake—Connor with undisguised hostility, Megan with her finger in her mouth as if she were four years old again. Jake, wearing that ratty old vest, stuffed his hands in his pockets and stared right back at them.

Hope went upstairs, presumably to change into something less dreadful. Vic shook her head, thinking of the pile of clothes she'd bought last week, which hadn't included pajamas. It didn't matter. Hope didn't seem to be wearing any of the new clothes.

"Connor? Megan? Jake wants to know if you two would like to go fishing."

Connor eyed Jake's fishing vest. "With him?"

"That was the general idea." Hers, at least.

"But we don't know him." Connor took a step away from Jake, as if he were contagious. "Who's this guy, Mom?"

Vic groaned, even though embarrassment had long since left the building. "I told you. Jake is an old friend from high school."

"Like a boyfriend?"

"A long time ago." She shot a quick look at Jake. His lips twitched, but he didn't say a word. Smart man. "But we're just friends now. He likes to go fishing, and I thought you might want to try it."

Jake shrugged. "If *you* don't want to try fishing, maybe your kids don't, either." He glanced up when Hope returned, wearing her usual baggy shorts and faded T-shirt. "Or maybe they want Hope to come along."

Hope practically bounced. "Really? That'd be—"

"I actually wanted to talk to Hope, alone, while you took the kids fishing." She looked keenly at Jake, who finally nodded his understanding, then turned back to the kids. "But if you don't want to go, just say so."

"Wanna go, Megan?" Connor whispered something in her ear. It prompted a puzzled frown followed by a vehement nod. "Yeah, we'll go. But we get to come back whenever we say."

Vic blinked, feeling oddly relieved. "If not sooner."

Ten minutes later, loaded down with snacks for a week and slathered with sunscreen, the kids pranced outside with Jake. Vic heard Connor's whoop when he spied Jake's truck.

Amused, she turned around—and bumped into Hope, planted in the middle of the hall, her lower lip jutting out.

"He's my dad, not theirs."

"As you keep telling me." Vic moved past Hope and into the kitchen. "But I hear you've already enjoyed some quality time with your new dad. At my gallery."

Hope followed her as she moved around the kitchen, methodically pulling out bowls, glasses, cereal, bananas, raspberries, and juice.

"Hope? Aren't you going to say anything?" She stopped in the middle of pouring Cheerios into her bowl. "I'm talking about you sneaking into the gallery with Jake the day I drove up to Bemidji. You forgot to mention that small detail."

Hope reached for the marshmallow Froot Loops. "I just wanted to help. When it looked like your dad was the one doing weird stuff, I knew you wouldn't like it. Then I started working here, and living here, and trying to get to know you better, and I didn't want to make you mad."

"How did you get keys?" Vic closed her eyes in the middle of slicing a banana, opening them when she realized she didn't need to lose a thumb. "I never gave you a set."

"I'm, uh, good at stuff like that."

She held up her hand, the knife still in it. "I don't think I want to know, at least not right this moment. But I need the keys returned, and I need to understand what you think you were trying to accomplish."

Head down, Hope shuffled to the refrigerator and grabbed a gallon of milk, then returned to the table and slopped it onto her cereal. "I was sure that Sean had been screwing around with your financials, and I wanted to catch him."

"Because?"

"To help you?" Her mouth already half full, she waved a heaping spoonful of cereal in the air. "I mean, he was screwing around with your husband. I hated that."

So did Vic. "It didn't concern you."

"Yeah, it did." Glancing up from her overflowing cereal bowl, Hope's eyes looked bleak. "I wanted you to like me. I wanted you to be my mom."

"Seriously?" Vic looked across the table at the young woman so unlike her. Except for the blond hair and blue eyes, they had nothing in common. "But you never do what I ask. You don't even wear any of the clothes I bought you, but you didn't tell me not to buy them."

As she realized what she'd just said, her breath caught. It sounded like Vic and her own mother, all over again.

Hope just kept shoveling cereal in her mouth.

"Don't you like the clothes?"

"I tried, Vic, really. You paid for my haircut, which looks like yours, and all those new clothes, which look like something you'd wear. And I wanted to be like you."

All evidence to the contrary. "But?"

Hope's spoon clunked into her bowl. "I couldn't do it. I mean, I want you to like me, and keep me in your life, but it has to be *me* you're keeping, not a clone of you."

The cereal tasted dry in Vic's mouth, and she stopped

trying to force it down her throat. A long swig of juice didn't help.

She pushed the bowl away. "So you don't want to be like me?"

"Um, no. I just wanted you to like me." Hope dropped her gaze to her lap. "Maybe even love me someday, the way you love your other kids. But moms should love their kids no matter what. Unconditionally."

Vic sat back in her chair, dazed. It was true, but this was also Hope.

After a long moment she got up, collected her dishes, and set them in the sink. Love Hope? She was still working on tolerating her.

———

AN HOUR LATER, Vic sat cross-legged on the floor of her office trying to make sense of the trust statements she found in her file cabinet. Thousands of dollars poured into the account, thousands out. And she hadn't touched a penny in years.

With her temples throbbing, she rose to her knees and fumbled in the top drawer of her desk for the Tylenol bottle.

She found it just as Dad walked into her office.

"Dad?" Startled, she tumbled backwards, her knees and ankles twisting beneath her, and yelped in agony.

He came rushing forward as pain spurted through her right ankle and she scrambled to stuff the bank statements underneath her. Dad grabbed her arm, pulling her upward, until she held up a hand to stop him.

"No. Thanks." She blew out a breath, wincing against the sharp pain. "I can take care of it myself."

Her ankle. Her FBI troubles. Dad.

"I can help you, Vic." His grip tightened on her arm as they pulled against each other. "That's what I'm here for."

"Oh?" Reaching under her butt, she grabbed the bank statements and waved them in his face. "Like you helped with my trust account?"

Letting go of her arm, he stumbled backward.

She tried to stand on her throbbing ankle but collapsed on the floor. Letting go of the bank statements, she watched Dad bend down and snatch them off the carpeting.

"Too late, Dad. I've already studied them in detail. I just don't understand."

He sagged to the floor, joining her. "I hoped I could fix everything before you found out. I'm sorry, hon." He reached for her hand, and she scooted away, bumping up against the file cabinet. "I love you."

She crossed her arms. "I want to know why you did it."

Whatever it was he'd done.

Her lower lip trembled, and she bent her knees, crossing her arms on top of them to hide her unforgivable weakness.

"What exactly do you know?"

Good question. She knew her whole world was turned on end. It was beyond surreal, but she realized that Hope and Jake, of all people, had been the ones to help her discover the truth about her family. And somewhere deep inside where it hurt far worse than any sprained ankle, she knew she trusted their word over Dad's.

She buried her exploding head in her arms. Her mistakes of twenty years ago versus the man she'd loved all her life. Dad. Her knight in shining armor. Watching him shake as he stuffed the bank statements back into the envelope, she bit her lip. "I don't know anything anymore. Why don't you clue me in?"

"It's a long story."

"With a happy ending?"

Shaking his head, he avoided her gaze. "The answer to that question is up to a lot of people, including you. The FBI and my old firm and some clients. And your mother."

"Mother? I thought you two were splitting up."

"I wanted to protect her." His knees creaked as he stood up, then helped her to her feet. When she sank into her chair, he paced the close confines of her office. "She tried to fix it for me, but I couldn't let her. Not again." He ran a hand over his face. "It's been the story of our life."

Vic blinked, understanding less with every word he spoke.

He gazed out the open door to her office, his hands clasped behind his back. "Your mother's father had wealth beyond anything you or I could imagine."

"So?" She thought back to her grandfather, who'd chatted easily with politicians and stuffy old rich guys but sat silently with his grandkids. Probably wishing they'd play with him but not knowing how to ask. "It didn't make him a happy man."

"It depends on your point of view." He kept talking over Vic's protests. "He set up all those trusts for his children and grandchildren. Patrice's trust meant she'd never be dependent on the poor, scrounging louse she had to marry."

"You? A senior partner in the biggest law firm in town?"

His answering smile was unbearably sad. "Not when I married your mother. Her dad figured I'd never make as much money as he did. I did pretty well, but I never found his success."

Vic frowned. "You found your own, and you made a lot of money. At some point, does it even matter?"

"More than it should." He stopped pacing and returned to her desk, propping on the edge of it. "Over the years, I started playing the market, trying to match your grandfather's gains. Your mother always kept a close eye on our bank accounts, though, so I sometimes had to be a little creative."

Sensing where this was going, Vic closed her eyes.

"You're right. Creativity belongs in the art world, not in law or finance. But it worked, at least until I hit sixty-five and they forced my retirement."

"You didn't have to leave the firm, Dad."

"No, but I would've moved to a smaller office and basically been treated not much better than an associate, if that." Crossing one foot over his other knee, he fingered the laces on his wingtips. "I know. Foolish, macho nonsense. Just what your mother said."

"But it doesn't explain why you moved all that money."

"I, er, borrowed money from client trust accounts over the years, using it for my investments. I always paid it back but needed a place to park my excess cash. Your mother would've noticed." He looked pointedly at Vic. "She doesn't share the loosey-goosey attitude about money that you and Ryder have."

She flinched. She and Ryder were loosey-goosey? Dad gave new meaning to the phrase.

"When I left the firm, I had to move the money. My first thought, unfortunately, was to move it into your trust account. Patrice would've been suspicious if I'd moved it into one of our accounts."

Vic finally popped the top on the Tylenol bottle and swallowed two tablets with a swish of water. "But Nat said that nothing happened to her account."

"No." He pressed the heel of his hand to his forehead. "I needed to open a new account, one your mother didn't know about, but I needed to move the money faster than that and couldn't send more than ten thousand dollars at a time."

Her eyebrows rose. "Or the FBI would notice?"

"I knew it was a possibility, and I didn't want to get Nat or Drew in trouble with their licensing boards." He waved a hand the moment Vic's mouth flew open. "I planned to fix it, honey,

I swear. Like I said, it really was my money." If so, it certainly took a circuitous route. "When I moved the money into my new account, I left a little extra in your trust, you know, as a sort of compensation."

She felt her face flush, and her hands balled up into fists. She wanted to hit something.

Hard.

Uncurling her fist, she slapped her desk. "I've still got tainted money in my account? No wonder the FBI is after me. How could you? Why me?"

He came around the edge of her desk, approaching her, but the look on her face warned him off. "I never meant to get you in trouble, Vic. I knew I could count on you to handle it."

Even though she hadn't. Even though she'd gone running to Dad, the person who'd put her in this fix in the first place.

"I don't want to handle your problems, Dad, and I don't want any of your money. Not a penny." She pushed back from her desk, then stood up on her painful ankle and pointed at the door. "You're in this all by yourself."

"Not exactly." The somber faces of the two men from the FBI appeared from around the corner, and one man stepped forward with handcuffs. "Warren Carlyle, you're under arrest."

———

THURSDAY AFTERNOON, home after closing the gallery early for the fourth or fifth time this summer, Vic answered the doorbell in spite of her misgivings. Nothing good had come of unexpected visitors all day. Since the kids had actually loved their impromptu fishing trip this morning, she considered Jake's visit a draw.

"Drew?"

"Hey, Vic. Yeah, I heard." He stepped inside, in a sportcoat and tie and probably on his way home from work. "Dad called, but not before Mom. And if you ask me, Mom's right."

"Is it true? She's refusing to make bail for Dad?"

He nodded. "Serves him right. Did he even ask you?"

"He couldn't say much as they led him away." He also hadn't called her since. "But if Mother won't help him, I will."

Despite everything he'd done.

"No." Drew stopped her when she reached for her purse and keys. "Mom knows him better than you do." He grabbed her keys and stuffed them in his pocket. "Yeah, I know. You've always been so sure that Mom doesn't know much or do anything right."

"Give me back my keys. And I never said that about Mother." Not in so many words. Or not to Drew, at least.

"Uh-huh. Well, Dad's in a mess, and Mom offered to help fix it, and he refused."

"So?"

"So they need to work this out. If Dad needs a lawyer, you or I can't help him, and Nat knows better than to represent her own father." Drew pulled her keys out of his pocket and set them on the front-hall chest. "You can have your keys, but don't help Dad. Mom needs to be allowed to handle this her way."

Vic's nose wrinkled. "But Nat said that she refuses to help him."

He laughed, even though nothing about this was even remotely funny. "She's just letting him stew for a while, maybe overnight at the most."

"Overnight? In jail?"

"He's so stubborn, it'll probably take him that long to admit that Mom's right." Drew walked past her into the kitchen, grabbed a can of root beer out of the refrigerator, and popped the top. "Marriage isn't easy, Vic, as you well know."

He guzzled the soda, his Adam's apple bobbing, then wiped his mouth on the back of his hand. She bit her tongue to keep from blurting out anything about Babs. Her tongue started to ache.

Drew caught her eye. "I know. I married Babs, and no one can figure out why. Sometimes I can't, either."

"I didn't say anything."

"Everyone does." He shrugged. "All I can say is, you have to be inside a marriage to have a shot at understanding it. Like Mom and Dad's marriage. Like mine."

She thought of Ryder and his homosexuality that still confused her. "Or mine. But *no* one understands that one."

"No comment." Drew chucked her under the chin. "Anyway, Mom knows Dad much better than you think. Seriously, let her handle it." He lifted his eyebrows. "Or next time I'll take the keys to your Boxster, and you'll never see it again."

"Good luck with that." She crossed her arms, not willing to agree with his analysis—or ready to lose her convertible. "If you do, you and Dad can spend some quality time together. In jail."

———

RYDER TOWELED off after a quick shower Friday evening at Sean's apartment, still trying to decide whether to go with him to a party or go home. The same debate he'd had with himself for weeks now. Despite the divorce. Despite the battles he and his divorce lawyer were waging with Vic, for reasons he didn't much understand.

Sean lay on the bed, naked and flat-out gorgeous, watching him. Not with real or even faked appreciation, whichever it had been, but with something Ryder had never seen in Vic's eyes. Contempt. He sighed, girding himself for battle.

"Are you getting dressed for the party? We don't have to be there for another hour." Sean patted the bed. "Play with me."

Ryder buttoned his shirt. "I can't play all the time."

"You play about ten minutes a day."

Ten minutes out of every fifteen was more like it.

"Not true. Anyway, I can't help it right now. Besides all my work, I do have a family." A family that needed him now more than ever. The law firm had buzzed all day with the news of Warren's arrest yesterday, along with rumors of Warren's shenanigans with client money, which couldn't possibly be true. Vic hadn't called, probably out of embarrassment, but he knew she'd want him there. Helping her through it.

"You haven't seen your kids in weeks, not since they left for camp in the middle of June. Am I right?"

Not exactly. "I've seen them."

Playing in Kenwood Park, riding their bikes around Lake of the Isles, eating ice cream cones at Sebastian Joe's. He felt like a stalker, but he'd watched them quite a few times since they'd gotten back from camp. Always from a distance.

Something else he didn't understand.

Lying on his side, Sean ran his hand down the length of his thigh. "Admit it. You don't know what to do with them, and they're doing okay without you." He ran his tongue over his lips. "So come. Play. I can make you feel better."

Ryder tensed. Wanting Sean, wanting his kids. At some level, although probably not a sexual one, wanting Vic.

The kids and Vic won. For once. "I have to go see Vic." Quickly, before his resolve dissipated like the early-morning mist on Lake of the Isles.

Sean's lower lip thrust out. "You know about Vic's baby, don't you?"

Baby? "She's pregnant? I don't think so." They hadn't had sex, not even lousy sex, in longer than he could remember. And Vic wasn't running around with someone. She wouldn't.

"Hope."

"Hope?" Ryder shook his head. Sean must be talking about Vic's summer intern, who'd lasted only a few weeks, and who was pregnant. Whatever. Sean had been angry at Vic before quitting the gallery, and that hadn't stopped. He was finally losing it.

"Hope is her kid. Vic's kid." Sean smirked. "Didn't she tell you?"

"Vic has been pregnant twice. Connor and Megan. Period."

"Sorry. Three times. That I know of."

"She would've told me." Like she'd told him about all her high school friends, including the one who died long before he'd ever met her. Her college professors. Her dance classes. Her first bike and first car. Her—

Appendectomy scar?

Sean slid him a knowing grin that wasn't even remotely sexy. "Is that who you're running home to? The woman who's divorcing you? The mother of three kids?"

"Whose kid is she?"

"My guess is Jake. A big, strapping, hottie of a guy, from what I hear. Owns Pendulum. Maybe she's been seeing him all these years."

"No." But he'd cheated on her for months and been tempted for years before that, and she'd never known. Was Vic someone he didn't know? Did that make her more . . . enticing?

Damn. If he was going to have a midlife crisis, he wished to hell he'd at least decide which gender to have it with.

"I just thought you should know. For your sake."

It didn't hurt Sean's prospects, either, to keep Ryder

around. He could keep tabs on Vic without using his sources in the art world and, unless Ryder missed his guess, without sucking up the nerve to ask for his old job back. It also kept him satisfied, with pocket change and trinkets to spare.

Ryder glanced around the bedroom, noting the new sheets, the new clothes scattered everywhere. A mess. An expensive mess. It wasn't time to go home. It was long past time.

He zipped up his pants, slipped on his loafers, and headed out the door.

CHAPTER 20

A s he stood on the front steps of Victoria's mansion, alternately knocking on the door and ringing the bell, Jake wondered why the hell he wasn't at Pendulum. Where he was supposed to be. Where he'd been almost every Friday night since he could remember.

It probably said something about his social life, sure, but the restaurant meant everything to him. He'd taken a broken-down saloon that mostly served potato chips for food and turned it into, well, Pendulum. His life's dream. In addition to Victoria. Vic.

He glanced up to see her peeking at him through a crack in the upstairs blinds. A minute or two later, she opened the door.

"No, I didn't come here to take your kids fishing." He held up both hands. Empty. "And I didn't bring you a damn gift. No Slinky, no Dilly bar, not even a newspaper."

She lifted one eyebrow. "I have plenty of newspapers."

"I figured."

"So what brings you here?" She smiled, sweetly, like the seventeen-year-old girl she'd been. "Was Andrea busy?"

"Funny. Can I come in?"

"Why?" She crossed her arms and stood on the threshold,

looking like a bouncer. No one was getting past her. "I've had a lousy week, and you didn't exactly help." Except for babysitting her kids in a wobbly boat they kept trying to tip. "And I'm a little preoccupied."

He ran a hand through his hair. "We need to talk, Vic. About Andrea. No one told you why I went out with her. Or a damn thing about it."

"Including you."

"I was pissed."

"Last Wednesday night, so was I. Livid. But I've gotten over it." She smiled again and didn't look one bit closer to letting him in the door.

"Are we going to have this conversation here?" His arm swept to one side, taking in the front lawn and her snooty Kenwood neighborhood. "In front of God and everybody?"

"Why not? That's probably who knows about you and Andrea, isn't it? God and everybody?"

"No." He looked down at the toe of his sneaker as he scraped it on the porch. "Hardly anyone does."

"Midge knew."

"From what I can see, Midge knows a lot more than she lets on. It's probably why she did so well in school." He jammed his hands into the pockets of his jeans, wishing he could click a remote and fast-forward through this conversation. "Listen. Yeah, I dated Andrea for a few weeks. After you left without saying goodbye."

"I said goodbye. I wrote you a letter."

The damned letter. "I told you I didn't read it."

"How convenient. That way you could date Andrea. Oh, wait. Did you say date or did you mean fuck?"

He took a step toward her, needing to make her understand how it'd been. He'd been seventeen. A guy. Not a saint.

"I never forgot you. In fact, that's why I went out with her."

From the look in Victoria's eyes, this wasn't helping, but he had to explain, even if it meant losing her again. "I needed to talk about you. Hear about you." He wondered how he could've acted like such a jerk with Andrea, even while he slept with her. "I wanted to be with you."

"And she was the next best thing."

"Yeah. I mean—"

"I think I've heard enough." She took a step backward and started to close the door. "Thanks, Jake. It's been a banner week, and I think you just made it perfect."

His hand caught the door a moment before she slammed it in his face. "Stop. Victoria. Vic."

They struggled with the door, his shoulder pressing on it, and inch by inch the opening widened.

"You were gone. Yeah, I fucked up." He winced as her bare foot connected with his shin. "But I loved you, Vic."

"Ancient history. Right now, I don't know if we can even be friends." She bit down on her lip as they both kept pushing. "If you want to be my friend, act like one. Not like some boy I used to date, a boy who put me on a stupid pedestal. I hated that."

As he froze, speechless, Vic stopped pushing against the door and flung it open. He tumbled inside, landing on the floor.

He scrambled to his feet before she could kick him again. "Where are your kids?"

"Hope isn't here, and the other two are at a neighbor's house." She walked to the kitchen, inviting him to follow, and he tripped after her. "They already ate dinner, so I don't know when they'll be back."

"But you can't go out."

She shook her head. "Not even if I wanted to."

"Please." He held up a hand. "You've made your point. I'm

the scum of the earth, and you're still residing high on that pedestal, all protests to the contrary."

Her hands went to her hips. "What is that supposed to mean?"

"Figure it out, college girl. Smith or Barnard, even."

"Vassar." She reached into the fridge and pulled out a bottle of Diet Coke. "Can I get you anything? A beer? Or did you prefer a keg?"

"Funny." Her sense of humor was older, edgier, and kept biting him. Not at all like high school, when she'd been the sweetest thing he'd ever known. He mostly preferred the way she'd been, but she did provoke him. Provocative was good. "I'll take a Coke if you have one."

She rummaged around and pulled out a can of Coke, setting it on the counter for him to retrieve. They spent five minutes that felt like a slow, painful hour sitting in silence at the kitchen table, drinking their sodas. She didn't even turn on the radio, which might've cut the tension. Probably her point.

"I guess I'd better be going." He looked at her long and hard, wondering whether this was worth it. Wondering what the hell he was trying to do. Catch her? The seventeen-year-old girl he'd known or the thirty-eight-year-old woman who was an angry, elusive mystery to him?

Maybe some of both.

He stood up, and she didn't stop him. She walked him to the front door, then waited while he tried to figure out what he wanted to say. If he had anything left to say.

He put a tentative hand on her wrist. "Vic, I want to—"

He inched closer to her, giving her time to say no. When she turned her head to one side, he settled for a kiss on her cheek. He wanted more. He wanted a woman who seemed unattainable. In some ways, nothing really *had* changed since high school.

She broke his grip and took a step backward. Put a hand to her cheek. Stared at his lips.

"I'm not sure what you want, Jake, but I can't seem to get past what happened with Andrea. And everything else." Gazing at her feet, she licked her lips. "Despite Midge's good advice."

"If I can get past Hope, why can't you get past Andrea? We've both dated since high school. Hell. You got married. You had two more kids."

"That's different." She crossed her arms, sending any arguments he might've made right down the toilet.

"Because it was you." He glanced out at his truck. Shiny and new. "You always say I live in the past, but you're the one who won't let go of it. If I'm willing to try, as adults, right now—" He paused, ready to beg if necessary. "Won't you at least think about it?"

She stared at him and didn't say anything.

He took a step closer. Leaned in, aiming for her lips. Watched her eyes all the way, hoping every instant that she didn't turn her cheek again.

She didn't. He pressed a soft kiss on her lips, barely tasting them, stopping before he forgot himself and took it too fast. He'd done fast before—twice now—and it had cost him far too much time with this woman.

She leaned forward and kissed him back. Tentatively, as if one of them might break. He kept his hands at his sides, not making any grabs for her, trying to keep from doing some dumbass thing that would send her packing again.

"Well, isn't this sweet?"

At the stranger's words, Jake flew backward, away from Vic, and almost collided with the guy. Not too tall, glasses, black hair. Khaki suit, pink shirt, and bowtie. Probably gay. Probably Vic's husband.

Flushing a bright pink, Vic ran a hand through her hair, and her voice trembled slightly before correcting itself. "Ryder. I—" She pointed at Jake, who thrust out his hand. "This is Jake. Jake Trevor. He's a friend of mine."

Vic's husband took Jake's hand in a firm grip. "That's what I hear. And the father of Vic's other kid." He glanced at Vic as she leaned against the door frame, looking sick. "Hope, right? I can't wait to hear all about it."

———

"So then he kissed you."

Vic nodded dully as she wrapped her arms around herself and stared thoughtfully at the flower bed behind her house, which needed weeding. Just like Vic's life. Despite her dad's more desperate problems, which had grown even worse when the FBI froze her parents' joint bank accounts, she'd spent most of the weekend replaying the catastrophe with Ryder and Jake. She'd done it again at work today, and it never improved on her.

Tess took a sip of lemonade through a straw. "And then Ryder showed up." Another nod. "And he knew all about Hope, which really can't surprise you, since Sean knows."

"I didn't say it surprised me. I said I almost passed out."

"From the heat, undoubtedly." Tess fanned herself as they sat in the backyard, watching the kids play pirate in their jungle-gym fort while Hope soaked herself in the plastic wading pool. "I can't believe we're outside when it has to be ninety degrees. We're living like savages."

"Or normal people." Vic called out to Connor when he clipped Megan in the side with his plastic sword. Glancing up, Hope belatedly said something to the kids and picked up the hose next to the pool, threatening to use it. "Whenever we go out lately, we end up at Pendulum."

"And your point is—?"

"That I prefer my own backyard." Vic leaned back in her chair, feeling a slight breeze on her damp neck. "No liquor. No greasy food. No creepy guys trying to grab my butt."

"No Jake."

"Right." She lifted her glass in the air. "No Jake."

"But he kissed you." Tess leaned forward in her chair. "The last time he did, you sent him packing for a couple of weeks. Did you kiss him back this time?"

She had last time, too, but Tess didn't need to know it.

"Barely."

"Now we're getting somewhere." Tess stretched out her legs and crossed them at the ankle. "No wonder Ryder had to check out the situation."

Vic frowned. "Why?" She glanced at the kids, still playing at a safe distance, and Hope, who appeared oblivious. "He's gay, Tess. He doesn't want me."

"He was with you all these years. You were safe and perfect and well-behaved, and now you're kissing other men."

"Like I said. Barely. But Ryder is still—"

"A man." Tess leaned back in her chair. "And a lot of men, straight or gay, really get off on a battle. Like they're warriors or something. Or cavemen. It's in their chromosomes."

"That has to be your strangest theory yet."

"Strange, maybe, but often true. Trust me."

Vic did trust her, oddly, where Jake was concerned. Tess hadn't told Vic about Andrea, which still annoyed her, but she didn't poach. Not in high school. Not now.

Frankly, she had to be able to trust someone. Someone other than Midge, who would faint if she heard most of the conversations that Vic and Tess shared. Despite all those years she'd spent studying biology.

"So what should I do?"

"What else?" Tess laughed a little too loudly, drawing quick glances from the kids and Hope. "Kiss him again. Admit it: the guy is hot, and he's perfect for you."

She shook her head. "He's still stuck in high school, where I'm the homecoming queen and he's the big football hero."

"Life was good then. Less complicated." Tess took another sip of lemonade, then glanced sideways at Vic. "Aside from cloak-and-dagger trips to Montana, of course."

Vic watched her kids, so blissfully unaware of all the drama ahead of them. She wished she could somehow keep them safe from it all. "I don't know what to do. This summer has turned my whole life upside down, and not in a good way, but . . ."

She trailed off, unable to express what she felt.

Or decide what she wanted.

"But it's your life. Warts and all." Tess gazed thoughtfully at Hope. "Don't worry. I'm sure Jake has a few warts, too, underneath that gorgeous body of his."

"Quit looking at that body of his."

Tess's bare shoulders shook with laughter. "Then you should. Like it or not, you two have serious chemistry, and you've already had a kid together." She shook a finger when Vic started to protest, then dropped her voice. "Yeah, it's Hope, but the fact is that you guys have a history. So figure out what you want, and if it's Jake? Bring him into the present."

"But how?"

"That's up to you. But you can do it if you want."

If she wanted. That was the crux of it.

She glanced over at Hope, splashing in the pool. The younger kids had accepted her—warts and all, as Tess would say—and they'd forged a threesome of sorts.

Like Jake and Hope and her. Another odd threesome, not quite a family, and yet—

"Hope?" Standing up, she poured another glass of lemonade and took it to the newest member of her family. She hadn't yet acknowledged to Hope that she'd officially accepted her, and it was time. Bending down next to the small plastic pool, she handed her the glass and a towel. "I thought you might want a cool drink and a break from watching the kids." To the extent she was. "Come over and join Tess and me. After all, you may be my child, but you're also one of the grown-ups here."

Hope stared up at her. "I'm . . . your child?"

Vic smiled. "Welcome to the family."

———

ANOTHER LONG MORNING at the gallery. Vic sat at her desk, staring at a box containing the new computer software that Hope had recommended, which she really ought to ask Hope or someone else to install. She wondered when she'd hear something from Dad, or even Mother, and wished she knew what had happened to the neat, tidy little life she'd had a few months ago.

Before Hope.

Before Ryder and Sean. Before Ryder left her, and she took her anger out on Sean, and Sean left the gallery.

Before Jake, although she wasn't sure Jake was a bad thing.

Before FBI agents invaded her gallery and took Dad away.

She still had two great kids, thank God, and she'd acquired an imperfect but mostly manageable bonus daughter in Hope. She also had Tess and Midge and Drew and Nat to lean on, and even Dad, when he wasn't in jail or otherwise messing up her life. And her relationship with Mother was no worse, even though she now knew that Mother was both more awful and less awful than she'd thought, which made her head spin.

She heard the chime of the main door to the gallery. Pushing back from her desk, she hurried out of her office just as Andrea reached it.

Andrea stepped inside her office, looking nervous but determined. "Vic? I need to talk to you."

Taking a step backward, Vic slipped behind her desk. "I don't really have time to talk." She pointed at the software box in the middle of her desk, even though she didn't have a clue what to do with it. "I'm busy setting up a new financial program."

Andrea followed her around the side of the desk. "We've been friends forever, Vic, and you have to talk to me."

"I don't have to." She frowned, remembering Midge's words and feeling about twelve years old. "No, you're right. We should talk."

Andrea glanced at the picture of Connor and Megan on the desk, then walked over to the only other chair in the office and sat down, clutching her Kate Spade purse in her lap. Vic waited for her to start. To apologize.

"I've always resented you, you know."

She blinked. As an apology, it needed work.

Andrea stared at her purse, her knuckles white from her grip on it. "Even before Jake, but especially that summer."

Vic shook her head, wondering when her relationship with Andrea had gone from awkward to toxic. "Are we talking about the summer I was gone? The summer you slept with Jake?"

A tight nod. "You went away to dance in your perfect little life, and Jake treated me like sloppy seconds."

Closing her eyes, Vic tried not to picture it. Reopening them, she pinned Andrea with her gaze. "I never had a perfect life, but I *did* have a boyfriend, and friends don't poach each other's love interests. Ever."

Even though Vic had already dropped him, or he'd dropped Vic, and their split had nothing to do with Andrea. She hoped.

Andrea's lips pursed. "I knew you'd act like this. That's why I never told you. Why we haven't been close."

"Because you resented me for reasons I can't imagine and had a fling with my boyfriend? That's why?"

"You were smart and cool and everyone wanted to be like you." A nervous laugh escaped Andrea. "Even though you set the home ec classroom on fire with your cooking."

Despite herself, Vic bit her lip on a grin.

"And there was the time you did that flip in gymnastics and you ripped out the seat of your leotard."

Remembering her utter mortification, Vic choked.

"And that time you threw your lunch tray at Jake, only you missed and it hit Mr. Haakenson."

"Oh, God. I'd forgotten." Laughter bubbled up as the old memories assailed her. "But you were the one who grabbed my elbow and made me miss."

Andrea crossed her arms. "So you say."

They stared at each other for a long moment before bursting into laughter. Andrea's purse rolled onto the floor as she leaned forward and braced her elbows on the desk. "God, those were good times."

Vic nodded. "And we had to go and fuck it all up."

"Especially you." "Especially you." They pointed at each other as their words joined in midair.

Wiping a tear, Vic shook her head. "You weren't so hot in home ec, either." She arched her eyebrows at Andrea, who still burned casseroles. "Some things haven't changed."

THE PHONE RANG THURSDAY AFTERNOON, and Vic picked up immediately. The morning had gone well and life felt a little better. Finally.

"Jasmine Gallery. Victoria Bentley speaking."

"Ms. Carlyle? I mean, Ms. Bentley?"

Oh, God. Here came another one. "Yes. Victoria Carlyle Bentley."

The woman coughed. "This is Marian Franklin. At Oakview Hospital in Kalispell? Montana?"

"Yes?" At this point, nothing that awful woman said could make Vic's summer worse. Two months ago, it'd been a different story, when the woman had practically knocked Vic flat on her face with two short phone calls.

"Someone asked us to undertake another examination of the records concerning the birth of your child here." She paused, and Vic heard the never-ending shuffle of papers. "Patrice Carlyle. I believe that's your mother?"

Vic frowned. Now Mother was going *way* too far.

"We've reviewed all the paperwork, including the DNA sample your mother provided on your behalf."

Gasping, Vic grabbed her glass of water, draining it. "I didn't provide a DNA sample or authorize my mother to give you one."

"Are you saying the DNA sample is inaccurate?"

From Mother? Unlikely. "No, but—"

"Then it appears that there has, um, been a clerical error. I'm very sorry for the inconvenience."

"Oh?" Whatever it was, it hadn't prevented Hope from charging into her life, uprooting everything, and forcing Vic to discover a new life. A less perfect life, but a more honest one.

The woman cleared her throat. Several times, until Vic thought she'd never say another word.

"As I said, Ms. Bentley, we made an error. I'm not quite sure how it happened."

Vic's breath caught. "What's the error?"

Another rustling of papers. From the sound of it, the woman must be swimming in them. No wonder she made mistakes.

"Here it is. Well, er, the fact is that, well, I hate to say this, but Hope McCulloch is not your daughter."

"What?"

"Hope McCulloch is not your daughter."

"*What?*" Vic screamed into the phone.

"Hope McCulloch is—"

"I heard you! Is this a joke? She worked in my gallery, she's my kids' nanny, she's in my house and in my life, and *now* you finally get around to mentioning that—oh, by the way—she's not my daughter? Two months later? And only because my mother made you?"

Vic drew in a shaky breath and blew it out. Drew in a deeper one, held it, calmed down. No, not really. "Who is she? And where *is* my child?"

"Hope is someone else's child. I'm not permitted to divulge that information, of course. But your baby—" The woman paused, and Vic almost fell off her chair while she waited. "Your baby died. At birth."

Just like Mother had always said. Jesus. She'd been telling the truth all this time.

Without another word, she hung up the phone. Put her head on her desk. And cried.

———

Five minutes later, Vic gripped the phone in her still-shaking hands. She should've waited longer to compose herself after hanging up on the woman from the hospital, but she had to have this conversation. She should've had it twenty-one years ago. Or twenty years ago. Or sometime in the intervening years.

"Mother? Why didn't you tell me?"

"Tell you what, Victoria?"

The telephone line crackled, or else Mother just sounded odd. Like she'd been the one crying, not Vic.

"About the baby. You went behind my back, even scrounged up a DNA sample, and talked to the hospital in Kalispell. They just called to tell me that Hope isn't my baby." She choked as she spoke the words. "My baby died at birth."

"I did tell you, dear. From the beginning."

"But—"

"I'm so sorry. I'm not sorry you didn't have to be responsible for a baby at seventeen, which would've ruined your life. But yes, I asked the hospital to check its records again and give you the news independently, so you'd finally believe me. I'm sorry for not telling you that. And for . . . everything."

"Everything" could include a lifetime of transgressions.

"But I still remember that day we were all at Drew's house, when we found out about Hope." Vic's mind reeled as she thought about Ms. Franklin's frantic phone calls in search of Hope's mother. "And you never said anything."

"I tried a few times, dear, but I didn't know what to say. You and everyone else in this family refused to simply take my word against a complete stranger's." As she paused, Vic heard her swallow hard. Or choke on something. "But I held your baby in my arms and gazed down into his sweet little eyes."

"His eyes? I had a boy?"

"Yes. A tiny little boy who wasn't strong enough to live. I

told the people at the hospital to name him Jacob, after his father."

"And you never told me?"

"I thought you'd have a more difficult time if you knew. If you saw him. Saw how beautiful he was."

"So you never let me. Just like you tried to stop me, my whole life, from all the other mistakes I could've made. All the mistakes I *did* make, despite your interference."

"Or because of it, I suspect." Her mother sighed, just as she'd sighed so many times over the years. "I'm sorry. I did my best. I tried to make the right decisions."

"It wasn't your decision to make."

"You're absolutely right."

"I am *too*—" Right. Vic faltered, finally hearing her mother agree with her. Acknowledge her.

"I made a mistake." The crackling now definitely wasn't the phone line. It was her mother, clearly sobbing. "I've made so many mistakes, but I always wanted what was best for you. I wanted to keep you from making my own mistakes."

"When did you ever make a mistake?"

Mother had always been perfect. A tough standard to live up to, and every look at her reminded Vic of it.

"Countless times." The sniffles were quieter now. "And I see now that I pushed you into exactly the same ones I made."

"You didn't have an illegitimate child."

A long pause. Had she? Impossible.

"No, but only because your father married me quickly enough, once I realized I was pregnant with Drew."

"But your wedding date— His birthday—"

"We've been married forty years, not forty-one. The anniversary date is right, but a year off." Despite the big forti-eth-anniversary party they threw last year. "My mother didn't—"

"—want you to be less than perfect."

"No. No, she didn't."

"Just like mine."

Her mother laughed softly. "Quite a family. Consumed with perfection and appearances and more than a whiff of deception."

"No kidding."

"I did it for you. Poorly, and wrongly, and quite foolishly, I realize now. It took your father's troubles for me to finally admit it."

Vic shook her head, wondering whether she'd spend the coming years visiting Dad in prison.

Mother cleared her throat. Unless she was still crying. "Your father has realized a few things, too, including how foolish he's been about refusing money from my trust account. I've never used it, and I planned to leave it to the three of you and your children. When the FBI seized our joint accounts, Warren finally relented."

Vic leaned back in her chair, half-expecting it to topple over backward any moment. "He didn't have much choice."

"No, but he made a good one. That's the important thing."

Dad was up to his eyeballs in trouble, but Mother acted so calm. So forgiving. Vic tapped her pen on her desk, wondering how she did it—and without Valium.

Mother cooed into the phone. "It'll be all right, dear. He's straightening it out. It's why he moved out. To hurt me, perhaps, but also to protect me."

Vic's head spun. "But why?"

"Because he loves us. Ultimately, that's what it's all about. And his pride, I suppose." Her mother sighed again. "He's spent a lifetime hearing about those trust funds that Daddy set up. I suppose your father wanted to compete with Daddy."

Vic shook her head, remembering her grandfather, who'd

inherited a large fortune in grain companies and built it from there. A sad, lonely little man at the end, but he'd done well by his family. The ones who still spoke to him, at least.

Mother spoke again. "Your father always hated those trust funds, even though yours bought the gallery and your house."

She felt a stab of both gratitude and chagrin about the trusts, but Dad had brought this on himself. "But Nat hasn't really used hers, and Drew reeled in Babs with his."

Her mother sniffed. "I don't know why you all dislike that poor girl so much."

"Babs is a nightmare, Mother."

"Perhaps, but I suppose I identify with her."

In a way she never had with Vic or Nat. And Drew was a boy, now a man, so she'd never worried about identifying with him. She just adored him.

"In any case, Mother, she's Drew's problem. Not Dad's."

"Quite true, dear."

This conversation was remarkable. Calm, and they'd even agreed with each other a few times. Vic blinked, wondering when she'd wake up from the weirdest dream of her life.

"What happens now? I mean, won't Dad go to prison? How much money did he take?"

"A fair amount. His old firm and its clients seem be rather forgiving, or perhaps they just want to keep their carelessness out of the news. Your father has already paid back everyone. His lawyer thinks he'll be able to avoid prison."

"And . . . will he move back home again?"

"Perhaps. If I let him." Her mother laughed, a small sound that startled Vic, then blew her nose. "Sorry, dear. Just a private joke between your father and me."

She'd never suspected her mother of engaging in jokes, private or otherwise, but decided not to share that thought. She felt as if their relationship had gotten a fresh start today, but it was still fragile, and she didn't want to destroy it.

"That's okay, Mom. I understand."

"Mom? You've never called me Mom."

"And you've never called me Vic. Isn't it about time we both tried something new?"

"Perhaps." Her mother paused, then laughed softly. "Yes, Vic, I believe it's past time."

CHAPTER 21

The rest of the afternoon and evening, Vic stewed over Hope, who was no longer her daughter. She'd never been her daughter. She'd just been a thorn in her side all summer.

A thorn who now watched her kids, her *two* kids, probably until at least August. But not indefinitely. In a matter of months, Hope would deliver a baby—no longer Vic's grandchild—and make a new life with her baby. Hope would be out of Vic's life.

Knowing that, Vic should've slept well.

Friday morning, she awoke bleary-eyed and out of sorts from a series of wacky dreams and nightmares to the sound of shuffling and heavy thumps. Pulling on a robe, she padded down the hall, pausing at the closed door to Hope's bedroom. Another thump and a hissed curse greeted her ears.

"Hope?" She knocked softly on the door, trying not to wake up Connor and Megan in case by some wild chance they'd managed to sleep through the uproar.

Silence. As she lifted her hand to knock again, the door swung open. Hope, her hair as gnarly as Vic felt, didn't bother to hide the open suitcase and overflowing duffle bag, the rumpled clothes strewn everywhere, or the streaks of yesterday's mascara running down her cheeks.

She wiped her runny nose. "Yeah?"

Looking past Hope's shoulder, Vic frowned. "What's going on? You're not leaving, are you?"

Hope just stared at her and wiped her nose again.

"You agreed to be the kids' nanny until the end of July." Or maybe longer, if Vic didn't find another nanny. "Did something change?"

"The hospital called me, Vic. I know." She stared down at the floor. "I'm not your daughter."

Pursing her lips, Vic ran a hand through her hair. Dozens of scattered thoughts flitted through her mind, much as they had yesterday. Part of her felt relief, yes, but she'd already survived a summer of Hurricane Hope. It was too late for ecstasy.

"I know you're not. But you're my nanny." For now, and maybe for a little longer than July. Swallowing hard, she uttered the words she would've once choked on. "I still need you."

"As soon as you find another nanny, you'll kick me out."

She had no interest in killing the fragile light flickering in Hope's eyes. Instead, she took a step past her into the room, inching between all the piles. "You still have parents who must miss you terribly." She held up a hand to cut off Hope's immediate denial. "And maybe an old boyfriend who regrets what he said."

Hope collapsed onto the bed, claiming the one vacant spot. "I haven't heard from my folks or my boyfriend all summer."

"Do they know how to reach you?"

"They could find me if they really wanted to."

Smiling, Vic tried to soften the sting of her words. "Like

you found me? I think we've learned that even computers can make mistakes."

Clasping her hands between her knees, Hope hung her head. "Some computer whiz I am, huh?"

"I *would* like you to set up my new accounting program." Vic approached the bed but, seeing no room, merely stood in front of Hope. "And I still need you as my nanny, but I also think you should make a few phone calls."

Hope's shoulders slumped. "For a new job?"

"No, calls that are much more important. To your parents, then maybe to your boyfriend. If I've learned one thing this summer—" She shook her head, wishing the lessons hadn't been so horribly painful. "It's that very few people in your life are irretrievable."

"Really?"

"Trust me."

Hope eyed the staggering heap of clothes on the bed and shoved it on the floor. Wincing at the mess, Vic took the offered seat as Hope gazed sideways at her.

"Thanks. I guess we *do* have a relationship, Vic, even if it's not by blood."

They definitely weren't bound by the same cleaning standards. Or taste. Or much of anything.

But they'd weathered a sea of battles together this summer, often against each other, and somehow survived. Together. Vic's gaze swept the room, finally landing on the pregnant young woman she'd finally and begrudgingly called her daughter. Hope had more battles ahead of her in the coming months.

She thought of Tess and Midge and Andrea and so many other good friends. Jake. Maybe even Sean. Family or not, they shared a bond. As she now did with Hope.

She nodded. "You're right. Biology is irrelevant." Her tenth-grade biology teacher would die of heart failure if he heard her. "No matter what happens, in some ways I'll always think of you as my daughter. Part of my family."

Hugging, they both fell off the bed.

———

Monday afternoon in the gallery's storeroom, Vic stepped around a dozen crates of artwork she hadn't ordered from artists she hadn't heard of. The delivery guy insisted they belonged to her, then fled before she could call someone higher up his chain of command. She shrugged as she turned off her cell phone. He'd be back. Quickly.

"Anyone here? Or should I take my business elsewhere?"

Startled, she brushed past a crate, banging her knee, and hobbled out of the storeroom. "Wait! I'm—"

Halting, she stared at Sean.

In sandals and shorts, much like the last time she'd seen him, and grinning from ear to ear. "Nothing like an irate customer to get your attention, Vic. Some things never change."

Even when everything else did. Curious, she took a step toward Sean, looking past him to see if he was alone.

"Don't worry. I'm solo and unarmed." He glanced around the gallery and whistled his appreciation. "Everything looks good. I guess you don't miss me."

Her gaze followed the same path, seeing the anticipated sales that hadn't occurred, the art that hadn't been delivered as promised, the occasional client whose demands exceeded reality. "Not true. Life has been . . . eventful."

"Yeah." Stuffing his fists in his pockets, Sean crossed the room to the only piece of his own artwork that hadn't yet sold. He touched the frame as he stared at the wild canvas. "Haven't quite finished getting rid of me, huh?"

He grinned sheepishly at her.

She nodded. "That's the last one, but I think it'll sell soon. A couple of clients are interested."

"Tell you what. Let's trade."

Her forehead creased in confusion.

"Me for my painting. I know I'm not much of a bargain, but I've had time to think." He glanced again at the canvas. "And now I know what it's like to work for someone else. What the hell. If you'll take me back, I'll even throw in the painting."

Vic thought of Ryder, and Sean with Ryder, and how being around Sean sometimes felt so painful now. But she felt worse when he wasn't in the gallery, helping make it work.

A trade indeed. "It's a deal."

He staggered backward. "Just like that? Without any discussion? I'm, uh, still seeing Ryder. Sometimes."

She sucked in a breath. "No details, please."

He put his hands on his hips. "And I'm still brash and arrogant and take too many latte breaks."

Her lips twitched. "No lattes for me, please."

He shrugged. "I can't promise it'll always be pretty."

"But this time we'll fix it before it breaks." Giving him a genuine smile, she was already bursting with ideas for the gallery that she hadn't dared explore without a top-notch assistant in place. Like, say, Sean. "It might not be pretty, but it'll always be colorful."

"You got that right, boss."

Finally. She did.

———

HE COULDN'T BELIEVE he had to ring the doorbell at his own house. Okay, the house he used to own. With Vic. He *really* couldn't believe Vic had changed the locks. She wasn't herself anymore. The woman he'd married.

Ryder stood on the front doorstep Tuesday evening, having come straight from work. Without going to Sean's. Without passing Go. Without collecting two hundred dollars. Ringing the doorbell.

Finally, Connor answered. "Dad?"

"Hey, sport." He bent down to Connor's eye level and roughed up his hair. Connor squirmed.

"What are you doing here?"

Ryder straightened, tugging on his too-tight bowtie. "I came to see you guys. And your mom."

"I'm not sure Mom wants to see you."

He looked past Connor into the front hall. "I'm not sure she does, either. But I'm here, and I've missed you. A lot."

"Where've you been? You haven't seen us all summer."

He blew out a breath, unsure how to explain the facts of life to a ten-year-old boy, especially when he still didn't understand them himself. "I haven't seen you here at the house, but I've been in the neighborhood. I missed you guys, so I watched you playing."

"Weird."

"Yeah." He laughed. "Pretty weird. I love you guys, but I'm not sure what I'm doing these days."

Connor stared hard at him, looking older than ten. "Like Mom, huh? Like when she was all sad an' stuff. An' took all those pills."

He nodded. "Kind of like that. We just handled it differently."

"You can say that again." Vic stepped to the door, looking vibrant in a sleeveless aqua silk blouse and skirt. She sent Connor back inside and closed the door. "Ryder? What brings you here?" She looked past him to his BMW, parked at the curb.

He dropped his head, feeling stupid. "I made such a mess of things. Screwed up everyone's lives. I'm sorry, Vic."

"I suppose they were bound to get screwed up. No one's perfect. Me, least of all."

"But you're—"

"Not." She waved a hand, stopping him. "And I'm tired of all the men in my life thinking I am. Or pretending they are."

His head spun, wondering how many men she meant. He understood, though, why he'd married her. Despite everything. Vic might not be perfect, but she was quite a woman. A thoughtful mother. A . . . good friend. He hoped.

He faltered over the words he needed to say. "I want to see the kids, Vic. Be involved in their lives. I've missed them. I've —" He tried not to stammer. "Missed you." He looked at his shoes, not daring to meet the questioning gaze of the woman he'd disappointed in so many ways. "I hope some day, after we start to move past all of this, we can be friends again."

"The divorce is happening no matter what you do, and we can't go back to whatever it was we had when we were married. Not for the kids. Not for anyone."

"I know." He nodded, surprised and grateful that she was even speaking to him. "I just want to be part of your lives."

Her hands were locked on her hips. "Then I have some bad news for you."

"Y-yes?"

She glanced at her watch. "Connor's Little League game starts in half an hour. If you want to see it, you'll have to move your butt."

"Gladly." And he did.

———

THURSDAY EVENING, Vic sat cross-legged on the living room sofa, her cell phone clutched in her sweaty hands. Staring blankly at the screen, she flailed for words.

Er, Mom, would you mind if I had a couple hundred friends out to the lake place on Saturday? On the spur of the moment?

The phone rang, and she jumped. Mom? She swiped right to answer with an unsteady finger. "Hello?"

"Vic? What are you doing at home? I would think you'd be at the summer house by now, getting it ready for your party."

The trill of her mother's laughter filled her ear.

Vic picked up her Diet Coke from its coaster on the end table and took a long sip while her brain melted. "What, um, are you talking about?"

"One of your high-school friends sent her RSVP by mistake to our house. It had Midge's address and phone on it, so I called her and got the scoop, as you say."

She frowned. "You called Midge and not me?"

"Don't worry, dear. You're my daughter, and I love you, but Midge knows everything." Mother—or Mom, as Vic mentally corrected herself—laughed again, sounding lighthearted despite everything still happening with Dad.

Her mom chattered into the phone. "It sounds like fun, and I'm offering to babysit. Connor and Megan can pack their pajamas and stay here overnight."

A first. Blinking, Vic swallowed a nervous gulp of her Diet Coke. "I'm sure they'd like that, but Hope is free on Saturday, and I already asked her to stay with them."

She froze, preparing herself for a tirade against Hope.

"I imagine Hope would like an evening off. Or you can ask her to help out at your party, although you might want to have someone else buy and serve the alcohol." Another small laugh as Vic cringed, flashing back to Hope's stellar performance at her first art opening. "Just a thought."

"You're on. How does noon on Saturday sound?"

"Fine, dear. We'll pick them up to save you the drive over here." As her mom paused, Vic rearranged her weekend schedule in her mind. "And don't hurry out here to pick them up on Sunday. I— Well, I thought you might want to spend some time with your friend. Jake. If you'd like that."

Vic nearly choked on her Diet Coke. "Thanks, but I'm not exactly seeing him."

"I . . . thought you were?"

"A few times this summer. Mostly with friends." Any additional details were on a need-to-know basis, and her mom didn't need to know. "But I've given it some thought, Mom, and I saw what happened to Dad when he married a wealthier woman. Jake and I would be exactly the same."

Her mom made a tsking sound. "I shouldn't get involved, dear." As she hesitated, Vic held her breath, trying not to remember all the times her mother had meddled. "But I believe you and your *father* sound the same, not you and Jake."

The air whooshed out of her lungs. "Dad?"

"Please don't be foolish. My money didn't cause your father's troubles. His ego did." She paused while Vic processed that. "My money helped *fix* his troubles. Not that I should mention that too often."

They shared a laugh. Maybe their first in twenty years.

"Now, go have your big shindig out at the summer house, and spend some time with Jake if you'd like. Don't worry. There's nothing that we can't clean or repair, just like I always did after those parties of yours in high school."

Diet Coke spewed all over Vic's lap. "You knew?"

"About your parties, and Drew's and Natalie's as well." Mom offered a faint sniff. "I may have made some mistakes in my life, dear, but I'm not stupid."

———

TIME TO REPAY A VISIT.

Late Friday afternoon, with the gallery in Sean's reliable hands, Vic made a quick stop at the Uptown Lunds & Byerlys, then continued up Hennepin Avenue to 36th Street and straight on into Lakewood Cemetery.

Climbing out of her convertible, she blinked against the bright sun and clutched the bouquet of daffodils, hiding them behind her back when she noticed the sign prohibiting loose flowers and anything not in an official cemetery container.

Carrie had never been much for rules.

No one stopped her as she wandered on foot to the north-west corner of the cemetery, paused briefly at Paul Wellstone's boulder, then veered left and headed over to the smooth char-coal granite of Carrie's headstone. A headstone she'd helped Carrie's mom choose in the awful days after the accident.

She peeled the plastic wrap off of the daffodils and pulled off the rubber band holding them together. Then she opened her hand, scattering them over Carrie's grave. Exactly how Carrie would want them, if she'd ever given death half a thought.

Unlike Vic, she probably hadn't.

Bending over the grave, she fingered a soft petal, pressing it to her cheek. "I'm glad I got to see you again this summer, Carrie, when I wasn't doing so well."

Hazy visions of Carrie during the wild journey she'd taken in her drug-induced coma came back to her. She blinked, and they were gone as if they'd never happened. But she'd seen and spoken with Carrie. She'd almost seen her permanently.

"You died doing what you loved. I remember your truck, your beaming face in that photo of it that you sent me, that jaunty wave of yours." Carrie had asked her to fly home on the spur of the moment and join her on her first adventure in the truck, as if Vic could've talked her parents into springing for a quick trip like that. Thank God she hadn't even asked. "I'm not sorry I missed that ride, but I've missed you. All these years."

A tear caught at the inside corner of her eye and dribbled down her cheek.

"I haven't lived my life as well as you lived your short one, and this summer I almost blew it. I'm so sorry. I don't know why I'm apologizing to you, but I'm sorry."

Picking up another stray petal, she balanced it on the tips of her fingers, then tossed it into the air, watching it flutter to the ground. Just how she'd always imagined Carrie dying after flying through the air in her truck.

She read Carrie's headstone and, with a sad smile, blew her old friend a kiss. "Anyway, thanks. I loved seeing you again, but I'm not ready to join you. I'm going to stay right here." Feeling a sudden breeze against her neck, she laughed. "Okay, not here in the cemetery. But thanks for asking."

─────

SATURDAY AFTERNOON AROUND FOUR, Jake gazed at the large yard sloping down to the lake, the tables strewn with flowers, and several stalwarts and hard-core party animals who'd arrived a good hour before the reunion was supposed to start.

Midge was running in every direction with her damn notepad, looking stressed but happy, and Andrea and her husband seemed to be helping her with last-minute details. Tess already had a drink in hand, *not* helping with anything. Vic was nowhere in sight.

He spotted Brandon Carruthers, who'd wisely skipped that first planning meeting for the reunion just because he hadn't been in their class—lame excuse—and walked over to say hi anyway. Piper Jamison, at Brandon's side, and Liz Tanner gave Jake a hug before Liz tried to introduce him to Brandon's older brother, David. Jake reminded her that they'd met at Pendulum one night last summer.

Liz and David seemed to be together now. He caught a glimpse of the major sparkler on her left hand and the way they looked at each other. Oh, yeah. Definitely together.

Tess sauntered up to their little group, hips swinging, and soon pulled Jake away from the rest of them. "Nice work on the booze, kid. I'll have to hire you for all my parties."

"Oh? Is this your party?" They shared a grin. "Where's Vic?"

"Powdering her nose, no doubt. Or just plain hiding, since she knows we're about to trash her parents' place."

"Just like high school."

"And yet not." Tess tilted her head, studying him.

He squirmed under the examination. Or under the bright sun, which was melting right through his Hawaiian shirt.

"Do you really want to go out with her again?"

He nodded, even though it was none of Tess's damn business. "I really do." He squirmed again. "If that works for her."

Laughing, she raised her glass in a toast. "I'm glad we have that settled. Now I can relax and enjoy the party, and you two can stare at each other all evening and be utterly unable to form an intelligent sentence."

He felt himself grinning. "Something like that."

She nodded at the summer house. "She's inside. And not getting any younger, if you know what I mean."

Without another word, he hurried toward the house, not that he needed Vic to get any younger. She'd done seventeen as well as anyone could, but he looked forward to getting to know her at thirty-eight. Watching her hit fifty. And eighty. Damn.

From behind him, Tess's warm laughter floated in the air.

———

"Jake? I was just coming outside."

Vic started to run a hand through her hair, smoothing out the tangles, but decided not to bother. The wind blowing off of Lake Minnetonka would wreck it soon enough anyway, and Jake might as well get used to her. Imperfect as she was.

"Looking for me?" His eyebrows danced.

She grinned as she turned toward the door. "Maybe."

"Look no more. I'm here."

She nodded outside, where a few dozen people had already appeared. If she'd named an earlier starting time, they would've arrived at sunrise. "Don't you want to join everyone?"

"Not yet." Grabbing her hand, he pulled her toward the wicker sofa with flowered cushions. "I wanted to see you first."

Feeling nervous somehow, she pulled free of him and twirled in a circle. "There. Now you've seen me." She headed for the door, only to be caught again by his hand on her wrist. "I think we should go outside and greet people. I'm the host, and I haven't seen a lot of them in twenty years."

"I haven't seen you in that long, either. Maybe, in a way, a whole lot longer."

She frowned. "You've seen me all summer." She thought of all the evenings she'd spent trying to avoid him—in Pendulum, of all places. Not exactly effective.

He brought her hand to his lips and kissed it. Lightly. Sweetly. Gallantly. As if she were still high up on that stupid pedestal.

"I saw you, but I didn't really see you. When I wasn't busy getting tangled up with Hope and her schemes—" He scoffed, but Vic saw a flash of regret in his eyes. "I kept seeing this cute seventeen-year-old who'd been my dream girl. In the end, though, I decided I didn't want her."

He dropped her hand, and she pressed it against her heart. "You don't?"

"Nope." He chuckled, which was more than a little irritating. And confusing, all things considered. "I want someone else."

Her gaze dropped to the floor. A floor that needed a lot more cleaning than she'd had time to give it.

"You." His fingers touched her chin, tilting it upward. "I want the grown-up version. After all, I'm not a kid anymore, and I was never into robbing cradles."

"That's a relief." Emotion flooded through her, leaving her unable to think. Instead, she punched him lightly on the arm. "After all, I don't want to visit another guy in jail."

"Yeah." He locked arms with her and marched her outside into the dazzling sunshine. "I was hoping you'd want to keep me around. You know, on a permanent basis."

She winked at him. "Let's see what we can do."

A NOTE FROM MARY

Thank you for reading *Seemingly Perfect!* This is the third and final novel in my Pendulum trilogy, and it's been a pleasure to send these characters out into the world. I dedicated Seemingly Perfect to my high school friends Sue, Lisa, Lynn, and Nancee. We spent a lot of time at the Villa Piazza and elsewhere (when I wasn't busy playing sports), and I thought of them when I first wrote this. Although Vic, Tess, Midge, and Andrea in this novel aren't in any way intended to represent my high school friends (or me), Carrie is indeed the fictional version of Nancee Eberhardt, who died in essentially the same way that Carrie did in this novel. I spent a lot of time thinking about Nancee as I wrote (and revised) this novel. I miss you still.

Also, although I didn't name it in this novel, the Spanish camp in Bemidji where Vic's kids spent three weeks is based on the fabulous Concordia Language Villages, where my own kids spent many happy summers, first as campers and later as counselors. I highly recommend it!

If you enjoyed this book, I would really appreciate it if you could leave a review wherever you buy or talk about books. Whether super short or longer, all reviews are good, and they help other readers discover my books. Thank you so much!

I also love to hear from my readers! Please stay in touch by signing up for my newsletter. You can also connect with me on Facebook, Twitter, Instagram, or through my website. For links, check out my bio on the next page.

Happy reading!

Mary

ABOUT THE AUTHOR

Mary Strand practiced law in a large Minneapolis firm until the day she set aside her pointy-toed shoes (or most of them) and escaped the world of mergers and acquisitions to write novels. The first manuscript she wrote, *Cooper's Folly,* a romantic comedy, won RWA's Golden Heart award and was her debut novel. Her love of Jane Austen prompted her four-book YA series, The Bennet Sisters.

Mary lives on a lake in Minneapolis with her family, too many Converse Chucks, and a stuffed monkey named Philip. When not writing books or songs, she lives for sports, travel, rocking out on guitar, dancing (badly), and ill-advised adventures (including dancing) that offer a high probability of injury to herself and others. She writes YA, romantic comedy, and women's fiction novels.

Seemingly Perfect is the third and final novel in The Pendulum Trilogy.

You can find Mary at www.marystrand.com, follow her on Twitter or Instagram, or "like" her on Facebook.

ALSO BY MARY STRAND

Cooper's Folly

THE BENNET SISTERS

THE PENDULUM TRILOGY

Made in the USA
Middletown, DE
05 June 2022

66673088R00213